ANTI-
HERO

ANTI-HERO

JONATHAN WOOD

TITAN BOOKS

ANTI-HERO
Print edition ISBN: 9781781168103
E-book edition ISBN: 9781781168127

Published by Titan Books
A division of Titan Publishing Group Ltd
144 Southwark Street, London SE1 0UP

First mass market edition: June 2016

10 9 8 7 6 5 4 3 2 1

A CIP catalogue record for this title is available from the British Library.

Printed and bound in the United States.

For Tami, Charlie and Emma.

My heroes.

1

Surely some things should be sacred? Surely. That hardly seems unreasonable. Yet, here I am diving for cover behind a gravestone.

Bullets tear into ancient limestone. Stone shards churn the earth around me. I scramble back, vault a tomb, tumble into a yew bush.

A black shape descends from the cloud-clotted sky. A miniature plane, a shadow with blazing barrels and the intention of making me resemble Swiss cheese. The tomb I'm using as cover caves as bullets chew through the lid. My yew bush gets a drastic trim. I sweat and curse.

Then engines whine. The plane veers away, searches for a better line of attack. I heave out my pistol, push a rogue yew branch out of my nostril, take aim.

I think it's a drone. The sort of thing the US government uses to piss off large portions of Pakistan. Except, I'm not in Pakistan. I'm in Oxford, England.

A drone attack. Here. Now. Nothing is sacred. Because—and I think I can say this with certainty—this is by far the weirdest funeral I have ever been to.

TWENTY MINUTES AGO

Rain falls. A priest mutters somber words. Slowly, with measured movements, I help lower my best friend's body into the ground.

"To tell you the truth, Arthur," says a voice in my earpiece, "it's a bit of an odd feeling, being at your own funeral."

To tell the truth, it is a bit of an odd feeling when a disembodied, digital copy of the man you're burying provides color commentary during the burial.

The body we're sending on a six-foot downward journey once belonged to one Clyde Marcus Bradley. Except it isn't his original one. Earlier in the month, the original was hijacked by alien mind worms, turned into the human equivalent of a fried egg, and then I shot it. Not something I'm overly proud of.

Anyway, Clyde's original body is rather indisposed.

However, for a number of really complicated reasons, we had a back-up digital version of Clyde on an ancient Peruvian mask, and a brain dead body that was lying around. Which, thinking about it, was a fairly fortunate coincidence.

So, Clyde went on a wooden mask. And that was OK for a while actually. Until he developed computer super-powers and might have gone a bit insane, and thought it was OK to overwrite other people's brains with his own. And *then* he got zapped, or broken, or… well, there was a time-traveling Russian magician involved. So Clyde was dead again. And that's why we have a body to bury today.

Where things get really complicated is the point where Clyde made numerous back-up copies of himself. And now they're talking to me at the funeral.

Not creepy at all…

Here and now are neither the time nor the place to deal with that oddness, though. Instead I attempt to shush Clyde—the commentator not the corpse—via the subvocal mike taped beneath my collar.

The difficulty of shushing subvocally should not be understated. My own attempt is met by a stern look from Felicity Shaw. Felicity, my boss. Also Clyde's boss. Also, my girlfriend. Though not Clyde's girlfriend. My life is decidedly odd these days, but it's not that odd.

"I mean," Clyde continues, "it's nice of everyone to come. Totally appreciate it of course. The last thing I want is to appear to be ungrateful. That would be terrible. And the flowers... Well, to be honest, I was never really a flowers person. I'm still not. Gosh, it's difficult to work out what sort of tense to talk about myself with these days. But that sort of ties into my point. Because, despite how lovely and touching this is, it does all seem a little unnecessary."

Except, "This isn't for you, Clyde," I point out.

"Well," Clyde replies, "it is *my* funeral."

But unless you're starring in an experimental seventies horror film, the point for helping the corpse usually expired along with it.

The way things stand now, as I understand them, three of the back-up versions of Clyde are active. All are in the possession of MI37, Britain's last line of defense against... well, things like alien mind worms and time-traveling Russian magicians.

MI37 itself consists of me, Arthur Wallace, head of field operations; Felicity, my boss and aforementioned girlfriend (a situation which at the very least rivals Clyde's existence for the most complicated thing I have to deal with on a daily basis); Kayla, a sword-wielding Scottish woman who technically reports to me, but mostly just intimidates me, and who has super-powers and issues; and

Tabitha, a Pakistani goth who fills the roles of both researcher and misanthrope.

I, Felicity, and Kayla own versions 2.2, 2.3, and 2.4 of Clyde respectively. He gave them to us on flash drives. Since then they have been downloaded onto and are co-habiting a server back at our office. I believe they're all watching this through a hacked spy satellite.

Tabitha stands separately. Tabitha... The proud owner of Version 2.1, Clyde's ex-girlfriend, and the woman for whom this funeral is really being held.

She stands at the head of the grave watching the coffin make its descent, gently shaking as the sobs wrack her body. As I understand it, goths have never been known for wearing cheerful colors even at the best of times. Today, Tabitha appears to have been rinsed of all color by the rain. Black dress. Black make-up. Black studs in her ears and in her face. The crimson swath of hair that graced half her head has been shaved away to leave a uniform quarter inch of black. A skull has been etched into the hair on the back of her scalp. The only colour variation comes from her white tattoos, standing out stark against her dark skin.

She's taken Clyde's death hard. I mean, normally if she shows an emotion that isn't frustration I know something is seriously awry. This public display of grief is indicative of some sort of internal shattering.

"Ash to ash," the priest intones. "Dust to dust."

Tabitha's body quakes with another sob. I think about putting an arm around her, but don't for fear that would just make it worse. Tabitha's spent so long keeping everyone at an emotional arm's length I don't know how to respond.

"She's still not talking to me," Clyde Version 2.2

says in my ear. "To any of us."

It would be an overstatement to say that I am completely at ease with the Clyde versions. Clyde is… He is dead. Interacting with a digital xerox of him… Well, the simplest actions take on existential meaning. Do I kill him every time I shut his application down? That's a fun thought to mull over late at night.

My relationship with him, though, is staggeringly functional when compared to Tabitha's. In a nutshell, they cause abject terror in her. We were only able to get versions 2.2, 2.3, and 2.4 onto a work server because she took several personal days after his death. I have a sneaking suspicion that her own version has been reduced to particulate by now.

She sees all of Clyde's more… aberrant behavior writ large in the smallest of the version's actions. In her eyes, they are all plotting the end of humanity, all poised to overwrite every brain they see. In fact, this is the first time in at least a week that I've seen her remove her hat.

Her hat is lined with tinfoil.

She's holding it—a small pillbox affair with a black veil to cover her eyes—but I can see the tinfoil poking out around the edges.

I may not be an expert on the subject, but I think I can definitely class "wearing a tinfoil-lined hat because of your boyfriend's demise" as taking it badly.

She made us all tinfoil hats too. She brought them into the office one day. Mine was a black baseball cap with a red anarchy "A" on the front.

"Wear it," she said, holding it out to me.

I took a moment to examine it. I noticed the tinfoil.

"Is that…"

"Antenna." She looked at me, her gaze flat and

hard, face expressionless. "For a small psi-resistor in the brim. Put it on."

"But it's tinfoil, right?"

Tabitha's gaze remained merciless. "Cheaper and lighter than copper. Easier to hide. Put it on."

I hesitated. Tabitha met my eye. I have met the eyes of things beyond human ken, defied them, and lived to tell the tale. This was way more intimidating. I put the hat on. It crinkled.

I have to wear it at all times in the office now. We all do. Felicity has a black straw bonnet. Kayla has a trucker hat. If one of us takes our hat off Tabitha freaks out. The hats also seem to disrupt cellphones and the office wireless. I think it's only a matter of time before Felicity sets fire to hers, Tabitha's mental well-being be damned.

Tabitha replaces her hat, takes a fistful of earth and scatters it on the coffin. I keep my cap balled in my fist. Tabitha is starting to look at me in frustration. But this ceremonial hat removal has been the first chance to check in with the office.

"Anybody try to blow up the world since we've been here?" I subvocalize. It's been about a week since the last attempt, a surprising dry spell for MI37, and I'm starting to feel suspicious. As if someone's trying to lull me into a false sense of security.

"No, nothing at all. Everything positively silent on the more-than-mundane front. Even mundane crime seems to be taking a day off. I think the most exciting thing that's happened so far is that Version 2.3 hacked into Tabitha's files."

When you are attempting to surreptitiously chat with an electronic copy of your best friend at his own funeral beneath the notice of his now paranoid ex-girlfriend, this is not the best news to receive.

I make a noise as if an invisible man had just given me the Heimlich maneuver. This in turn causes Felicity to take an anxious step toward me, Kayla to roll her eyes, and Tabitha to grab her hat. The priest pauses mid-spiel to give me an odd look. I try to pass it off as a sob.

Tabitha is staring desperately at my hat now. Felicity has replaced her bonnet. Kayla's foil-lined trucker hat is in place.

"He did what?" I manage to say beneath my breath.

"He misses her." A pause. "We all do."

Part of me thinks I should be more sympathetic. If this was Clyde, really Clyde, if it was the man in the coffin I would be. But these… versions. I get why they fight Tabitha's point-of-view, but I wish they could do it in a more respectful way. The way I think meat-and-bone Clyde might have done. "If Tabitha finds out, she's going to take an industrial magnet to your hard drive," I hiss.

Tabitha, for her part, is starting to mouth words at me across Clyde's open grave. "Put. It. On."

"It's worse than you think," Clyde tells me. I fail to see how this is possible.

"She's working on a programming code to debug the brains of people telepathically mind wiped by the dead me."

I'm actually relieved. Normally when I see no way for things to get worse, the world surprises me with its resourcefulness and warped sense of humor. This revelation is merely worse for the Clyde versions' chances of reconciling with Tabitha. Me and the rest of the world are emerging remarkably unscathed.

"Do you think that I should send her flowers?" Clyde asks.

"Put. It—"

I can't deal with this. I put the hat on. It crinkles.

This, I think, is probably the weirdest funeral I have ever been to.

I reach down, grab a fistful of dirt, look at the coffin. And even though I just stopped talking to some version of Clyde, I feel the loss. That is my friend lying there. My eyes sting. Saving the world sucks sometimes.

I let the soil drop from my hand, down into the hole.

The lid of the coffin explodes.

What? What just...? What?

For a moment everything is completely still. The priest in the middle of signing the cross. Kayla in the middle of reaching for her fistful of dirt. My hand still out. My palm still open.

How? I wonder. *How did I manage to make exploding soil?*

Then it comes down at us, swooping, engines shrill, machine guns rattling. Dirt, and wood, and stone fly, mashed into a fine paste of detonating detritus by the oncoming drone.

It drops out of nowhere, hurtles forward. A tiny contrail streams out from one wing.

I fling myself at a gravestone, half somersault over it, land upside down in mud and dying flowers as the drone's machine guns turn the grave marker from holy to holey.

Judging this cover to be, in technical terms, for shit, I lunge across open ground, vault a low tomb, and fall into a yew bush.

The drone comes on. I duck lower, feel the heat and wind of the bullets shredding the world around me. And then the moment passes and I'm still breathing.

I grab the pistol from my shoulder holster, try to take aim. The thing is moving furiously fast. I give leading-the-target the old college try, but I might as well be shooting at the moon.

"Wait until it's closer," Felicity yells. She's behind what's left of a cedar tree and a significant amount of bullet-generated wood pulp.

I'd point out that waiting until it's closer significantly ups the chances of my being turned into pâté, but unfortunately I know that Felicity knows that. Not that she doesn't care. At least I assume she cares. The whole dating thing seems rather dependent on the assumption that she doesn't want me turned into flavorful meat paste. But this is a work situation, and with work, the whole avoiding death thing usually ends up taking less precedence than it really should.

I scan for Kayla. It's always good to know where your friend with super-powers is in situations like this. Saving your arse being the optimal place in my opinion.

She appears to be halfway up a tree.

While significantly further from my arse and its proximal saving zone than I'd like, she does have her sword out. I too am the proud possessor of a sword, but I have yet to work out how to conceal it on a daily basis. Along with speed and strength that would make Wonder Woman blink, Kayla also seems to have the skill to hide a three foot katana on her person regardless of the outfit.

The black dot is growing bigger again. And louder. And deadlier.

It closes on us. Like a lightning bolt flung by a heavily bearded deity. We are a shooting gallery of targets, all lined up in a row. Bullets chew up the ground, racing toward me. I fling myself sideways, firing blindly. Something terrifyingly hot blows my shoe off. I spin and yell.

I come up, gun still raised, blink mud from my eyes.

Kayla is in the air. Behind her, the tree she climbed sways back, bending from the force of her leap. The drone is coming in low and hard, closing the distance. Kayla's whole body is a curve, sword high, feet extended. An Olympic gymnast committing beautiful, graceful suicide.

Closer. With each millisecond, closer.

She snaps the sword down.

And misses.

For the first time in my life, I see Kayla miss.

The drone dances away, spins down between trees, a defiant barrel roll. Its guns still blaze. Paving a path of bullet holes.

Kayla slams into the ground behind the drone, skids through the dirt, never losing her balance for a second. She stares after the machine in hatred.

I pull up my gun, but my eyes aren't on the drone. I'm looking for Felicity. I'm making sure she's OK.

And there she is, performing a pirouette of her own, as her cedar tree becomes a stump. She comes around the toppling trunk, pistol raised, barrel barking. A beautiful economy of motion.

God, my girlfriend is a badass.

Then the drone speeds by, outpaces her ability to aim, sweeps low. The air cracks in its wake and it banks hard, seeming to skid through the air.

And Tabitha. Tabitha, momentarily forgotten in the confusion. She stands at the foot of Clyde's grave. Frozen there. Staring at the drone devouring the distance. She's got one hand up clamping her hat to her head.

I snap my eyes from Tabitha to the drone. *Lead the target.* Felicity's words echoing in my memory. I've been putting in a lot of time at the range since Clyde died. Failing to save the life of your friend tends to cause that sort of behavior. And Felicity is keen for me to not follow in his footsteps. Her voice: *lead the target.*

I lead it. I fire. The gun cracks and jumps in my hand. Again.

Bullets eat the ground before Tabitha. Eight feet away. Six. Four.

I fire again. Again.

Tabitha flings herself backwards, through the air. Down. Down into Clyde's grave.

Three feet.

Again. Again. Three shots until the magazine runs dry.

Two feet.

The last shot leaves my gun.

One.

The path of the drone's gunfire deviates, swings wildly away. The angry chatter of the guns clicks to an abrupt halt. The pitch of the drone's engines scales octaves. And smoke. There is smoke in the sky.

I hit it. Jesus. I actually hit the bloody thing.

It screams out of the air. Less a meteor now, and more a wounded bird. It plows toward a wall, low stone marking the cemetery's boundary. And then it detonates. The percussive blast ripping through the air. Shrapnel scours through damp earth. Fire billows—a phoenix's last flight.

Felicity. My first thought is for her. I move forward.

My shoeless foot skidding through the mud.

She climbs up from behind the destroyed cedar tree, grabs me. "Nice shooting, Tex."

I kiss her, heart and pulse hard in my throat. Hold her to my chest. All around us: the wreckage of the attack. Steaming chunks of metal embedded in shattered gravestones. The priest lying in the fetal position praying at the top of his lungs. Me and my girlfriend, holding each other, holding smoking guns in our spare hands.

No question. Weirdest funeral ever.

2

"What, in the name of all feck, was that?"

Kayla is pissed. Well, Kayla is always pissed, but she appears to have slid closer toward the rabid-animal-fury end of the scale than usual.

"A drone," I say. "It was an attack by an unmanned drone."

Kayla glances at me, then Felicity. "I honestly do not have a feckin' clue what you see in him." To me, "Of course it was a feckin' drone. Feckin' why?"

Somehow, knowing that Kayla is on my side is never as reassuring as I think it should be.

I shrug.

Felicity steps away from me, gives us both a slightly suspicious stare. "If either of you pissed off any governments recently, now is the time to come clean." It strikes me as a little sad that she's not joking.

I try to clear my head, but adrenaline is still flooding the engine. I want to just shoot or run away from everything. "A malfunction?" I manage to suggest. "Some test gone horribly wrong?" It has to be something like that. Drones don't just attack people.

Felicity shakes her head. "The government doesn't test armed drones anywhere near major urban centers."

Kayla nods. "What Wales is for."

I reach up to the anarchy cap, still perched slightly

absurdly on top of my head. "I'll check in with the versions. See if they're picking up any chatter."

"No!" a voice screams.

We all spin to stare at Clyde's grave. There is Tabitha, dirt-spattered, splinter-strewn, clambering out of… Jesus. That's… I don't even want to think about it. She was in her boyfriend's grave. Why on earth could I not have hit that damn drone a moment or two earlier?

"It's him," she says. She's wild-eyed, hanging on to her hat with one hand, using the other to flap madly at us like a grounded fish. "It's them." She glances up at the skies, while heaving herself bodily out of the grave. "The versions," she hisses.

"Oh." Felicity's face is a mask of sympathy. "Tabitha. No." She goes toward her, arms out. "It's not them. You're safe. It was just—"

Except I don't get to find out what it just was, because at that point a Mercedes plows through the gap blown in the cemetery wall by the detonated drone, and careens between the graves toward us.

3

The Mercedes—a silver, growling thing—bucks over the sodden ground, over uprooted stone, through shrapnel-dug trenches. It rears over Clyde's grave. Felicity seizes me around the waist, flings me sideways. I bite dirt. The car crashes down.

A tire buries itself in the open grave, spins wildly. The back tires kick, the Mercedes lurches forward, twists, tilts down, drives itself into the earth. The rear tires kick once more, but one's up in the air now, and the other just sprays mud.

Lying sprawled, I grab my gun, jab it at the car. I stare down the barrel. But I don't know who to shoot at. What to shoot at. The car is empty. The driver's seat void of manic ne'er-do-wells with kamikaze urges.

"What in all hell?" Aliens I have dealt with. Sorcery has become more than passing familiar. But homicidal machinery? That is a new one.

In the face of this weirdness, I hit upon a reliable battle plan. "We have to get out of here," I say.

"Well put." Felicity clambers to her feet then gives me a hand up. "We figure out what the hell this is later. Right now we just bail."

Tabitha is staring at the car. "It's them," she wails. "It's Clyde."

But it's not. It can't be. Clyde is dead. And I was just

talking to the versions. They are far from homicidal.

Except something did just autopilot a car at us. Something... hell, it must have hacked into the car's computer, taken more control than I thought it could.

But who?

I think back to Felicity's question. *Have* I pissed off any major governments? I did cancel my subscription to a few junk email lists I'd found my way onto. But I can't imagine that any major retail chains would take that this badly, even in this economy.

We need to get out of here. But can we even trust our own cars? Will Felicity's Satnav turn rogue? Try to instruct us to death? Turn left off this cliff now?

I'd rather not chance it. In fact I'd rather be a good mile from anything with a computer. Except we're in the middle of a city, the countryside nowhere in sight. The whole options thing is looking very limited right now.

The best hiding places I can figure are the houses, shops, across the road that rings the cemetery. They at least would provide moderate cover from vehicular projectiles while we plan the next step.

"OK," I say. "We're getting out of here," I say. "Whoever's trying to kill us, needs to try a damn sight harder."

This seems a popular suggestion. We move. Kayla accelerates past me, leaps up on what's left of the cemetery wall, surveys the scene. I keep pace with Felicity. Tabitha is between us, wide-eyed and silent now—a state bordering on catatonia. She's not bleeding heavily from anywhere obvious, but the fact that she just spent some quality time in her semi-dead boyfriend's grave could account for the symptoms, I suppose.

Another crunch of steel and stone from behind

us. I glance back. A Jeep has breached the wall and is struggling over the craters and liberally strewn grave markers. I point my pistol, open fire. Smoke starts pouring from the Jeep's hood.

The rest of us make it to the wall ahead of the floundering Jeep. We vault it. And then we pause and we stare at the road. At a road full of even more cars. Our only route of escape looks remarkably like a death trap.

Vehicles have slammed to a halt in the middle of the road. People stand around open car doors staring. They have cellphones and bewildered expressions.

Surely not every car has a computer in it. And those that do... well, they can't all control the steering. I think.

Hell, I don't have any better plans right now.

Plus, beyond the cars lies a store selling televisions of the dubious knock-off variety. A widescreen monstrosity in the window shows a slowly revolving shot of the Statue of Liberty staring imperiously out at the world. Shelter.

I point at it, using the universal language of fleeing. We lunge into the street. Concerned citizens approach us. Kayla punches one in the throat. They stop approaching.

Their cars, however, don't.

A parked Honda lurches forward. I see its owner gesticulate wildly, mouth open in what must be a yell. His car is silver, in need of a wash, and aimed directly at my legs.

I jump, take the hit on my hip. Pain shoots through me. My shoulder comes down on the hood and I roll up the windshield. The car barely had time to accelerate but on top of everything else it hurts. I seriously need to restrict the things coming at me to cotton swabs and rubbing alcohol.

Then a second car shoots forward. The pedestrians are panicking now. Driverless cars slam together. Something crashes into the Honda, sending me rolling to the tarmac. A van bears down. I roll more, try to align myself between tires. Keep my head down.

The van thunders over me, hits something else and shudders to a stop. I lie, face in the tarmac, breathing in short gravelly breaths. I am alive, I remind myself. Still alive. I need to move.

Something plows into the van's side, shoves it sideways. Tires bear down on me. My rolling takes on a desperate edge. Something crashes from the opposite direction. My cover becomes distinctly narrower.

I scramble forward. My fingers rasp against asphalt. More impacts all around me. The car above my head shaking and shuddering like an epilepsy victim. Then I'm beneath another car, this one slung closer to the ground. The exhaust pipe scorches me through what's left of my jacket.

Then the curb is before me. Full of milling feet. I get an arm out. A shoulder. Someone grabs my hand, heaves. I slip up and out, shoulder protesting.

Felicity is there, holding my hand, helping me from my knees to my feet. She grabs me in a savage hug. And I'm not the only one in this relationship fearing for the other's safety, I see.

It's always nice to have something to live for so clearly defined for you.

Then a sound from behind. Another screech of metal, a grunt of over-exerting engines.

Someone grabs me around the shoulder, bowls me

over. I roll, come up staring at where I just stood.

A car vaulted the others. Its hood now occupies the space where my head used to be.

I stare at my rescuer. Kayla. She holds both Felicity and me. "Feckin' idiots." She shakes her head.

Tabitha stands in the store doorway, still staring and wide-eyed. I depart Kayla's grip, shove Tabitha forward and in. We need to get away from the display window. I don't want some errant vehicle sending death-sized shards flying at us all.

The store is dark, narrow, mostly illuminated by opposing walls of TVs. They all show some laminated-looking presenter standing in Times Square, being assaulted by neon and billboards.

We push deeper in. A terrified looking man with too much gel in his hair and too little slack in his T-shirt stares at us, wide-eyed. We stand, eyes locked for a moment. Like panicked gunslingers at high noon. Slowly he extends his left arm, points to a TV.

"You want a Sony?"

Then every screen in the store goes white. Everything in the store is suddenly cast in bright unflattering light. The reflection from the man's greasy hair is almost blinding. There's a high-pitched whine building in the room. I see Felicity's hand go to her mouth. I'm glad I was too vain to get metal fillings.

Then an explosion behind us. We spin as one. A TV blown out. Glass shards scattered on the floor. Wires spitting sparks in the set's empty corpse.

Then another. Another. A whole column of them on one side of the store. Then the column facing it. And then, racing down the store, closing down on us, detonation after detonation. The whole store filling with flying glass and plastic shrapnel. TV remotes fly across the room. Circuit boards spin like shuriken.

I could really use a break from running away from things, right now.

4

I move. Something whips through my hair. Over my head. I stumble, roll, scramble up. Something opens up the back of my hand, and it stings like I jammed it in a bee hive.

There's a back door in front of me. Kayla kicks it open. I slam into an office. I kick the door shut. MI37 members and a terrified television sales man mill about the room. Just to add to his confusion, I grab the computer sitting on the man's desk and fling it out the window.

"What the hell?" he screams, high-pitched enough that I expect Felicity to check her fillings again.

Kayla cocks a fist and looks at Felicity. She shakes her head, but the man backs up fast.

"Are we safe here?" I scan for threats. But obvious shelter is starting to look pretty sparse on the ground.

"Wireless signal. Somewhere without one." Despite the syntax, it still takes me a moment to realize it's Tabitha's words that I can just make out. She stands apart from the rest of us, still not making eye contact with anyone, staring out the shattered window, into the despondent concrete yard beyond.

She's still thinking it's the versions. And it's not them—I'm sure of that—but that doesn't mean it's not something like them. Someone who's in the machines, hacking at computers. And it doesn't mean Tabitha's not right about shelter. We do need to be somewhere without wireless.

The countryside is still too far away. Houses and stores are now clearly out of the question.

Where the hell else?

I scan the depressing little yard behind the store. And there, in the middle of it. Our answer. A manhole cover.

"Underground," I say. "Beneath the earth. The sewers or something."

Felicity looks at me. It's not a happy look. Which is fair enough. No one likes going into the sewers. But at least we get paid for it.

So up and through the window we go, with an eye to the heavens in case anyone wants to send another drone at us or hurl a 747 at us for good measure. But nothing breaks the cloud line.

Kayla heaves the manhole cover loose with a burst of rust and stone dust. Insects scrabble to hide from the sudden light of day, like tiny mundane vampires. I stare into blackness and try to focus on my desire to prolong my life until lunch time.

I jump. My feet hit the floor in a splash of cold water. The smell hits me right back. I blanch and think that maybe taking a Mercedes to the face wouldn't be so bad.

Kayla lands almost on top of me. Felicity and Tabitha opt to take the ladder I missed. We stand together, huddled, all trying to breathe through our mouths. Felicity leans against me, her head resting on my shoulder.

After five minutes it seems like no one's trying to kill us anymore.

"What the hell was that?" My voice sounds tinny in the tight dark space. Not that I really expect an answer. But this much confusion and bewilderment—I can't keep it inside. What could we have possibly done to piss off someone that powerful?

"Clyde," Tabitha says. She's changed, here in the dark. Her silhouette stands taller now. She is held more rigidly. Her voice has changed too. It doesn't tremble. It's flat and cold. "It was Clyde."

"It can't have been the versions," I start.

"It—" Tabitha starts.

"Not here," Felicity's voice cuts her off sharply. "Not now." She pushes away from me. "What we do now is we concentrate on getting out of this, very literal shithole." She looks about her, points off in one direction. "The office is this way."

There's not much else to be said. We start walking.

ONE UNPLEASANT HOUR LATER

We haul ourselves out of another manhole cover remarkably close to MI37 headquarters, near the Oxford train station. We are shivering, stinking, bleeding, and somehow, I realize, all of us are *still* wearing Tabitha's tinfoil hats. Felicity's bonnet resembles a drowned scarecrow draped over her head.

I touch my baseball cap as Felicity punches the six-digit code into the office's unassuming front door. Tabitha flinches as I do it.

"How the hell has this not fallen off?"

Tabitha shrugs. "Slight electromagnetic field. Your body has one. Everyone does. Opposite charge. The hat has. Static cling basically."

An angry goth on the cusp of some severe

psychological scarring she may be, but Tabitha has got some serious mad professor skills.

"You OK?" I ask her.

"The versions. Just need to delete them. Then I'll be fine." She says it flatly, like she's telling me she needs a cup of coffee.

"No," I say. "This wasn't them."

She's not looking at me. "Today. Burying all of it. Buried him. Going to bury them. No more Clyde."

"They would never try to kill you," I say. "They—" Her look cuts me off. *They love you*, I was going to say. But she doesn't want to acknowledge that. And even now I'm not quite willing to force the subject.

"How sure?" Tabitha presses her advantage. "A hundred percent?" She shrugs, backs up a step. "I'm not. But I delete them, I'm sure it's not them ever again."

Ah, the violent extremist version of "prevention is better than the cure." Time to nod, smile, and prepare the sedative. I glance at Felicity. We're out of the field, so technically this is her territory.

"Tabitha," Felicity says. "No one is deleting anyone without a debrief and an investigation. And yes, pending that investigation, deleting the versions is on the table. But there needs to be demonstrable reason."

Tabitha opens her mouth to object, but Felicity rides over her.

"Depending on the debrief, yes I may quarantine the server while we investigate, but that is as far as I will go for now. And before you say another word, consider that I have had bullets, cars, and the internal organs of a flatscreen TV hurled at me today, that I am covered in liquid feces, and that my patience is starting to wear just a tiny bit thin."

I swear I see Kayla smile at that. Tabitha, on the other hand, grimaces, and starts examining her nails.

FIFTEEN MINUTES LATER, CONFERENCE ROOM B

Apparently when Felicity said there would be a brief break before the debrief she intended for us to wash up, not collapse in a chair and wait for our limbs to lock up. When she comes into the conference room, she has managed to change and wash most of the shit out of her hair. I, on the other hand, feel like a crap-coated mannequin.

She gives me a sympathetic smile, goes to sit next to me, then wrinkles her nose and moves a chair down.

"You OK?"

I think about that. "I knew today was going to be a little odd, but this isn't exactly how I imagined it all playing out."

She crooks a smile, but it doesn't last long. Maybe because I'm having trouble sharing it with her.

"You worried?" she says.

That, I don't need to think about for long. "I'm terrified. That was an assassination attempt. I mean, it has to have been. And whoever it was, they were not playing around in the slightest. I can't even think of who has that sort of firepower."

Felicity momentarily looks as if she's chewing a lemon slice. "Clyde?" she says eventually.

I shake my head, vehemently. "That doesn't make any sense. The versions are weird, yes, but they have been nothing but benignly Clyde-like. And the crazy deep-end version of Clyde—who, I want to point out, was only around for a day or two, after a lifetime of being pleasant and helpful—well, he's dead. We were all there. We saw him die. And beyond that even, sure he did some weird inhuman shit at the end, but nothing that was ever on this scale. He overwrote a brain or two. He didn't send military drones after people. And all the questionable stuff he did was, you know... it was aimed at saving the world. Whatever the hell happened today, it did not smack of saving the world."

Felicity nods slowly, digesting. "Something like him. Him but worse. Something that can hack computers. Any computer it seems. That can send a massive power surge to a specific shop in Oxford if it wants to."

"Maybe," I nod. "But does it have to be some computer intelligence? Couldn't it just be someone with a computer and way too much power?"

She nods. "There aren't many people like that though."

I nod too. She's right. We've riled up a big nasty, and we don't even know who or what. The worry shows on Felicity's face.

"What about you?" I ask. "Are you OK?"

"I think the word you used was terrified."

"Is it stupid," I say, "that this threat feels scarier because it's terrestrial? That it's not some sort of mythical beast come to life?"

Shaw smiles, slides over to the closer chair. She takes my hand, smiles softly. "A little bit," she says.

The conference room door bangs open. Tabitha stands there, holding a laptop at arm's length. She stares at our twined fingers.

"That shit. Stop it." Tabitha has been decidedly opposed to public displays of office affection since her own relationship took such a colossal nose dive. Felicity pulls her hand away.

Tabitha sets the laptop down gingerly then shoves it at me, and steps away.

"Wire it up. Start it up."

It's the Clyde Versions' laptop. Their home away from the server. And as Tabitha is the only one of us with both a good working knowledge of computers and a physical body, then she's the one who set it up. She still handles it like it's nuclear waste, though.

"Ethernet cable," she says. "Need to plug it in. Killed office wireless. Firewalled to fuck. We are."

I'm not sure that someone or something that can remotely drive cars at us is going to really care about our firewalls, but it's better than nothing I suppose. And… "Does that mean I can take my hat off?" I ask.

Tabitha grunts like I just physically hurt her. I decide to take that as a yes. The fact that she doesn't respond by trying to scalp me, makes me think that I was right. Felicity scrapes her mangled bonnet off with a sigh.

Kayla slouches in as the computer whirs to life. She's as filthy as I am but seems to be suffering less physically. She slides into a chair, as loose and limber as ever.

On the computer screen, a small black box appears. A cursor winks once, twice. Then the whole screen goes black. And then, resolving out of the darkness: something not entirely dissimilar to a college dorm room. Three beds. A massively overburdened bookshelf. A few Klimt prints.

A man's head pokes into the frame. Scruffy beard, slightly disheveled hair, square glasses, innocent expression. Then the man's identical twin appears. And then another.

The three Clyde versions peer out at us.

"So, sort of wondering, as one does," says one of them, "about what in the name of all that is good, green, and holy happened out there?"

In a small guilty place, I think I should know which version is speaking, but they are, quite literally, identical. The clothes aren't exactly the same, but each one of them is wearing cords, and a shirt, and the same tweed jacket. It's basically impossible to distinguish them.

Not unsettling at all, that.

"Did a drone attack you?" asks another. "Definitely looked like a drone."

"Very drone shaped," says the third.

"A military drone, that is," comments the second. "Not the male bee. Unless it was a male bee that happened to be shaped like a military drone. Though…" He cocks his head on one side. "… a touch unlikely."

"A very salient clarification." The third one points to the second one.

The first turns around. "Don't mean to interrupt, you two. More of an interjection really. And, yes, obviously, appreciate the accuracy of the question. But, I was thinking, you know, again, just a potential suggestion, but should we sort of listen and see if they confirm it first?"

The third one points to the first. "Excellent idea. Love it. All ears." He puts his hands behind his ears and pushes them out.

Office meetings have become decidedly longer ever since we got three Clydes instead of one.

"Why?" Tabitha stares at the screen as if hoping to crack it.

"Hello," says the second Clyde. He looks at his feet. "Good to see you, Tabby. You look fantastic. Glad you're OK. I was really rooting for you."

"Me too," nods the third. "Heart in mouth.

Metaphorically. Binary code in the recycle bin may be a closer analogy. But, you know. Totally glad. We're all glad. And you really do look lovely too. Really like the hair."

"Why?" Tabitha screams at them. "You murderous little fucks! Why'd you try to kill us?"

Which, I suspect, is not exactly how the versions saw this going. They recoil from the screen.

I need to not be weirded out by them, and to focus on keeping MI37 functional. "Look," I say, trying to play the peacekeeper, "this isn't an interrogation."

"A magnet to your pissing hard drive," Tabitha growls.

"We wouldn't!" protests the first Clyde.

"Never," says the second. "Never ever."

"You know how we feel," says the third. "Subtlety is not our greatest asset. You know that. You loved us, Tabby. We love you."

"Shut up!" Tabitha snaps. Her fingernails are digging into the surface of the table. "I loved Clyde. Clyde, you are fucking not."

"Let's just calm—" I start.

"Enough," Felicity snaps. "This is not a witch hunt, and it is not a couple counseling session. Clydes, I want to know exactly what you saw. Not just on the ground. Digital chatter. Energy spikes."

"Lie. They fucking will," Tabitha says. "Save their arses. 'Til they're ready to try again."

"Tabitha!" Felicity snaps. "For the last time. We are not making any snap judgments. I personally find it very unlikely that Clyde, any bloody version of him, is on a MI37-oriented murder spree."

Tabitha snaps around at her. Somewhat to my surprise, I feel my fists bunch.

But then a voice cuts into our conversation. A voice out of place in a secure government facility, because it's a voice I don't recognize at all.

"Well, Director Shaw," it says, "that assessment may be rather a misstep, I'm afraid to say."

5

We all spin to stare at the new voice's source. Even Kayla. My stomach sinks as I turn, bottoming out somewhere around my knees. The last time someone showed up at the door of our conference room unannounced, things did not exactly proceed well from there.

He's a tall man, even has a few inches on me. Narrow frame, though there's some breadth in his shoulders. Angular cheeks. Black hair swept low over his forehead in what, I suspect, is a rather obvious move to hide a receding hairline. A wire brush of a mustache. The sort that Hitler made unpopular. Good suit though. And a briefcase. And an umbrella.

"Who the hell are you?" Felicity snaps.

Which means she doesn't know him. Which means he's not an ex-boyfriend. Which means he's definitely a step up from our last unannounced guest. I immediately like him just a little bit better.

"Name's Duncan Smythe. Lovely to meet you all. No need to stand up. I'm fully briefed. I know all your names, backgrounds, all that sort of stuff. The people who put these briefing documents together are terribly thorough, and so it only seems polite to read them. I'm from the British consulate to the United States of America, by the way. And sorry to burst in so unannounced. Again, the door codes were in the briefing jacket, and well, you know as well as I do that you don't have a doorbell." He speaks fast and clipped, despite the ripe vowels. A moneyed, educated voice. The sort you'd expect to hear on an old BBC show telling you about how we're beating the snot out of Rommel.

"I have a damn phone," Felicity points out.

I look back and forth from her to the newcomer. He seems entirely unfazed by her anger. Not that it is anger exactly. I've seen Felicity angry, and this… well, this is a dry heat. It's more like she's establishing a dominance pattern. The alpha dog of the pack making sure her status is recognized.

Kayla has the same bored, bemused expression she's had since Tabitha started haranguing the versions. Tabitha seems like she's just anxious for this little moment to be over so she can get back to the aforementioned haranguing.

And me, well… I don't know. If I had to put money down, I'd say Smythe is the sort of person who comes with answers, but not the sort of answers anybody likes.

"Yes," Smythe says to Felicity. "I have your phone number. Another of the many itemized pieces of information I was provided with." He nods in the direction of his briefcase. "Between you and me, it's a little bit of overkill actually. But, given the events of the morning, our schedule has moved up a little bit, and so, and again this is with the utmost apologies, the following meeting has become rather urgent."

"Following meeting, my arse," says Felicity. "If you want to come back—"

The tall man smiles apologetically, pops open his briefcase, and pulls out a small red file folder. He passes it to Felicity.

She eyes it suspiciously but silently. She unwinds the piece of red string holding the folder closed and pulls out a sheet of cream paper. Classy paper. The sort of paper that you'd expect a man with a voice like Smythe's to hand out from small file folders.

Felicity looks from the paper to Smythe, then back at the paper. She returns it to the folder and hands it back to him with a tight little smile entirely absent of mirth.

"Proceed," she says.

Smythe nods politely. I have a sneaking suspicion that the alpha dog thing just got derailed.

"Sorry," says one of the Clydes from the laptop. "Bit difficult to see from back here, what's going on?"

Felicity's eyes snap to the laptop like an eagle sighting prey. And I knew I wasn't going to like Smythe's answers.

"Should he be here?" she asks.

Smythe shrugs. "According to my briefing documents none of your versions have been compromised."

"Can't be sure," Tabitha declares, though I suspect she's clueless about what either Smythe or Felicity is referencing. But she's smart enough to spot an opportunity when it presents itself. "Better be safe. Shut them down."

To be honest, I'm not entirely opposed to her argument. I don't believe the versions tried to kill us, but computers have been turned against us today. What if they were corrupted?

But Clyde was my best friend…

But the versions aren't Clyde. Not quite.

Felicity shakes her head at Tabitha. She sits, and pulls the laptop over toward her, out of Tabitha's reach. She points the webcam in Smythe's direction.

"This," Smythe says, hanging his umbrella on the back of his chair, and laying down his briefcase, "is, for the record, information classified as top secret. Which I realize is rather redundant for people like yourselves, but they make me say these things. Dotting i's and crossing t's and all that red tape malarkey.

"I am here representing the British government, and its US consulate, to speak to you about a joint mission with the CIA for which your expertise is required."

"CIA?" Tabitha immediately looks suspicious. That said, Tabitha wears a tinfoil hat these days, so if anyone was going to look suspicious it was probably her.

"The Americans?" There is significantly less antipathy in Felicity's voice. To be honest it sounds a little more like excitement.

Smythe inclines his head at Felicity and ignores Tabitha's heckling.

"You are all, of course, familiar with Clyde Marcus Bradley," he says.

"I am," says one of the Clydes. A smile twitches across my face. It feels like an irresponsible thing to have done.

"He's dead," Tabitha says.

"Indeed," Smythe smiles broadly. "Very much so. We have it on file. Deceased earlier this month. October ninth to be precise. The Didcot incident." He smiles again and nods at the laptop. "However, it does seem to be having a little trouble sticking."

There's a noise from the laptop, something like a gulp. "This isn't an undead rights thing is it?"

Smythe reaches into his briefcase, retrieves a small bottle of water, cracks the seal, and sips.

"While this matter does intimately concern you,"

he nods at the computer, "it is not exactly about your rights. Or if so only indirectly so."

"Is it about that thing we downloaded?" one of them says. "Because that link was misleading, and I really had no interest in violating copyright. I'm generally opposed to anything that involves the word violating. Pretty strict principle in fact. Though—"

Smythe clears his throat. "Maybe I should continue and that would clear muddy waters," he suggests.

"Oh yes," says a Clyde.

"Good idea," says another.

"Sorry," the third throws in for good measure.

Smythe arches dark eyebrows. "Indeed." He sips his water again.

"Mute them. I can." Tabitha suggests. "Happy to."

Smythe's eyebrows arch in her direction now. I get the impression he's used to dealing with the sort of smart efficient people who put together extensive background documents on other people, and not with... well, us.

"Six copies of Mr. Bradley's personality were created," Smythe tells us. "The original copy, in Peru, came into being on October sixth."

"Version 2.0," a subsequent Clyde version adds.

"Indeed," Smythe says, and this time I expect to see ice cubes form in the water.

"Sorry," says Clyde.

I'm fairly sure Smythe is reconsidering Tabitha's offer of the mute button.

"Everyone shut up and let the man speak." Felicity is leaning forward in her seat.

"So, yes," Smythe continues, "Version 2.0 was created in Peru. Then five copies of that version were

made. One is in the possession of Miss Mulvani."
Smythe nods in Tabitha's direction. Which means that
I was wrong in assuming she'd destroyed hers.

"Three are represented here," he appears to force
himself to acknowledge the laptop. "And one was given
to Miss Devon Alman, Mr. Bradley's former partner.
She has however destroyed her copy. That leaves five
copies in existence."

And I've been assuming Smythe is a smart man, but
that seems like a pretty basic math error.

"Four," I correct him. "There are four copies left. The
version of Clyde on the mask, Version 2.0—that was
destroyed. He was killed."

Smythe smiles in an entirely surprising way. Like a
very jolly shark.

"Really, Mr. Wallace?" he says. "Is that so?"

I look around the room, rather nonplussed. I see
similarly blank faces. I mean, we just buried him. We
were pretty convinced of his status as a dead man.
After all, we were there. We saw it happen. The mask
that housed Clyde's personality, that *was* Clyde, was
split in two when a time-traveling Russian magician
pulled the power out of it at exactly the same moment
that I, in an attempt to save Clyde, sort of… well, I
haymaker-ed him.

Honestly, it seemed like a valid plan at the time.

But we were there, and we saw him die, so I go with,
"Isn't it?"

There is a grating noise from across the table.
Tabitha's knuckles are the shade of white that I imagine
exists at the heart of the sun. She appears to be literally
crushing the table beneath her hands.

Even Kayla looks mildly interested now.

Smythe doesn't say a word.

"This morning?" I ask, refusing to wholly believe it. "At the funeral? That was seriously Clyde?" I think about that for a moment. "No," I say. "No. He's dead." I insist it at this tall, smooth little diplomat with his made-for-DVD personality. "He's dead."

Smythe shrugs. "Personally, Mr. Wallace, I don't know. You say he's dead. The CIA claim he's hiding out on a server farm somewhere on the North American continent, hacking federal government servers like a child picking candy out of jars."

"It's not possible," I say.

But—

"Yes." Tabitha drops the word like a tombstone. "It is. If he downloaded himself in time. Before the mask broke."

"It's not possible," I say again. Because... because... No. Except, is it just I don't want it to be true? Dealing with the fact that my best friend is three digital copies of himself is hard enough without having to deal with his super-powered, murderous evil twin. I drop my head to the table.

No. Just... no.

"What evidence exactly do the CIA have?" Felicity asks.

And I love Felicity Shaw. The voice of reason in the insanity my life has become.

"Well, I'm sure they'll tell you." I look up to see if Smythe has another sharkish grin, but he's shuffling papers back into his briefcase. Putting the cap back on his little water bottle.

"What do you mean?" And any hint of being offended by Smythe taking the alpha dog role is gone. But her excitement seems tinged with a little anxiety now.

Smythe retrieves one final item from his briefcase before snapping it closed. A simple manila folder this time. He places it before him. "Your flight details," he says. "To America. You're leaving tomorrow. Heathrow. British Airways. Of course. Business class, I think you'll find. The Americans are footing the bill."

It's moving too fast. Everything is always moving too fast in this job. The Americans want us to... what? Find and kill Version 2.0 of Clyde. A version that this functionary is saying tried to kill us this morning. A version that I worked alongside. That, hell, I had a hand in creating. A version I counted as a friend.

And yet... And yet...

I wish that Smythe's story didn't make sense. That it had plausible deniability. But there is a terrifyingly implacable logic to it all.

I look at Felicity. She does not seem to share my feelings. Instead Christmas seems to have come early for Felicity Shaw. Personally I don't see exactly what there is to be excited about.

"Is there anything else we need to know?" she asks.

Smythe considers this, head cocked to one side. "You should try to move about the cabin at least once an hour. That'll stop the blood pooling. Good for the heart. It's a long flight."

He pushes back his chair, stands up, smiles perfunctorily. "I'll see myself out."

And he leaves us there, sitting in the crater of yet another bombshell.

6

FELICITY SHAW'S APARTMENT. EVENING

Felicity and I sit opposite each other in her living room, and try and work out what to say.

It's been a quiet few hours since Duncan Smythe left Conference Room B at MI37 headquarters. Felicity dismissed the others so they could pack. We worked out if we wanted pasta or curry for supper. I finally washed the fecal matter off myself and applied rubbing alcohol to my various abrasions. And then this—sitting in a chair, and trying to work out where our heads are at.

"Do you believe it?" Felicity asks me finally.

I stare at the magazines on the coffee table—copies of *The Economist*, and *National Geographic*, because Felicity Shaw is not a frilly or fluffy woman. And she certainly has a way of cutting to the chase.

"I…" I say, which pretty much sums it all up. And then, eventually, "I don't want to."

Felicity smiles. "That's not exactly answering the question."

"Do you believe it?" I respond, which still isn't.

Felicity smiles again. She sees through me the same way most people see through windows.

She puts her feet up on the couch. There's a framed Georgia O'Keeffe print behind her looking floral and ambiguously suggestive. Some of her hair has fallen down in front of her eyes. She pushes it back.

"I knew Clyde…" she shrugs, "for a long time. I recruited him out of Cambridge University four years ago. I promoted him to field agent. I briefed and debriefed him a hundred times."

"Debriefed sounds dirty," I say.

"You know you use humor as a defense mechanism?" she asks.

Like a window.

"I knew Clyde longer than you," she says, "though never as intensely as you did, if that's the word. Whatever died when we fought the Russians, wasn't the man that I recruited. The man I recruited was already long dead. The Didcot incident, or whatever Smythe called it.

"And," she continues, "the man I recruited, that I promoted, that dead man, he could never have done any of the things we saw today. But whatever he became, whatever was left of him after he died… I don't know. It seems like it's on the scale of possibility. I don't even know what the versions are capable of. They seem harmless, but even the original Clyde, your friend, my recruit, wasn't harmless. That man knew enough magic to level a house. And if that was corrupted…" She trails off, but I think it's just because she'd rather not follow that line of logic out loud.

"So you do believe," I conclude for her.

She shifts on the sofa, sinking into a slouch. "I'm saying I don't know. I can't know right now. But I know that the CIA wouldn't be shipping us across the Atlantic if they didn't have a damn good reason."

The CIA. Jesus. I shake my head.

Felicity shifts in her chair. "What?" I ask. I know her

well enough now to know when she's hesitating about saying something.

"Just... you know, the *CIA*." That, I think, effectively sums up what Hollywood has told me about that agency.

"Is it wrong for me to be a little bit excited?" Felicity asks.

"Excited?" I try to fit that word into the scenario facing us. The scenario where something vast and powerful that may or may not be our former colleague and friend is trying to kill us. I struggle.

"I mean," Felicity goes on, without waiting for me to find the right words for what I'm thinking, "the Americans. The CIA. They asked for us. For MI37. A month ago our agency was on the verge of being shut down. Now a super-power is asking for our collaboration. This is huge."

She bites her lower lip, not enough to show teeth, just the corner of it tucked away. She has a slightly faraway look in her eyes.

And I guess I hadn't really thought about anything in those terms.

"So..." I venture, "we should have our lives threatened by our friends more often?"

She flaps a hand at me. "No. I didn't mean it like that." She shakes her head slightly. "It's just... They're taking us seriously, Arthur. They're taking me seriously. Do you know how long MI37 has been out in the political cold? Trying to do anything at all? This could change all of that. Proper staffing. Proper budget."

And I do see it, at least a little. MI37 has been her life for... Well, I'm not exactly sure how long. Around twenty years, I think, but I don't actually know how

Felicity got involved in this line of work. Still, I can understand why the sudden legitimacy of MI37 would be a big deal for her. She has a lot more invested in it than I do, and I like this job.

But… excited?

I close my eyes. I should be happy for her, even if I can't be for me.

"That's good," I say. "That'll be good."

With Felicity being the keen observer of human behavior that she is, and me being about as guileful as a brick, the lack of enthusiasm is noticed.

She grimaces. "I'm sorry. Obviously there could be better circumstances. I know that. Of course I know that. And I hope it's not Clyde. Just like you."

I nod to that.

She tries to erase her frown with another smile. "You still haven't answered my question. If you really think it's him."

I knew she'd noticed that.

I debate whether I actually want to answer. "The versions couldn't do it," I say. "Wouldn't. Regardless of how they feel about me or you. They are head over heels in love with Tabitha. They would never do anything to hurt her."

"But Version 2.0?" Felicity presses.

I open my mouth.

He was my friend. Even Version 2.0. Even after the man's meat body died. He was my friend. And, yes, he did some questionable things at the end. But he was my friend.

He made a woman kill herself.

I close my mouth.

He was dealing with the serious psychological

trauma of no longer being corporeal, and none of us helped him. We just went on like things were normal. And we never really acknowledged that he had died. We never even tried to come to terms with it. Just ignored it. And wouldn't that piss even the calmest man off.

But he never complained. Never said a word. And he was fighting alongside us right up to the end.

I open my mouth again. I fail to progress.

"Perhaps," Felicity suggests, leaning forward, "before you answer that question, you should consider that you are still wearing your tinfoil-lined hat."

I put a hand up. And she's right I am.

I put my head down, massage my temples.

"God help us," I say. "If it's him. God help everyone on earth."

7

I wait until Felicity's asleep before I fire up the laptop. I'm back in the living room, sitting on the couch, the little computer balanced on a stack of newspapers.

I'm not sure if it's the right thing to do, but I want to talk to the versions. To, well… to my version, though I feel uncomfortable about using the possessive when talking about… well, whatever the hell the versions are.

When Clyde… Version 2.0… When he died, I chatted with 2.2 a few times. But each time the distance between what was going on and genuine human interaction seemed to yawn wider. Until I couldn't take it any longer.

And, in the end, I'm using the wired connection. And I've still got my baseball cap on.

After thirty seconds of waiting, the version's face appears. The window on my screen puts him in the same disarrayed room as he was in earlier.

We look at each other for a long time.

"Sooo…" he says after a while. "That was a little bit awkward, wasn't it?"

Normally I'd smile. If Clyde was… was… screw it, if he was a person sitting opposite me, then I'd smile. But he's not. And it's as obvious as it ever was right now.

"Did you know?" I ask. "Did you know it was him?"

Clyde looks shocked. "Of course not!" He shakes

his head vehemently. "I was…" He hesitates. "Well, there's basically the uncomfortable fact that I was created. And that happened prior to Version 2.0 going off the proverbial deep end for a swim in insanity stew. I mean, I don't even know how he went into your head and put in all that sword-wielding stuff."

And there's a topic I'd been trying to mentally dodge. The fact that Version 2.0 has already been in my brain, has already done something irreparable.

But he was trying to help, that's the thing. I had a sword. A flaming sword at that. It was, after Felicity, the coolest thing this job has given me. Except I didn't know how to use it. And knowing how to use it against time-traveling Russian sorcerers could help save the world. So Version 2.0 went directly into my brain and gave me a migraine and an encyclopedic knowledge of how to use the weapon.

I close my eyes. "Why would he do it?" I don't really expect an answer. But surely the versions know 2.0 better than any of us. "He always tried to do the right thing. That's why this doesn't make any sense to me."

"It doesn't make any sense to me either," 2.2 says. "I can't imagine a scenario where I'd want to kill you all. Not that I want you to think that I spend my time thinking of those sorts of scenarios. Except for today. But that was only for around ten minutes. And, well, you know, there were extenuating circumstances."

Again I feel the distance between a real conversation and whatever this is opening up before me.

Abruptly, I feel very tired. Outside, beyond the plants Felicity has stacked up on the window sills, Oxford seems very quiet and distant. The world holding its breath.

"What do we do?" I ask him. "If it's…" I was going to say "you," but… "If it's him." I shake my head. "I can't believe he's just gone evil. That's not what happens to people. He must have a reason. Probably a good one."

Version 2.2 shrugs—a long hunching of the shoulders. "We find out his reason?" he says.

But that's not the end of it, of course. We don't stop there. And even if he has a really great reason, I doubt anyone from MI37 is going to roll over and let this Version 2.0 kill them. We're the sort of people who get obstinate about that sort of thing.

I feel an impasse coming on. One where we try and delete someone who does not want to be deleted. And if Clyde… if Version 2.0 is behind today's attack, then I can't imagine this going very well for us.

And Felicity is excited about it. I understand her point of view intellectually, but still…

I don't want to do this anymore. To have this conversation anymore. I thought it would help and it has not.

"I should go to bed," I tell Clyde.

Clyde shrugs a few more times. "Just…" he starts then stops, looks down at his feet.

"What?" I ask him.

"If… Well, say it was Version 2.0, and these CIA chaps and chapesses are right. And say it isn't that he's got some startlingly good reason for trying to off his very best friends, and all round good people, which I feel I should stress is how we really do feel. All of us. At least me and the two others I know. But let's say this Version 2.0 just doesn't feel that way about you, and he is, not to put too fine a point on it, an evil bastard.

But, in that scenario, well, and this sounds a little silly now I go to put it into words. Like speaking the lyrics to a song you really like out loud. I should be so lucky, lucky, lucky, lucky. I should be so lucky in love. For example. I'm pretty sure I sounded stupid there. But just to repeat that whole experience. I guess, I just wanted to check, we'd still be friends, right, Arthur?"

I look at him. This picture of my friend, that talks and acts just like him. And can there be a digital copy of friendship?

But I don't ask him that, I just say, "Yes, of course." And then I close the laptop, and go to bed.

8

HEATHROW

Getting on a flight to New York does not go as well as planned.

The first plane we board experiences "technical difficulties" which sound and smell a lot like the plane's computers detonating. Then we're told to meet an incoming flight at another gate, until it comes out that somehow the plane has been accidentally rerouted to Honolulu. And so, with Kayla muttering a mounting number of curses and threatening to disembowel air stewards left right and center, we head back to the ticket desk just in time to see every computer in the airport go down.

At that point, Kayla is not the only one about to get her rage on. Beleaguered men in bright yellow jackets tell everyone that everything is fine and will be fixed in a moment. Their visible sweat belies their promises. The entire airport seems on the verge of a riot. It doesn't help that Tabitha is looking darkly at the sky and muttering, "He's watching us, the bastard."

I pull my baseball cap down just a little bit tighter.

We head out of the terminal to get some fresh air, and to avoid the impending violence.

We stand there, kicking our heels, and rubbing our hands in the late October chill, and watch as an expensively shiny limousine pulls up in front of us. The back door opens and Smythe steps out, smoothing his mustache.

"Spot of bother with the computers, so I'm led to believe."

Kayla takes a step toward him. "If I find out you're feckin' around with us, then I swear to God, you will find yourself using your lower intestines as a feckin' belt."

Charm, I have been told, is Kayla's middle name.

"I'm sure that won't be necessary," Smythe says without even the slightest blink of an eye. The man has balls, I will give him that.

"Is it him?" I ask. "Is it Clyde?"

Smythe contemplates this, Kayla still invading his personal space. "I honestly couldn't say. They don't brief me on that kind of thing."

"Fucking with me," Tabitha comments. "Sending us up against an artificial intelligence. All the computers blow. Hmmm…" She tilts her head to one side, places a finger to her chin. The middle finger, I note. "What could it be?"

Normally we let Felicity do the talking. This must be why.

Smythe nods in the face of Tabitha's invective. "A definite correlation of events, I grant you. But I'm not going to determine any causative links based on that sort of evidence. Above my pay grade, as the saying goes."

I glance at Smythe's car again. He has a driver. Based on my own government salary, his pay grade seems a little high to me. That said, I get the impression that people like Smythe are not always entirely forthcoming with little things like the truth.

"Are we getting there today?" Felicity only lets a

sliver of frustration slip into her voice. "Or are you here to tell us to go back home?"

Smythe looks uncharacteristically uncomfortable. "The Americans have arranged something." The word "Americans" seems to cause him particular problems, as if he is saying the sentence around a word lodged between his teeth.

"So we're going. Terminal?" Felicity says. She is brusque and unflappably efficient. She is, I think, very admirable. I step a little closer to her.

"I'll drive you," says Smythe with a magnanimous, if slightly put-upon smile. With an arm he offers the interior of his car.

We drive in relative silence. The brooding anger of Heathrow's crowd pressing up against the car windows.

And yet, I have to say having someone screw around with our flight is significantly better than that person throwing large metal objects at my head.

And then I realize that I'm about to get into a large metal object entirely dependent on the sort of computers that Version 2.0, or whoever else it might be, likes to diddle viciously.

I've been in a plane that fell out of the sky, and it wasn't so much fun that I'd like to repeat the experience.

"I don't think we can go," I say suddenly.

Everyone looks at me. Smythe in particular seems to think this is a poor suggestion. Felicity wrinkles her brow.

"He's going to crash the plane," I say. "It's about the only thing he didn't throw at us yesterday. He's already screwed with an enormous number of planes today. How will this be hard for him?"

Tabitha looks at me with a long hard stare.

"Swim the Atlantic. We will," she tells me, "if that's what it takes. Delete him. What we *are* going to do. Help me. What you are going to do."

Occasionally I think Tabitha is in a fight with Kayla for being the scariest person on this team.

"Actually," Smythe says, with the same forced air that he told us about our new flight arrangements, "the *Americans* seem to think their plane will be safe."

This sounds dubious to me. I let my face express that.

Smythe gives an uncomfortable shrug. "Truth be told they may be right. One of their DARPA secret projects."

I mentally check the acronym. Something, advanced research projects, something. Mad military science, the internet would have me believe.

Smythe looks as if he's swallowing something unpleasant. "We didn't exactly know they'd flown it here until they pointed it out to us on the airfield."

There is a collective raising of eyebrows.

Smythe grimaces. "Bloody show offs."

THIRTY-FIVE THOUSAND FEET HIGHER UP

While this plane may be a multi-million dollar expression of military might and stealth, no one seems to have thought to put a single comfy seat in it. Black sleek lines, mirrored surfaces, and no headroom—the interior of this thing is a triumph of geometry over ergonomics. From the outside, it also resembles a metal paper airplane more than anything that can do Mach two ever should in my opinion.

On the plus side, no one has flung this thing at the Atlantic yet to see if it bounces.

AND BACK DOWN AGAIN

I descend from the stealth jet legs akimbo. The JFK airport tarmac is surprisingly sunny, though the temperature is doing little to match the sun's promise. Planes and grass and low buildings spread off in all directions.

Felicity steps down after me and slips an arm around my waist while she cracks her neck one way and the other.

"You half expecting this place to blow up?"

"A little more than half," I admit. There are a lot of large metal objects with computers in them here.

"He hasn't been aggressive since the funeral," she says. "We've no reason to think he couldn't have continued the attack. Maybe he's changed tactics. The Heathrow incident was virtually peaceful."

Him. She's already using that as the pronoun. Not it. Not them. Him. As if it's already a fait accompli that Clyde is the one behind everything.

But maybe that's the smart thing to do. Mentally prepare for the confrontation now, rather than deal with the mental whiplash later.

Maybe…

The others have disembarked too. Tabitha shields her eyes against the low sun, scans the foreign landscape, and points.

"Contact. Ours. There."

We turn to look. There's a man wearing what appears to be a standard-issue CIA man-in-black suit crossing the tarmac toward us.

Seeing our collective gaze, he raises a hand and gives us a broad wave in a very un-man-in-black way.

"Yo!" I hear him shout over the tarmac. "MI37 dudes!"

My brow immediately furrows. This feels weirder than jet-lag alone can account for. I turn to Felicity.

"Did he just call us—"

"Yes," says Felicity, looking a little concerned, "he did."

"I could kill him from here," Kayla comments.

Which seems like a drastic solution to our problem. If it even is a problem.

"Surely," I say, "someone disguising themselves as a CIA contact would not go as far off stereotype to call us dudes, right?"

Felicity cocks her head. "Your argument," she says, "is that he's so unlikely a CIA man, he has to be one?"

I think that through. "Yes."

Felicity shrugs. "Decent enough theory."

"Thanks."

"You're welcome." She pecks me on the cheek. "Now let's go see what he has to say."

"No worries," Kayla says as we set off, "I can kill him up close too."

We cross the tarmac, cold winds sweeping out of the deceptively sunny sky. Say what you like about the damp in England, at least its winds aren't armed with razor blades. I wish I'd packed a thicker coat.

Our CIA man is waiting by the sort of slick black car Smythe favors. He's young and strikingly handsome. Sharp cheekbones, dark eyes in lightly tanned skin. His hair is dark and shiny in a way that is usually reserved for TV ads. He wears it surprisingly long for a man in black—down to his shoulders, and the wind buffets it about his face. He has to push strands out of his eyes twice before he can extend his hand for Felicity to shake. I see pale green tattoos poking out from under the starched white shirt.

"Dudes," he says again as he pumps Felicity's hand. "Very cool to meet you all. Totally, I mean…" He puts his spare hand to his forehead and mimes a small detonation. "Read your files last night. Mind blown. Trippy shit, man. Trippy as hell." He extends a clenched fist toward me—a slow motion punch. I stare at his hand.

"Fist bump?" he asks me. "No? That's cool." He nods. "Very cool." He grips my hand in a firm, warm shake. "Didcot incident." He winks at me. "Freaking awesome."

For some reason—and I am not sure if I agree with my face on this one—I am smiling.

He turns to Kayla. Hesitates. "I wasn't… Do you actually shake hands?"

Kayla just looks at him. The way the sun looks at the desert.

"Righteous."

And seriously now? But my smile keeps on growing.

Skipping Kayla, he turns to Tabitha, grins. He has very white teeth. Of course he does.

"Do not tell them I said this, but our tech boys are literally wetting their pants to get to meet you. It's insane back at the shop. Totally insane." He holds out a hand. "Very excited to meet you."

Tabitha stares at his hand for a moment. As if she's making a decision. And then she grabs it and gives it a firm shake.

"Pleasure," she says. "All that shit."

The CIA man winks. He actually winks. Something Tabitha did convinced him that winking was the right thing to do. And somehow, and this is the part I really do not understand, the bastard was right.

Tabitha doesn't exactly smile, but she doesn't rip his arm off and shove it up his arse either. Overall, I think this guy is batting above average.

His arm retrieved from Tabitha's grasp he extends it toward the car. "My name's…" He hesitates then gives a grin. "Well, everyone just calls me Gran. Chariot is totally awaiting us. You dudes want to take a ride?"

He gives the impression that he'd actually be totally fine with us saying no. I'm not sure if that means he's a really decent bloke, or just terrifyingly deceptive. But I find I don't want to turn down his ride. Despite the suit and the car he seems genuine in a way someone like Smythe has probably forgotten exists.

I try to get a quick read of Felicity's feelings as we slip into the car, but she's clamped down with a carefully neutral expression. She could have fallen in love or could be preparing to kill the man.

Occasionally, my girlfriend is a little bit scary.

No one else goes for the passenger seat, so I take it, sitting next to Gran.

"So," I say, "what part of the world does the name Gran come from?" He doesn't seem exactly like the elderly-maternal-relative type. "Is that European?"

He starts to laugh.

"Not European then," I guess.

"Dude, Gran isn't my real name," he says, still grinning. "My folks went with Calvin Wilfred Monk the third. Bit of an uncharacteristic absence of cool on their part."

I do the mental math. "Yeah," I say. "I'm not one hundred percent seeing how that shortens down to Gran."

"It's short for Granola," he says. "Like the breakfast cereal."

This is worse than when Clyde explained magical theory to me. "You're nicknamed after a breakfast cereal?"

"I think maybe, like, we've got some cultural associations getting in the way," he says. "Granola is, you know, associated with a certain lifestyle this side of the pond."

"High-fiber living?"

Gran tempers his eye roll with a chuckle. "It's the whole hippy thing."

A hippy CIA agent. Sadly it sort of makes sense that if MI37 is going to deal with any member of the CIA it would be the hippy one.

"Are there…" I hesitate, not wanting to offend, but it's just too bizarre to not probe further. "Are there many hippy CIA agents?"

"Erm…" Gran thinks on this as he drives us onto a small route between hulking aircraft. "I guess it probably, like, correlates to the percentage of hippies in the US total. I mean, I know the TV likes to, you know, show the CIA as a bunch of evil suit clones, but… well, that's fucking Hollywood, man. You can't believe everything they tell you."

I refrain from telling him that that's been my basic survival strategy since I started at MI37.

Still, for the most part I like this man. God knows if he's any good at his job, but he is personable, and pleasant, and seems handy with a smile in the same way Kayla is handy with a sword. And, to be honest, I find the former skill puts me more at ease.

"So," I say, resisting the urge to glance over my shoulder at Tabitha, "you guys think you're up against Clyde."

"Yeah." Gran nods regretfully. "Total bummer, your

dude going all batshit on you. He sounded like a real nice guy. But…" He shrugs.

Whether the motion is meant to recall Clyde or not it does, and I find my knee-jerk need to defend the man is activated again.

"Do you have any proof it's him?"

The back of the car goes very quiet. I can imagine Felicity shouting at me that we need to make a good impression with the big boys, but I keep my eyes off her and on Gran.

The CIA man seems to think that now is an OK time to take his eyes off the road and return my appraising stare. This causes me to break mine and scan for oncoming death threats.

"Totally see where you're coming from, man. Totally do. I mean, I get it. He was a friend. It's… Look, it's like this. The government has seen, like—and I'm not even shitting you on this—a five hundred percent increase in hack attempts since your buddy went all apparently dead. And it's not just that. The big mind fucker is that they've almost all been successful. You know how many of the usual attempts get through. Like nothing, man. It's tiny. It's crazy. We're like, really good at keeping our shit locked down tight. We're a government. We're the man. That's kind of what we do.

"But whoever started knocking on our firewalls is, like, laughing at us, man. Just taking stuff apart at the code level. At speeds people can't do it. Like regular meat people. And we're never hacked the same way twice. So some digital thing is just ripping through our stuff, like it's sport, man. Code bleeding and tattered on the ground. Digital slaughterhouse. And people don't write those programs that fast. It just doesn't happen. And these attacks are happening all simultaneously. All hours. All the time."

Gran's eyes depart the road to engage me again. "It's an AI, man. Like, a totally ridiculous badass-as-shit AI. Like, drop acid on top of acid mindblowing AI. Insane. And so, we look into the list of available, you know, crazy insane AI badasses, and our list says Clyde Marcus Bradley and, like, that's it man. That's who we've got." He shrugs again.

I glance toward the back of the car. And I think we all get that this is not a good story Agent Gran is telling us. This is not something that we will tell our grandchildren by crackling fireplaces in our winter years. But it's Felicity who looks truly horror struck.

"But…" she manages. "Nuclear codes…"

"Oh, dude!" Gran throws his hands up in the air, and the car careens wildly for a moment. "Don't even start. That would be, like…" Again the hands show the mental explosion. "Nah, we have those on a computer waaaaaaay off the grid. Not even funny how locked down that shit is."

Felicity looks significantly relieved.

"But," I say, still not entirely willing to give into the cold cruel grasp of logic, "it's still not necessarily him."

"Oh no." Gran shakes his head with enthusiasm. "No, no, no, no, no, no. No. Totally could be someone, something else. Maybe the Chinese managed to sneak something by us. Some terrorist cell. Bill Gates may have gone off the deep end. Totally happens. Bunch of totally viable alternatives. It's just, you know, this guy Clyde—massively, massively likely it's him."

Oh. OK then. Well…

Gran pilots the car out of the airport and onto a

sprawling road of rushing cars and trucks. Manhattan juts sharply out of the horizon, glistening, scraping at the sky. A teetering testament to capitalism and industry.

"Come on, man," Gran says, following my eye line. "Let's go to the capital of the world, settle in, and work out how to erase your friend from the face of the earth. It'll be totally awesome. You'll love it."

9

Yellow taxis; herds of pedestrians; billboards screaming—Gran bludgeons his way through New York traffic.

Even after we exit the canyons of steel and glass of midtown and skim past the great green lacquer of Central Park, the city keeps its sense of the alien. It is as if someone had heard of a European city but never actually seen one. Everything is so familiar and yet so insistently *not from home*. There is a feeling of having stepped through the Looking Glass. We drive past a place called Alice's Tea Room. It doesn't help the impression.

"Where are you located?" Felicity asks from the back of the car.

"Area 51?" Gran says. "About three hundred feet beneath Columbia University. It's—"

But I interrupt at that point. "Area 51?" I ask. Pop culture alarm bells are ringing in my head.

"Yeah, man." Gran nods. "Our division of the CIA. We have that whole name-legacy thing. It's no biggie. Really."

No biggie? Area 51 is like solid conspiracy theory gold. It's a name that summons grainy video images of alien Grays on dissecting tables, and visions of sweaty middle-aged men hunting through New Mexico desert while exchanging probing stories. And… "You're beneath Columbia University?" The home of the Manhattan Project. My incredulity meter is red-lining.

"Yeah, man," Gran says. "It's pretty awesome. Research resources for our kind of stuff are just totally magnificent. And the place is mad with recruitment choices. Plus students are always holding. It's great."

From Felicity's expression—glimpsed in the rearview mirror—that last criteria is not one that she is overly concerned about.

"Area 51?" I'm shocked to hear Kayla's Scottish brogue chime in. "Like in the movies?"

"Well." Gran shrugs again. "Like, yes on the name. But the movies are… you know. Whole Hollywood thing again."

As much as I like Agent Gran, I think he and I have different opinions on the merits of big studio movie productions.

"But," Kayla persists. "Feckin' Roswell."

Gran rolls his eyes. "Aw, man. We are, like, never going to live that shit down. Total, just, like, nightmare. I mean totally before my time. So, mea not very culpa, but…" He facepalms.

"Wait," I say, because this is something I really want to get straight. "The CIA really did recover an alien space craft at Roswell?"

Gran looks at me and blinks. Twice. Slowly. "No, dude. Course not. I mean… you've met aliens. Fucking weird as shit they are. This Gray bullshit…" He shakes his head. "Man, I would love bipedal aliens, man. That'd be awesome."

Again, given my experience, not an opinion I completely share.

"Nah, Roswell, was like…" He stops. "Wait, how does security clearance work with you guys being contracted?"

We all turn to Felicity. She looks stumped.

"Screw it." Agent Gran waves a hand. "The Area was messing around with all this cyborg stuff back in the late forties after the war. They had this ship that was, like, fifty percent organic. Like, some agent totally restitched into the mechanics of it. Really early example of total interface bodyscaping. Before they worked out, you know, like all the psychological ramifications of turning someone into meat wallpaper and pasting him over an engine and shit. Dude went batshit. Had to shoot the poor bastard down. Set us back, like ten years."

Total interface bodyscaping. At least now I know what I'm going to wake up screaming about at four in the morning.

"And here we are, dudes." Gran steers the car off the road, and down into a narrow chute with a sign proclaiming PUBLIC PARKING. $23.75.

We swing down ramp after ramp. The world is lit by strips of moldering yellow neon. Graffiti becomes increasingly inventive.

"Home, sweet home," Gran says.

The parking garage's bottom floor is inhabited solely by cars covered with dust sheets. Most of the neon strips have gone out, leaving the place shadowy and desolate. The mad bustle of New York suddenly feels very far away.

Gran pulls into a grimy looking parking spot. I stare out the window, but it's hard to make anything out through the gloom. I pop my buckle and go to open the door.

"Wouldn't do that, dude."

And then the bottom falls out of the world.

10

There is a flash of light and a grinding of machinery, and then darkness falls again. Darker shadows flick by the windows and the pit in my stomach is still opening.

I do not… I wouldn't call it a shriek. But it might be a rather high-pitched gasp. Fortunately for my pride, I am not the only one.

Then comes a juddering halt, and our movement becomes lateral. I grab the car door as we are shunted sideways, and the car rocks to a halt.

"Sorry," says Gran. "Totally should have told you about that. But, you know, this way was more fun."

Rather than darkness, the car now sits in a light airy space. There is a clean, space-age sheen to the light gray walls, the broad lights that shed clean blue light. Neat ranks of cars identical to ours sit in the sort of shining rows that seem reserved for Turtle Wax advertisements.

"Jesus," Tabitha mutters looking at the volume of other cars as we get out of our own. "Must be tons of you."

"Well," Gran shrugs. "You know, like, we're a pretty small department."

"How many?" I can't see why they would need fifty of these cars all lined up.

"This office?" Gran shrugs again. "Erm, maybe, like, five hundred of us."

Holy shit. Five hundred. This office? They have more than one office? Clyde Xeroxing himself effectively doubled the working staff of MI37.

Felicity nudges me. I slide my eyes over to look at her. She leans her head up and breathes, "This is so cool."

A retina scanner—markedly more shiny than ours—opens a sequence of three steel doors, each one a foot thick or more.

"Feckin' ridiculous," Kayla mutters. "Poncy bastards."

The open doors reveal a broad corridor that looks as if it was molded from one continuous piece of gray plastic. Everything has a slightly slippery, modern sheen to it. Stripes of bright orange, blue, green, and yellow are painted down the sides of the wall. Orange branches off down a side corridor, blue down another. In the distance the space seems to open up onto something that is either an aircraft hangar or a genetics laboratory. Men and women in labcoats and stark white hazmat suits bustle back and forth. Clipboards and manila folders are clutched.

Standing just inside the corridor, beaming widely, is one such clipboard-clutcher. He is a short, slightly overweight man, with a round face, circular spectacles, and dark hair plastered to his pate. A wispy mustache is refusing to grow on his upper lip.

"Ah," he breathes as we enter. "Our honored guests. So nice to meet you." He reaches out, shakes each hand in turn. It is a little like trying to shake hands with a dead fish. "Wanted to extend my welcome. I am Basil Kensington, inter-agency liaison. Really did want to meet you at the airport, but I had an unfortunate incident with a jello in my office that needed resolving."

As nonsensical as this is, Agent Gran seems to take

this as a cue to look off into space and whistle.

Mr. Kensington grimaces. "You've had the erm… pleasure of Agent Monk's company."

"Monk?" Kayla squints angrily at the little man.

"He means me," Gran says.

"Should feckin' say so then." Kayla falls back into line.

I don't quite have the nerve to point out that he already did. Meanwhile, Felicity's look shoots enough daggers in Kayla's direction that I think we should recruit it and make it a field agent.

Personally, I'm just shocked by this sudden display of verbosity on Kayla's part. Normally she's good for about one death threat a day and that's it.

"Yes." Kensington smiles humorlessly. For some reason he makes me think of a sentient cabbage. "Now, I don't want to be a pest—"

That's clearly untrue.

"—but there is a little bit of paperwork to cover before you go any further. Really should have been signed earlier on but…" Kensington titters lightly then shoots a death stare in Gran's direction. Gran keeps on whistling. "It's all very standard stuff. Basic gag order on discussing what you see here. Confidentiality. Agreement for a brain scrub if you breach contract. Giving you temporary access to—"

"Wait," I say. "A brain what?"

"Oh." Kensington looks up. "A brain scrub. Typical procedure. A general restructuring of the frontal lobes to redact memories and personality."

"Redact personality?" I think I understand, but I'm rather hoping I don't.

Kensington nods. "It's standard procedure."

Tabitha takes a breath that is clearly going into her lungs purely to pick up the obscenities she keeps there before being flung back into Kensington's face.

Felicity quickly steps in front. "That will be fine, Mr. Kensington."

"Deputy Liaison Kensington," he corrects her.

Felicity closes her eyes. And I know this is a big deal for her. That she wants this to go well. But we have also been dating long enough for me to recognize the expression she wears when she's forced to deal with imbeciles that she knows she's not allowed to kill.

It's funny, I don't remember any of my previous girlfriends having that specific one.

"Sorry," she manages, "Deputy Liaison Kensington." She even manages to avoid leaning on the word "Deputy" too heavily. It really is quite impressive and far more than the man deserves. "We'll happily sign the agreements."

A thought occurs to me. "What about the versions?"

The way Kensington smiles makes me think it causes him pain. "They will be limited to wireless inaccessible devices only for the duration of their stay in the United States," he says.

He contorts his face into another smile. "And then once you've signed that and we've completed the cavity search—"

Wait. What now?

"—then I can give you an office tour. I think you're going to find everything here vastly superior to anything you're used to back—"

I think Tabitha and Kayla are about to get into a race to see who can force feed Kensington his own spleen first, and no amount of diplomatizing by

Felicity is going to be able to stop it.

"Oh." Gran stops whistling abruptly. "Did Majors track you down, dude?"

And everything stops for a moment. Everyone wondering what the play is here. Felicity looks to Gran the same way an alcoholic eyes up an unattended whiskey bottle. The tentative chance of salvation.

Kensington is the first to move. He whirls on Gran. "What?"

"She was totally looking for you earlier. Meant to mention it, but it just… you know." He taps his head. "Poof." He shrugs. "Something about a spot inspection in… Crap, what section was it?"

Kensington turns a shade of purple that I generally associate with internal organs. He starts to splutter as if something inside him is broken.

Gran steps forward and retrieves the clipboard from Kensington's suddenly lifeless fingers. "You know what, dude?" he says companionably. "You go track down Majors, and I'll sort this all out. Divide and conquer. Be awesome."

If looks could kill, Kensington's would cause Gran's liver to burst out his chest and attack him with a knife. The deputy liaison whirls away, hips gyrating wildly.

Gran watches him for a moment, his whistling briefly resumed. He looks down at the clipboard. "You want to skip this and just see the cool shit?"

"Yes." Tabitha is definitive.

Felicity takes the clipboard with a small sigh. "I'll just sign for all of us."

11

As we go down the corridor I grow no closer to deciding whether the room at its end is a hangar or a lab. I am staring so intently I almost miss a young woman in a military uniform as she emerges from a corridor.

"Oh, I'm—" I start to apologize and then I stop short. Something profoundly violent has been done to this woman.

For the most part she looks perfectly normal. Rather pretty in fact—big eyes, pale skin, a small button of a nose, but a great mass of machinery is jutting out the back of her skull. It looks as if an engine block has been smashed into the pale blonde locks that grace her head.

"Oh, I am sorry," she says. A TV-perfect American accent. And then she turns and walks away.

I stand staring after her. The others pause with me, follow my gaze.

Gran nudges me. "Dude, your girlfriend is, like, right there."

Felicity has started to shake her head. I get the impression this is not quite living up to her expectations. But I'm still too distracted by the girl to reassure her.

"Is she OK?" I say. I stare at the mass of machinery jutting from the woman's perfectly coiffured mane.

Gran looks at me, confused. "What do you mean?"

I am nonplussed by the question. "I mean," I say,

"the big bits of metal in her head. How the hell did that happen? How did she survive?"

Gran starts laughing. "Seriously, dude?"

More nonplussing. "Seriously what?"

"She's a class five, man," Gran says, as if this explains everything.

I go with, "Erm?"

Gran claps me on the shoulder. "It's a categorization thing, dude. Taxonomy of life forms. Internal jargon, et cetera, et cetera."

"Life form. Taxonomy?" Tabitha looks at Gran sharply. "Human?"

"Class one." Gran's hand indicates us all. Tabitha nods as if that makes sense.

"So she's…" I look again after the girl. And she was so… Her skin was so real. I could see pores. I saw her eyes widen, startled when I bumped into her. But she's, "… not a class one?"

He gives me the benevolent expression Clyde used to give me before readjusting my sense of reality. "Class two is other higher life forms. Birds, beasts, fish, and all of those groovy things. Class three is what we call, you know, lesser life forms. Bit of a judgmental category. But bacteria, viruses, fungi. Class four is extraterrestrial. I mean, we are called Area 51, so we should have something for them."

"Yog-Sothoth," Tabitha says.

"Bless you," I say.

She flaps a hand at me. "Fictional fungi out of space."

I am still clueless.

"Lovecraft. Horror writer. Thirties."

And I am familiar with the man. But… No, I don't see where we're going.

"That would be a class three-four hybrid," Gran says, because he is, apparently, already better at translating Tabitha-speak than I am.

"But what about class five?" I demand. Hypotheticals are lovely and all, but we still seem to have failed to get to the point.

Gran looks at me. "Class five is synthetic. Dude, she has half her mechanical brain sticking out the back of her head. What did you think she was?"

I look again. The girl is just rounding the corner with a rather attractive swing of her hips. Except she's a robot. A not-person.

"Jesus," I say.

"I know, man," says Gran. "Bit creepy the first few times, right?"

And yes, yes I do know. I brought three of them over here on a computer with me. And compared to that thought... A robot is... Well, yes, it is creepy that someone programmed attractively swinging hips. But at least you can reach out and touch her. I mean, not in a sexual way. Just, I could shake her hand if I wanted to. On the scale of creepy things I deal with, she's not that much of a blip.

Tabitha is staring at Gran. I have trouble reading the expression. "The money," she says. "Where does it come from?"

Felicity rolls her eyes. Maybe this is the inter-agency equivalent of asking the man how much money he makes on the first date.

"Legacy of JFK and Reagan," Gran says.

For once, that sounds like the beginning of an answer I could actually understand.

"JFK," Gran continues, "because he was, like, really

oddly obsessed with this idea of boning alien chicks. All sort of weird memos about space condoms. I shit you not. And Reagan because… well honestly, man, I don't think anyone should have let Nixon try to download his personality into the poor actor in the first place. That shit was bound to degrade eventually. And the whole interfacing issues… Nightmare, man. Total nightmare."

Or, alternatively it could be another answer that sends me cross-eyed.

"Feckin' ponces," Kayla says, though exactly who or what she's addressing, I'm not sure.

"Dudette," Gran says to Tabitha, ignoring Kayla, "you think this shit is cool, you should see our mecha."

"Mecha?" I ask.

"Suits," Tabitha says. "Giant robot battle suits."

Holy shit. I really do want to see their mecha.

"Not a patch on what the Japanese have, though," Gran says with a shrug.

"Well," Tabitha says. "Sasaki-san. They have him. You don't."

I have absolutely no idea what she's talking about. But apparently Gran does, because his eyes light up like light bulbs.

"Exactly, man," he says, in spite of Tabitha's fairly obvious gender. "Man, no wonder the tech boys want to talk to you."

And Tabitha actually smiles. For the first time since Clyde died, she smiles. She may still be wearing her tinfoil-lined hat, but she smiles.

SEVERAL MIND-BLOWINGS LATER

I always found the adage "money doesn't buy you happiness" to be a basic, decent philosophy for life.

A good general guide to the workings of the world. On the other hand, having surveyed Area 51... Well, money does buy you some really cool toys.

Once we are completely bewildered by super computers, laser guns, digital personality constructs, and other space age awesome, Gran leads us to more familiar territory. It is a sad thing to have to admit to yourself that you find comfort in conference rooms, but when your day job involves monster killing and AIs capable of hacking military drones and throwing them at you, your teenage self can just go suck it.

"I hate to get all Kensington on you dudes," Gran says, "but we probably should do some work at some point."

Felicity smiles. "More than happy to get down to it."

I collapse into an ergonomically curved plastic chair next to a conference table that sprouts from the floor like a particularly useful mushroom. Jet-lag is starting to kick in. Still, I get the feeling that this AI issue is a problem that won't wait to be slept on.

"So." Gran takes a position at the head of the table. "The Area dudes and dudettes are thinking your old co-worker Clyde is all responsible and shit for looting our digital coffers."

I remember Clyde discovering his digital self, discovering that he didn't need to sleep anymore. What would that do to someone? Becoming another type of life form. That slow dawning realization that you are not human anymore. I remember Agent Gran's story of the Roswell incident. *The psychological ramifications of turning someone into meat wallpaper.* In some ways Clyde's transformation was as radical. He was a wooden mask. We all thought of him as a person because someone was wearing him. But he was just a mask. Wallpaper for a man's face.

Could that have pushed him over the edge? Could Gran and the rest of the Area 51 team be right? They seem to have the resources to make educated guesses.

"But," Gran continues, "having figured out, you know, like the whole suspect numero uno thing, where we're having a less groovy time is the whole actually-understanding-what-the-hell-he's-up-to thing."

I may be grasping at straws, but it strikes me that if they don't know what Clyde's doing then the idea that he's up to no good is just an assumption. And I'll concede that raiding the US government's digital coffers may not be the smartest thing to do, but Clyde always was a voracious reader...

OK, maybe that's a stretch too far.

It's time for a different tack. Back when I was a police officer, I learned you could find out a lot about the perpetrator by looking at the specific crime committed. What was done. How it was done.

"What's the AI taking?" I ask. "What's it reading?"

Gran looks at me and shrugs. "Anything, man. Everything."

The mental gears churn. Trying to get into the head of the villain. It's a while since I've stretched these muscles. The policeman I used to be is a corpse lying on the ground, and here I am administering the breath of life.

OK. Clyde. Clyde the bad guy. God, there are so many problems with that. But one of them is that for all his bumbling and absent-minded professor routines, he is frighteningly smart. One doesn't just bumble one's way into Cambridge University.

"He could be purposely trying to cover his tracks," I say.

Felicity nods, encouraging. Usually a good sign.

"But if he's trying to do that," I'm thinking out loud, "he needs tracks to cover." Felicity nods again. "Where did he hit first?" I ask.

Gran presses a seemingly random spot on the conference table, and a panel slides away to reveal a computer keyboard buried in its surface. I blink in surprise. Then he taps a key and I get to blink a whole number more times as one entire wall reveals itself to be a monitor, coming alive with light.

He scrolls through files, pulls up a document. There is a large "Top Secret" label at the top. Below is a long list.

"OK," Gran surveys the list. "First few hits seem a bit tentative. Low security targets. Totally didn't make our radar 'til we went back, looked at the pattern. Crazy level of sophistication in the hack. Totally gave it away in retrospect. But he's hitting some of our sponsored labs out in San Francisco, Chicago. Then Alaska. Next he tries his hand at the Smithsonian institutes—"

Oh shit. Oh shit.

"Then the Library of Congress."

My eyes flick up and catch Tabitha's. And she knows it too. Right there. Those two targets. As soon as the hacker works out he can crack in, he goes for the books.

"It's Clyde," Tabitha says.

"We don't know..." But I'm half-hearted.

"You feckin' know," Kayla says.

I look at her. And for once she's not looking daggers or sword blades at me. Just something faintly grim. A woman who had already accepted an ugly truth. Waiting for me to catch up.

I glance at Felicity. My last port in the storm. She reaches over and squeezes my arm, and looks sad for me. Because she knows. We all know.

There has to be a reason. I need there to be a reason.

"Where next?" Felicity asks. "Keep going down the list."

"Few more museums and libraries," Gran says. "This is all like, over two or three days, mind. But then the big one. Put him on our radar. DARPA. Defense Advanced Research Projects Agency. Went in and just, man, scoured that place. Took a copy of everything. Like, everything. We even worked it out halfway through. You can't hide traffic like that. And they couldn't stop him. They were pulling plugs out of servers at the end but it was too late, man. It was fucking crazy."

"Feckin' science nerd." Even now he's a supervillain, Clyde has not managed to elevate himself in Kayla's eyes.

A supervillain. Clyde. It just doesn't make sense. Even looking at the list of places he's hit. It's all so typically Clyde. Nerdy, high-minded, and essentially harmless. Just someone whose curiosity doesn't have the same boundaries as other people's. How do you go from that to someone who uses a military drone to attempt mass murder at a funeral?

Felicity squeezes my arm again.

"Where does he go after DARPA?" I ask.

Gran scrolls down. "Increasingly random after that, dude. More science labs. But infrastructure stuff too. Power grids. Sewage lines. The political buildings. Embassy offices, that sort of thing. Then he went into the FBI. For some reason he's mostly left us alone. Homeland Security, though, man. He loved them up almost as much as he did DARPA."

Homeland Security? Why on earth would Clyde be curious about them?

"Random," I say. But… I look at the list again, and I can't quite put conviction into the word. I chew my bottom lip.

"What is it?" Felicity asks.

"Well…" I chew on it a second, because I don't like it. "It could be random," I say. "A purposeful covering of tracks. Creating something too big and messy for us to pull apart."

"Or?" Felicity prompts.

I hesitate. Because I don't want to admit it. Not to myself, not to the room, not to my memory of Clyde. But… "Or, well, he's the king of tangents, but he's also incredibly good at synthesizing all of those tangents. So maybe it's not all random. Maybe it's all related. Maybe he's planning something terrifyingly large."

12

Gran bounces up out of his chair. "See, I totally knew bringing you dudes over was the right idea. This is the good insight shit I was talking about, man."

He holds up his hand and aims it at Tabitha. She stares at it for a moment, and then tentatively reaches out and high fives him.

"Nice." Gran grins.

And Tabitha grins back. This may be the most smile-dense day Tabitha's had since... I cast my mind back. Since... Since she and Clyde hooked up actually.

Wait.

Nooo.

I look at the two of them. And Gran *is* good looking. But...

No. Just. No.

I glance at Felicity. And I know she's seen it too, because I can tell she's trying to restrain herself from facepalming.

But then Gran goes and ruins the relationship before it can even begin.

"OK, dudes," he says, "I'd love to just fire up the Clyde versions now, if that's cool."

"No," Tabitha replies so quickly there's almost a sonic boom.

Gran snaps his head around to look at her, eyes wide. I swear, I hear Kayla chuckle.

Felicity leaps smoothly into the liaising breach. "Tabitha, please just shut up and cooperate. We're done with this discussion."

Well, kind of smoothly.

"No," Tabitha repeats. "Spawn of evil mind-controlling AI. Not safe. Not cool. No."

"Well, to be fair," I point out, "they were created prior to the whole, and still potentially questionable, going evil thing. They're from an earlier psychological model." I'm not sure if that last bit would stand up as expert testimony, but I'm pretty sure a morning TV show host would buy into it.

"Full of bullshit. You are." Tabitha is evidently still getting in contact with her inner morning TV show host. "Same person. Same endpoint. Inevitability."

But if I'm full of bullshit then so is she. "That's determinism horse crap, I say. People are more complicated than that. It's probabilities and environment and a thousand—"

"Look—" Felicity says, trying to cut the argument off before it can really get going.

She fails.

"They're not people!" Tabitha shrieks. Everyone stares. The red spots on Tabitha's cheeks seem out of place in her uniform of black and white. "They're programs. They're code. It's math. They go bad."

I try to work out if I really do disagree with her, or if my defense of the versions is misplaced loyalty for a friend I'd like to see actually tried before we all condemn him.

From the end of the table comes an odd popping sound. I turn and look. Kayla has managed to produce bubble gum. She blows a second bubble. It pops as we all stare.

"Feckin' buckets of stress you lot are," she says.

"Look, dudes," says Gran. "I totally realize that, you know, the whole situation is like this really heavy thing for you." Gran is trying his best to be serious and emotionally grave. It is clearly not his comfort zone. "And the Clyde versions, man." He shakes his head. "That's like… so not helping. I can see. But, I mean, I don't mean to be a dick, or 'the man' or anything," which seems a hair disingenuous considering that he is with the CIA, "but from an outsider's point of view, you are in possession of some software that could really, really help us deal with another piece of software that is making a mockery of your friend's memory."

"Software?" Tabitha repeats the word.

Gran nods. "That's all, dudette. Ones and zeroes and all that groovy shit."

And, goddamn it, despite it all, Gran has managed to make the situation OK for everybody.

Well, everybody except the Clyde versions, I suppose.

"This room is firewalled, like, to hell and back." Gran shrugs. "No way out. Nothing for him to grab. It's a safe room. Cross my heart." He performs the motion with exaggerated care.

"Fine." Tabitha relents, opens a bag, pulls out the versions' laptop and slides it over. Gran taps another invisible panel in the table which opens to reveal a large number of cables. He spools one out and connects it to the laptop. A moment later, three Clydes stare at us from the massive wall-screen.

"Hello!" says one.

"How do?" says another.

"You must be Agent Monk," says the third extending

a hand. Then he retracts it. "Oh, can't shake. Silly of me."

"Still getting used to the disembodied thing," the second says.

Again the sense of things sliding headlong towards the uncanny…

"Hello to you too, Tabby," says the first, with a tentative smile.

"Fuck off," Tabitha informs the version.

All three Clydes slump. Though what they were thinking would happen, I don't know.

"Feckin' idiots," Kayla chimes in, apparently assuming the mantle of team peanut gallery for good now.

"Could we just…" Felicity starts, but then just shakes her head. I don't think we're quite living up to her hopes.

"Dudes," Gran says by way of introduction. "Not sure if your software is totally calibrated to our synthetics interface protocol."

The Clydes look at each other with varying degrees of confusion.

"Come again?" says one.

"No worries." Gran smiles. "We'll download a copy to your reference database. Peruse that and this whole tête-a-tête thing will be smooth as an Olympic swimmer's legs."

"Erm… OK," says one Clyde. "Sure this will all make sense at some point."

"Righteous," Gran nods.

One Clyde looks at me with something like panic on his face. I have no idea if it is a genuine emotion or just a simulation of one. Still, this does seem an odd way for Gran to have started this conversation.

Gran keeps talking. "We're also going to provide

you access to a whole ton of classified material perused by the software program known as Clyde 2.0," he says. "You'll be, like, running a standard pattern recognition search through them. We're looking for, like, anything scoring a six or higher. Interim report when you hit the fifty percent mark. Groovy?"

Two of the Clydes look at each other. "You know," one whispers to the other, "TV sitcoms led me to believe I would find it easier to understand Americans."

"This is all going to make sense once we read the protocol document, right?" says the third.

"Don't mean to be nit-picky about this whole interfacing thing," says the one who whispered. "Not that picking nits seems like a terrible thing, of course. Keeps gorillas and the whole primate class relatively clean as I understand it. At least that's what David Attenborough tells me, and he's not known for being a big fat liar. But anyway, assuming negative connotations apply to the act—not aiming for those. But that said, and albeit us having only known each other for about forty-five seconds, is there any chance we can dispense with the whole standard protocol, which is a tad confusing, and explain all this to me in words of a limited syllabic number, and possibly with diagrams?"

Gran opens his mouth.

"Shut up," Tabitha says to the versions before Gran can say anything. Then she leans over to Gran. "Interface protocol I've been using. Mostly."

All three Clydes lean forward peering close to the screen. Their noses distort as if approaching a fish-eye lens. They eye Gran suspiciously.

If they just shouted, "I don't like you," they could not be more obvious.

Felicity cannot suppress her sigh.

I should probably say something, defuse the situation. Except, I'm not completely sure where my sympathies lie. Perhaps treating the versions like software is for the best. Stop us confusing them with… with Clyde. Real Clyde.

Nobody says anything.

"Fine then," says one Clyde, sagging back from the screen and collapsing in an easy chair. "We'll be happy to give the protocol a good old-fashioned perusing." A stack of documents appears out of nowhere next to him. He picks it up and starts reading.

"Groovy," Gran says. "All settled then."

JUST BEFORE JET-LAG WINS

The CIA put us up in a rather nice hotel a little north of Times Square. Night falls but the sheer density of nearby neon and LCD denies it, keeps the world stuck in a permanent twilight.

Felicity and I share a room, proving that the CIA files on us are remarkably thorough. I don't exactly object to the sleeping arrangements, but I am slightly worried that Gran has read an "Arthur Wallace inserts tab A into slot B" version of my relationship with my boss.

Bags unpacked, I collapse on the bed. Felicity sits next to me. With one hand she plays with my hair.

"Well," she says, "the hotel part is going better than expected anyway."

I smile, reach up to the hand in my hair and squeeze it. "Tabitha and Kayla not behaving as you'd like?"

She looks at me for a while.

"What?" I protest my innocence.

She shakes her head. "You did good, Arthur," she

says eventually. "Well… better than them."

Which is not exactly the most enthusiastic praise.

"I think Gran likes them," I say. "Actually if you're going to worry about anything I'd worry about him liking Tabitha a little too much."

And that does make her smile. "I don't think he's up to the challenge," she says.

"I don't know," I say. "Worse decisions have been made on the rebound."

Felicity nods. "Well, that's true."

I furrow my brow. "That sounds like personal experience."

She shakes her head. "I suspect you don't want to know."

Felicity Shaw is an insightful woman.

I sit up, wrap an arm around her. "We save the world," I say. "It's what we do. MI37 won't let you down." I kiss her. "Scout's honor."

She eyes me. "Were you ever even a boy scout?"

"Two years in the cubs," I offer.

Another smile, but a thinner one. "You're skating by on a technicality."

I shrug. "It's worked so far."

The smile rallies momentarily then slips altogether. Felicity bites at her lower lip. "We will make it work here," she says. "We have to. I am not going back to the way things were. I am not."

There's surprising passion in her voice. This means a lot to her. MI37 means a lot to her. Not just me and her. There is something about the institution itself that is integrally woven into the fabric of her. And I am reminded again of the idea that I don't even know that much of her history with the institution.

"How did you get started with MI37?" I ask her, leaning my head against her shoulder.

"What?" She leans away, unceremoniously dumping my head so she can get a better look at me.

I shrug. "I don't know. So much of what we do is about the now, about responding to the immediate threat. I want to know you better. MI37 is under your skin. How did it get there?"

She looks defensive, searching for the criticism.

"I think it's sweet," I protest. "I just want to understand it."

She hesitates a moment, and then finally says, "It was because of my sister." A look of sorrow crosses her face.

"You don't ever talk about her," I say. I've only heard of her sister once before, and that wasn't from Felicity but Kayla.

Felicity looks away. "It was a long time ago."

She doesn't want to talk about it. That much is obvious, and maybe if I was really going to do the thoughtful boyfriend thing properly I would back off, but this feels important, some critical part of her I should know. "What happened?"

Another hesitation. A working of the jaw. "She was called Joy," she says eventually.

Joy and Felicity. I nod, encouraging her to go on.

"We were twins," Felicity says eventually. "Not, you know, all these in vitro fraternal twins you see nowadays. We were identical." A slight smile. "The boys used to double take when we walked across the bar."

And that I can believe.

"She was always more academically inclined than me. Read more. Remembered more. Some twins... it's like they're the same person, really. But that wasn't us. More…" She hesitates again, looks at me, as if checking to see if I'm worthy of this, but I must pass the test because she carries on. "More like two halves of one person. At least that's how it always felt to me. She did the books, I did the sports. That sort of thing.

"But, well, that sort of thing has repercussions, doesn't it? And you don't see it when you're young. But then university looms, and you realize that being captain of the hockey team, or the tennis team, that isn't going to get you into the same university as actual good grades, and that someone you thought was integral to you is on a different trajectory altogether."

She stops, licks her lips. "So Joy went off to Imperial College, and I was just scrambling for anything close by. I ended up at the University of Westminster, which I wouldn't say anything against. Not at all. It was just…"

Felicity reaches up to her eye and flicks errant dampness away.

"I'd always thought I was the strong one, you know? Because I was in better physical shape than Joy was. It was foolish really. Somehow thinking physical strength equated to mental…" She shakes her head. "I was over visiting Joy at Imperial all the time. I had more friends there than at Westminster. I think some of them thought I actually went to Imperial." She smiles at the memory. "We made it work. Joy did. She was…" But she trails off. That thought, it seems, is not for me.

"Anyway, in her second year she started dating this boy, Mark." Some tremor of emotion runs through her face at the name but it's gone too quickly for me to identify it. "He was older. A post-grad student. He…" She licks her lips. "He," she starts again, falters. She looks up at me.

"He was writing a thesis about some early English occult texts."

Oh. Oh dear. And I suppose I knew that Joy Shaw wasn't going to make it out of the story alive. But... Jesus. Her boyfriend.

Felicity shakes her head. "I don't blame him," she says. "Not anymore. He didn't know. It was all theory and bullshit to him. Just some old beliefs. A little foolishness. But he found things... texts. They led him to groups. To people who knew things that weren't just theory and bullshit."

She grimaces. I reach out and squeeze her hand. Her fingers feel cold and hard.

"Joy got scared," she says. "And I was so eager to be the hero. To be the strong one again. I'd been taking jujitsu classes since I was twelve and she thought, well... Mark wasn't exactly the athletic type. Joy thought I could help him.

"She didn't want him to know, though. I don't think he was proud. Just... he wouldn't have seen the seriousness of the situation. God, he had good grades, I know, but he was stupid, Arthur. So very, very stupid." She shakes her head again. Old regrets that won't come loose cling to her. "I was no better, of course." She seems to find a little humor in self-recrimination.

"Anyway we all went to meet these people. All three of us. I was interested, or so Joy told him. And she was coming so I didn't feel weird. Such silly lies. If I hadn't gone..."

She closes her eyes for a moment. "I'm sorry," she says. "This is a very long answer."

I squeeze her hand. "It's OK."

Another head shake. "No, it wasn't." There isn't

so much a ghost of a smile on her face as there is the bloody corpse of one. "There were Progeny," she tells me. "Six of them."

I blanch at the name of the alien mind worms we dealt with a month ago. The ones that started this whole mess with Clyde. Vile maggot-y things with tentacles that infect people and live in their hindbrains. Once you're infected there is no cure. Your mind is no longer your own. You're essentially a corpse who hasn't stopped moving yet.

"We got there," Felicity says, "and straight away they infected him," she says. "Then they infected..." She swallows hard. "They infected Joy. They killed her. Right in front of me. And I didn't know it. I just knew something was in her head. But I got away. Kicked out one's legs. Crushed its windpipe. Blinded a second. Broke the jaw of a third. And then I was out. God, I was so scared, Arthur." She presses herself against me.

"I called the police. Of course I did. I didn't know better. I was gibbering and screaming, and I called them. Took them an hour to arrive on the scene. I don't think the officers believed me. And when I took them back to where it had all happened there was no evidence at all. They just left me there. Just... left me."

She draws a very long and not at all steady breath.

"I filed a missing persons report the next day. And then, the day after that, a nice man from MI37 came to see me. And he told me about what was going on and he asked me to help. And I was still scared, but what he told me, Arthur, God it made me so angry. So very angry at what had been done to Joy."

She speaks to my chest now, not looking up at me. Trapped in history.

"I showed the agents where it happened. And they made some calls, and correlated some things, and we drove a few places. And then we found them. Found the Progeny. They were all together in a flat in Clapham. All of them except the one whose throat I'd crushed. I think it was that detail that made MI37 recruit me, actually. It was a pretty bloodthirsty agency back then."

Her arms are around my waist and she squeezes for a moment.

"Mark was there. Joy was there. And…" She trails off, and she's so quiet for so long that I think she's done. That's all she'll tell me, she'll let me fill in the blanks myself.

"They shot her, Arthur. I watched them do it. They captured them all, tied them up, put them against a wall, and shot them from a distance. To keep us safe from infection."

Felicity swallows hard. "She was screaming at me the whole time. Screaming that she was my sister. Asking me how I could do this to her. But I saw what happened when they were shot. I saw the aliens in their heads. And I knew she wasn't human anymore."

"That's awful," I say. My arms are as tight around her as hers are around me. "No one should see that."

"I know," she says. There's unexpected firmness in her voice. "Anyway, MI37 were ready to be done with me after that. It was thank you for the help, have a good day. They honestly thought that would be it. But," and suddenly her face is as hard as a rock, "I knew no one should ever have to see what I had seen. That it should never have happened. I knew I should have been stronger when Joy and Mark got infected."

"No—" I say, but she rides right over me.

"I knew I was going to do everything I could to stop it happening to anyone else. So I didn't go away. I didn't say goodbye. I insisted they take me on. I demanded it." She chuckles mirthlessly. "Broke a guy's nose over it.

"They took me. And that's what I did. I stopped other people living my nightmare. That's what I still do."

She pulls away from me, swallows, wipes her eyes.

"Damn," she says, looking at the make-up on her hands. "That's why I don't tell that story."

I hug her. Hard and fierce as I can. "You do good," I say. "You do such good."

She hugs me back, a little brusquely, then pulls away. "I know," she says. "I'm glad you know. And I'm glad the government is remembering it too."

I nod. "I'll be on my best behavior tomorrow. I promise."

She smiles, dabs at one eye again. "Thank you." She stands up from the bed, busies herself by starting to take apart her pistol. She pulls a cleaning kit out from one drawer. Gun maintenance—a good sign from Felicity Shaw that a conversation is done.

"What about you?" she says after a while. "All this talk about me, but how are you, Arthur?"

I think about that for a while. And in some ways my worries seem petty after that, even if they are perhaps a little more immediate.

"It's nothing," I say.

She turns, looks at me hard. "I asked you. Tell me."

I shrug. But she is my boss after all. "It's this Clyde stuff still," I say, slightly embarrassed. "We keep on throwing around phrases like bad guy," I say, "but... well, it's all relative, isn't it? Before all this... when Clyde overwrote that woman's mind, that was evil, but we didn't condemn him then, because he was fighting toward that same goal we all believed in."

Felicity doesn't say anything, just moves from one gun part to the next.

"So," I say, "what's changed? When did he become the 'bad guy'? What if he's the hero in all this? I mean... we're working with the CIA. They're hardly known for being the fuzzy-wuzziest of bears."

Felicity puts her gun parts down, turns in her chair to face me. She makes sure that I'm looking directly at her deep brown eyes. "I've been doing this for a while, Arthur," she says. "Trying to do the right thing with all my heart. And you know what I've discovered defines heroes?"

I think about that. And maybe that's what I've been trying to figure out ever since I joined MI37. I wish I'd known I could have just asked.

"Sacrifice," Felicity says. "Sacrificing personal interest for the greater good. That's what you do. Every time you risk your life to save the world. That's the sacrifice you offer up. That's what Clyde used to do. But let me tell you now, trying to kill us in a cemetery was not heroic. Whatever this Clyde 2.0 might be, whether he used to be our friend or not, he is not a hero, he is not the good guy. That's you, Arthur. You." She turns away, goes back to her gun with a certain ferocity.

My heart feels large in my chest. I look at her, this good strong woman who has done so much for the world despite what it has done to her. This woman who has done so much for me. And I cannot help but cross the room and kiss her—my personal hero.

She kisses me back. And then the kissing progresses, and then, in a little while, we lie back on the bed together, and we forget all our worries for a time.

13

AREA 51 HEADQUARTERS

We all disembark from Gran's shiny car. Tabitha took shotgun this morning, sitting up next to the CIA agent and being unusually verbal. The fact that their chat was so dense in tech jargon that it became the conversational equivalent of a circuit board meant I lost some of the finer points, but it definitely seemed to be a friendlier exchange than any I've managed with Tabitha to date.

I, on the other hand, was perched between Kayla's rock and Felicity's delightfully soft place. I preferred Felicity. Though, it has to be said, Kayla did not give me a single death stare for the entire ride, which is perhaps the longest she's ever managed.

Kayla and I have never managed to be on the best of terms. She introduced herself by way of stabbing me in the lungs. I responded by accusing her of trying to kill her step-daughters, which, it turned out, was as wrong as it was hurtful. Things have improved since then, though I'd never describe them as friendly. But since Clyde's funeral her behavior has actually verged on the side of warmth. I am beginning to become a little suspicious.

As we exit the car, instead of making for the entrance to Area 51, Kayla instead heads for the trunk. She punches the lock with savage efficiency and it pops open. Gran looks a touch concerned.

"Need better locks," Kayla informs him.

Gran's, "Groovy," sounds a little less than genuine.

Kayla reaches into the trunk and pulls out a sword in a scabbard. At first I assume it's hers. It's a touch odd—Kayla always seems to have a sword on her, usually tucked under a flannel shirt—but it's not half as odd as when she tosses it to me.

Then I realize it's my sword.

I am rather proud of my sword. I found it in the ruins of Chernobyl, buried beneath an ancient Russian military installation. I'll be the first to admit it looks a bit on the beaten up side, but I always think it makes up for that by being *wreathed in goddamn fire*.

But I didn't bring it with me. I left it in England, because of, well, because wandering around foreign agencies with a flaming sword seemed a little pretentious, to be honest.

"How did—?" I start.

"You forgot it," she says. "Feckin' idiot." She looks away for a moment. I try to catch the expression on her face. I expect a death stare, but instead it seems something between a grimace and… embarrassment? When she looks back at me, her expression is carefully neutral. "Anyway, you'll need it for lessons."

I take a moment with that one, but don't get very far. "Lessons?" I venture.

She rolls her eyes. "Me. Teach you. Sword. Lesson." She cocks her head to one side, as if regarding a particularly stupid dog and trying to get down to its level. "Are you following me?"

And her accent is thick but… "You're going to teach me how to use a sword?"

"Yes," Kayla speaks slowly. "I am going to teach you how to use a feckin' sword." She shakes her head. "Can't tell which of us is the bigger feckin' idiot."

Regardless of the thawing in our relationship, it cannot be denied that every single time Kayla has come at me with a sword she has been aiming to kill me. And now she wants me to volunteer for the experience?

I look at Felicity. Felicity can deal with Kayla. She can save me from this death trap. Except she has never been very supportive when it comes to my issues with Kayla. She shrugs at me.

"But..." I desperately pedal for room. And I need to keep my promise to Felicity. I need to make a good impression. I need to keep this civil. I scramble for an excuse. "Clyde downloaded everything I need to know into my brain."

It's odd to say that like it's a good thing.

Kayla just shrugs. "We'll see."

"Awesome, dudes." I look to see Gran giving us a thumbs-up. And this is hardly the time for his level of enthusiasm. "We don't have anything to do 'til your versions turn in the interim report anyway. I'll set you up with a room."

For the first time since I have met him, briefly, and rather unfairly, I hate Agent Gran.

ONCE AN INTERIM REPORT HAS FAILED TO APPEAR

I stand in a large bare room. It reminds me of a school gymnasium, except instead of ugly brown brick and sneaker-scuffed wood, the whole thing is constructed of the same gray plastic as the rest of Area 51. I have started to think of it as the architectural equivalent of a unitard.

"OK." Kayla discards her shirt to reveal the tight

green tank-top underneath. Her frame is thin and muscular in a way that makes me think that body fat is as scared of her as I am. Her scabbard is slung across her back, she whips out the katana in a movement so fast I can't trace it.

She strikes a pose, sword held upright bisecting her face, one shoulder aimed at me, feet wide apart. Not exactly a defensive stance.

"Get ready to meet me," she says.

I swallow instead.

"Stop wasting time, you big feckin' pansy."

Unfortunately for Kayla, I have grown very comfortable with my overpowering fear of her. Challenging my manhood in this fashion is unlikely to work.

She rolls her eyes again. "I'm going to come at you in five seconds whether you've drawn the feckin' thing or not."

That, though, does work. I sling the scabbard away and bring up the sword in front of me. A wave of red light ripples up the blade, ignites at the tip, and flames swallow the blade. A great gout of fire flashes up toward the gymnasium roof, then the sword settles down to a steady burn.

Kayla regards me from her side of her katana, a critical expression on her face. "That's the wrong grip," she tells me.

I check my grip against the swordfighting encyclopedia Clyde dumped in my head. I'm pretty sure I've matched it exactly.

"I don't think…" I start.

"Not your hands." Kayla shakes her head. "You're holding it feckin' fine. It's the grip. You're using the wrong grip."

"But—" I say.

Kayla steps forward and moves her sword in a small, extraordinarily quick move. Then my arm sings with excruciating pain and my hands open like they've been stung.

My sword flies up and away, a flaming javelin. It comes down point first, perfectly spearing a small, track-driven robot scuttling along the edge of the room. The thing spits sparks and dies.

"Crap," says Kayla, "they're going to make me pay for that, aren't they?"

FORTY-FIVE TERRIFYING MINUTES LATER

I am sweating, aching, have nearly voided my bowels a total of seven times, and yet I am remarkably whole. All my limbs are still attached, all my organs remain unpunctured.

The thing which has really taken the soundest beating is my confidence. Once Clyde put the requisite information in my head I thought I might be able to at least vaguely handle myself in a fight. Kayla hasn't even been going super-speed and since we started, I think I've managed to disturb exactly one hair on her head. It lies at a slight angle to the rest of her bangs.

She regards me as I lean on the hilt of my sword, panting and slowly burning a hole into the gymnasium floor.

Eventually she nods. "Not bad," she says.

It's not the first time this lesson she's caught me off guard, but at least it's the kindest blow so far. I look up at her. "Really?" That is not exactly how I'd describe my performance.

She shrugs. "Well, I beat you shitless. There is that.

But you do know your stuff. It's only it's," she taps her head, "up here, not," she taps her arms, "down here." She thinks about this and nods to herself. "Stop thinking. You'll do better." She nods again. "Your problem in general actually."

And then she smiles.

Kayla MacDoyle smiles at me.

Not a maddened baring of the teeth as she lunges at me, or a satisfied smile as she hoists me over some battlement into a fiery pit. It is undeniably a friendly smile.

Unfortunately, my fear is so ingrained at this point that her baring of teeth immediately, and mindlessly, causes me to genuflect. I am, and I think this speaks well of me, immediately ashamed of this reaction. But at that point I have already flinched and it is already too late.

Kayla stares at me, and for a moment I think I glimpse genuine hurt. Then the emotion is savagely murdered by anger. "Oh, go feck yourself, Agent feckin' Wallace," she says.

And then she *moves*.

I don't even see it. It is a blur, and then her sword is against the back of my neck. I can feel her breath behind the blade. She is behind me and I don't think I've had time to blink in surprise yet.

"If I wanted to feckin' hurt you," Kayla murmurs, her mouth inches from my ear, "you'd be feckin' dead."

"I…" I start. I know I have misjudged. I know I have let my lizard brain rule when I should have used something with a few more higher functions. But my fear of Kayla is something deep-rooted, based in the very fabric of the universe. She is intimidating in a very profound way, and I cannot shake that from my system.

And this sudden change in demeanor… It has no origin. I have done nothing different. I don't understand.

All of which I should say to Kayla of course. Interspersed with profuse apologies. But by the time I turn around she's already at the door.

She's going so fast, she almost runs over Agent Gran. The way a steamroller might run over a hippy commune.

"Yo," he says, though whether it's a greeting or an expression of surprise I am still too discombobulated to tell.

"Feck off," Kayla tells him.

"Totally," Gran says, failing to get out of the doorway. "Except, you know, wondering if you'd mind, erm… fecking off in the same direction as me. Your Clyde versions—they have a hit."

14

The Clyde versions' three heads peer down at us from the massive wall monitor—the world's nerdiest Cerberus guarding the gates to geek hell.

"Data report," Gran says in the oddly perfunctory manner he seems to reserve for the versions.

The versions peer over Gran's head at the rest of us, clustered on the far side of the conference table. Tabitha looks pointedly at her six-inch platform Doc Martens.

Kayla on the other hand stares fixedly at the versions, casually emanating waves of hate toward me. Felicity keeps looking back and forth between the two of us. And how the hell am I going to explain how I screwed that one up?

To make good, I decide to help with the whole going smoothly thing here. "What did you find?" I ask the versions.

The versions, as one, smile at me. The phrase "inhuman synchronicity" passes through my mind and I bat it away.

"Well," one of them starts, addressing Gran, "first of all, we all wanted to say thank you for the reading material. I mean, talk about fascinating. I tried to go as fast as I could, but well, I mean, you've got stuff here about the psychometric evaluations on alien slave AI—"

What might be sarcasm in other people is enthusiasm in Clyde.

"—and it is hard to just flip and data scan through that. So thank you, and apologies. But we had a really wild time with this. I mean, if you can imagine a wild time, say, I don't know what people do, probably there would be hookers involved, and cocaine, I imagine. Well, imagine that, and then multiply it by, probably like six, that seems like a good number, well that's what it was like on this server last night when we hit the DARPA papers. Amazing."

Gran holds up a finger. "Per protocol and shit, your servers *will* be completely scrubbed once you deliver the final report. All memory totally redacted. Just so you understand."

"You are terribly serious about this whole protocol thing, aren't you?" says a Clyde.

"Maybe," Felicity suggests, "we could just get to the bit where the Clydes tell us what they found."

"Oh yes," a Clyde says. "Totally getting there. Sorry about that. Meant to be heading from a to b, and got all distracted by c along the way. But getting off the detour and back—"

"Just feckin' tell us."

I don't think Kayla's temper is wearing thin because of the Clydes, though. I try to make apologetic eyes at her but she isn't looking at me.

"Right." All three Clyde versions genuflect slightly.

"Emails," says one of them.

"From me," says another.

"Well," says the third. "From evil me. Version 2.0."

"He's sending emails?" I say, which admittedly is

exactly what they just said but it seems odd enough that I want confirmation.

"Oh yes," says one Clyde.

"Indubitably," says another. Presumably because he is a version of Clyde. I can't think of another reason.

"We didn't see—" Gran starts. It's the first time I've seen him look slightly flustered. Hippy or no, he seems pretty invested in his agency.

"Well, it's not like he signed it 'love and kisses, Evil-Me,'" says one Clyde.

One of the versions, I notice, is looking intently at Tabitha as this zinger is delivered.

"Some very clever encryption involved," actually interjects the third Clyde. "Even if I do say so myself. As I assume it is myself, or some version of me that is responsible. Not sure if that's self-congratulatory or not anymore. If it is then I do apologize, and if it's not, don't totally mean to seem like I'm admiring the bad guy, but just want to note he is terribly good at the encryption thing. I mean he's way ahead of me. Of us. We haven't even figured how to overwrite minds."

"Not that we've been trying!" shouts another one, looking slightly horrified and desperately waving his hands at Tabitha as if to reveal there are no evil plans hidden there.

"Idiot," says the other Clyde.

"First thing he's said I agree with," comments Kayla.

"Let's focus, shall we?" Felicity suggests.

"Well," says the Clyde who made the snafu, "all we're trying to say is that the encryption is very good, but it is also very different from anything the CIA is using in its other emails. Sticks right out once you notice it. *If* you notice it." This last sentence is accompanied by another pointed stare at Gran, while the other two try to furtively examine Tabitha's response. She is busy fiddling with her own laptop and ignoring them.

So Version 2.0 is in the US government servers, sending emails. Trying to hide them. So the next obvious question is... "Who's he sending them to?"

All three Clydes smile with a certain degree of smugness.

"Also encrypted," says one.

"Very cleverly," adds the chatty one.

"Totally broke the encryption," says the third not looking anyone in the eye but looking proud enough of himself to suggest that he thinks Tabitha might be impressed.

"Wait," I say. "The replies used the same encryption as the ones Version 2.0 sent out?"

"Yes," the Clyde versions reply in unison.

"And they're not from Version 2.0?" I check.

"Would seem odd for Version 2.0 to email himself," says one. It's a valid point.

"So," I say, "whoever Version 2.0 is emailing with, he's shared his encryption program with them. So they're in league with him." I look at Felicity for my typical sanity check. She squeezes my hand.

But Tabitha looks less amenable. "Trap," she says. "Big obvious one. Walking right into it. You idiots are." For this, she finally graces the Clyde versions with a disdainful sneer.

"How so?" I ask.

"Encryption," she says. "Different from the CIA encryption. He could make it the same. But he doesn't. Wants it to be noticed. Because it's a trap. A big obvious one." She stares at me. "Duh."

"Oh," says one Clyde.

"I didn't think…" says another.

"Well, if Tabby says…" says the third.

They look completely deflated. And there's a chance Tabitha is right. But Tabitha has even more trouble dealing with the versions than I do.

"Wait," I say, "it *may* be a trap. But we don't know. We can't know. Who was he emailing?"

"Trap bullshit," Tabitha insists. "It is."

I look at her. Sternly, in fact. "Look," I say. "Would you still be as insistent that it's a trap if Felicity brought this to us? If Kayla did? Or is it just because it's the versions suggesting it?"

"Yes," she snaps. But there is a moment of hesitation.

"We *don't* know," I tell her. "Now, Clyde," I look up at the screen. "One of you. Who are the emails sent to?"

This display of intra-agency civility earns me another hand squeeze from Felicity.

The Clydes all look at each other, then the middle one turns to me and says, "Doctor Victor Mercurio."

"You know him?" Felicity fires the question at Gran like a gunslinger in a high noon showdown.

Gran looks blank. Tabitha's fingers are already flying over her keyboard. I'm already moving on, though. The next obvious question in the chain.

"What were the emails about?"

"His research," Clyde says. "Dr. Mercurio is in the middle of some absolutely insane botanical science for the US military. I had no idea they were even investigating in this area. Turning an enemy's vegetation against him, et cetera. And, well, obviously some moral qualms about the whole death and mayhem inherent in that, but if you think of domestic applications… Rapid growth of crops, rapid counteraction to deforestation, all that. It could be very neat long term. Very hippy and groovy actually."

Then the Clyde seems to remember himself and glares at Gran. "If you're into that sort of thing, of course."

"Hippies everywhere, man." Gran gives him the peace sign. "Peace, love, and growing monster plants."

I look over at Tabitha, fingers still blurring over her keyboard.

"You know where he is?" I ask her.

"New Jersey," she says. "Lab there. Across the river." She looks up at me. "Total trap though."

Gran looks over at her, and gives her a great big lazy smile. "Groovy, man," he says. "Let's, like, totally set it off and kick ass and shit. Be awesome."

15

NEW JERSEY

I have to admit, I was rather hoping we would get to bring one of the mecha. Though I suppose there's a chance that a giant death robot might tip our hand a bit.

Instead, we are traveling—to quote Gran—"Totally incognito, man." This essentially means we have swapped the anonymous black car for a dull orange VW camper van. Despite this oddly noticeable low-profile vehicle, Gran is still wearing his standard-issue CIA suit. I am not entirely sure we have achieved our goal.

We pull up outside a small, gated-off commercial building that has had a three-story arboretum grafted onto it. It sits a little outside a town I am reliably informed is called Hoboken. For the record, there are no hobos.

Felicity pushes open the van's back door and I step into the chill October wind. The now-familiar weight of my pistol bounces against my chest. Then, seeing Kayla—still grim-looking—step out, I reach back in and grab my sword.

I sort of stare at the scabbard.

"Erm," I say to her tentatively, "I'm never sure exactly how to wear it."

She hesitates a moment, then looks at me darkly.

"It's my help you're wanting now, is it?"

I try to convince my balls to leave the protective shell of my body. "It would be much appreciated."

She looks at me a moment longer, then shrugs. "Take your jacket off."

I hesitate a moment, then manage to stifle my natural need to question everything and just comply.

"Now your shoulder holster." I do. "Give it here. And the sword." She unbuckles the strap of the holster, feeds it through the scabbard, rebuckles, and holds the thing up for me. "Stick your arm through," she tells me.

I approach and, with surprising delicacy, she replaces the holster on my torso. She looks at me, appraising. "How is that?" she asks.

The weight is a little off, the holster riding a little high and forward, but to my surprise, the jerry-rigged contraption is relatively comfortable.

"It's…" I start.

"It'll feckin' do. But don't wear the jacket. You'll need one with more room in the back." Kayla nods to herself and turns quickly away before I can say more. She heads toward the gates and with little apparent effort, jumps a ten foot wall onto the far side.

Someone claps me on the back. I turn to see Felicity. "Looks like you've made a new friend," she says.

I look at Kayla, picking the gate's lock with her fist, and contemplate that.

"Why the sudden change of heart?"

"I've been telling you since you joined that you've misread Kayla. She's a kind woman. And you've saved the world twice now. That earns a little respect, I'm sure." She pecks me on the cheek. "Stop worrying so much."

So instead, I go through the gate Kayla just beat into

submission, and walk into Version 2.0's trap.

The lobby of the laboratory building is quiet. An empty desk. A dead computer. A lonely Munch print on a beige wall. The whole building seems quiet. Just the air conditioning humming its mechanical ditty.

Tabitha flicks open her laptop, punches a key. "Wireless," she says. "Still up." She takes mental inventory of our heads. She still has her pillbox number from the funeral. I still have on the baseball cap. She reaches into the depths of her laptop bag and retrieves a small green beanie. I see the glint of an aluminum foil lining as she holds it out to Gran.

"On," she says simply.

"It's got a psi-resistor inside," I say as Gran turns it over in his hands. "So Version 2.0 can't overwrite your brain."

"Groovalicious." Gran slips it on. "Thanks, dudette." He claps Tabitha on her shoulder.

Another smile. Eyes a little lidded as she looks at Gran.

And she likes him. There is just no denying it. She likes him. God, as if working with Clyde versions wasn't weird enough.

Yet it feels odd to be out in the field without Clyde. Without some version of him. Part of it is a practical concern—Clyde was our equivalent of heavy artillery— but it's more than just that. Clyde was our emotional backbone, our smile with verbal diarrhea. As I push a door open with my gun barrel, I keep wanting to check my nerves by glancing at him, working an AA battery around his mouth.

But he's not there. Can't be there.

I swing the door open. Kayla flicks through it. The

room beyond is lined with long tables, large chunks of gray-white equipment perched expensively upon them. The seats are empty, neatly tucked in below the benches.

"How many people are meant to work here?" Felicity asks.

"Twelve total," Tabitha responds without even consulting the laptop this time. "Including Mercurio."

"Do they happen to do nocturnal experiments?" I check.

Tabitha's look says "Trap" more eloquently than she ever could.

At which point the door at the far end of the lab opens up.

Three guns and one sword snap in the door's direction.

A man in his late fifties, balding, prematurely white hair slicked back in two great wings behind his ears, stops and stands very still.

"Victor Mercurio?" I ask.

"Looks like him," Tabitha tells me.

The good doctor stands there, still frozen, staring at us.

And then, abruptly, he smiles. His whole body relaxes. "Oh I am so glad," he says. "You came."

Even if this was my first day at the rodeo, I think I would still be able to tell that that is not the best thing he could have said.

"You," Tabitha whispers at me. "I told you."

"Get ready," I say.

"Oh," Mercurio waves a dismissive hand, "we have time. I really didn't want to rush you at all. Trying to be considerate and all that. May have misjudged, and in that case, well… in my defense I assumed you would have questions."

I ignore him, look for other entrances to the room.

"Dude, I am totally all over your six," Gran informs me. It seems a less efficient use of the parlance than the military originally intended.

Mercurio walks to a table and takes a seat. "Really, it's no trouble," he pats the stool next to him, "I am completely at your disposal. I mean, there has to be something you want to know."

He wants to keep us here. He's delaying us. And it's just like Tabitha said—a trap. And this delaying tactic is part of it. But there really *are* things I want to know.

"Why?" I ask. And there are so many whys. Why is one of my best friends trying to kill me? for example. But I go with the safer, "Why side with Clyde 2.0?"

Mercurio gives me a grandfatherly smile, one that would not be out of place in an ad for old-fashioned butterscotch candy. "Ah, yes, I thought that might be an issue. Totally understandable misunderstanding. Assuming that boils down to the whole you-not-recognizing-me thing."

That catches me off guard. I peer closely. And besides his resemblance to a better groomed version of Christopher Lloyd from *Back to the Future*, he seems unfamiliar.

"Have we met?" I ask.

"Yes, Arthur," he says. "Of course we have."

OK, I am officially spooked now.

"Not here." Felicity breaks in. "We need to get him off site. This is where he wants us, so it's not where we want to be."

"Agreed," Tabitha says.

"He can bring it feckin' on." It's good to know that while her attitude to me may be changing, Kayla is as enthusiastic about violence as she has ever been.

Felicity moves behind Mercurio, keeps her gun trained on him. "Put your hands behind your back."

He complies without complaint. But I'm still caught by what he said. It worries at me like I'm the ball and he's the terrier.

"Who are you?" I ask him as Felicity cuffs him with a plastic tie.

He gives me another grin. Something that is both impish and a little sad. "You don't see it?" he asks. He shrugs. "Or perhaps seeing is what is getting in the way. Maybe, and really this is just a suggestion, don't mean to impinge on your personal freedom of will and all that, but if you would consider closing your eyes, then perhaps…"

And then I don't have to close my eyes. Because I already know who talks like that.

But it can't be. It mustn't be. My mind denies it. Because… Because… But…

"Clyde?" I say.

Everyone in the room freezes. And Mercurio smiles. The grandfather is all gone now. Only the imp remains.

"In the flesh," he says. "Or, well… someone else's flesh, I suppose."

Oh. Oh no. Oh Clyde.

16

I just stare at him. At Clyde. At Version 2.0 sitting in the body of Victor Mercurio. But the good doctor is not in the building. His mind has been taken, flushed from the system. Clyde has killed him.

No. No. Not Clyde. I can't think this is Clyde. This is some twisted sick version of him. Something else, something different.

Except then he shrugs at me. One of those very expressive shrugs he always gave. "Life's a bitch, isn't it?" this one says.

And yes, yes, yes it is.

I turn, look at Tabitha, try to see how she is dealing with this. If she's dealing with this. God, I can't even think what this is doing to her.

She holds a hand out to me. "Your gun," she says simply. "Give it to me."

But I can't. Not because we need him to question him. Not because it would be profoundly psychologically damaging to allow Tabitha to kill him. Not because I am opposed to the loss of human life.

Because it's Clyde. Despite it all. It's Clyde.

"No," I say. "We need him."

Tabitha's face almost bulges. A visible build-up of rage and hate and anger, straining at the limits of her self-control. The volcano the moment before it blows.

"Not a him!" she shrieks. "Him is dead! A machine. A program. A fucking zombie. Shoot him. In his motherfucking head. Do what you do. It'd be more than a kindness. A fucking necessity."

Gran steps forward, puts a hand on her shoulder.

She shakes him violently off. "Do not fucking coddle me."

God. I look again at Mercurio. At Clyde. At Version 2.0. At whoever the hell it is grinning at me like Charles bloody Manson.

I touch my hat. My tinfoil hat. And suddenly it doesn't seem so paranoid or so stupid. It seems vitally, vitally important.

"Yes," Mercurio, or Version 2.0, or whatever godawful hybrid this is says, "those things are rather well made actually. Total kudos to Tabby on those. Very innovative, and good to see her living up to her potential. Though, and I do apologize for the self-trumpeting, but I will work them out. Just give me a day or two."

It takes me a moment but… that's a death threat. Right there. And it shouldn't be a shock from a man—a thing?—that tried to kill me a few days ago, but… God.

"How's the sword thing working out by the way?" he asks me conversationally.

"Wouldn't judge you if you feckin' showed him," Kayla says. And, God, for just that moment, I am tempted.

We all just stand there. Even Felicity with her gun still pointed at his back. Her hands are shaking, I see.

All just standing here…

"We're still here," I say. "He's still keeping us here."

"Shit," Felicity curses.

"Let's move." I wave my pistol toward the door we originally came through. "Come on."

Gran turns the door handle. Pushes. Doesn't get through.

"Locked," he says. He looks confused. "I didn't…"

"Not a problem," Kayla informs him.

Her fist flies out. The door shudders, the metal bends slightly… but it does not fall.

Kayla stares at her fist, at the door, looks confused.

"DARPA has been working on these very cool locking mechanisms recently," Mercurio comments.

Kayla crosses the room in less time than it takes to draw breath. Her fist is up.

"No!" Felicity snaps.

Kayla pauses.

"Not unconscious," Felicity says. "Not that way. We need to get in there and see what Clyde's done to him. We can't risk damaging his brain."

"Could I just chop out his tongue?" I get the feeling Kayla is all done joking.

"Later," I say. "We need to be moving."

Of course our exits are limited at this point. In fact we're down to just one. The door at the far end of the lab. The one what's-left-of-Mercurio entered through. The one I'm guessing he wants us to go through.

Bugger it. I start moving toward the door. "Tabitha," I say, "get us a blueprint. Chart us a course."

She doesn't respond for a moment. Just stares at Mercurio. Works her jaw. Her eyes are very bright and very wet. But she doesn't blink. Just stares. Mercurio smiles at her.

She flings her gaze away from him so hard I fear

she'll do herself harm. But then her fingers start to fly across the keyboard.

With Felicity and Kayla at my side, I push the far door open, and get ready for the trap to spring.

17

"Oh man," says a voice, "you have got to be having a laugh."

I freeze. My eyes scan the room. I'm looking into the laboratory's arboretum—standing around three times as tall as the lab at my back. A cluster of tall trees is surrounded by an ugly tangle of bushes. A distant glass dome lets gray light sluice down.

I scan left. Right. Nobody. And yet somebody with a pronounced cockney accent is talking.

Cockney? Wait. This is New Jersey. What the hell is…

"Arthur, mate. Over here!"

And then one of the trees waves at me.

One of the trees.

I only know one talking tree, but it still takes a moment for all the pennies to line up and drop.

"Winston?" I say.

Winston is… God, how do I explain Winston? Back when Clyde was a regular person, with regular goals that didn't involve killing me and my co-workers or taking over the minds of American botanists, he created Winston. Literally created. Because Winston was a golem, a created man, a creature crafted entirely out of books that Clyde had found lying around the Bodleian Library. Into these Clyde invested an animating force from another reality. And its name was Winston.

Then Winston hung around in the Bodleian, eating shwarma, and scanning for rogue spell books. And that was pretty much that.

Except then we had to take Winston to London, and the time-traveling Russians, who I know I've mentioned before, got involved and turned back the clock on the books that made up Winston. And all those books were made of paper, and paper used to be trees. So Winston became an animating force inside a tree. "Ent," was his word. The last I saw Winston he was being kept in a basement beneath MI6's London headquarters, essentially because he couldn't shut up.

Winston, it should be mentioned, has a rather unique personality.

"You keep following me around like this," Winston says, his bark-crusted face breaking into a grin, "I might begin to think you've gone gay for me." The wooden whorls that form his eyes bulge knowingly. Then he winks. "Hello, Felicity, love," he says. "Totally didn't see you there."

"What the hell is going on?" she says. Not unreasonably. I make way for her to come through the door.

"Winston's here," I say. It's obvious, but I'm still trying to get over the fact that Clyde's mind is here in another man's hijacked body. This additional reunion seems a little much.

"The hell?" Tabitha asks, again not unreasonably.

"You know," Winston comments, "you are not taking the grandeur of this reunion in exactly the spirit I might have hoped."

At this point Kayla, Gran, and the handcuffed Mercurio–Clyde hybrid muscle their way into the room. More confusion, and cursing follows.

"You know what?" Winston finally breaks out. "Hang the bloody lot of you anyway. I was happy here without you. I'm special here, I am. I'm appreciated. There's not many tree-men about, you know? Course you don't. You don't care for nobody but yourselves. I'm rare and unique. I have lovely foliage. Him." He thrusts a branch at Mercurio. "He cares about me. He wants to know about me. I like him."

Which at least gives the chaos some direction. "Dude," Gran says, "this guy?"

"Course that bloody guy, whoever-you-are. Don't recognize you. Maybe being a tree is messing with my memory. I don't know. But him—Doctor Mercurio, who you, by the way, appear to be treating without the due respect a genuine tree-lover really deserves."

His eyes flick left. "Not a tree-lover like that, by the way. Get your mind out of the gutter."

Kayla groans. Winston carries on regardless.

"He requested me to be sent here from London special, he did. Flew me over on a military jet. Used hydroponics to keep me alive on the trip over, they did. Very fancy. Hippy bollocks of course, but very fancy."

I try to take this all in. Mercurio requested Winston to come here. Mercurio who researches turning vegetation into weaponry. Had Clyde overwritten Mercurio's mind when the good doctor did that? Or was it happenstance? I don't know. I can't know right now. But what about Winston would interest either of them? And what about Mercurio interested Clyde?

Is this another delaying tactic? My paranoia is starting to sky rocket. Too much is happening on too short a timeline. Why does me being off balance always seem to coincide with terribly bad things happening to the world?

Kayla is circling the room looking for the best exit. Tabitha is shouting random blueprint information at her. Gran is orbiting Tabitha and Mercurio like a worried parent. Felicity is trying to keep her gun aimed at Mercurio but Gran keeps getting in the way. Mercurio is smiling like a Cheshire cat getting a blowjob.

I stare up at Winston. Winston the talking tree. His mouth is a cracked hole in the trunk. His arms have leaves. And yet he is somehow the center of calm in this scene.

"Why did he want you?" I manage to ask through the clamor of chaos. "Why specifically?"

"Well, his research, mate," says Winston, calming down now someone seems to want to pay attention to him again.

"And what's his research about?"

"Oh, it's those things," Winston says. "What's the word? Mad about them he is."

"What bloody word?" I ask. Adrenaline overwhelms my civility.

"Steady on, mate. Steady on. Don't get shirty."

If my blood pressure gets any higher I think my nose is going to erupt like Vesuvius. The next conversation I have with Winston, I'm going to bring a chainsaw.

"It's on the tip of my tongue," Winston says. "Not that I have one, but you get my meaning. God," he laughs. "Stupid of me to forget it. I am one."

"Tree?" I say, increasingly desperate. Something bad is going to happen. I can feel it in my gut like a lead weight. This is all too much coincidence.

"No."

"Asshole?"

"Fuck off, mate," Winston says with relative geniality.

"Oh wait, that's it. Golem. He's mad about golems."

"Doors are locked," Kayla shouts from the far side of the trees. "All of them. The fecks."

"Oh, I can fix that," says Mercurio.

Felicity jabs him in the side of the head with her gun barrel. "You don't—"

And then comes an audible click from every single door. The sort of click one associates with a lock coming undone.

"Oh shit," Felicity breathes.

And then the golems start to pour in.

18

It's a swarm. A biblical plague of them. Ugly misshapen things. Bulbous limbs. Lumpy irregular heads. Their legs whirl in wild uncoordinated arcs, dragging and tearing them forwards.

Version 2.0's golems. His army.

They are made of vegetables, fruit, gourds. Vines twist between cantaloupes and bunches of grapes. Branches hew together into a neck where a bunch of bananas perch lopsidedly. Pineapple fists. Pumpkin chests.

It should be comical. These stupid, poorly rendered things coming towards us. But there is such desperate fury in their mad scramble. Such a willingness to tear their compatriots apart just so they can get a little closer to us, a little closer to ripping us limb from limb, that I can find no humor in their approach.

To be honest, they're terrifying.

Pistols crackle to life. The air fills with lead traveling at very terminal velocities. Fruit pulps. Seeds and peel spray. Concave curves become convex. Juice splatters.

The golems do not slow for even an instant.

The bullets punch through the golems easily, but without effect. Their trajectories are useless pinpricks as our assailants tear toward us. Their impact is too small.

I wish Felicity had brought her shotgun. But it is back in Gran's incognito camper van. Not far away, only too far. I wish that someone wasn't going to have to explain to my parents that I was beaten to death by a fruit salad.

I look down at my pistol—suddenly a useless little thing. I jam it back into the shoulder holster and brace as the horde descends.

My shoulder holster.

My shoulder holster hanging too high and too far forward.

Because of the great bloody flaming sword strapped to my goddamn back.

I whip it out in a great sweeping arc. And I know to put my right foot just there. Pivot my hip just like that.

I cleave a vegetable man through the midriff. He falls in two separate halves. My blade carries on, buries itself in the leafy torso. The smell of burned spinach fills the air.

Kayla dances through my field of vision. No salad was ever chopped finer. With one hand she drags Mercurio behind her.

With a roar, Winston wades into the fray. He towers over the golems. His fists plow great trenches through the oncoming masses. And maybe Version 2.0 was gone from MI37 just long enough to forget exactly how we bring the goddamn pain.

The golems keep coming, though. Keep jamming themselves with greater and greater ferocity through the open doorways. A creature made almost entirely of pineapples comes in low, tackles me around the waist. I bring the hilt of my sword down on its neck, dislodge something vital. The thing falls apart, takes me down with it. I lie in its sweet smelling corpse.

Then something grabs my sword arm, wrenches at

it. I bellow and heave, but the thing has a vicious grip. I swing a fist at the mass of vegetation assaulting me and something pulps beneath it.

This has absolutely no seeming effect. Only the most massive of trauma seems to slow these things. I punch again but my sword arm is still pinned.

I can see more coming at me, ducking under Winston's flailing arm.

Shit.

Then, with a yell that would curdle blood, Felicity appears. Leaping through the air, mouth open, hair flying. Felicity Shaw, Amazon warrior. Gun in her hand.

She collides with the golem's back, clings there, unshakeable. Her mouth is open in a mad war cry. Her pistol comes down, again, again. She's using it like a club. A mad rodeo rider caving in her steed's skull.

The golem shudders suddenly and the pressure releases.

Three more golems are almost on me. I wrench up my sword arm with a yell, rising on shaking knees. The blade whips by Felicity's head with a roar of flame, slams into fleshy bodies. The golems spill to the ground.

More are clambering up Winston's body, tearing at his bark and branches. I can smell his sap mixing with the scent of mashed berries and crushed cabbage. He claws at his body, to free himself of them, but his limbs are blunt and awkward.

"Goddamn little fruit salad bastards!" he bellows.

Gran is back to back with Tabitha. She swats golems' heads with her laptop. I see one go down and think that the Lancashire cricket club maybe missed out on a star batswoman.

The attacks continue though, relentless and

unremitting. Gran has grabbed a branch from somewhere and bludgeons away as best as possible, but the pair are on the verge of being overwhelmed.

"On me!" Gran yells. "Dudes! On me!"

I tear a flaming hole through the crowd toward him. Vegetable bodies sizzle, spit, and collapse. Kayla churns a path from the opposite direction, her blade a blur. Mercurio stumbles, dragged along in her wake.

The golems are still coming, still filling the room as fast as we can empty it. How many of these bastards did 2.0 make?

Winston still smashes away at the center of the room. A limb skids over my head. A flying body almost sends Kayla sprawling. He's as much a threat to us as he is to the golems.

"I wouldn't even bloody deign to put blue cheese dressing on you!" he bellows.

"We've got to bail, dudes!" Gran yells and bludgeons at the same time, beating one golem down then another. Kayla reaches over him, skewers a bulbous cabbage head. I slash the hand off a cauliflower man about to seize Tabitha's throat.

"On three—" he yells.

But wait. "Where's Felicity?" In the crush of things I have lost track of her.

Then I see her. She stands just inside the sweep of Winston's arms, waist deep in vegetable matter, beating golems back with the butt of her gun. Pistol whipping reality back into line. Her face is matted with fruit juice and blood. Her skin is split above her eye.

I don't even think, just go for her. And in that lacuna of thought, my sword comes alive. It twists, leaps, jumps. My sword dances. My blood sings in my ears—a full-throated heavy metal roar. The sword's flame whips from red to blue. I sear a gaping hole through the vegetable men. Arms, legs, and leafy guts leap flaming into the air as I make my way toward the woman I love.

She stops as I hack my way to her.

"Holy crap," she says.

I'm panting, barely aware of what's going on.

"You OK?" I manage.

"Been worse." Considering the circumstances, that's actually quite the statement.

Another wave descends on us, and for a moment the pleasantries are put on hold. I hack madly at the oncoming assailants. Something smashes against my forehead, sends me to my knees, but I manage to get my blade through its guts.

"The others?" Felicity says as Winston's flailing buys us a moment of calm. She's sporting a slash above the other eye now.

I glance back across the seething floor. Kayla, Mercurio, Gran, and Tabitha have been pushed back against the wall. Tabitha has switched from offense to defense. She holds up her laptop to fend off blows, its case cracked and bent. Gran's branch has snapped and he's using it as a particularly ineffective flail. Kayla is the only thing keeping them alive and Mercurio keeps trying to get in her way. She elbows him hard in the nose and he staggers back, nose pouring blood.

"Shit," seems to pretty much sum up the situation.

"You take point," Felicity tells me.

I do, carving a path forward as best I can.

"Get off me you dietary disasters!" Winston yells somewhere above me. "Fucking root vegetables. You're just jealous of my stature!"

I make it back to the group. Blood is getting in my eye. My arms ache from the weight of the sword. Assuming we make it out of this, I need to find out about Kayla's workout regimen.

"The hell?" Tabitha snaps at me. "Teamwork?"

"Dude," Gran says, with significantly less venom, although he is busy stabbing an eggplant with the stump of his stick, "need to stick together. You know?"

"I was," I pant, trying to duck a blow and catching it on my shoulder instead. "Was sticking Felicity back to us."

"Can we feckin' go yet?" Kayla asks.

We make our move. Tired and ragged, Kayla dragging Mercurio by his collar. My sword slashes are increasingly wild. The golems keep on and on, mindlessly swinging for us. This has become a war of attrition.

If only Clyde was here. Clyde the original. Clyde my friend. Blasting holes through the crowd, instead of sending it to kill us.

"Fuck!" Tabitha howls. And then she's down. A rogue thing of vines and grapes seizing her by the ankles. Then they're on her, beating, clawing.

Gran and I both start smashing away. My sword flickers back and forth. His broken branch stabs and skewers. I'm terrified I'll accidentally gut Tabitha, but the other option is to let the bad guys do it. By the time we beat the crowd back, her head is lolling.

God, don't let her be dead. Don't let her be…

"Still breathing," yells Gran, slinging her over his shoulder in a fireman's lift.

I straighten. And then there is half a forest lunging at me. Something of brambles and thorns. The loosest approximation of a fist plunging at my head. I try to get my sword up, but all I have time to do is gasp.

Felicity's elbow comes out of the same region of nowhere as the golem. She hurls herself into it, a feral whirlwind of flailing arms. The pair sprawl, tussle, tumble. Only Felicity comes up. "Don't make me make a habit of that." And she kisses me.

I stare, slightly bewildered, trying to get my bearings.

Kayla doesn't have time for that. "Here." She shoves Mercurio at me. "You watch his feckin' treacherous arse." She grabs her sword in both hands and starts hacking harder.

The door is only a few feet away. I have my arm around Mercurio's throat, parrying past his body. My slashes are increasingly lazy, increasingly ineffective. We're nearly out of here, but the golems have almost overwhelmed us.

"Here we are again," Mercurio says in Clyde's voice. "Back in the thick of it again."

"Shut up," I tell him. Tell it. "Just shut up."

A foot to the door. Just a few golems between us and the dash to freedom.

We burst forward, crash into a startlingly empty lab. The equipment all lies smashed on the floor. There is the stink of rotting vegetable matter. Trampled lettuce leaves line the floor. This is where he was keeping them. Mercurio. Clyde 2.0. He jammed this place with them.

There's a door at the far end of the lab. We surge toward it. More golems are on our heels, streaming after us.

Kayla smashes against the far door, but it refuses to budge. She curses with vehemence, smashes against it repeatedly. The door starts to buckle, but far too slowly. I scan the room, desperate.

"Window!" I yell.

We break left, toward the square of light and freedom. I shove Mercurio at Felicity, and Kayla and I form a rear-guard. Behind me, someone smashes the window. Freezing wind howls through.

One golem goes down. Another. But three more are circling round to the left. I turn and slice, an aching two-handed movement.

"Tabitha clear!" Gran yells behind me.

My blade gets stuck in a pineapple and for a moment I lack the strength to yank it free.

Behind us I can still hear Winston screaming. "I'll feed you all to fucking rabbits!" But there's no chance to go back for him, no way to get him out of the arboretum. And he'll be OK. He has to be OK. We'll come back. We'll send in the reinforcements.

"Mercurio clear!" Gran yells.

Kayla leans over me, splits an oncoming golem in two, which lets me keep my brains inside my head for a little longer.

"Felicity clear!"

I see the golem coming at Kayla a split second before she does. It's snuck past us, circling. It raises a massive lumpy gourd of a fist.

I slam my blade forward, lunging underneath Kayla, catching the thing in the gut, and ripping sideways, eviscerating it.

The golem tumbles.

"Dudes, come on!" Gran bellows.

Kayla looks at me. "Ta," she says. And she's smiling again. I'm almost too tired, but I manage to flash one back. Then she's gone, out the window, into the cold and the wind.

"Come on!"

I stagger back. Up onto a bench, Gran grabbing me from through the window, heaving me out. I land in a heap. A golem lunges at the open window. Mad and scrabbling to get to me.

This is what Clyde left for us. This is what he wanted us to find. This is all he has for us. This mindless, spasming frenzy.

Is that it? Is that the why? Has he lost his mind? Is this golem a metaphor for what is going on with him?

Kayla's sword snaps out and decapitates the thing.

"Come the feck on," she says, and pulls me toward Agent Gran's van.

19

ONCE THE BLOOD HAS DRIED

The Area 51 infirmary is a narrow rectangular room, staffed entirely by robots. Or synthetic people. Or class fives. Or whatever the hell I'm supposed to call them. There seem to be too many varieties of life form these days. What happened to good old-fashioned bad folk?

A woman with slightly shiny, rubbery skin applies a fresh ice pack to my head. Felicity sits next to me with a mannequin man stitching up the right side of her head. The servos in his arm squeak every time he pulls the thread out. He has apologized for it twice. Somehow that makes it feel even weirder than it did before.

He apologized for that too.

Gran, Tabitha, and Kayla are here. Gran is receiving the ice pack therapy and playing with his smartphone. Tabitha lies in a genuine hospital bed with a bandage around her head. She seems much more concerned with her laptop's injuries than her own. She's been poking at the machine with a multi-tool since she regained consciousness, parts of its anatomy are spread on the pristine sheets around her.

Kayla is a little scraped but has threatened bodily harm on the next robot that approaches her.

Gran looks up from his phone. "All right, dudes,"

he says. "That's it. Wireless network in Area 51 is officially down."

"Good." Tabitha doesn't look up from her repair work.

"Rest of the US will be all taken care of and hunky-dory in twenty-four hours. Well, you know, apart from all the rabid corporate dudes all pissed and stuff about, you know, work." This seems to strike Gran as a slightly absurd concern.

Still, I have to give Area 51 credit. Dismantling the wireless network of an entire nation, against everyone's will, inside of twenty-four hours is an impressive feat. "What will you tell everyone?" I ask. "A solar flare?" I remember the British government's cover story for cutting all power to London. The city is still recovering from eight hours of darkness.

"No, man." Gran shakes his head. "Environmental stuff never flies so well here as with you guys. Total shame and everything. But we always wind up saying it's some terrorist thing or doodad, or something. National security ups compliance by, like, I don't know, a shitload."

"Oh." I nod. "OK." Brutal but efficient, I suppose. Maybe that's the CIA for you.

"That mean I can take off this stupid feckin' hat then?" Kayla asks. Possibly not the highest priority question, but a favorite for the home crowd.

All eyes go to Tabitha. She works a screwdriver attachment deep into the circuitry of the laptop and flips something smoking across the room. It bounces off a mannequin man's head. He blinks but makes no other comment. Neither does Tabitha.

"Feck it then," says Kayla, yanks her trucker hat

off and tosses it into a corner.

When Tabitha doesn't start screaming, I pull mine off too. It joins Kayla's in the corner. Felicity slings the bonnet aside with a sigh of relief. She has the worst hat hair. It is rather adorable looking.

There is silence for a moment. We seem to no longer be able to avoid the subject, but no one wants to broach it.

I take a breath, then dive in.

"So then," I say, "what are we doing with Mercurio?"

Gran looks at Tabitha for a long time before answering. She doesn't look back.

"Under, like, sedation," he says. "We're running a whole bunch of scans. MRI, EEG, all that mad science stuff. Tweaking the dials, man. Then we'll have some psych guys come in. Head shrinking dudes. They'll do some awesome talking stuff. We'll totally get you the transcripts. Video too if you want. But, I'm assuming…" he trails off. "Then…" He trails off again.

Then what?

He looks at Tabitha again, but I don't know why. And then to Felicity. In turn her gaze meets his then travels to Tabitha. It is the eyeball equivalent of a Rube-Goldberg machine.

"Are you up to it?" Felicity asks Tabitha.

Tabitha takes the bent and twisted base of her laptop. And then with a savagery that I have seen lurking before, but never seen unleashed, she twists the metal. There is a crack and a violent pop. She shakes the sheet. It is remarkably flat. She looks up and meets Felicity's eyes dead on.

"No need for it to be conscious," she says, avoiding the personal pronoun. "Keep it quiet. I'll debug its brain."

Debug… And then I remember. From the funeral service. Chatting with the versions. One of them had gone onto Tabitha's server and found out she was figuring out how to fix the mind of someone overwritten by Clyde. It had seemed so paranoid then. An innocent age.

Well… an innocent week or something.

"Will there be anything left?" I ask. "Of the original Mercurio, I mean. Or is that all…" I hesitate because it's a horrible thought. "… gone?"

She looks at me. A stare as emotionally dead as the one the robot stitching up Felicity is giving her.

"Don't know," she says. "Maybe. Better that than…" And despite the emotional deadening she still can't complete that sentence. Maybe that's a good sign.

A monitor beside me suddenly blinks to life. A Clyde version smiles happily at everyone from the screen. "Could I help?" it asks. "Couldn't help but overhear. Well… in all truth I could have helped, but I was busy working out the interface for the intercom program. Plus this place is bugged just about everywhere. These Area 51 people have no privacy. But maybe that's how they like it."

"The hell is he doing there?" Tabitha asks, jabbing her multi-tool at the screen. "Restricted to conference room." The multi-tool swivels threateningly to Gran. "You promised."

"Dudette," Gran says, "totally not my call. Kensington and his whole seniority thing. He gave your versions access to our full domestic server. I was all, 'psychological sensitivity.' And he was all, 'yadda yadda,' and, 'I don't give a pompous shit.' Dude has some serious issues with mellow-ness. But, yeah.

They're, like, about and stuff on the premises now."

"No." Tabitha repeats it again. "No discussion. No debate. Just no. No versions."

One thing you have to credit Tabitha with—she is really in touch with her negative emotions.

In many ways, I think she's right. A man whose mind was overwritten by, well, by someone almost identical to these things, these versions... he just tried to kill us.

But... am I really looking at this rationally? What if I divorce emotion from reason. These versions are not the one who tried to kill us. They took a different path. They make me uncomfortable but to ignore their basic utilitarian usefulness is idiotic.

I take a deep breath. "Actually," I say, "we do need them. Or we need someone. We almost had our arses handed to us. We had to send in a back-up squad to rescue Winston. And having our own trio of Clydes could tip the edge in our favor. There might be some insight they have. I mean, Jesus, the more people we have on this the better, right?"

For a moment everyone is very still and very quiet as they wait to see if Tabitha is going to murder me.

"Thank you, Arthur," the Clyde version breaks the silence. "May not actually physically have a back now, but it is nice to know that you have it metaphorically."

Tabitha flicks a pointed glance at Felicity. Who shrugs. "He's got a good point," she says.

"Fine." Tabitha flings back her sheets, gathers up the remnants of her laptop. "Fucking fine. In the field. Saw who you two are really interested in protecting." She gets out of the bed, and while a little unsteady on her feet, she manages a pretty convincing stalk toward the room's exit.

As she passes the monitor, the Clyde version says, "Tabby..."

She plunges the multi-tool into the monitor. It detonates with a hiss of cracks and sparks. She doesn't spare it or us a glance as she exits the room.

20

LATER

The CIA has apparently deemed it unsafe for us to return to our hotel prior to the deactivation of the nation's wireless networks. Instead they provide board in the form of a small square room made of the same molded plastic as the rest of Area 51. The place also has the same slightly antiseptic feel as the rest of Area 51. Felicity tells me to stop moaning and help her unpack.

She has plucked a pair of my underwear from the suitcase, and is folding them in half when I ask her, "Do you think Tabitha was right?"

"About what?"

"About us in the field. About me being too concerned with your safety." I'm at a small desk where I just finished connecting our laptops to the Area 51 wired network.

She smiles. "I thought it was rather sweet that you came to my rescue. Very knight in shining armor of you. Though I do seem to remember me saving your delightful derrière a couple of times as well." She reaches back for another pair of my underwear.

She is being slightly coy. And she is not letting me fully in.

"That was much appreciated," I say. Because it really was. It's nice to not be a corpse right now. "But you didn't abandon our teammates to accomplish it." I lean forward in the desk chair. "I mean, did you need me? Would you have been OK if I hadn't come for you?"

She shrugs, and puts the underwear down. "I don't know, Arthur. I think, honestly, it's a minor issue. We were in a fight with a former co-worker. Things were bound to get weird. I know I certainly wasn't at my A game." She shrugs. "I think the important thing to focus on is that, despite it all, nothing bad did happen. We all got out alive." She smiles, sympathetic. "Are you OK? You're not normally this worried about your performance."

I go to say I'm fine, and then I hesitate. I *am* more confident than this usually. Felicity herself has chewed me out for things, and I've been fine with them. What is it this time?

But I know. Of course I do.

"I abandoned three teammates for the sake of just one, today." That's a shitty truth, right there. "But it was you. So of course I abandoned them. But that could have been disastrous. Except I don't know how else I could have done it."

Felicity steps forward, pushes a hand through my hair, sweeping it back from my forehead.

"What do you want me to say, Arthur? That this will get easier?" She looks at me, firm and sharp. "It won't. This is going to be awful."

For a moment, there is a slightly haunted look in her eyes, and for a moment I see a visual echo of the face that told me about the time she watched as agents shot her sister.

"You will regret things, Arthur. I'm sorry but that's the way it is. You will make sacrifices." She swallows hard. "But they'll be necessary. That's why you'll make them. That's how you'll learn to live with them." She flicks her wrist at the corner of one eye.

I close my eyes, try to get myself under control. I am being selfish. I know the sacrifices Felicity has made. The one I made today should barely even register. And yet there's still a knot in my gut. Maybe honesty is the best policy.

"You said…" I start and then hesitate. It's not an easy thing to say, either to Felicity or myself. "You said heroes are defined by sacrifice."

"I did." There's something about her face that is both firm and soft. I don't know how she does it, only that it melts my heart.

"But… I…" I shake my head. "I don't think I could sacrifice you."

For a moment I think she's going to say something, but then either she doesn't trust herself or me. I honestly couldn't say which.

"And the thing is," I manage to continue, "I don't think you would ever really be able to forgive me if I saved you at the expense of the greater good."

She tries to smile but it falters. She leans in, presses her head against mine. "You'll make the right call, Arthur," she says quietly. "In the moment, that's what you'll do."

She puts her lips to my forehead, kisses me. A benediction perhaps. "I have faith in you, Arthur," she says. "Please have some in me. I can take care of myself."

I hold her, tight and close. Hold her and feel her real, and solid, and warm. She squeezes me back tight.

But she didn't answer me. Not really. And maybe that's confirmation in itself.

* * *

ONE LONG NIGHT LATER

"Full of shit. You are."

At the beginning of my relationship with Felicity, she assured me that it was possible for exes to have a healthy working relationship. Apparently, Tabitha and Clyde did not get that memo.

"Well," says a Clyde version, "while I do appreciate the anthropomorphism, which is really very sweet of you, and I do certainly want you to know that you're entitled to your point of view, and in many ways I do see where you're coming from, and I am in fact even considering agreeing, I think completely ignoring the thalamic entrypoint is perhaps a little hasty."

I suspect that was meant to make sense somewhere, but the version lost me at, "I do appreciate the anthropomorphism."

We just have one Clyde version with us for this operation. The other two are mining the servers we rescued from Mercurio's labs. This one speaks out of a monitor that hangs from the ceiling on a jointed arm. It is angled to face down on a slight angle. It affords the version a better view of Mercurio's body.

The good doctor lies unconscious and bound on the operating table beneath him. His head has been shaved and the white hair replaced with a thick layer of electrodes. One of the infirmary's walls is doubling as another massive monitor; numerous windows give life to the electrodes' measurements.

Tabitha stands with her back to the man and the monitor—both versions of her old boyfriend. It's probably the most mentally healthy way to face them. She scans the screens with an acid expression. Gran and I have taken up our spectator position at a respectful and hopefully safe distance.

"What are you seeing?" I ask. Wading into this fight is probably less potentially lethal than going up against the golems yesterday, but I'm still glad I'm wearing my pistol.

"Certain amount of neurological damage," the Clyde version says, attempting to peer at me from his screen. "It looks like Evil-Me came in through the thalamus, which is sort of a routing center for the brain," continues the version. "It's sort of like the brain's King's Cross just without all the bad shops and hookers after midnight. Not that I'm judging the way in which anyone makes money. Except, well, there is the whole legality issue, so well, maybe judging it a little bit. Personally I'd always thought selling a kidney would be my plan for dealing with long-term financial disaster. Less of an option for me these days, but money is also less of a concern, so—"

"The thalamus," I cut him off.

Gran chuckles.

"Oh right, yes," the Clyde version says. "Well, originating there, we have some burn damage. Looks like Evil-Me came in a little hot and zapped Mercurio. Burned out some nerve bundles. A bunch of them lead from the thalamus to the hippocampus, which is sort of a subrouting station for the whole memory thing. If we're still all aboard on the whole train metaphor. Pardon the pun. God, I love puns. Did we ever discuss that when I still had legs?"

"Not so much."

And did he love puns when he was alive? Is that true? Or is... No. I have to stop this.

"Shut up," Tabitha says, without turning to the monitor.

"Oh sorry," says Clyde. "Wrapping up. Anyway Tabby and I were just discussing where best to get started with our coding. Origin point or main site of injury. Professionals at work."

"Professional," Tabitha corrects. "And software."

"Totally." The Clyde version nods vigorously. "Whatever you say, love. Oh damn, I didn't mean that. Being professional. Oh wait, I'm the software. Totally being software. Zero, one, one, one, and all that."

Tabitha growls in frustration.

Gran leans over. "You know, dude," he murmurs, "with your team's, you know, track record and stuff, I always just figured you guys would be... I don't know..." He searches for a diplomatic word.

"Functional?" I suggest.

"I guess so."

"Me too." I nod.

We share a smile. Then I notice Clyde looking over. He doesn't exactly scowl—that's not in his nature— but he does not look exactly pleased.

Should I be scared of that? Of what evil might lurk in him?

On the bench, Mercurio twitches.

"The fuck?" Tabitha snaps. She finally turns to face the monitor, dark eyes flashing.

I smell danger and am almost grateful for the excuse to stand up. "What's going on?"

"Mercurio. Fried by him." Tabitha stabs a finger at Clyde's monitor. "Almost," she allows.

I go to Mercurio's side. One of the side effects of my job is that I have developed an unhealthy habit of walking toward danger.

"It was a minor miscalculation in the amplitude,"

Clyde protests. "Totally minor. And I corrected it. I did."

"You're a machine," Tabitha says. "Math, not a problem you can have. Call bullshit."

I massage my forehead. I have to make Tabitha's relationship with the versions functional when I can't even manage that myself.

"Look," I say, "let's just calm down and work on this."

Tabitha seems momentarily unsure whether to send her spiteful looks in my direction or the version's. She settles on the version.

"Fuck up and I fry you," she states, leaning back over the body.

I came here because I thought I might learn something, but so far we're just probing at the edges of how uncomfortable one man can be made to feel. "Perhaps we should leave," I suggest to Gran.

Tabitha shrugs as if she couldn't care less about anything in the world. Then, "Gran could stay," she says. "Maybe."

I wish I knew if she was doing this out of some genuine, albeit improbable sense of connection with Gran, or if she was just doing it to spite the Clyde versions.

"Actually I'd prefer it if Arthur remained too," says Clyde. Possibly to counter Tabitha's move, or possibly just to spite me for siding with Gran.

I suppress a groan, and settle in for the long haul.

THREE AGONIZINGLY DYSFUNCTIONAL HOURS LATER

I finally manage to escape the room. I make it about three paces beyond the door before I just have to stand there rubbing my temples and hoping that's more effective than beating my head repeatedly against a wall.

I'm so absorbed in the activity that I don't even

notice Kayla until she taps me on the arm and scares the shit out of me.

"Sword lesson," she says.

I am so not in the mood. I just want to lie down and rinse my brain with some jazz and trashy action movies for about four weeks.

"Come on, you big Jess." She proceeds to drag me, apparently without any real effort. "Be cathartic."

She has my sword waiting for me back in the large gymnasium. I seem to remember leaving it in my room. I worry there will be a fist-shaped hole in the door.

She comes at me a few times. Slowly enough. I parry.

She shrugs. "Thinking too much," she says. "Still."

I flick the sword at her, irritated. "It's in my nature."

She smiles. Another friendly smile. And it's not so scary this time. "So think," she says, "but about something else."

I stare at her. "You're attacking me with a sword. What am I meant to think about? How sweet the hereafter will be?"

Another shrug. "You're the talky bastard. Talk. About something. Gets boring, I'll decapitate you."

I think that was what passes for a joke with Kayla. Which does beg one question.

Jab, parry, thrust.

"Why are you being nice to me?"

"This, a-feckin'-gain?"

Harder jab, more desperate parry, thrust batted away.

"No," I say, beating a retreat. "I mean, we've never been on the best of terms. This seems a little... out of character."

Kayla twirls around me, graceful in a brutal sort of way. I twist, manage to meet her blade, but stagger back under the ensuing onslaught. She smashes her sword toward me. I fumble up a block, but she bears weight down. My blade is forced dangerously close to my face. I can feel the heat of it, almost searing my skin.

"You did save the world last week," she says. "Fairly impressive. Plus, like you said to Tabitha and the versions, we're stuck with each other. Can do this hard or easy."

I would nod, but that would take the tip of my nose off.

"By the way," Kayla mentions, "you should be kicking my feet out from under me about now."

Her leg smashes into mine, and I tumble to the floor. My sword spins away.

"Not in your sword manual?" Kayla taps the side of her head.

I lie panting on the ground, waiting for my tailbone to stop yelling so loudly at me.

She gives me a hand up. But she's got me thinking about the number Clyde did on my own brain as she starts to come at me again. Three quick blows later and I'm on the ground again.

"Distracting yourself too hard now," she tells me. "Talk."

I get my sword up. Kayla circles me. Predatory. And I start talking just to keep the fear at bay. Intellectually, I may know Kayla and I are on polite terms now, but my subconscious only accepts these things in writing and has a four week backlog.

"It's Mercurio," I finally admit.

"Poor feck," Kayla says.

She lunges fast and hard, and I am not entirely sure how I survive.

Feint and thrust. Parry and block.

"We just came from… We were taking Clyde out of him. Or the evil version. Version 2.0. But what about Version 2.0 himself? What if we could debug *him*? Take the evil out somehow. Turn him back into…"

I just about get my sword in the way of a blow that would have made me a foot shorter.

"We've got three of him al-feckin'-ready." Kayla's swipes are vicious. "That's no enough for you?"

And… No. No it's not. And I'm ashamed to admit it, but they're not Clyde. Somehow, as messed up as it is, Mercurio is more Clyde to me than they are.

"You want my opinion?" she asks me. "We skewer the feckin' a-hole."

"He's a computer program," I point out.

"Then we skewer his feckin' hard drive in its feckin' a-hole. You want to do the heroic thing? You make him feckin' gone. Rid the world of evil. It's feckin' simple."

Kayla comes at me then, fast and hard and for a moment I can't talk, can't think about anything. I am just my swordblade moving back and forth.

Finally I manage to launch an offensive strike of my own. "But don't heroes save people too?"

"Are you feckin' stupid?" Kayla curls her lip, smashing my sword aside. "He's not people. Just said it yourself, he's a feckin' program."

"What about hope?" I ask. "We just abandon him even if there's a long shot chance?" I'm getting heated now. Kayla smashes my sword aside but I go with the motion, pivot on my foot, and duck, stabbing under my arm as my back goes to her. There is the clash of steel but Kayla grunts.

Then she stops. No movement. Holy shit, did I?

I glance over my shoulder. Kayla has my sword caught between her palms. It is less than an inch from her neck. My sword spits fire against the skin of her hand. She pushes me away. Hard.

"Oh crap," I say, "I'm—"

But she nods, shaking off the scorched palm. "Good," she says. "You weren't thinking. Just fighting."

And she's right. I wasn't thinking about the sword at all. It was like that moment in the arboretum of Mercurio's lab when I was fighting to get to Felicity. Simple.

"Wait," I say, "were you just baiting me?"

She looks at me like I'm the one who almost received a serious blow. "Are you fecked in the head?" she asks. "More Clyde? Shoot the bastard and be done."

Which is an awkward moment for Clyde's digital figure to suddenly appear, peering up from the floor below us.

Seriously, is nothing in this place not a monitor?

"Hello chaps. Chap and chapess. Chapette? Is that how that unpleasant little CIA man frames it? Odd thing to say. Sort of underhand and philandering if you ask me. Which you didn't, of course. But for future reference if you ever do want to ask me."

"Why the feck are you here?" Kayla doesn't even need a sword to cut to the point.

"Oh." Clyde places palm to forehead. "Yes. Sorry. Version 2.3 and I were just helping Felicity go through Mercurio's computer equipment and we found Evil-Me and we need to go kill him. Almost forgot to say. Good thing my head is digitally coded onto my shoulders really. But she wants to do the whole briefing thing. Come on."

And with that he's gone.

Kayla looks at me, pointedly. "More of him?" she asks. "Fecked in the head, you are. Seriously fecked in the head."

21

We stand in the Area 51 conference room and stare up at the three Clyde versions. They are all looking slightly too pleased with themselves. There's the crackle of anticipation in the air. Even Tabitha seems to have wiped some of the antagonism off her face for this one. Though there's a chance that's because she is standing remarkably close to Gran.

"So," Felicity says, "where is he?"

Him. We're going to confront him. Clyde. Version 2.0.

And then we're probably going to kill him.

God...

"Well it wasn't an easy task, let me tell you," says the first version. "I mean, one doesn't want to pat oneself on the back—"

"Especially if one doesn't have a back," points out another.

"Well, it's a metaphorical back," says the first.

"Totally following along with the logic here," says the third, "and I don't want to derail things. Think you guys are off to a totally blazing start. But I don't think we should question our anthropomorphism in public." He gives a nod in our direction. "Doesn't set a good precedent. Just a thought of course."

"A good thought, though," says the first.

"Fabulous thought," says the second, clapping the third, apparently without irony, on the back.

"I asked, where is he?" Felicity repeats the question, this time with force.

"Well, on the surface of Mercurio's files there wasn't much apart from his research. Weaponizing vegetation, with a strong focus on the golems we fought. But also stuff about massive growth spurts, and deadly fungus attacks, and all that delightful mad science stuff, which, I have to say, really reaffirms my faith in the American nation. Someone has to be sponsoring mad science, and it's good to see the world's super-power taking charge in the field. But anyway, that's essentially all chaff, and flotsam, and other words for unwanted stuff we don't need to care about. But anyway, below that was a whole second layer of files, but you know what was really fascinating?"

I suspect I will regret this but I grudgingly ask, "What?"

"It was more chaff, flotsam, and the other word!" shouts the third Clyde, rather excitedly. One of the other ones gives me a thumbs-up.

"But," says another Clyde, "then we found the *third* layer."

"Where the feck is this Version 2.0 feck?" Kayla suddenly shouts.

"Oh, wait," says a Clyde. "I thought we started off with that."

"No," Kayla breathes, "you feckin' didn't."

All three Clydes gulp.

"Well then," one of them says, "long story short, we found the IP addresses he'd been bouncing the email off, and tracked them down to the point of origin."

"Which is feckin' where?" Kayla has actually drawn her sword.

"Here." Clyde's face disappears off the screen and a map of the world appears. It revolves slowly, the camera beginning a slow zoom. Continents resolve into countries. The gross anatomy of our world spinning past, rivers, mountain ranges, rain forests.

Then we start to zoom in. North America. Central America. Mexico. The camera keeps on zooming, the focus tightening. Cities start to spawn on the map, like bacteria on an agar plate. One growing larger and larger, rushing up to us. Mexico City.

Clyde. We're going to see Clyde. And I killed him once before.

No matter what Kayla says, no matter how things went with Mercurio, I don't want to repeat that moment. Clyde will have his reasons. We will be able to reason with him.

Streets and thoroughfares fill the screen. But we rush toward the city's outskirts. Toward the breaking down of urban order. A twisted, tumor-like growth of houses. And then beyond, a great spreading pustule of desolate land.

"Bordo Poniente Landfill," the Clyde version intones. "Officially closed in 2011 but still filling up."

"He's there?" I ask. I try to understand it. Clyde is a computer program. How the hell can he be hiding in a massive landfill site?

"Trap," Tabitha intones.

"You just say that," I say, attempting to lighten the atmosphere a little.

"I point out the fucking obvious," she says.

But I actually genuinely disagree. "No," I say. "It makes no sense for him to be there. That's why it makes sense."

"Not, like, totally sure I'm following your logic." Gran looks like I may have broken his brain.

"Look at it," I say. "It's nothing. There's nowhere for him to be. He can't be there. So he has to be. It's camouflage. He's hiding."

And this is the part, I realize, where I should smile, and clap my hands and be down to business, but it is only with great sadness that I can say, "We've got him."

22

FLYING SOUTH

Apparently Agent Gran is not messing around this time.

Squatting before our cramped uncomfortable net seats in the back of a huge transport plane are two massive mecha. They are armed so heavily they must be approaching the density of a black hole.

"Oh," breathes Kayla. It is the first time I think I have ever seen her look even vaguely impressed. "I have to get me one of those."

Two CIA pilots look down at us from the enhanced height of the mecha. The man is small and wiry with thick-rimmed glasses. Not that I notice that as much as the fists the size of office chairs, and the four-inch thick sheets of steel covering his body. He stands about seven feet tall in the suit. And he's dwarfed by his partner.

She's a tall woman, and looks like she starts the day by bench-pressing Hulk Hogan. Her mecha is broader, heavier, and covered in way more machine guns. Three barrels poke over her right shoulder. The smallest one appears to shoot bullets with the same diameter as my palm.

I'm pretty sure what's on her left shoulder is a missile launcher.

All in all, the Area 51 boys and girls do have some

pretty impressive toys. Patriotism has its time and place, but these guys do seem way better equipped to deal with Clyde than we do.

Gran stands before the two pilots, doing his own unique version of a brief. "Collected dudes," he starts, immediately hitting completely the wrong tone.

The woman grits her teeth. "Just tell us what the hell we're dealing with, Gran." She sounds efficient to the point of coldness.

"Oh, nomenclature," Gran says. "Groovy. Erm… disembodied class five threat."

Class five, which means they're treating Version 2.0 like a robot. Which sort of makes sense given the whole being on a computer thing.

"Threat level?" asks the woman. The CIA do seem to love their jargon.

"Erm…" Gran counts his fingers, then looks up brightly. "Unspecified," he says.

"You shitting me, granola-boy?"

"Gina, dudette, would I do that to you?"

I'm not entirely sure I would be so flippant with this woman, Gina. She has that same I-would-really-love-to-rip-out-your-colon-and-strangle-you-with-it look that Kayla has perfected. And with the suit on she looks equally capable of pulling off the feat. Though possibly the hands are too large for the really fine motor movements required for a proper colon-strangling.

Funny the things stress makes you think about…

The bespectacled CIA man works something around in his mouth and then spits out a long brown streak of tobacco. "You ball park us?" he asks.

"There's been no, like, totally direct engagement. Proxy warfare and all that ungroovy shit. But could potentially be a category three."

The woman looks dubious. "You fucking with me, Gran," she says, "and I swear I'm going to come back here, shove my hand up your ass, and wear you like a puppet."

Kayla looks as if she approves of this sort of feedback.

"What's a category three?" I venture. The woman looks at me like I'm bird crap that just fell on her shoe.

"Oh," says Gran, "Gina, Joel," he waves to the mecha pilots, "you should totally meet MI37. Liaising from the UK and all that. Very chill folks. Very groovy."

The woman's face does not soften. The man nods, albeit grudgingly.

"Category three is a state-level threat," he says.

"State level?" I ask.

The woman groans as if I pain her.

"Oh, well, you know," Gran says. "Like, capable of blowing a hole in the world that's the size of the average US state."

I contemplate that for a moment. That is the level of damage they think Clyde could inflict? Clyde? Bumbling, grinning Clyde?

Clyde who sent a horde of golems to try and kill us all. Who programmed homicidal tendencies into a military drone.

Could he do that? Would he?

"What in the name of hell," asks Felicity, "is a category one threat then?"

"Oh," Gran says. "It sort of goes up, like, geographically. Category two is country size hole. Category one is a continent. Not totally metric or anything, but it sort of gives you a sense of scale and shit."

Felicity seems to think about this. "So a nuclear bomb…" she starts.

"Category four—city wide hole."

Holy shit, they have Clyde one category up from a nuke. My sense of reassurance slips. They're only sending two mecha against that?

Tabitha chews her lip and looks at the pilots. "Clyde's going to tear them apart," she mutters.

Kayla just nods.

BORDO PONIENTE LANDFILL

We stand in the cesspit of humanity. Everything is trash. It defines the landscape. Its fumes infect the air we breathe. It swirls and swills in the trickles of water that flow from nearby cloaca.

But it is not the scale, nor the stench, nor the sense of the place seeping through the soles of my shoes that makes my gorge rise.

It is the humanity. It is the women and men and children scurrying through this detritus. They are covered in the stains of filth. It is in their hair, their pores. It is deep beneath their fingernails. I see a boy no more than eight pulling a fistful of rusting metal from a pile of broken bottles. It comes loose with a spray of violent green fluid. He shoves the still dripping mess into a shopping bag, wipes his brow with his polluted fist and blinks the dripping sewage from his eyes.

"Jesus."

Of course, I knew this sort of place exists. We all know. There are the TV documentaries. There are the pleading ads. There are the celebrity spokespeople looking into TV cameras with happy, filthy children perched around them—a cheerful counterpoint to a melancholic face with staring eyes.

I knew it, but only in my head, not in my gut. And, God, I was not prepared for this.

Felicity has tied a handkerchief around her face, obscuring her nose and mouth, but she cannot keep the horror out of her eyes. Kayla is doing her best to look impassive and heartless but her eyes track the children and her hands tremble slightly. With one hand, Tabitha clutches her laptop like a talisman. Gran holds the other.

So… I guess, well, they… Yeah.

But that's just something I cannot deal with right now.

The only ones who look impassive are the CIA pilots, but that's because they've closed the cockpits of their mecha suits and all I can see is blank steel. Bastards probably have air conditioning and perfume dispensers in there.

"Maybe he picked here," says Kayla, "because he knew there's no feckin' way we'd want to come."

"I'll, like, get the eye in the sky to do another sweep." Gran manages the sentence before his gag reflex kicks in again. He stifles a heave with his forearm. The bottom of his suit pant legs are turning from black to an ugly shade of purple. He manages to control himself and touches a small plastic bead in his ear.

"You dudes see anything from up there?"

The cargo plane that brought us in is doing low sweeps back and forth above the landfill, riding updrafts of rotten air.

A static-filled voice comes back over my own ear bud. It says something like, "Gffffnshhhhkzzzzshfzzz."

"Roger," says Felicity.

I look over to her. "You understood that?"

She shrugs. "I'm fluent in military radio chatter." She points ahead and to the right. "Might be some sort of structure one click south-east of here."

We slog on and through. This place gets worse. The trash piles are deeper, the people thinner—emaciated limbs and desperate eyes. They stare at the hulking mecha with an odd passivity, as if they have been robbed of any sense of wonder.

"Why would he come here?" I ask Felicity.

Felicity shrugs. "I'm not sure. But he's going to have a reason."

A reason. That's what I need Clyde to have for all of this. I look around. "Maybe he wants us to see something..."

"What shits we are, letting people live like this?" Felicity looks skeptical.

"Holy shit." It's the female mecha pilot's voice coming through my earpiece. She's ahead of us, standing on the crest of a dune of plastic drinking bottles, smashed circuitry, and rubber hoses.

We clamber up beside her and stare down. There is a depression in the field of filth, a shallow bowl perhaps a kilometer in diameter. At its center, its deepest point, there is indeed a structure. A square building, the size of a small family home.

It's not exactly the traditional bricks and stucco construction though. The walls are made of cans, mulch, and smashed TVs. The roof is sheets of rusting steel, patchwork tarpaulins. Balding tires, piled high, form columns before a pitch black rectangle of a doorway.

"It's a temple," I say, suddenly recognizing the design. "Like an old Greek temple. Just..." Well, there's only one way to say it really. "Just made out of shit."

"Arrogant fuck," Tabitha says, and while she is a bit one-note on the whole Clyde issue, it's hard to parse building a temple to yourself as an act of humility.

"Still think this is a trap?" I ask.

"So he's here." Tabitha shrugs. "So what? Still a trap."

"He puts up anything between us and him," comments the male pilot, "and we fill it with more holes than Swiss cheese in a mouse hole."

"Goddamn, Joel," comes the woman's voice. "You are still the worst fucking poet I know."

The man's mecha turns to face hers. One massive fist jabs at her. "I was published, Gina. Goddamn published."

You know, one day it would be nice if just someone could conform to a stereotype.

"How about," Felicity suggests, "we focus, lock, load, and go in and get the bastard?"

"Published," says the pilot as the two mecha stomp down the slope toward the temple of trash. Felicity and Tabitha follow in their wake, while Kayla goes out wide, scouting clockwise along the rim.

I catch Gran's arm. He turns to me.

I'm staring at that little temple. I know Tabitha is seeing it as some pompous gesture, some self-aggrandizing bullshit. But I wonder if there's more irony and sadness in it than anything else. Maybe it's less the creation of an arrogant man and more the creation of someone who's looked around him and thrown his arms up in despair.

"If there's a chance," I say, "to talk to him, to try and bring him back to sanity, let's do that, OK? Before we shoot him. Let's see if we can rescue him." And I know Kayla and Tabitha would disagree with me, hell, maybe even Felicity would, but it still feels like the right thing to do.

"Sure, dude. Path of non-violence. Groovy shit. I dig you." Gran nods as if I am the beardiest of yogis.

He still pulls his gun though.

That said, so do I.

23

We get halfway down the slope toward the temple and I start to feel like we've all been a little paranoid. There are no visible defenses. No zombies whose minds Clyde has overwritten. It's just dirty, crap, and depressing. And it's going to take more than melancholy to stop us now.

"I'm not buying this whole trap thing," I tell Tabitha. "This is camouflage. Pure and simple."

Tabitha rolls her eyes.

"Arthur has a point," says Felicity. "We didn't even notice the structure until we had a plane directly on top of it. No one is looking for anything here."

"Have you two never even feckin' heard of jinxes?" Kayla throws up her hands.

This is the point at which Clyde should pipe up and tell us that jinxes are actually caused by stress points in the fabric of reality, and are actually geographically driven events, rather than dialogue-driven ones. Or something like that. Except if Clyde did pipe up right now, it would probably be to tell us how exactly he's going to kill us.

Instead of any of that, the female pilot says, "We've got movement to the east."

Which may actually prove that there really are such things as jinxes.

We all turn. The mechas' machine gun barrels start

to spin, ready to spit death. But there's nothing. Just one of the many piles of trash collapsing, rumbling down the gentle incline of the slope.

"It's nothing," Gran says. He starts moving again. The others follow.

But someone... something... disturbed that trash. I keep scanning the rim of the pit.

The trash keeps tumbling down, picking up speed and mass as it falls. Like a snowball building to an avalanche. The others keep moving, but I take my eyes off the ridge to stare at it.

Something is wrong with it. Something I cannot put my finger on. But I have learned that waiting to work out exactly what is wrong is usually a fatal error in this profession. Brace for a walloping first, ask questions later.

"Weapons ready," I shout to the team.

"What is it?" Felicity stops and looks at me.

"I don't—" And then I do know. I know exactly what is wrong. The trash isn't falling down the slope. It's falling on a long diagonal, falling sideways *around* the pit. It is falling directly toward us.

"Incoming!" I bellow.

Too late.

The sheer size of the trash fall only hits me as it careens through the final hundred yards. It is a crashing wave, a surfer's wet dream sketched out in rotting vegetables, smashed toasters, and junked coffee pots.

The barrels of the smaller mecha blaze into life, spitting fire and death. Plastic bags perforate, loose cans spin away. But the mass is not slowed.

There is an explosive hiss as Gina's mecha lets loose with a missile from her shoulder. It burns through the air. Closes the distance in seconds.

And then the trash wave leaps into the air.

It is a massive, thrashing thing. A tangled mess of tentacles in the lead, a long sleek body tapering away behind.

It arcs effortlessly, almost absurdly over the missile.

The rocket smashes into the ground a hundred yards behind the trash monster. The explosion is loud enough to drop me to my knees, hands pressed to my ears. Shrapnel and shit rain down around us.

The arcing trash monster smashes down to the ground, a second detonation, sending the slope we stand on spilling and slipping all around us. I roll twenty yards downhill before I slam into the remains of a washing machine and stop with a grunt of pain.

The two mecha spin around.

"The hell did it go?" Gina's voice barks.

"Need a visual!" yells Joel, the male pilot.

"In a circle!" Felicity snaps. "Now! Facing out. Scan for movement."

I scramble into line next to her, jam my gun out at the world, look left, right. She stands behind me, breathing hard.

"Is Clyde trying to kill us with a giant trash squid?" she asks. She looks as if she genuinely wants me to say no.

I want to say it too. I really do.

"I've got no visual!" Joel shouts. His mecha has its back to Gina's. They circle slowly, the rest of us gathered at their feet, trying to match our circling to theirs.

"Feckin' jinxing bastard," Kayla throws in my direction.

"Trap," Tabitha adds. "Told you."

Because apparently it is just not enough for only a giant trash monster to beat up on me today.

I open my mouth to refute these accusations.

The ground beneath me heaves, erupts upward.

The trash squid bursts from the depths of the refuse, tentacles splayed wide. It embraces Joel's mecha, engulfs him. Its massive body thrashes up at such speed the pair are carried into the air. They hang for a moment. Then they slam down. The shockwave rocks me.

Trash tentacles start to tear. The mecha's guns blaze. I dive to the ground. Colossal shells gouge through the beast's hide. But it's like shooting the vegetable golems. No individual part of the beast is important. There's too much redundancy in the system.

"Joel!" I hear Gina scream. She points guns, missiles, fists. But the mecha and the beast are too tightly entwined. If she hits one, she hits the other.

A massive sheet of metal is torn from the mecha with a protesting scream. I hear Joel spit curses through the radio transmitter.

"Fuck it," cuts in the woman, and she just dives on them both.

Massive fists rend and rip. More tentacles erupt upward, smash down with earth shuddering force on the mecha's back. I hear screams and howls stabbing through my ear bud. I rip the thing out even as I stagger away, trying to get out of range of gunfire, and flailing fists, and squid shrapnel.

The squid hits a box of ammunition. The explosion lifts me off my feet, dumps me five feet downhill. My ears ring and the world screams.

"The temple!" I can faintly hear someone yelling. Felicity.

"Come on, dudes!" Gran runs past, skids to a halt, shoves out a hand, drags me to my feet. "Move!"

I move.

A tentacle torn free from the beast's body flies into the air, rains down in its constituent parts. Milk cartons and hubcaps bounce off my back. Kayla swats a car bumper from the air. Tabitha takes a coke bottle to the forehead and blood starts streaming down her face. Gran stops pulling me and grabs her.

"The temple!" Felicity is still yelling.

We tear downhill, away from the epic brawl behind us. That fight is out of our weight class. The temple looms. An ugly black rectangle of an entrance. I was scared of the dark when I was a kid, but then I grew up and learned there weren't monsters under my bed. Then I joined MI37, and realized there were.

Still, there's nowhere else to go. And we came here with a mission.

And then the ground ripples. And I realize Version 2.0 is not the sort of man who has just one giant trash squid to defend himself. And I have a lot more to be afraid of than the dark.

24

The second squid lunges up from the surface of the landfill. Its tentacles flail. I drop to my knees, skid. Unspeakable filth scrapes my skull. The squid is above me, skims over my scalp. A beak of rusty iron shears snaps at me. I feel the wind of them closing.

Then it is gone, plunging back into the refuse.

It is smaller than the one currently tearing the mecha apart. Perhaps a third of the size. About twelve feet from tentacle to tail. Still plenty big enough to remove my entrails from their warm, fleshy housing.

I spin, watch the surface of the landfill boil as the squid squirms away.

It is not the only disturbance in the surface. One, two, three more.

"Oh shit." I am never at my most eloquent in these situations.

"We've got to move!" I yell.

"Your feckin' sword!" Kayla yells.

She's right. Guns are no good here. I slam the pistol back into its holster, rip the sword from its scabbard on my back. Flame gushes into the already boiling sky.

"You take Felicity and Tabitha," I snap to her. "I'll guard Gran." As much as I'd like to be the one protecting Felicity, there's no denying Kayla is the better swordsman. Felicity will be safer with her.

We push forward as fast as we can, feet slipping and sinking in the loose trash. The temple is tantalizingly close. The ground boils as first one trash squid crosses our path, then another. Tabitha yells as something skirts around the back of her feet.

This is a hunting pattern. They're forcing us into a tightly packed group.

Behind us machine guns roar and metal screams.

Three roiling shapes hem us in. They spin round us faster and faster, drawing tighter.

"Where's the feckin' fourth one?"

I realize where the moment Kayla's question ends. It's still too late.

I dive sideways, knock Gran to the floor. I swing wildly with the sword.

The fourth squid erupts from the ground beneath our feet. I see its tentacles bearing Kayla, Felicity, and Tabitha skywards. I hear the gnashing of its steel trap beak.

"No!" I bellow.

I gain my feet as the three other squid rise up out of the surface of the landfill. Tentacles massive and waving. Towering, sunlight glinting off the edges of jagged cans and split steel. And there, above us all, that one leaping, arcing squid. And Kayla stands atop it. Dancing on its lashing tentacles, swords slashing wildly.

One tentacle falls. Another. Another. And a yell, and a scream. Tabitha plunging back toward earth.

The squid around me lunge. I whirl my sword in a tight arc, smashing through one tentacle, jarring off another, bouncing, spitting sparks, slamming into the squid's body. I rip the blade sideways, almost losing it as the beast thrashes. An ungodly scream comes from it, like feedback on a guitar. Its thick tail smashes into me, a bulldozer to the shins, lifting me off the ground. I bellow and howl. And oh, and ow, and fuck that hurts.

I come down with a crash. Limbs jarred. My sword spills. Kayla is standing over a trash corpse, lacerating metal. Gran is crouched over Tabitha firing desperately to no avail.

Felicity? Where the hell is Felicity?

Then I see her, lying to Kayla's side. Unconscious? God, she better only be unconscious.

I find my feet, my sword, my will to fight. I go in low and hard, charging, bellowing. Gran has a gun. Felicity has no one. A squid comes at her. I go at it hard and fast. Screw the fact that the beast is twice the size of me, this thing is not messing up my love life. I can do that perfectly well on my own.

My blade snicker-snacks through whirling limbs. Then a blow to my forehead sends the world spinning and I go to my knees. But at this point in life I can say I've lived through worse. I'm up, still yelling. I hack and slash. I get Robert E. Howard on its ass. If Felicity, lying at my feet, was wearing a chain mail bikini instead of a pants suit, then this would be some teenager's midnight fantasy.

As it is, I just get bitch slapped in the face with a milk carton.

I come up in a rising blow. My blade catches the thing where its guts should be, and I just rip, tear into it, feeling the resistance on the blade and yelling at the joy of it. I wrench the sword free. Bottle caps, and oil, and foul putrescent water splash out in a gush. The thing wavers for a second, a great toppling tree suddenly sprung up in this desolate wasteland, and then it crashes to the floor. Timber, motherfucker.

I spin around. Kayla is standing over Gran and Tabitha. Another squid corpse is down.

"I thought you said I didn't have to feckin' worry about Gran."

And maybe she has a point, but she's lacking a sense of timing.

"Later," I say. "We have to get to that goddamned temple."

The mecha are still thrashing away at big daddy squid, but the fight's almost been beaten out of them. Limbs hang at angles. Servos spit sparks. I wish we could help, but I don't think we can. I bend down, pick up Felicity. "Let's move."

"Yeah," says Kayla, "but I still don't know where that feckin' fourth one is."

Oh shi—

It comes out of the ground and smashes into Kayla's side. Like a train car emerging from nowhere. She flies through the air. A broken bird.

The squid skids over the surface of the landfill. Gran opens fire. His bullets rip uselessly through the loose body. It whirls, tentacles held out in a flat arc, whipping through the air at obscene speed. I glimpse rusting chains, bicycle cogs, glass shards.

In the split second before it hits me, I think how I never really took the time to truly appreciate the way my head is attached to my body. The neck is truly one of the body's great unsung heroes.

Then the limb explodes. Trash and shit form a stinging rain that breaks over me, but which, very noticeably, does not kill me.

I blink in surprise as the roaring in my ears registers. And then I see Gina's mecha sitting up, its one functional arm raised and pointing in my direction, smoke drifting from the still rotating barrels.

Static buzzes from the bead in my ear.

"Yippee, Kay—"

And then the monster squid's tentacle erupts through the mecha's chest in a spray of steel and wires.

Gina's voice goes dead.

25

"Run!" Gran bellows. "Dude! Run!"

But I stand for a moment. Stare. At the monster rising out of the ground. Joel's mecha bounces, broken, along its long body. Its whirling tentacles spear Gina's machine, lift it high into the air, and then, dismissively, flip it away. Gina's mecha lands like a meteor, metal booming and breaking.

The squid circles, looking for fresh meat.

"Run!"

Finally life comes back to my legs. I spin, Felicity's unconscious weight on my shoulder giving me momentum. Gran and Tabitha are dragged by Kayla as she accelerates at ridiculous speed toward the temple.

I have to run.

So I do. Felicity's body bounces awkwardly, slowing me.

Behind me—a roar like a speaker blowing out. A roar that I feel in my gut. And the monster squid has found its prey.

"Run!"

The temple is so close. I can see the distance between myself and its shadow shrinking. Shrinking.

"Run!"

Yes. Yes. I got that goddamned memo. But it is hot, and the ground is loose, and Felicity, though I would never tell her, is kind of heavy—

"Run!"

Hell to that. I dive, a short stunted arc through the air, skidding over the ground, ripping my suit and my skin on the jagged ground.

I feel something massive move behind me. The whisper of the air the thing displaces.

A tidal wave of trash hits my legs, barrels me forward, rolling me over Felicity, her over me, driving us forward. Into darkness.

There is a crash as the leaping squid lands on the far side of the temple.

Felicity and I lie just inside its doorway. I pant, gasp, and bleed.

Someone comes and stands over me. "Come on. Get up then. We haven't got all feckin' day." Kayla.

"You know," I say, once I have finished getting up, and groaning, and making sure nothing is going to try and kill me in the next two seconds, "I think I preferred it when you were more belligerent and less lippy."

"Never underestimate my ability to remove your balls any time I feckin' choose to do so."

I decide to abandon conversation and get my bearings.

The temple, such as it is, is really just a small dark room that smells like shit. On the plus side, the squid seems reluctant to come in.

Felicity is still unconscious at my feet. I kneel and press a hand to her forehead. It is damp with sweat, but I can see the gentle rise and fall of her chest. "Do we have any water?" I ask.

No one answers me. I glance over my shoulder. "Is everyone OK?"

Tabitha and Gran are crouched against one wall.

Tabitha leans forward, looking around Kayla. "All right," she says. "No thanks to you."

This, I feel, is kind of unjustified. "I seem to remember hacking apart several more squid than you did."

"Funny," she says. "None of the ones threatening me." She snorts. I can't tell if it's of anger or derision. "Felicity did OK."

This again?

"Kayla had you," I protest.

"Priorities," is all Tabitha says in return.

"Look," I say, standing up. "We are standing in what is supposedly the home base of a man who just sent magic trash squid to kill us, is this *really* the time to do this?"

"Dude has a point," Gran says.

Tabitha growls, but seems prepared to let the subject drop. Which lets me get back to the important concern of my unconscious girlfriend.

"Dude," says Gran, as I kneel, "is it really time for that?"

I look over at him. "She's our director. And there's nothing here. We're trapped in a trash temple, and I think her consciousness could really help us."

"There's stairs," Kayla says.

"What?" I peer into the gloom. It's a one-story structure. I have no idea what anyone is talking about.

"Shaw. Only eyes for her. Self-imposed blindness." Tabitha, it seems, is not completely over that.

"In the floor, dude," Gran says. "Next to me and the dudette. This place goes subterranean, man."

So we need to entomb ourselves in crap to find Clyde? Fantastic. Still, I'm not sure that devalues my original point. "We could still use Felicity's help."

"We should get this job done, man."

He's being insistent. And he had my back with Tabitha despite their… well, who knows what that relationship is exactly. But I would guess they are further along the sliding scale of intimacy than Bert and Ernie. So maybe he's coming from a fairly rational point of view.

"Someone will have to carry her," I say finally.

"Not a problem." Kayla bends and hefts Felicity without apparent effort. She looks a little bruised and battered in the dim light, but otherwise she seems no worse for wear.

"All right then, let's do this."

We descend. The smell, and the heat, and the darkness intensify. Felicity lets out a dull moan, but when I check her, she's still out. I whisper her name. Kayla shushes me.

Gran produces a flashlight with a red bulb. He sweeps it down the stairs, lighting a corridor.

"Dudes, you smell that?" he asks.

"Way too much," I whisper back.

"No, man." He shakes his head. "Not that. Something sweet."

I have been doing my best to avoid inhaling. After a moment to steel myself, I take a sniff. The pungent smell of decay is still nearly overwhelming, but he's right, there is an edge of sweetness to it. Something almost floral.

Curiouser and curiouser.

We hit the corridor. It has distinct mine shaft qualities. If the tunnels in mine shafts were dug through geological strata of human shit, anyway. Here is a rich seam of old batteries. Here we can extract all the decomposing orange juice cartons we'll ever need.

After a short distance the floor grows spongy. Just as my gag reflex is about to kick in, Gran flicks his light down and I see... "Is that moss?"

Gran reaches down, touches it. He is a braver man than I. He pulls up a tuft and holds it to his nose. "Yeah, dude. Smells fresh."

How did Alice get out of Wonderland again?

The tunnel twists and turns. I lose my sense of where we are. Tabitha flicks open her laptop and eyes it like it's a Geiger counter. "Wireless signal. Still none," she says. She's clutching her foil bonnet in the same hand that holds the laptop.

Another twist in the corridor, and suddenly we can see faint light coloring the walls. The edges of old crisp packets glisten in reflected light. The moss feels thicker.

"What the hell?" I say.

We approach the turn cautiously. But there's no denying it. Light is shining. It has a blue, slightly harsh edge. Like sunlight on an autumn day. It would be out of place on top of the landfill, let alone this many feet beneath its surface.

"Lock and totally load, man," says Gran, pulling his pistol.

I seem to remember him promising me we would try and talk to Version 2.0 first. Still, wariness is probably the better part of valor. I pull my gun too.

We go round the corner as a pair, guns extended. But there is no boom or crash. There are no golems leaping out of walls. No mindless men.

There is a garden.

The ceiling is lined with lightbulbs. The same natural light ones Felicity has in her windowless office to keep her orchids healthy. But so many more. It turns the filthy roof into an artificial sky. Beneath it, roses bloom, bushes thrive. Azalea, hydrangea, lily, species that exceed my grip on plant names. The place is lush and suddenly the warmth seems almost comforting. I reach out and run my hands through spiky leaves of a yew bush. They feel soft and delicate against my palm.

"What is this?" I ask.

"Trap," Tabitha says, but she sounds hesitant this time.

"I don't know, dudette." Gran looks around, a puzzled look on his face.

I look up at the fake sky once more. Bulbs. Which means a power source. And if this is Version 2.0's true home, he is not a man who wanders among the rose bushes. He is a machine. A program. He needs computing power. I shield my eyes from the glare, and try to look beyond, to the truth beneath.

"Electric wires," I say, pointing. "Leading that way." My finger follows the path of the wires toward the back of the garden cave. "They'll lead us to him."

Guns still drawn, we press on. Our path takes us down a second corridor floored with moss. It has ivy walls too. The same flat bright light as the garden has above us. I can see how filthy we look, how out of place we are surrounded by this beauty.

Two more garden caves, each beautiful, but we're heading downhill the whole way, so I'm not yet convinced this is a wild goose chase. And finally, a door, wooden, covered in chipped turquoise paint—the sort that you find in either a high-end catalog or in a rotting shed at the back of an overgrown yard.

"If that's another one of those feckin' DARPA locks…" Kayla starts.

But I turn the handle and the door opens easily.

The room beyond is oddly devoid of leaves, petals, and roots. It almost comes as a surprise now. And a disappointment. Not that the room is a return to the refuse world we descended through. But now organic lushness is replaced with old world opulence. Heavy furniture thick with scroll work is scattered about the room. Thick rugs lie on the floor. Tapestries hang on the walls.

Against the far wall, raised up a little, like a throne upon a dais, is a daybed. Velvet pillows and cushions are piled upon it. And there, perched in this fabric nest, reclines a young girl.

The girl stares at us, serious and unsmiling. She is Mexican, I think. Around eight or nine—round cheeked, and her black hair cut in a bob, held back by a black velvet headband. She wears something that resembles a school uniform.

She looks up as we come in.

"Oh good," she says. "You made it. I was a bit worried."

26

I push sweat-slick hair from my eyes, and consider whether I am really the sort of man who can point a gun at a child. I am not. But I don't put the thing back in its holster.

The girl blinks. "OK, I can see, given what you had to go through to get here, that might seem a little disingenuous, but I really am glad. Cross my heart. I really promise that I did want to see you all again before the end."

"You're, like, under arrest," Gran informs the girl.

Except it's not a girl, is it? Oh, Clyde. Oh, Jesus. A girl? A child? My fists are shaking. What was she doing? What made that seem OK?

"Not to be overly antagonistic," says the child with Clyde's clear plummy English tones, "—and I do realize that's a little hard to totally ignore but if we could—de-emphasize it—what I was going to say is that you can't arrest me."

Gran makes a scoffing noise.

"Well," Version 2.0 says, "there's the whole issue with jurisdiction and you not having it. And anyway, I am not here to fight you, no matter how this seems. I'm here as an ambassador."

"Technically and stuff," Gran says, "you have to be, like, recognized as a state by the UN to have an ambassador."

The girl that is Clyde cocks her head. "I don't want to be a wording maven. Though I'm sure they have their place in society. No judgment on their chosen craft, just not something that coincides with my current interests. But, what I was trying to say is—do you really think you are going to be able to negotiate better terms with me based on a lexical technicality?"

I keep staring at the little girl speaking another man's words. Like a human loudspeaker. It makes my gorge rise. "What the hell, Clyde?" I say. "What the hell?"

"Well…" the girl says, "technically speaking I'm not the Clyde you are referring to." She is very self-assured. Very calm. "I realize it's a little confusing, and I wish I had the time to explain everything fully, I really do, but for now let's suffice it to say that I am just an affiliate of the one you called 2.0. An incomplete copy of the whole."

An affiliate? Jesus. Version 2.0 is franchising his brain now?

And somehow none of this seems to have distracted Agent Gran from his lexical arguments. "Little dude," he says, "if you think this is a negotiation, you should be, like, aware that the US government totally doesn't negotiate with terrorists."

The girl sighs. It's an overly dramatic gesture. A little girl's gesture. Jesus.

"Again, I am going to have to get all definitional with you. And I'm not trying to insult anyone's intelligence, or anything at all like that. Please don't think I am. I just want us to be clear about terms. There could totally be confusion on my part too. I'm more than happy to admit that. But when you call me a terrorist, Agent Gran," says the girl, "that, to me at least, suggests you think there's a power differential in your favor. And

I really want to assure you that's not the case in any way. And this is very presumptuous of me, I know, and I'm sorry about that, but I think you've got this all backwards. It's typical of me really. Not explaining things right. I should begin at the beginning. Set out precedents and all that."

God, it's so like listening to him it hurts. If I closed my eyes I could almost believe that this was the old days, Clyde doing some eerily accurate impression of a little girl.

"So," says the little girl that is Clyde, "with apologies for being such a stickler about this, but just to make sure we are all clear on this: I am not negotiating my surrender with you. You are negotiating it with me. Does that make sense?"

"Can I kill it yet?" Kayla asks. She's lain Felicity down and has her sword gripped in two hands.

Maybe I should say yes. Everything about this feels wrong. The world spinning on the wrong axis.

"What's going on, Clyde?" I ask. "Why are you doing this?" It feels wrong to call the little girl Clyde. But what else do I call her?

The little girl turns to me. And there is a look of such fondness on her face. It's an awful thing to see.

"Oh," she says. "The whole questions and motives thing. I skipped that, didn't I? And that's the whole point of this in a way too. So you can understand. It probably shouldn't be important to me, but it is. You and me... Well... We were good friends, right, Arthur?"

"I..." My throat is thick. I can't get words out. "I..." I try again. "My friend," I manage. "This." I gesticulate at him. At her. At the body. "He wouldn't do this."

I sound like Tabitha. Maybe, despite appearances, she is actually frozen in the grip of overwhelming emotions twenty-four-seven.

I glance over at her. And she is frozen now. Her mouth works slowly. Something is building in her, I think. And when it blows, it will not be good.

"This girl?" Version 2.0, or the franchise of it, or whatever, is addressing me. "Do you know what this girl's future held, Arthur? I mean, she was barely held together when I found her." There is the sound of outrage in his voice. More emotion and anger than I've ever seen in Clyde before. "She grew up here. In this filth. Her whole life drowning in the toxins of humanity. She was more disease than human. She was dying too. Slowly and painfully. Day by day. She has cancer, Arthur. She's riddled with it. She'll last another week or two. And it would have been awful. Awful. And now she doesn't feel anything. She doesn't know. She's not here anymore. I gave her peace, Arthur. It was the only thing anyone decent could give her. And there are no decent people here, Arthur. None at all. And I know you had to go through hell to get here, and I'm sorry for that, but all I can say is that you don't guard your home with squid golems when you're surrounded by wonderful people."

He's visibly upset. "But that's my point," he says. "Do you see, Arthur?" 2.0 shakes his head. "Probably not. Not yet. I'm probably making a hash of it all. Wandering up the conversational garden path. And garden paths have their merit, they can be quite beautiful, but I brought you here so you would see. In the hope I can be clear for once in what I shall refer to as my life. I came to you as this child so I could."

He taps his chest. Her chest. "I saved this girl. And it was an awful monstrous way to do it, but in the end it was the only way. The problem is awful and monstrous. It demands that kind of solution. Humanity, you see, Arthur, is that kind of problem." He sweeps an arm up and around. The girl is wearing dark nail polish. A crimson that is almost black.

"This is humanity's legacy, Arthur. This place. This girl. Not to be dramatic, but all that will be left in its wake are death, and disease, and pestilence. And do people throw their hands up and wail at their inadequacies? At the horror they have wrought on the world?" The girl's face is contorted, is nothing but rage.

"No," she spits. "It is an inconvenience. A fucking inconvenience, Arthur. This! History! The future! It's an aggravating afterthought. People poison this planet. They tear it apart. They take, and they take, and they take. And this is what they leave behind. These temples of shit. Like ugly signatures. They kill themselves, poison their children. And they do it because it's convenient. Because it's easy. Because they are fucking monsters, Arthur. People are awful and monstrous."

Her breath is coming hard now. She's sitting up on her knees on the day bed, spitting invective.

And I realize that he has never once said, "we."

"So what do you think the solution is, Clyde?" I say. "Are you the solution?"

I know this point in the movie. This is when the hero talks quietly and pulls out his big stick. This is when he takes his friend to the river bank, sits him down, nice and calm, and puts a bullet through his brain.

I can see Kayla edging wide, finding the most direct route of attack, the predator starting to circle.

"The solution, Arthur?" The little girl looks at me with sad eyes. "The solution is just maths."

Not exactly what I was expecting. So far Clyde has been throwing some pretty big guns at us. This had better be some pretty terrifying calculus.

"I know I've never been the bastion of steadfast opinions that so many others are," the little girl says. "I could always see around a problem, I suppose. See the other side. Not trying to brag. I think it was a bit of a flaw really. But I am certain about this, Arthur. Maybe I was waiting for this. Waiting for the thing to be certain about.

"Humanity's burden upon this earth is now so great," Clyde says, "that it simply cannot be undone. You are taxing it to its breaking point, and even if governments were willing to force it—and whether your brain is a supercomputer or not, I think we can all agree that they're not—absolutely no amount of deceleration will stop the damage fast enough. It has to just stop. The pollution. The overpopulation. The deforestation. All of it. It just has to stop. I've looked at everything. Everything, Arthur. I just want to do the right thing."

And there would be a reason. I knew there would be a reason. I had just really hoped I'd like it.

"What is the right thing, Clyde?" My voice isn't quite even, though whether it's anger, or sadness, or just confusion, I don't know anymore.

"The hero saves the world, right, Arthur?" he says.

"That's right," I nod. And how much has he been spying on me? Those words sound too close to my own.

"The problem is, Arthur, we've been lying to ourselves. MI37, I mean. All of you. Me. We don't save the world. We never did. We saved humanity. We always saw saving the world from humanity's selfish, selfish point of view.

"I'm beyond that now, Arthur."

Clyde's voice coming from the mouth of a little girl. A girl whose mind he ripped away. And no matter what her situation, you can never convince me that was a kindness. Yes, I think we can agree Clyde 2.0 is beyond humanity now.

"To save the world," Clyde tells me, "I have to sacrifice humanity."

27

Oh shit. Oh shit and quite spectacular balls. Clyde has not so much gone off the deep end as he has buried himself somewhere in the bedrock beneath the base of the Marianas Trench. And how the hell do I talk him around from there?

"It's not like the species is going to last much longer anyway," Clyde says, as if realizing he's punched too hard, and is now regretfully holding out a jar of salve. "Honestly, my most generous estimate gives humanity about a hundred years. And I really do want to give you all the benefit of the doubt. But by the time humanity is scientifically and politically ready to do something about the problem, it'll be too late." The girl shrugs apologetically. "It's already too late right now. And I realize this sounds harsh, but well, that's the nature of the beast at this point—it's just a question of how much collateral damage occurs."

And, God, it's all delivered so calmly, so simply. I so often wanted Clyde to just speak to the point, to just spit out what he had to say, but I never imagined it would be so many terrible things.

"So that's it?" I ask. "There's no hope for us?" There has to be a way to change his mind. There has to be. There has to be hope here.

"No," Clyde says, irrevocably. "Just hope for every

other living thing on this planet. It's maths, Arthur. Sacrifice seven billion, to save so, so many more."

I open my mouth, but…

What if he's right?

Of all the things going on here, that's what really damages my calm. Because he <u>does</u> have a supercomputer for a brain. He *will* have done the maths. He *will* have given us the benefit of the doubt. And everything is probability, I know, but… God, what if he's right? What if humanity's death is the only way to save the world?

Aren't I meant to save the world?

What does the hero do? What does he sacrifice?

No. There has to be hope. There has to be. I won't just accept this. I can't.

"Can I feckin' kill it yet?" Kayla asks again.

"No!" I say at exactly the same time as Tabitha says, "Yes."

"Tabby," says the little girl.

"The fuck up," she spits. "Shut it."

The Clyde version shakes her head. "I wish the world had more time, love. I wish that I could make you understand."

Tabitha's hand reflexively goes to her head.

"Not like that. Never like that. Not you." There is such heartache in the little girl's voice. "I know this has got very morally complex. Labyrinth metaphors and bumping into wall metaphors abound, I'm sure. But, I just…" The girl hesitates, shrugs twice. "You will always be my biggest regret, love. I know you can't forgive me, but I hope you can understand me."

"Bringing a gun," Tabitha says. "Next time."

"That won't stop me." The little girl even looks apologetic.

"I will hack you to hell. Then back again." Blood makes Tabitha's dark cheeks bright.

But the girl's big eyes meet Tabitha's. And the sadness in them seems capable of drowning all the hate Tabitha pours at them.

"I love you, Tabby," she says. "But I will kill you." A sad, simple truth.

Sacrifice. Personal sacrifice. God, Clyde is utterly convinced he's in the right on this one.

And then I realize Clyde's planning to kill Tabitha far more imminently than I realized. The girl puts her hand to her mouth. "*Ashat mal corlat—*"

"No!" I yell.

From the corner of my eye I recognize Kayla hitting hyperdrive. "No!" I yell again, at her now. We need this girl. We need Clyde. There is too much information here. There is too much of a chance to understand him, to have him understand us. Talk him back to humanity.

Humanity. He's declared war on all of humanity.

God, he even has a convincing argument.

I need time. But Kayla moves fast enough to break the sound barrier, and I don't know if my words can even reach her now.

"Wait!" I yell. But it's all over except for my screaming.

Kayla stands behind the girl. A fistful of hair is in her hand, holding the girl a full foot off the floor. The sword, in her other hand, is at her throat.

"Another feckin' word," she says. "Please. I'm feckin' asking you to do me the favor of giving me an excuse."

The little girl doesn't say anything. Doesn't even squirm.

From the look on Tabitha's face, I think she's going to be sick.

"Look, dudes," Gran says. "This is getting, like, pretty heated. Why don't we all just choke down the chill pill, dial it back a notch—"

Kayla flicks her gaze at Gran. "You keep feckin' talking and you're next."

No matter how much nice she makes to me, Kayla will always just be a little too much in touch with her rage for me to be one hundred percent comfortable with her.

OK. I try to take a breath, to take stock. Whatever Gran's phrasing, he's right. It's time to get out of here. There's just a few last things.

"Search the place for a hard drive," I say. "Any sort of digital storage."

"While I kill it?" Kayla nods at the girl she still holds aloft by the hair.

"No." I say.

Both Kayla and Tabitha turn on me.

"We take her... him... her. We take her back. We question her. We talk more. We learn what's going on. And then we debug her. And fix her. Save her." I'm gabbling now. Trying to hold it together in the face of all these revelations. And Clyde always did know how to pull the rug out from under my expectations. "Just clear this place out and then we leave."

I don't want to talk to Clyde anymore after that. I don't want to look at the girl he's possessing.

Instead I look at Felicity while Tabitha and Kayla search the rest of the rooms. Gran keeps his gun trained on Clyde. Felicity has a large bruise on the side of her head. I push her hair back around it. She moans, blinks her eyes.

"Hey," I say. I can't keep the relief out of my voice.

She blinks harder, faster. I put a hand on her chest, over her heart. "It's OK," I say. "We're safe. We found him."

Felicity takes a breath, calms herself. "Everyone OK?" she asks. And while her voice is a little shaky it'll need more than a bout of violent unconsciousness to keep Felicity Shaw from getting down to business.

"Physically," I say.

Felicity closes her eyes. "OK."

Except it's not. I take the time to explain why to her.

I'm just wrapping the story up when Kayla re-enters the room. "Nothing," she says.

"Just batteries." Tabitha stalks at her heels.

Felicity stands up with the curse. She is surprisingly steady as she advances on the girl. "Why did you have us come here? Why the trail of breadcrumbs?"

There is a sinking feeling in my gut. We should get back to New York.

But this Clyde isn't wearing Mercurio's Cheshire cat grin. Just sadness. "I just wanted you to understand is all," the girl says. "I felt I owed you that."

"Fucking machine." Tabitha can't bite back the bile. "You are. Owe nothing. Just delete yourself and be done."

The girl's smile is rueful.

"Where are you, Clyde?" I ask. "Where are you hiding?"

"I can't tell you that."

Or won't. But even if I was as amoral as Clyde seems to have become, I don't think I could torture it out of him. And he knows me well enough to know that.

A waste. It's all a waste.

"Let's get out of here," I say.

* * *

A HUNDRED FEET UP

We stand at the temple entrance. The five of us and the girl. Outside the massive trash squid is still smashing the remains of the mecha.

"Goddamn." Gran stands framed in the doorway. "I knew those guys. Joel had a wife and kid. Goddamn."

He doesn't sound like a hippy in that moment. Just a very angry man.

I look again at the girl. At the merciless killer in her head. At my friend.

Gran advances on the girl. "You said you wanted these dudes here so you could explain. And you've explained. But that squid is still there. So now you call it off?"

The girl looks a little shame-faced. "Well…" she concedes. "Having done the whole explaining thing, I was sort of moving forward with the killing humanity part. Which, I mean, not to beat around the bush, you're part of."

"So it kills us?" I'm horror-struck. Again. Truly and fully. I keep saying cold-blooded in my head, but there's a difference between hearing it and being faced with it. Maybe it would be better if hate was motivating Clyde. Megalomania. If it truly were madness. This cheerful, apologetic logic makes everything so much worse.

The girl shrugs. "Like I said, Arthur. It's just a question of how much collateral damage there is."

Shit. Just shit.

"OK," I say, turning to Tabitha. "Weak points. Flaws. Anything. There's got to be a way around this thing."

Tabitha looks at me, her face pale but her voice steady as a steel bar. "Animating force. Quickest way to remove it: kill the summoner."

She looks right at Clyde. Right at the little girl.

But we need her. We need to talk to her. *I* need to talk to her. There is another solution to this. We can find it. We can.

And I'm about to say that, but Gran's gun is already drawn.

I'm about to say that, but Gran has already shot the little girl.

28

Her head snaps sideways as a great flap of blood and bone hinges open. A mess of skull, and brain, and fluid bursts out, sprays the wall. Her body folds, small, and tired, and useless. An empty shell of a thing. Even Clyde is done with it now. Even us.

She's dead before she hits the floor.

Outside I can hear the squid collapsing. Raining down in its constituent parts. Just as dead. Just as useless. But I don't look at that. I just look at the dead girl.

Weren't we meant to save her? Isn't that what the hero does?

"Good feckin' riddance." Kayla spits at the little girl's corpse.

Jesus. Just... Jesus.

Am I the one wrong here? Am I seeing this all skewed. Is this just another villain lying defeated at our feet. Is this victory?

Shouldn't I know that?

I look at Gran, tucking his pistol back into his holster.

"You said we'd talk," I say. "You said we'd rescue him."

"We talked." Gran doesn't look at me, but there's no hint at remorse. "Now I need to go and talk to Joel's wife."

And that's it. No more to be said. Just a trash pile to

trudge across, and an extraction point to reach.

The flight back to New York is long and quiet.

AREA 51 SLEEPING QUARTERS

"You're not looking overly happy, Arthur, old chap."

I stare at my computer screen. There's a chance this isn't going to help. Felicity would probably tell me it wouldn't. But she's off doing a debrief with CIA top brass. And I want to understand.

"Evil-You had a chat with us today," I say. And I tell my version, 2.2, about what Clyde 2.0 did and said in the Bordo Poniente Landfill.

2.2 is quiet for a while at the end. Then he says, "That's rather cold logic, isn't it?"

I nod. That it is. "But it is logic."

Version 2.2 thinks about that. "So he's right then," he says. His voice sounds tinny through the speakers. "We join his side, and execute humanity?"

For a moment I'm worried he's serious. But just a moment.

"What does that make us, though?" I ask him. "If he's right and we're fighting him."

"I've done a lot of reading recently," says Clyde. "Think I mentioned that. Since this whole non-corporeal thing. And I've done a lot of reading about global warming, and climate change, and environmental stuff. It was always an interest of mine. I always was of the opinion that recycling was a good thing to be doing. I mean, we do it with ideas and fashion trends, so why not with refuse too? Stands to reason, I thought, though admittedly my thoughts are not always the ones that one should put a yardstick next to, but I don't think I was entirely alone on the general positive nature of recycling."

I sit and wait for him to get to the point.

"But something that did rather come to my notice was that there are a lot of differing opinions on this whole environmental end-times scenario thingamajig."

I mull on that. "So Version 2.0 is wrong?" I ask. "There is no global warming?"

Clyde shakes his head. "Of course there's global warming, Arthur. You don't melt half the ice caps in a few decades and claim it's just business as usual. Well, not unless it would cost you a lot of money to change from business as usual. But even disregarding the more inane political aspects, it's not like there's a universal voice shouting, 'no more questions, chaps, we've got it all figured out.' Assuming all scientists spoke like me. Which they don't, thank God. Still be waiting for someone to get around to the Enlightenment if they did."

In some ways it's comforting to let Clyde's patter wash over me, even if it's filtered through this filter of Xerox weirdness. At least it's not a murderous ramble. That said, I would rather like to get to the point before Version 2.0 brings the apocalypse upon us.

"So 2.0 is wrong, and I can rest easy sending him to hell?" I check.

"I don't know," says 2.2, in a less reassuring way than I'd hoped. "Evil-Me might be spot on the money. And he is a terribly smart seeming chap. And I think he may have exceeded my hardware limitations. Parallel processing up the doodad, I rather think. But that regardless, it takes some hefty cahones to just dictate that you've found the spot-on perfect science and know all there is to know, full stop. Rather antithetical to the old investigative spirit, that is."

"So we might still be the good guys?" It's sad that it all keeps coming back to that. But it is nice to think you're fighting on the side of the angels even in a world where the angels have all had their wings clipped.

"There's a chance," 2.2 concedes.

"Fifty-fifty?" I venture.

Clyde pulls a face, his glasses wobbling on his beaky nose. "Well…" he hedges, "Version 2.0 is a supercomputer genius type."

"Twenty-five percent chance we're the good guys?" I have a sinking feeling in my chest.

"Yeah," says 2.2, employing his rather disastrous version of a poker-face, "twenty-five sounds very reasonable."

"Fifteen?" I am so crestfallen, I think I shall have to pick my crest up off the floor and dust it off.

"I'd feel very comfortable saying there's a ten percent chance we're not going to doom the world by fighting Evil-Me," Clyde tells me with a far wider smile than should ever be used when delivering those sorts of odds.

I close the laptop and fail to feel better about anything.

AREA 51 GYMNASIUM

Apparently my little workouts with Kayla have started to attract an audience. A small gaggle of men and women in labcoats stand at one corner of the room staring as we face off against each other. I half expect to see someone waving betting slips. If that does start up, I could probably turn having my arse kicked into a rather profitable sideline.

Normally I'd be disinclined to perform in front of an audience, but after seeing a girl shot in front of me and my chat with 2.2, I need to blow some steam off.

"Talk," Kayla says, then comes at me like a lightning bolt.

I just about get my blade up, but the blow pushes me six skidding feet back over the gray plastic floor and leaves my arms numb to the elbows.

There is a brief smattering of applause from the crowd.

Kayla charges me again. I dodge to the side this time. Kayla skids to a halt beside me. There is more polite applause. Which is nice. Then Kayla sweeps my legs out. The applause turns to giggles. Which is less nice.

"Need to keep moving," she says as I pick my sorry self up off the floor.

"Thanks," I say, without really meaning it. "That's—" I cut myself off with a savage lunge at her midriff.

She bats my sword away and I stagger past her. She puts the boot into my arse as I go, just to let me know what she thinks of that.

I come at her hard and fast then. Screw words. I concentrate on breathing, on footwork, on my grip. Keep the blade under control. Quick, sharp brutality. Feeling the burn in my arms and my chest. Trying to sink into the information in my head, to drown in it.

Kayla parries every blow. But I drive her back. Slowly but surely.

Finally she smashes my blade away. My arms ring to their shoulders. "What the feck are you fighting, Arthur?"

I stare at her, panting. "What?"

"Are we here to feck around? Or to learn shit so you can save people from evil bastards?"

I stare at her, confused at the sudden anger. "What are you talking about?"

"If you're here, you're here to fight me. But you're not fighting me. So get it out. Talk about it or whatever it is the feck you do, and let's get back to business."

I am acutely aware of the audience behind me.

Kayla stands in the ready stance. "Come on, you feck," she says.

I shake my head. Take a pose… Then hesitate before coming full ready.

"He shot a girl," I say.

Kayla comes at me, whether I'm ready or not. "Course he did," she says, beating me back over the ground she'd given. "She was a feckin' shell of a thing, possessed by an evil feck. What else would you do?"

"Save her." I manage to get some firm footing behind me and hold off the advance. "Debug her brain."

"Say that's even feckin' possible," Kayla says, as she weaves around me, searching for a way through my guard, "then you have a wee girl dependent on the CIA for health and home. How the feck does that story have a happy ending?"

She comes in low and hard. I leap the blade, but lack the grace to land in an Errol Flynn-esque backflip. Instead I come down and catch the flat of Kayla's blade with my arse. It sends me reeling, but I'm still together enough to hear the crowd's, "Ooooh."

"Killing little girls, possessed or no," I say, "hardly strikes me as your average good guy behavior."

"Who the feck said anything about being good guys?" Kayla comes at me even as I finally find my feet beneath me. Her blows are short, sharp, and savage. "Good guys are comic books and popcorn movies. They're feckin' fake. We don't do the right thing, Arthur. We do the necessary thing. How the feck have you not figured that out yet?"

I parry, parry, riposte, spot the opening, and step in under her guard.

Her fist catches me hard in the balls.

I go down as neatly as if she'd fileted me. Bones become rubber. Muscles giving up in one ugly squeak of mashed masculinity.

She looks at me lying on the ground. "We do what's necessary to win, Arthur. That's it." She shrugs. "Now get up."

It takes a while. And it is done gingerly.

Kayla gets in the ready pose. I get in the please-don't-hit-me-in-the-balls-again pose. To call it defensive is possibly not as accurate as calling it close-to-fetal.

"Gran was right to shoot her," Kayla says to me. "Right feckin' thing."

"But…" I manage. I take a breath. "But he said we'd talk."

"How the feck would talk help?" And she comes at me.

There is no mercy here. I can't track the blade. It's all I can do to guess where the next blow will be and jam my sword at the interceding space. My arms sing with pain as Kayla batters me about the room.

"Dead little girl. With your dead friend feckin' her in the head. And it's not even your dead friend. Just a feckin' copy of a copy. Not even the real deal. As real as he gets now. So there's not even any point to the talk."

"We could've saved her," I pant. "We can save him."

"What?"

Kayla actually stops. Stops and stares at me. "Are you feckin' gone in the head?"

I stand there panting, barely able to stand, sweat

pouring off me. My blade flickers and gouts flame.

"We can save him," I insist. "We can talk him out of this. We can get through to him. He's Clyde."

"You," Kayla says, and her sword travels so fast it's invisible. Somehow, operating on an instinct I didn't know I had, I meet the blow. It smashes me sideways across the room.

Kayla is there to meet me. Already swinging.

"Stupid."

Another blow, reeling back in the other direction, arms screaming in pain.

"Dumb."

Her blow meets me. My defense is so weak I have no idea how I'm hanging onto the blade.

"Feck."

Somehow, from some deep, deep, poorly-conceived-of well of knowledge, I manage to parry the blow. I don't stagger. Don't reel. I parry and stand.

"He has to die." Kayla hacks at me. "Be done with. Or he'll kill us. And you'll stand there and let him. Like you almost let Tabitha die. Twice now. To save what you think is the right thing to save. The good guy thing. Not the necessary thing." She looks me in the eye. "You don't fight for love. For a friend. You fight for humanity. You kill Clyde. Plain as feckin' day."

"No." Grunting, panting, I smash back at her. The flame of my blade flickers blue. I whip it faster and harder. I exist in a halo of flame. Kayla and I smash together and away. An angry, intricate dance of aggression. Both of us on the edge of control.

"We fight for more than that. Otherwise we are Version 2.0. What we fight for defines us. We fight for what's good because that's what gives us the right to fight."

"Truth, justice, and the American feckin' way? You've been abroad too feckin' long." Kayla's sword falls in hammer blows. Beating me to my knees.

So I kick her in one of hers.

She stumbles.

"No," I say. "Nothing that grand. Hope." I smash at her, at her one-armed guard. "Hope of being better people." Smash. "Hope of a better future." Smash. Hell, ten percent is still a chance. Smash.

She finally beats away my blade, comes up, blade rising. I duck, spin, stab.

There is the feel of my sword hitting something thick and meaty.

Something starts to sizzle and burn.

I stare.

"Oh," Kayla says.

And there she is. She is right in front of me. Her mouth is a small circle. Her eyes are wide, mirroring the shape. There is my sword. Skewering her straight through her gut.

She drops her sword. It lands with a sharp clatter on the smooth, shiny floor.

"Oh feck."

And she collapses.

29

"Kayla!"

Mine is not the only scream. Behind me people mill and shriek.

I rush to her. She lies there, my sword sticking right through her. The point is jutting out of her back forcing her to lie at an angle on the floor. She is punctured through the upper left of her abdomen. The liver. Fuck. Fuck. Oh fuck. I've killed Kayla.

My first instinct is to rip the sword free, but then some half-remembered piece of information from an Oxford PD first aid course makes me hesitate before removing the object from a puncture wound. Something about causing the wound to bleed. And perhaps the sword is cauterizing the wound even as we speak. Though is that a good thing? This needs to heal. God, this has to heal.

I can't have killed Kayla. I can't. She can't die. She's Kayla. She's a bloody superwoman. You can't kill Superwoman. That's written in the Comic Books Code, right? And, God, this is real. This is real. Of all the unreal shit I have to deal with… this is real.

"Help!" I scream. "Help!"

One wall of the gym, massive and obliterating, comes to life as a monitor. Clyde's face eclipses everything. "On it, Arthur. Already alerted folk. Already on their way."

"Medic!" I scream. The Clyde version's words aren't sticking. Clyde. The bad guy. Except I'm the one who's gone and killed Kayla. Jesus. I've... No. She can't be dead.

"They're on their way, Arthur." Clyde's voice is soft and soothing. But my knees are in a pool of Kayla's blood. And that's not soothing at all.

I pick up Kayla's head, cradle it. Reality is a gear that I cannot engage. I try to remember first aid. Press the sides of the wound together. The heat of the blade makes it too hot, but I try anyway. I can smell my flesh singeing along with hers. And it seems such a small, paltry gesture.

"Paramedics here in five, four..."

"Step away! Step away!"

I don't. I can't. Until a white-suited paramedic physically hauls me off the body.

I watch as they do their work. Felicity comes. Tabitha and Gran too. They watch. Felicity puts her hands on my shoulders and knows enough to not ask me yet. To just let me stare in shellshocked horror as they rip the sword out. As they slam bandages to cover the gush of blood. As they fix the oxygen mask and hustle her out of the room.

LATER, BUT STILL TOO SOON

Once I regain the power of speech, they take me to a room and they talk to me. Kensington, the little pompous liaison; then a small business-like woman who reminds me vaguely of Felicity, except she pretends to be more friendly and is actually less so. Whether it's counseling or an interrogation, I can't really tell.

"Will she be all right?" I ask over and over again. And

no one tells me, not the woman; not Kensington, though he makes sure to let me know that this sort of thing never normally happens here, and then looks at me as if I am a house guest who just took a crap on his Oriental throw-rug; and neither does the genuine nurse who probes and prods at me; nobody until Gran comes in, and looks at me, and says, with uttermost gravity, "Dude."

"Is she OK?" I ask again.

"She'll be OK, man. Righteously tough cookie. Like a post-apocalyptic Twinkie."

"Twinkie?"

Gran looks at me. "You guys had an empire the sun never set on and no Twinkies. History makes no sense to me, man. None at all." He shrugs. "It's just candy, dude. Candy that's resilient like a cockroach."

I think that the British Empire may have been wise to leave behind any type of confection that can be compared to a cockroach.

And then what Gran said hits me through the barriers of emotional numbness I've been building up while waiting for this moment.

"Wait," I say. "You said she's going to be OK?"

Gran nods. "Totally, man. We have like top grade medical folk here. Creepy good, actually." He shakes his head at some memory he is kind enough to not share.

"Thank God." I sink my head into my hands.

"Dude," he says, sitting down across the table from me. "May not be the moment, but it's, like, pretty epic that you could actually stab her in a fight."

I close my eyes. Epic is not exactly the word I would have picked. But now my immediate concerns for Kayla's safety are fading, I have a chance to think of other implications of this moment.

I stabbed Kayla.

In a fight.

I beat her.

Except that can't be right. She must have let me. Or been not really trying.

But I remember those last moments. When we started to lose control. Started to just go at it.

And I beat her.

"What happened, man?" Gran asks.

I've gone over it enough times now that it comes out almost by rote. "We've been practicing swordfighting," I say. "She makes me talk so that I can be... I don't know. To get stuff out of the thinking bit of my brain and into the instinct bit. So we were talking about Clyde, and we disagreed. And things got heated. But, God, I swear I wasn't trying to stab her. I didn't think I could stab her. She's Kayla. She's not someone you can beat." I put my head in my hands. "I really just wanted to win the argument."

"Training accident," Gran says. He nods sagely.

"What?" I look up from the gray tabletop.

"It's a training accident, dude." Gran shrugs. "They happen, man. They suck, but they happen."

I remember Kayla lying on the floor. Being beside her, my knees sticky with her blood. And I am not sure I can be so wholly dismissive.

"I just wanted her to see that there might be hope. That we might still be able to resolve all this." I don't know why I'm still explaining. Gran has accepted what I've had to say. Except I'm not sure he really understands.

I remember Gran shooting the little girl.

"I didn't want to hurt her." I try to put every ounce of conviction I have into those words. So he hears them. "I don't want to hurt anybody. I don't even want to hurt Clyde 2.0. I want a peaceful resolution."

"Dude," Gran nods. Like I'm the TV preacher, and he's the middle-aged woman with a phone and a credit card. "If we can talk this thing out, I will be the first one to pull out the hacky sack. All over that shit, man. I hear you."

He smiles. Warm and friendly. Just a nice hippy in a CIA suit. "Look, man. This was a shitty thing to happen. But it's no one's fault. And I know you want to beat yourself up, but you're not the bad guy here. We got enough of those already, right? We're all on the same side, man. All fighting to save the world—"

"Humanity," I say.

Gran gives me a quizzical look. "Version 2.0 is fighting to save the world. We're fighting to save humanity."

Gran blinks at me. "Dude," he says. And I think he'll say more, but he leaves it at that, and instead says, "Look, man, Felicity is waiting outside for you. Has been for about two hours. Why don't you just go chill with her, shake this thing off, and we'll all come back tomorrow and be groovy as balls. Sound good?"

"Yes," I say after a moment. Felicity. Chilling. That genuinely does sound about as good as things will get under these circumstances. Everything except the bit where we're groovy as balls, actually. I don't ever want things to be that. Yuck.

30

A NEW MORNING

I wake up with Felicity's arm draped over me. The alarm clock reads six thirty in the morning. Time to wake up. Time to go back to all this.

I close my eyes again and stay in bed.

Ten minutes later, Felicity stirs. She retrieves her arm, rubs her mouth, her eyes, blinks slowly at me a few times.

"You feeling better?" she says, voice still heavy with sleep.

"Yes," I say.

"Liar."

"I will be."

"Liar."

She rolls from her side to her back, blinks at the ceiling a few times, then stretches. I hear joints popping. She rolls back to me, pushes my hair out of my eyes.

"You're not meant to be happy about it, Arthur. Just to be able to deal with it."

I close my eyes, wonder if I can go back to sleep for a bit. "I can do that," I say.

"Can you start now then?"

I open my eyes, look at her. And it seems a little too early in the morning for a look that mocking.

"So far," I say, "I am responsible for more casualties

on our team than Version 2.0. I am not feeling so heroic today. Is there any chance I can have some slack?"

She sits up, looks down, ruffles my hair. "Will Version 2.0 give you any, or will he press the advantage?"

"I'm not dating Version 2.0."

"No." Felicity's voice is without humor. "He's trying to kill you."

I groan. Right now that sounds like another good reason to stay in bed.

Felicity's hand runs down through my hair, over my cheek. Her skin is soft. "Bad things happen all the time, Arthur. And I don't mean general bad things out in the big wide world," she gestures with her hand, "but very specifically things that happen to us. And they're terrible, awful things. But do you know the reason why we keep on winning? Why MI37 saves the world?" She doesn't wait for a response. "Because we keep on going. We keep pushing. That's why I recruited you, gave you the position I did. You keep on pushing."

I glare at her through slitted eyelids. *Don't like it. Just deal with it.* I lick my lips. "'Keep on pushing,' doesn't happen to be a sex reference, does it?"

She bats at me with her hand. "Get out of bed," she says.

There's nothing really to do but comply.

AREA 51

The newspapers are full of the wireless internet news. Pundits rage on television. People camp out in downtown parks. They curse and spit at Big Brother governments. The right and left are finally united in the single point of view: this sucks.

From the Area 51 conference room we watch the

head of Homeland Security sweat through a speech he didn't write to defend a policy he didn't come up with.

"Afraid this isn't making us totally popular," says Gran, clicking off the screen.

I would answer but he's holding Tabitha's hand and that makes saying anything that isn't, "You're holding Tabitha's hand" rather difficult. I preferred it when the TV was on and there were moving pictures to distract me.

"So," Felicity says from across the table, "your policy makers would prefer a psychotic artificial intelligence attempted to kill all of humanity just so they can watch cat videos on YouTube?"

Gran shrugs. "Depends who the psychotic votes for."

Maybe there aren't so many cultural differences between the US and England after all.

"People will comply?" Tabitha asks Gran. "You seriously think?"

Gran shrugs. "No choice, dudette. We really are going a bit Big Brother on this one actually. Dudes are stringing up this network of wireless signal blockers all over the country and stuff. Cellphone reception's going to be for shit too."

Tabitha looks at him, quizzical. "Network of wireless things to stop wireless networks? Seriously?"

Gran goes with a second shrug. "Mad DARPA genius science, space, alien technology, magic doodad. Maybe."

Tabitha shakes her head.

Honestly, I find that answer makes about as much sense as any of the ones I usually get. And personally, I don't care how it's done, or how many awkward speeches the head of Homeland Security needs to make. My concerns remain closer to home.

"How's Kayla doing?"

"She's stable." A Clyde appears where the Homeland Security bloke was a few moments before, and answers before anyone else can. "Though I was very good about not peeking at her medical records. We all were. Very conscious of the whole good behavior thing, I promise you. No psychotic killers in this crowd. Which, now I come to say out loud makes me sound exactly like a psychotic killer. Well, maybe not exactly like one. That's probably more of a grunting, knife-wielding sound. Maybe some mad gibbering. At least that's if *The Texas Chainsaw Massacre* is accurate. Which I concede, now I think about it, it might not be. Not exactly documentary footage, I suppose. And now I probably really do sound like a psychopath. Probably tell you about my mother next. Not that I will. Because she was a charming woman with nothing... Oh wait, doing it. Stopping now."

To be fair, it would probably be much more worrying if the Clyde versions didn't babble like lunatics.

Felicity flicks a quick look in my direction. Checking to see how I'm holding up. I give her as reassuring a smile as I can manage. It is good news about Kayla.

"OK, let's refocus," she says. "Version 2.0's stated intent is to wipe out all of humanity. And right now he hasn't given us much reason to doubt him. So how is he going to do it?"

"Well, we know the weapons at the evil dude's disposal," Gran states, apparently deciding to exert a little bit of leadership since he's the one on home turf. "Mind wiping and golems."

An unpleasant thought crosses my mind. "Wait..." I say, "there could be something else." I look over at the

Clyde versions. "Were there any doomsday devices in the DARPA files?"

"Surprisingly few," one version says to my great relief. "And none of them really viable either."

"Would a supercomputer be able to fix them?"

The version winces as he scans his databases.

"Honestly, man," Gran interjects, "we really aren't into the whole doomsday thing anymore. Very passé from a security point of view. Mutually assured destruction is totally uncool. When we find them we're more into the destroying-all-evidence thing these days. We've got a whole branch for just, you know, assassinating evil mastermind scientists and stuff. Not the most fun people for dinner parties, but, like, all over the ruthless-efficiency thing."

Tabitha seems to think this is the moment to lean over and kiss Gran on the cheek.

God, if government-sponsored scientist death squads are one of Tabitha's peccadillos, then I think maybe the Clyde versions' affection is misplaced.

They, for their part, stone face it through the kiss. Possibly more successfully than I do.

Felicity takes it upon herself to rescue the situation, bless her. "Mind wiping all of humanity in one fell swoop feels a little cumbersome," she says. "And shutting down the wireless networks will have put a crimp in any plans along those lines. So I think that's the less likely option. On the other hand we've seen him use golems to great effect. And in large scale."

I try to picture the scenario. New York, the city above us, suddenly filling with faux-men. All the blowing trash rising up against the citizens. They could be everywhere immediately. It would be chaos.

I know it was my suggestion, but a doubt crosses my mind. "Summoning that many golems would require ridiculous amounts of electricity," I point out.

"Dude was looking at a lot of infrastructure shit, though," Gran points out.

"Power grid?" Tabitha asks. Gran nods.

Felicity's head swings up and down in time with the CIA agent's. "Any sort of operation on the scale Version 2.0 was talking about would require massive amounts of planning."

I think back at the sheer amount of information Version 2.0 sifted through in the week leading up to this. And it's too much to grasp in one go. We need a way in.

And then I see one. "What about Mercurio?" I ask.

"Trap," Tabitha snaps, disengaging from Gran's cheek. "Sprung. Escaped."

I think about that. And to a point she's right. But only to a point.

"But why him?" I ask. "Clyde knew how to create golems before he hooked up with Mercurio. Winston is proof of that. It could have been anyone he picked. Why Mercurio?"

"Well." Gran looks unsure. "Mercurio was like all into golems and stuff. Maybe he had all the junk and stuff he needed to make them right there. You know, like, not somewhere else."

Something rattles in the back of my mind. "You said something about weaponizing vegetation though, right?" I look up at the versions.

"Oh yes," says one. "But really the focus of his research was harrying troops. Nothing massively offensive. Unless he was experimenting on Brussels sprouts. That would be offensive. No idea why anyone would go near those things without a hazmat suit, to be honest."

Which seems like an excess of information.

"But weaponized vegetation does tie into this whole green environmental thing, right?" I say. This suddenly feels solid to me.

Felicity is nodding. Even Tabitha leans her head in grudging assent.

"Will he talk to us?" I ask. "If we get him out of his coma."

Gran shakes his head. "Had some psych boys come and talk to him. Didn't go spectacularly well. I'm pretty sure the written evaluation actually contained the word batshit at one point. We're kind of still working on the whole professionalism thing with our psych guys though."

Tabitha seems to be about to say something, then hesitates. It's not usual for her to show reluctance to speak her mind.

"What is it?" I ask.

Tabitha hums and haws for a moment. "Debug him," she says, not meeting anyone's eye. "Could try to do that."

Her code. She's been working on code to get Clyde out of people's heads. Which could be perfect.

"Would he remember anything?" I ask.

Tabitha shrugs. "Untested code. Might kill him."

Oh. So there are less than perfect outcomes here too.

Felicity leans forward on the desk. "Do we really have any other options where Mercurio is concerned?"

No one has anything to offer.

Felicity meets everyone's eye in turn. "Then we have our next move."

AREA 51 LAB

Mercurio lies as I saw him last, flat on his back on a table, arms and legs restrained, head covered in electrodes. There is a little more stubble on his cheeks, perhaps, but otherwise he is not much different. A man reduced to a science experiment. What an awful way to end up.

Tabitha bends over her laptop, typing madly, occasionally cursing out the Clyde versions.

Is this the right thing to do? But I don't know. Maybe it's close enough. To quote Felicity, it is a call I can live with. We just have to wait and see if Mercurio can live with it too.

"OK," Tabitha says. "Ready."

She doesn't wait for me to quiet my qualms or my conscience. She just hits a button on the keyboard.

Mercurio's body convulses. A great shuddering of the limbs runs down his body. His torso twists, bucks. His head smashes back against the table. Again. Again. Again. Leather restraints strain and creak.

Then he stops. Lies rigidly, back arched, balanced on heels and skull.

"Is that meant to happen?" Felicity asks. She is looking a little less certain of this plan now. I take a step toward her, but as much because her physical proximity comforts me as vice versa.

Tabitha shrugs. "Pioneering science. Breaking boundaries, and shit."

I think hanging out with Gran is starting to affect her vocabulary. Still, it does seem a bit of a cavalier attitude. "This is a man's life," I point out.

"No." She turns on me, eyes fierce. "Mercurio's dead. Only Version 2.0 in there. This isn't medicine. It's resurrection."

Which rather reframes things for me. It also fills me with the urge to shout, "It's aliiiive!" at the ceiling, but I restrain myself.

Tabitha's computer emits a loud ping. Tabitha punches another button. Mercurio sags back against the table. His chest rises and falls fast, the air rushing in and out of him.

"What now?" I stare. He's definitely alive. But as Clyde has proven there are different degrees of that.

Tabitha steps forward, peers at his face. "Mercurio?" she says. "Doctor?"

And maybe having Tabitha be the first person this guy interacts with isn't the kindest thing on earth. I step forward, hoping others come with me. "Doctor, can you hear me?"

He lies there, panting, eyes flicking back and forth, wide and panicked. They come to rest on me.

"Doctor Mercurio," I repeat, speaking slower and louder. "Can you hear me?"

His brows furrow, but his panting relaxes, some of the tension goes out of him. He works his jaw, seems to be trying to say something.

Tabitha, for a fraction of a second, glances up at the Clyde versions on their hanging monitor. "EEG," she snaps.

"On it."

The wall monitor flickers and a vast image of Mercurio's brain appears. He turns his head in that direction, stares.

"It's OK," I say to the doctor. "You're with friends."

Gran raises his eyebrows at that one. I shrug back. It's not like I'm going to tell the man the truth.

Mercurio rolls his head to look back at me. His eyes

are big, almost innocent. His jaw works again.

"Uffle?" he says.

There is a moment when we all just look at each other.

"I'm sorry?" I say. That doesn't seem like it's the sort of thing anyone intends to really say.

"Urf marr?"

I am reduced to squinting and looking puzzled. Felicity shrugs at me. "You got any translation software?" I ask the versions.

"Oh," says one. "Good thinking. Should have been on that. Pulling up the interface. Give me a second. Settings…" He hums and haws as a new window opens on the wall monitor.

"Auto detect," says another.

"Funny phrase that," comments the third. "Makes it sound like some sort of Sherlock Holmes derivative. Deer stalker hat and a fine command of French. Not like that at all, of course."

"Murfa wal?" Mercurio asks. His eyes still have that large innocent look. "Wetto?"

"Erm," says the first version. "OK. That's giving me…" He puts his head down; reams of code appear on the wall monitor, disappear again. He shrugs. "Nothing."

The version looks up at the assembled crowd. "Well," he says. "I am not the world's largest fan of absolute statements. Operating in the field we do, one is likely to find that the sky—having previously been declared to be blue—is now an off-shade of maroon. But that aside, as far as I can tell that's not a language."

"Oogle," says Mercurio.

I look over at Tabitha. "OK," I say. "What's wrong with him?"

Tabitha's bile levels seem to be unusually low. She regards Mercurio with a slightly worried look. "Brain scan," she snaps to the versions. A yellow, green, and red portrait of the man's brain quickly appears on the wall.

"Flerp?" Mercurio asks.

"Well," says one of the versions, "if one wants to focus on the positive—and I always think that a sunny disposition can cheer up a room—I'm pretty sure he's not Version 2.0 now."

"He's a fucking vegetable." Tabitha steps forward and pokes Mercurio with what seems like an unnecessary amount of aggression. Her jaw is clenched in frustration.

"Urf," Mercurio says.

"If we could avoid obviously derogatory statements…" Felicity sighs and glances at Gran.

"Well." I stare at Mercurio rather sadly. "We have kind of made him stupid, haven't we?"

Felicity sighs again. "I would rather not jump to any snap conclusions. This could just be the result of some damage to his verbal structures. We have no idea what else could have been left intact."

Mercurio is repeatedly putting his finger in and out of his navel while making soft cooing sounds.

"Seriously?" I ask.

Felicity blanches. "OK," she says. "What the hell went wrong?"

"Now?" Tabitha asks. "Less than a minute in? Full experiment analysis? Just pioneered new science. Might take me a moment."

The versions huddle, seem to disagree on something. It's a muttered affair that seems to mostly involve the word, "sorry." It takes me a moment to realize this is the first time I've really seen them not be in total unity about something.

One version breaks free of the others. "I'm sorry," he says, "and first I would just like to fully acknowledge the enormous difficulty of achieving what Tabby was aiming for. In fact, that this went as well as it did and didn't end up with the good doctor's head detonating like a claymore is rather a testament to her prodigious skill."

"Shut it," Tabitha snaps, not looking at them. "Before I format you."

"But there's a chance the code needs a little work," the version finishes under the stern gaze of his compatriots.

"Duh," says Tabitha.

"Duh," repeats Mercurio. He plunges his finger into his ear, pushes, winces, and removes it, wearing a sorrowful expression.

"Is there any chance," Felicity says, "that we can recover any of what he knew?"

Tabitha doesn't immediately reply.

"I see," Felicity says. Her voice is tight.

"Good learning experience," Tabitha says without looking up. "Work out the kinks. Next time: fail better."

"Yes," Felicity breathes, her eyes on Gran, "but if we could skip the failing altogether, that would be great."

ONE LEVEL DEEPER IN THE AREA 51 COMPLEX

"OK," I say, holding up a large pencil sketch, "this is kind of upsetting."

Mercurio now being off the table as a source of information, Felicity, Gran and I have decided to take a look through the possessions recovered from his lab and apartment. Meanwhile, Tabitha and the versions are trying to work out where they went wrong.

Hopefully they are having more luck than us. So far our biggest discovery has been that the good doctor was really into cat pictures.

It appears to be a slightly unhealthy obsession. There are cat calendars. Cat one-a-day calendars. The saved pages of cat one-a-day calendars. Printed out pictures of cats. Doodles of cats. Posters of cats. And in my hand now is one extremely unsettling and frighteningly detailed sketch of a cat stretched out on a beach wearing a bikini.

It is while I am transfixed by this distressingly large image, and realizing that it is not only supernatural horrors that one cannot unsee, that Gran taps me on the shoulder.

I flinch violently, and then screw the sketch up and fling it away from me as if it's a live grenade.

"Dude," Gran says, "that's nothing. You should see his version of cats playing poker."

"I can't imagine that being worse."

"It's strip poker."

I blanch. Over from behind a stack of boxes, Felicity makes gagging noises.

The storage room containing Mercurio's possessions is surprisingly cramped and gloomy for Area 51. Instead of the sterile scrubbed feel it smells musty and damp. Brown cardboard boxes are stacked to the low ceiling in a mad confusion. Gran and I huddle in one small clearing. Felicity has clambered over to another.

"It's weird," I say, yanking a pile of relatively safe looking scientific journals out of a fresh box. "I figured if he was a plant guy that he'd be more into... I don't know. Cat nip, rather than cats."

Gran nods. "Love is a funny thing, man."

"Yeah," I nod. Though I'd really rather not think of Mercurio's feelings as being ones of love. Strong affection is really as far as I am comfortable considering.

"Speaking of," Felicity says, "you and Tabitha seem to have hit it off."

Gran nods, grinning. "She's groovy, yeah. Bit early maybe for the big L word. But, you know—" He grins, sheepish and roguish all at once.

"She just came out of a fairly tumultuous relationship." Felicity is doing that thing where she sounds like someone's mother. It's probably wrong that I find that kind of sexy.

"Yeah, yeah." Gran nods sagely. "Working with her to kill the ex, so... aware of the whole minefield thing. But, you know, the healing power of love and all that. Kind of near and dear to my personal philosophy."

He looks at us both, the laconic stoner look suddenly slipping away.

"And," he says, the word pregnant, "I'm not, like, the only dude who's, erm, fraternizing and such with a co-worker."

Felicity looks at him sharply. One of her eyebrows is raised. While our relationship is not exactly a touchy subject—we have been quite open about our status— Felicity is not one to suffer having her decisions challenged lightly.

"No, man," Gran holds up his hands defensively. "Not judging. Love is a beautiful thing. Fill the world with it, I say. Cats and dogs living together. Total harmony." He holds up his fingers in the classic peace sign.

"So," I say, shooting for subtext, "we'll smile and be happy for you and Tabitha."

"But I'll gut you if you hurt her," Felicity adds. "I

protect my own, Agent Gran." And there is no room left in her voice for any doubt.

Gran is shaking his head. "No, no, no, dudes. Totally all over the making Tabitha happy thing. Very into that actually. Like… well, you don't want details."

I momentarily thank all that is holy that he stopped there. This job is hard enough without having to deal with hysterical blindness.

"It was actually the whole protecting-your-own thing I wanted to focus on for a moment."

The defensive look is back in Felicity's eyes. It's probably in mine too. Either that or the guilty look, because I think I know where this is going.

"Look, dudes," Gran says. "I love that you guys have clearly got the groovalicious thing for each other bad."

And here it comes…

"But—"

There it is.

"—you know, in the field, it's like getting to feel a little dangerous when you have my back, man." Gran's laugh is awkward. His usual affableness diminished. "Like I dig that Felicity is your first priority and vice versa, but, man, there's quite a decent chunk of prioritizing going on with that, it seems, you know." He shrugs awkwardly.

Shit. Because he has a point. Love doesn't belong out in the field. That's essentially what he's saying. It puts every other life out there at risk.

I look at Felicity. And how can I not? How can I not protect her?

"Are you saying that our relationship is affecting our efficacy in the field?" Felicity has gone very stiff.

"Oh man," Gran pushes his hands through his hair.

"I hate this shit. Look, I'm not doing anything formal here. Just having a chat with some groovy people. That's all."

I look at Felicity. Because if I look at Gran he might want me to meet his eye, and I don't know if I can right now.

"We..." I start.

"I look after my own," Felicity snaps. At Gran. At me too. There is unexpected tension in her voice. And I know she doesn't like to be challenged, but this seems beyond that point. "I keep my own safe. *All* of my own. And that includes you, Agent Gran. Everyone is safe on my watch. Do you understand?"

And with that she storms out of the room.

Gran looks miserable. And maybe it confirms Gran's argument but he is still not my first priority. I hurry after Felicity.

SEVERAL CORRIDORS AWAY

I catch up with Felicity, put a hand on her shoulder. She wheels on me.

"Hey!" I say, almost raising a hand to fend her off. And then I see the streaks of make-up in the corners of her eyes. "Hey," I say again, but softer now. I reach out to her. "Are you OK?"

She wipes at her eyes furiously. "Yes," she snaps. "Of course."

I regard her for a moment. In the hopes that she stops taking me for a fool.

She seems to concede that fact. "I don't want to talk about it," she says.

"Come on," I say. "I'm a part of this too." Which might be a bit presumptive of me, but I am an increasing fan of the pronoun "us," and would like to help shoulder some of the pain.

She regards me, jaw working hard. And I feel so sad for her in that moment. Gran, without meaning to, has hit a structural weakness in her steel foundations. And I don't know exactly what it is, but I am so sad to discover it was there at all.

"Is this about your sister?" I ask as gently as I can. It is the only thing I can guess at.

Felicity clenches her jaw for a moment. "I protect my own," she whispers fiercely.

In the end, that sounds a lot like, "yes."

"I know you do," I say. Because I genuinely believe her. Because when she has my back, I believe down to the bone that my back is fine.

Felicity draws a breath, holds it for a moment, and then releases it the same way a kettle releases steam. I'm half surprised she doesn't whistle.

She shakes herself. "I'm being ridiculous," she says.

"No," I say, because Felicity is stronger than that, because she doesn't need denial. "You're recognizing the danger we're up against. You're—"

"No," she says, "I'm not." She shakes her head. "I know exactly how dangerous this is. That's why..." She hesitates, and seems to retreat from whatever went unspoken.

"Why what?" I want so much to understand, to help her bear this weight.

"You said," she says, not meeting my eye, "that you worried that if you saved me at the expense of the greater good I wouldn't forgive you."

I nod. I sort of remember that fairly well. "And you reassured me," I say, "that I'll make the right call."

"I know," she says. "And I still believe that."

"There you go, then," I say. QED, and logic, and all the things Clyde used to reference.

"No." She shakes her head, looking very sad indeed. "I think you would. But I don't know if I would make the right call, Arthur."

"While I find that hard to believe," I tell her, "I would still be there for you. I would very easily be able to forgive you."

"Yes," she says. "But I would never be able to forgive myself."

"Oh."

And I feel her pain so sharply in my own chest. I pull her to me, and she comes, wraps her arms around me.

"I swore never again, Arthur. No one under my watch. No one. I swore."

"I know. I know. But we'll be OK," I tell her. "We'll make the right decisions. We'll make them together." And, God, I wish I had more than platitudes for her now. I wish I had certainty. But that has never been my gift to give.

Felicity pulls away from me. Rubs at her eyes once more, a look of self-recrimination on her face. "I know. We will. Of course." She sniffs. "I'm being ridiculous."

But she's not, and as we head up through the corridors of Area 51, I don't think either of us are reassured.

31

SEVERAL HOURS LATER

We regroup for a lunch meeting. Sandwiches and wraps are laid out in a room labeled Epsilon-3. Considering how much the CIA love their nomenclature, I assume the epsilon signifies that this is a floor for dysfunctional visiting groups

The Clyde versions take up a large portion of one wall of the lab. Tabitha has angled her laptop so her back is to them. I sit next to Felicity, who has still not entirely recovered her calm and won't look at Gran.

A couple of men and women we don't know—all with ponytails, I note—sit at the far end of the lab, looking uncomfortable.

I remember Felicity's desire for us to appear competent and pleasant and decide to break the ice as best I can. "So, how's it all going?" I ask as jovially as the atmosphere will allow.

"Awful," Tabitha says at the exact same moment that the Clyde versions chime, "Great."

"Fuck off." Tabitha gives the versions the finger over her shoulder.

I smile and try to muscle through. "Work out anything about what happened with Mercurio?"

Tabitha grunts. "Yeah. Found two things."

"Oh?" I brighten.

227

"Diddly and shit."

"Oh." I readjust my brightness to its earlier levels, try Gran instead. "You find anything in Mercurio's effects suggesting at the larger plan?"

"No, dude." Gran shrugs. "All the personal notes are on the same shit. Rampant growth of ground cover, yadda, yadda. Weaponized fungus, et cetera, et cetera."

Weaponized fungus. Jesus. Still, maybe the obvious is staring us in the face. "Is there anything in there," I say, "about how this could be scaled? How big an area could he affect with this?"

"Well, it'd be the standard limitations," offers a Clyde version. "Power source related. The more electricity he has the larger the area he can affect."

My teenage self would disown me, but, God, I hate magic.

I force my gray matter to chug and whir. "Wasn't there something in the files Version 2.0 originally looked at? Before we came on the case. Something to do with infrastructure. With the power lines or something?"

"Yes." The three Clydes nod in unison.

"So," I say, "theoretically he could hack into the US power grid, and turn plants on people over a massive area. Like the entire US."

"Shit," Felicity and Tabitha say in unison.

Gran's eyes go wide. And then he shakes his head. "Nah, man. Our infrastructure is, like, for shit. Total disaster. No way you could go in and just digitally rejigger the thing. Wouldn't work."

"Clyde zombies," Tabitha says.

It takes me a moment, but I realize this is what we're now calling the recently mind-wiped.

I glance at the Clyde versions, and none of them look

happy about the term, but none of them look willing to nay-say Tabitha either.

"There would need to be, like, hundreds of them," Gran says, still back on Tabitha's Clyde zombies theory. "All over the country."

"Yes," Tabitha agrees.

"Shit," Gran says. His calm is definitely being disturbed here. "Jesus, could we even spot them?"

"Oh!" says a Clyde. "Burn pattern."

Despite herself Tabitha suddenly sits up very straight.

"Burn what?" I ask, looking at her. I still prefer to deal with flesh and blood folk than the versions.

"Mercurio's head," she says. "His brain. Burned neurons where Clyde went in. A distinct pattern. Would show up on MRI."

While this seems like good news to me, Gran's head slumps to hit the table. "God," he says. "Now I have to MRI everyone touching the power grid. Like, I wasn't unpopular enough already."

It is probably not as good a sign as I would like that this causes Felicity to smile.

"Ahem."

Our eyes all snap to the doorway. Kensington, the pompous little man who greeted us to Area 51 and who made some ugly insinuations about Kayla's injury yesterday, is standing there.

"Yes?" Felicity asks him, which is definitely more polite than what I was going to say.

He gives us all the most perfunctory of smiles. "I was sitting in my office and I realized that I had never given you the full tour of Area 51."

"Gran—" I start.

"An official tour," Kensington rides over me, "from the *deputy* liaison—" There's emphasis on the title. "I think you'll all be surprised by how advanced we are here compared to what you're used to." He unconsciously smooths his hair. "Probably some things you're not really used to seeing back in a, err... more parochial outfit."

Whether it's a conscious effort to be insulting or not, I don't know. Either way I think he's got about six seconds before I punch him in the throat.

Then something on the wall behind him catches my eye. A better alternative. "Wait," I say cutting him off, "is that mold?"

I point to a dark patch I've spotted on the pristine gray wall behind him. A black stain, almost like a blob of dripping spray paint.

For a moment Kensington seems unable to speak. I don't think I could have insulted him more had I chosen to kick a baby in front of him. There is at least a mild chance his head is going to detonate.

Gran stands, peers past Kensington. "Dude," he says by way of confirmation.

"No," Kensington manages. "No." He remains with his back firmly to the mold, unable to acknowledge it.

It's petty of me, but I am quietly proud of the fact that while it may be shoddy, and run-down, and underfunded, and have a really neglected air, and be in desperate need of some really basic amenities, and... well, I am quietly proud MI37 isn't moldy.

"Dude," Gran says again. He sounds far more concerned this time. Then a third time. "Dude!" Recoiling. Disgusted and alarmed.

As he pulls back I see the stain again. It's bigger

now. And getting bigger. It bubbles through the wall, an uneven smear of black and purple. The wall beneath almost boils, layers of plastic peeling back, sloughing away. Something beneath, furry and dark, pushing out. An odor like rotten eggs.

"The hell?" I say.

"Back," Felicity barks. "Down."

"No," says Kensington again. Finally turning. The sight seems to rock him back on his feet. "It can't be."

He steps forward toward the thing, a bulbous column of dark purple fur.

And then it explodes.

A spray of a fine dark powder. Like a breath exhaled. The black fungal structure already collapsing upon itself, sagging down.

The spores billow in the air, about Kensington. He coughs, splutters, spits. He claws at his mouth, his nose.

"Jesus!" I manage, as eloquent as ever in my shock.

"Back!" Felicity barks again. And I comply. Hell, do I comply. All of MI37 does. We know that tone.

But Gran doesn't. "Kensington?" he says, the concern over-riding the disgust. "Dude? You OK?" His hand is on the deputy liaison's shoulder.

Kensington still hacks and coughs, down on his knees, his back to us. The exhalations become thicker, wetter. I hear something splatter against the floor with each cough.

"Urrrr," Kensington rumbles.

That doesn't sound good.

"Urrr," Kensington rumbles again. And with that he staggers to his feet. His motions are jerky, something off with the gross motor functions. Some joints too loose, others too stiff. His back is still to us. And then he turns.

His eyes are black. Totally black. His mouth too. His lips the darkest purple. The stain leaks from the corners of his eyes, down his cheeks, like sodden mascara. It's on his chin, like a meal sloppily eaten.

"Urrr." He grabs Gran by the collar and buries a fist in the CIA agent's face. His nails are purple too.

"Shit!" Felicity's gun is in her hands before I can track the movement.

"Wait!" Tabitha shouts. Kensington is dangerously close to Gran. But then the shot is fired.

Kensington's head detonates like rotten fruit. He tumbles to the floor. Cranium scatters everywhere. A great spray of blood. Black blood. Bits of brain mashed against the floor. Half of them covered in black fur.

My gorge rises.

"Shit, man," Gran is saying. "Shit. Shit. Shit."

He and I are rather on the same page. I go with, "What the hell?"

It's Tabitha who answers, voice numb. "Fungus," she says. "Alien, mind-controlling fungus. Fungi from Shug-Yoggoth. Fuck. Clyde is trying to kill us in the nerdiest way possible."

32

It takes me a moment before I realize. She's right. This is it. This is the attack.

Jesus. We were going to MRI the world. Wasn't that the plan about eight seconds ago? We were going to do it before Version 2.0 had time to sort everything out.

Except he has.

This is it.

This is the attack.

Shit. My sword. It's back in the sleeping cube this morning. I left it there after... Kayla.

"No." Gran is shaking his head. "We can't be under attack. We can't." He sounds like Kensington looking at the mold.

Kensington. The dead man on the floor. I point to him. "I think we have some pretty good evidence to the contrary." Panic can make me a smart mouth.

Gran shakes his head again. Except there are screams now coming from further down the hall.

And then another, "Urrr," from much closer.

We spin. Look down the lab. At the other researchers having lunch here. The ponytail crowd. God, I hadn't even...

Fungus wilts against the wall behind them. I see the dark spores staining the laptops they were using. I see their black eyes and purple lips. Something black, viscous, and ugly leaking out of one of their noses.

They stumble over each other toward us. Not a full-on zombie shuffle, but it definitely has uncoordinated undertones. Haste marred by lack of coordination. One of them grabs the corner of the table and hauls itself toward us at stuttering speed.

No. This can't be happening. These are just people who work here. They...

Felicity's gun snaps out another four shots. Their heads go pop, pop, pop. One woman staggers left and takes the bullet in the shoulder. She spins around then stumbles toward us. Her blond hair is hanging limply on her head. Her roots are getting darker by the second.

"I look after my own," I hear Felicity whisper.

Bang. She fires again. Catches the woman in the temple. The woman drops with half her head missing.

Gran doubles over and is quite noisily sick.

I stare around the room. Five bodies. In a matter of seconds. We just killed five people. I felt shitty yesterday because I *injured* Kayla. And these people... Jesus, they were just... normal people. Seconds ago. And now they're dead. They were infected for less than thirty seconds. And we... Felicity... Shit.

There are more sounds from beyond the room. Grunting angry noises. Screams. Yells. Barks of command. No gunfire yet. But it's going to come. I know it will.

How many people are going to die today?

All of us. That's Clyde's plan.

All of humanity. To save the world.

And maybe he is right. Maybe that's the way it has to be in the long run. But I can't stand around and watch it.

"We have to get out there. We have to help people evacuate."

I don't wait for anyone to acknowledge me. It's not even a command that demands compliance. It's a statement of fact. A statement of who we are. In this moment of crisis I have no doubt about that. This is what has to be done. The big picture is going to have to just sit down for a while, kick off its shoes, and fucking wait.

And then, as soon as I take my first step toward the room's door, it slams shut.

"I'm sorry," says a familiar voice. "I'm afraid we can't let you leave just yet, Arthur."

No. No. No.

I turn slowly, stare.

I stare at the versions.

33

"Clyde?" I say.

But of course it's Clyde. I can see it's Clyde. Just not the version I thought it was.

Tabitha clutches her laptop like a talisman and moans. Gran crosses to her, wiping vomit from his mouth.

"Hello, Arthur," the versions say in perfect unison.

My mind races. This place is firewalled, lacks wireless, and should generally be completely impregnable. "How the hell did you get in?"

"Well…" Another of the Clyde versions smiles, "you brought me here, Arthur."

"Mercurio," says the second version. "Traps within traps. One to hide the other."

Mercurio? I try to think. Was there something in his brain… When they scanned him.

"Files," Tabitha moans. "The fucking files."

"I overwrote your versions' software the moment they plugged into the first hard drive you recovered from Mercurio's office."

"Sorry," says another, with an apologetic shrug.

Oh God. He's here. And he's apologizing to me. Apologizing that he's going to try to kill me again. "You have to stop this," I say. It's all I can think to say.

"Why?" The corrupted Clyde versions look genuinely confused. "I'm pretty sure I explained all this to you. I sat through the whole debrief about it. I mean, I don't mean to criticize, I really don't—it's not a very noble thing to do, especially under these current circumstances—but you really do need to pay more attention. That was the whole point of Mexico, to explain it all to you. Well, that and buy time to hack into the security countermeasures installed in this place. They really are quite amazing."

Outside I hear a dull thudding sound, speeding up to a blur of continuous pounding.

Gunfire.

Very large caliber gunfire.

"Oh no." Gran has his head in his hands.

I look at him. "What is it?"

"Arthur," says Clyde before Gran can reply. "I appreciate that given our different perspectives, you may not be able to appreciate the true awesomeness of this now, but, seriously, their security countermeasures include wall-mounted machine gun turrets. It's crazy cool."

Oh God. He's butchering people out there.

"Felicity," I say, fighting the need to hyperventilate. "The door."

"On it." She takes aim. The whine of the ricochet is almost lost in the sound of the shot, but we all see the neat bullet hole appear in the wall the Clydes are occupying.

"DARPA doors," one Clyde comments.

"You have to stop," I parrot. It's still all I can think to say. "You have to. Now."

"How about I wait about ten minutes and then stop," says one Clyde.

The guns continue to thunder. In ten minutes no one out there will be alive.

Felicity shoots again. Another ricochet punches a

hole in the screen. Why the piss did I leave my sword back in the room?

Because I stabbed Kayla yesterday.

Thank God they shipped her off site.

There has to be a way out of here. I stare at the blank room. The locked door. The bodies on the floor. They're rotting away at incredible speed, purple fungus eating away at them. There is no way out.

"Let us out," I say. It's an unlikely option, but it expends few enough resources that it's worth a shot I suppose.

"It's not a good place to be out there, right now," says one Clyde. "You're better off in here."

"What are you going to do with us?" Gran asks.

"Well…" The Clydes look at each other, a little sheepish. "Kill you," admits one.

"We did say it's a better place to be, *right now*," says the third Clyde, rather lamely.

My mind is still reeling. Trying to process this abrupt shift in fortunes. And why are we separated from the rest of Area 51? Is Version 2.0's regard for our skills so high that he doesn't want us to get out of here? That doesn't seem entirely likely.

"You don't want to kill us," I say. I look at them. And I see it's true. "You don't want to at all."

Clyde shrugs. "I know that, Arthur. I just have to."

"Why?" I demand. "Who's forcing you?"

The Clydes shake their collective heads. "You know no one's forcing me, Arthur. I have a choice before me. Kill the species that was once my own plus my friends, or kill all species plus my friends. Neither option is exactly what I would call fantabulous, but those are the ones I have. And I've chosen. And I am firm in my choice."

"So kill me," I demand.

"Wouldn't encourage him, dude," Gran suggests.

"Arthur..." Felicity is clearly less confident about this path than I am.

"Keep on the door," I tell her, not looking back.

"I'll kill you last," says Clyde. "Of everyone in th is building, you'll live the longest. That's the best I can promise to you."

"We're going to stop you," I say. It's mindless, groundless optimism, but it feels like I've found a weak point and I press on it as hard as I can.

"You can't," a Clyde says.

"We will."

"And what if you did?" a Clyde asks. "What then? You'd just be condemning the world to its end."

"I can't believe that," I say. "I can't believe there's no hope at all."

"It's maths!" shouts one. And now this is the second time I have seen Clyde lose his cool. Something about this issue has burrowed deep beneath his skin. His body goes very rigid. His cheeks are bright spots on his face. "It's not hocus-pocus, Arthur. It's not imaginary. It's just maths. And it's going to happen."

"You cannot know that," I say. "Not for certain. Nothing is inevitable."

The fury on the Clyde's face burns hotter. Burns brighter. The other two step away, step out of existence. It is just this one. This angry projected man, with his fists clenched, and his teeth bared.

"I am," he says.

And then the screen goes blank.

34

There's silence in the room for a moment.

Gran goes ahead and breaks it. "Holy hell, dudes."

Tabitha stands up shakily and wraps an arm around him. "Totally gone," she says, staring at the screen.

I can't tell if she's talking about the versions, or their minds, or Clyde in general. And then I realize that this means there's nothing left. The versions were the last remnants of him. And they're gone. Clyde is dead.

Except he's alive. And he wants us dead.

I can't sort it out in my head. The truth of it all. How I feel about it. There's not time for that. I need to focus on here and now.

"The door?" I ask Felicity.

"I don't know how many times I can almost kill us all with ricochets before you accept it's not going to open," she says.

I close my eyes. Try to find a center that will hold. The stench of the rapidly rotting bodies doesn't help. I can hear gunfire and screams swirling outside.

A hundred feet below surface level. A door that's sealed and impenetrable. And we need a way out. The center isn't holding.

I open my eyes. I'm staring at one of the bullet holes Felicity accidentally shot in the wall. I could have sworn I started out facing the door. The sense of vertigo—

Staring at one of the bullet holes in…

"The wall," I say.

"What?" Tabitha looks at me as if I may be as far gone as Version 2.0.

"Bullet holes," I say. "In it. The door is impenetrable, but the wall isn't. We can make holes in it."

Gran grins. "The air ducts, man. We find them, we can crawl through them. Get out of here."

"Exactly." I turn to Tabitha. "Can you get us the blueprints for this place?"

I'm still getting the you're-funny-in-the-head look. I mirror it.

"Blueprints," she says. "On local server?"

"Yes."

"On local server infected by 2.0?"

Oh shit. She goes online and we lose our one electronic resource. And we still don't get the blueprints.

"OK," I concede. "No blueprints." I press my hands to my forehead. Think, Arthur. Think. How do we find the ducts?

Felicity points her gun and shoots. Fourteen trigger pulls, as she turns in a slow, controlled circle. Fourteen holes in the plastic-steel walls.

"Thought that might get us started," she says.

It strikes me that Felicity's penchant for casual violence may have been previously masked by Kayla's presence.

Gran paces the room, putting his hand to each hole. At the sixth he says, "I got cold air, dudes."

Which means it's time to make that hole bigger. Felicity's pistol isn't much use for that, and I have the feeling we should be conserving ammunition. This is where we could really use Kayla with her sword skills. In the meantime, I have to improvise.

"Flip the table," I say to Gran.

"What?"

"He told you to flip the table," Felicity snaps.

Gran blinks then does as he's told.

"You better have a bloody plan," Felicity says, quieter.

"Getting there."

The table legs are long, straight, metal. Perfect. At least they would be if they weren't bolted to the tabletop. Then I remember.

"Multi-tool," I say to Tabitha. The tool she was using to pick away at her laptop while she was sitting in the hospital bed being bandaged.

"Break it and you're a dead man," she says as she hands it to me.

I quickly unbolt the table leg, heft the thing, and slam it into the bullet hole.

The hole isn't large, but by the fifth blow, I've widened it enough to get the table leg in. Then it's just a case of levering the thing back and forth. Gran comes and helps me and together we see-saw the thing up and down widening the hole, tearing at the metal.

It is not fast work. And how long did 2.0 give us? Ten minutes? Perhaps. If the Area 51 employees take a long time to kill. God. I try not to think about that.

It must have been at least five minutes. The hole Gran and I have widened must be about a foot in diameter now. Not big enough.

"Get me another table leg," I say to Tabitha. She must be feeling desperate because she just complies.

Thirty seconds later, there's another table leg in my hand and I start battering at the hole. It's a little like wielding a short, badly balanced sword, I realize. Nothing you'd really want in a fight, but I know the right strokes to use to apply pressure and widen the hole.

Another minute and the air duct lies exposed, running vertically through the wall. A gaping hole offers access.

"Up or down?" asks Gran.

"Is up viable?" I ask. "Because if it is, that's the way to the exit, I believe. Going down feels like working our way deeper into the problem."

"I'll give it a shot." Gran ducks into the hole, just the lower half of his legs still sticking into the room. Then he bunches his knees and jumps. His feet kick, once, twice, and then are hauled out of sight.

"There's a lip," he says. "Not too bad a jump."

"Come on then."

I give Tabitha a boost first. She's nearly a foot shorter than Gran and me. I hear her breath of relief as Gran's hand clasps hers and she's hauled out of sight.

Now it's just Felicity and me in the room. Kensington and the other scientists are just purple stains on the floor. She kisses me hard on the lips.

"We're going to be OK," she says. I think it's for both our benefits. "We're going to keep finding solutions. We're going to fix this."

I nod. "Never give up hope." She kisses me before I give her a boost up.

Then, for a moment, it is just me in the room, in the scene of our most recent failure. Perhaps things can only get better now. Perhaps.

I tuck the table leg into a belt loop and follow Felicity up into darkness.

35

The air duct is tight and narrow. It also smells a lot of Felicity's shoes. That, admittedly, may be because they're six inches from my nose. For all her positive features, Felicity Shaw has yet to develop rose-scented sweat.

As daring escapes go, this one is a little bit heavy on continually banging my elbows and knees and a little light on going faster than speeds that would make a snail scoff. We shuffle forward, Felicity occasionally asking Tabitha to refrain from kicking her in the face.

"You know where we are?" I call forward to Gran. As the elbow banging hasn't attracted the attention of any Clyde zombies yet, I go ahead and assume they're not going to be bothered by the occasional shout.

"Not spent that much time in here," Gran calls back, "so, you know, me and the layout not one hundred percent simpatico, but, like, above where we were."

It occurs to me that maybe Tabitha is serially attracted to the lexically challenged.

Another thought occurs. "You know those security countermeasures Version 2.0 mentioned?" I say. "Are any of those in the ventilation system?"

"Erm…" Gran says. "Not really my department, dude."

"Would make sense," Tabitha says with what strikes me as way too much matter-of-factness. Especially as the main security countermeasures we know about so far involve very large bullets.

"What sort of countermeasure exactly might make sense to you?" Felicity asks. She at least sounds appropriately concerned.

"Noise sensors. Motion sensors. Heat sensors. Thermal imaging. Pressure sensors."

Which is a nice way of saying we're screwed. Except, "Wouldn't we have set something like that off by now?"

"Depends. Spacing. Paranoia levels. Not near a point of ingress so—"

Suddenly the duct is flooded with very red light.

"So, like, about this far apart?" Gran asks.

Oh balls.

"We need an exit!" I shout in a startling display of stating the obvious.

Felicity's gun is very, very loud in the tight space.

"Probably, like, not quite a big enough hole," Gran says.

"Working on it!" she snaps. The gun goes off again. My ears start ringing like they're the phone and I'm the lazy secretary. There's banging and crunching from up ahead.

The red light intensifies, darkens. I have the feeling it might be getting hotter in here.

"Kick!" Felicity shouts, presumably to Tabitha. Then, "Not me, you idiot!"

More banging. More crashing. A worrying hissing sound.

"Some sort of green gas heading toward me," Gran says as if commenting on the overcrowding at a local beach.

The gun fires again.

"My fucking foot!" Tabitha yells.

The only reply is more banging, and then a tearing sound, and then, a yell, and a scream, and the duct tilts, and suddenly my face is plowing into Felicity's boots, and I am scrabbling at the walls, but they are smooth as steel and blank, and the seam is too narrow to grab, and I am falling.

My face breaks my fall.

My face breaks.

My nose is a smear of pain across my face. Blood, hot and wet all over my face. I come up on my hands, grunting and spitting. My teeth hurt. How the hell is that possible?

"Move! Now!" It's Felicity. Her voice cutting through my pain.

I blink. Where the hell am I? It turns out to be a corridor. Above us, an ugly tear mars the smooth wall. The duct spills out of splayed plastic.

And filling the corridor...

"Clyde zombies," Gran says, "at, you know, top of the clock. Big and little hand... Oh, fuck it dude." He opens fire.

Six Clyde zombies stumble toward us, slowed by poorly coordinated limbs. Their jerking progress looks like it should be slow, but they close the distance with surprising speed. Their gums are pulled back in rictus smiles. Their throats work, a dry clacking noise.

Gran's bullet plows through one's arm. The shot spins it around but doesn't drop it. It keeps coming, thick dark blood oozing from the wound. One of them opens its mouth, the grimace of its smile becoming a leer. Its mouth is full of purple fur that leaks down its chin, staining its blood-spattered work shirt. Black tendrils grow out of the corners of its eyes.

"Shit!" Gran fires again. A solid gut shot. It slows the Clyde zombie down for all of six seconds.

Felicity opens fire too. Bullets graze shoulders, crack clavicles. One head shot opens a creature's skull with concussive force. The body drops away, ending in a ragged stump of neck. The spine glints white in the ruined flesh.

But they are too damn close.

I yank the table leg out of my belt loop and set to work. It's a dull, blunt thing. But while I cannot slice a leg in two, I can crack the hell out of some bones.

My initial gambit leaves two on the floor. They try to scrabble up as I roll away, but the extra joints I've put in their legs don't give them much leverage. I come up, but I've misjudged the distance and one is inches from my face. I feel its hand claw at my gut.

I expect some sort of terrible cold. The mockery of life from the grave. Instead the skin of the creature is almost scaldingly hot. I recoil, lashing out blindly with the table leg. The point of it jams into the thing's mouth, keeps pushing back.

It is like pushing my finger into a peach. Soft reluctant resistance. Then the head detonates.

Brain and bone cover me. Black blood mixing with the mess still spilling from my nose.

And God, and Jesus, and even the Holy Ghost if he's hanging about, I hope with everything I have that that crap is not toxic, doesn't transmit the spores. I cannot become a mindless fungus man today. I cannot. I have weekend plans.

Something grabs me by the collar. I spin, still spitting out chunks of my last opponent. An ugly purple-white face lunges at me. My table leg whirls through the air.

But the zombie is collapsing before I connect. Felicity stands behind it, gun held in outstretched arms, its barrel smoking. Apparently one bullet to the torso may not put one of these bastards down, but ten to the chest will rupture enough internal organs to slow them.

Then one of the ones whose leg I broke gets an arm around my ankles and attempts to enact revenge.

I go down hard. My nose takes more punishment. I do some screaming, and flail about with more wild abandon than I think Kayla would really approve.

When I come back to my senses, there's another guy with an exploded head lying next to me, and I am covered in way more filth.

"Jesus." I stand. I am drenched in other people's blood. It's soaking through the shoulders of my jacket. I feel like throwing up but that would be yet another undesirable fluid on my clothes. I choke the urge down.

Gran and Felicity's guns are smoking. Tabitha is crouched behind her laptop, which is spattered and smeared with the same crap as my face. There are six bodies on the ground. Three are missing their heads.

"Are you OK?" Felicity looks at me, concerned. "Come here."

I smile, despite the pain. It is nice to have someone care for—

Her hand snakes out, grabs my nose, and wrenches it back into place. I bellow.

"It'll heal better this way," she says as I punch a wall. "So I can at least always love you in a really shallow way."

I think it says something about our relationship that despite everything, despite the pain, and the bodies, and the general hopelessness of our situation, what really catches my attention is, "Did you just use the L-word?"

Felicity Shaw, director of MI37, the British government's answer to all that goes bump in the night, does not quite meet my eyes. She opens her mouth as if to say something, and then just blushes.

"Jesus. Fuck." Tabitha shakes her head. Her disapproval might carry more weight if she wasn't just coming out from cowering behind her laptop.

"We need to move, dudes," Gran says.

It's probably good there's an outsider to MI37 here. Someone to sit above all the soap opera crap and get us on our feet and moving.

"Where are the sleeping quarters?" I ask. I knew when I went into the computer lab this morning, but the geography seems foreign now. There's a lot more smoke and dead bodies than there were then.

"One floor down," Gran says. "We need to go, like, up and out, man."

"My sword," I say.

Felicity wraps an arm around me. "Do you need it? You just killed three men with a table leg."

I am not sure if I'm more concerned by the fact that I did that or that Felicity seems to be a little bit turned on by it.

But it is a flaming sword…

Jesus, there are dead bodies on the floor rotting at an unnatural pace, and my biggest concern is the absence of my cool flaming sword?

"Let's get out of here," I say.

"Suppose you can't be a dumbass every decision you make." It's not exactly approval in Tabitha's voice but it's nice to know we're on the same page.

We head down the corridor toward a short flight of

stairs. I take point along with Gran. Felicity has the rear, her pistol drawn, but she has to be running low on ammunition at this point. Even her handbag can't hold *that* many clips.

Gran and I brace ourselves at the top of the stairs, where they turn at a right angle.

"You ready?" he asks.

"On three. One, two—"

We both turn on the appropriate number. There is a moment where I get to glimpse the bodies, the blood spattering the walls, the dull red light, and then the whine of speeding barrels registers.

We duck back just as bullets smash into the wall. One of the wall-mounted guns Clyde mentioned blazes to life. I swear I felt the heat of lead ripping past me. If my heartbeat gets any faster I'll be able to set a techno track to it.

"Not that way," I suggest.

We double back, take a left, a right. There are signs of wilted fungal growths hanging limply against the wall. Purple stains stretch around them. In some places there are larger stains on the floor. The remains of zombies the uninfected members of Area 51 must have killed.

There are bodies that haven't rotted too. Bodies with bullet holes. Bodies with bite marks. The whole place reeks of rot and copper. I want to spit the stink out of my mouth where it seems to sit like a cloud.

"Fucking massacre," Tabitha says.

And she's right. This was done with remarkable, brutal speed. A completely clandestine, supposedly impregnable CIA installation deep beneath New York City, and Version 2.0 took it out in minutes. How long will it take him to take out an unprepared, defenseless city? How long have we got? A handful of hours, maybe?

How long does the whole human race have? Are we all still alive tomorrow? How wide is the attack he can coordinate?

I don't have any answers. Just gnawing fear.

Gran opens a door for us to go through, then slams it again. He puts a hand over his mouth. When he's recovered, all he will say is, "Not that way."

"Where are the zombies?" I ask. This place is too quiet.

"Maybe they break down," Felicity suggests. "After a few minutes or so the fungus is too much for them to sustain."

It's testament to how bad things look that I'm hoping that is true. When a higher body count is better for you, things have definitely gone awry.

Jesus, these were people. Were people with families and lives. All of them. And I've killed… Jesus, I killed three of them with a table leg. And I know it was too late for them. That their minds were gone, that they were fungal monsters, but… God. I killed people today. And it's not the first time I've done it. But the line seemed clearer back then. The side of it I stood on.

We reach the end of a corridor, and Gran points. "That door is, like, to a stairwell."

We eye it. It looks calm and innocent as doors go. Almost too innocent. "Exactly where I'd put a security countermeasure," I say. "In a stairwell."

"Me too." Gran nods.

There is a pause. "We have to risk it anyway, don't we?" I say.

"I think we're going to have to." Felicity nods.

"Fucking rat trap." Tabitha appears to be reaching

her breaking point. "Doesn't have to kill us. Just starve us. Coward's way."

Considering there's a decent chance Version 2.0 is listening to us, I'm not sure I would have gone as far as insulting him directly. Still, there is no peep out of any of the speakers. No rationalizations or apologies. Just silence.

Like in a tomb, for example.

"Screw it," I say, "I'll open the bloody door."

I stand to one side, so that, when I open it, any bullets that emerge flow past me rather than through me.

I am not quite as prepared for a zombie horde.

36

They surge through the doorway—a struggling, seething mass. Bodies upon bodies. Like a blown pressure valve. Fighting to get past each other. Grunting and hissing. Their hair falling out. Milky eyes. Black eyes. Fungus spilling from their mouths, ears, nostrils. Creeping out from under their fingernails. They smear themselves on the doorframe as they pour toward us.

Bloody zombies.

Well, not zombies exactly. Not risen from the grave, feasting on human brain matter. Not a seventies commentary on consumer culture. But as far as mindless automatons seeking to kill me go, zombies is close enough.

There's just enough time to hear someone scream, "Shit!" and then I'm running. Feet mashing against the floor. Only ahead of the zombies by merit of the fact that I don't have to cram myself through a doorway. There is no bottleneck for me, only the full flood of panic and the open corridor.

Felicity, Gran, and Tabitha have a good head start. I am reminded of the adage that you don't have to run faster than the bear, just faster than your friend.

I'm not the one running faster.

We round one corner, another. We are just ahead of the pack. Left. Right. Left again. Grunting and cawing screeches after us. Right. Right. Only the hindrance of their stuttering limbs keeping us ahead now. Left. My breath ragged in my chest. Left. I'm still trailing the pack. The weakest of the herd. Right again. This place is a maze. Left. Left.

"The hell," I manage, "we going?"

"Just…" Gran flails his arm. "Away." He sounds no better than I feel. Felicity clutches her side. I risk a glance over my shoulder. The bastards are not slowing down.

Shit. Shit. Think.

Suddenly something familiar. Something that locates me. The tear in the plastic wall. Where we emerged from the air duct. This is back the way we came. Back to the beginning. To the…

"Want to do something really stupid?" I gasp.

"No." I'm surprised Tabitha wastes the breath on me.

"Next left," I pant. "Then right. Then wait at the corner."

"Wait?" Felicity looks at me like I'm insane. There's a chance she's right.

"We have to let them catch up before we go round the corner."

"Dude, are you, like… you know…" Gran pants. "Stress and its impacts."

We make the left. Thirty yards and then the right.

"We get to that corner, and we wait," I insist. "Then when I give the word, we turn and duck."

"Duck?"

I just nod. I don't want to give too much away. Because they'll object to the stupidity of my plan. But if it doesn't work it's at least a better way to die than being eaten alive.

We make the right. Sprint. Hit the end of the corridor. I hold up my hand. To my enormous relief, everyone stops.

We can hear the horde behind us. Not just their guttural moaning, but their limbs. Their bodies smacking off the wall. A wet squelching sound.

I double over, trying to catch my breath. My muscles start to freeze. Tabitha flirts with the corner, caught on the edge of indecision.

The horde rounds the bend.

They are hideous. A mindless stretch of fungus and man, blurring the line between flora and fauna. The same stuttering steps. Arms stretched out. Mouths pulled back. That moan, that grunting desire for us, for flesh.

Tabitha twitches. I grab her arm.

"We *have* to wait."

"Fucking crazy." Her eyes are wide and her breath coming fast.

They come on. Faster. Closer. The cawing clack of murder on what's left of their tongues.

"Seriously having issues with this plan now, dude," Gran says.

Just a little longer. Just a little longer.

I see one. Eyes wide. No white. Its teeth are black. It's wearing a jacket with shoulder pads. There's blood on its tie. It's almost on me,

"Arthur!" I think I just lost Felicity's confidence.

Just two more seconds.

The arm of the zombie is a yard away. A foot.

"Now!" I yell.

No one needs to be told twice. We burst around the corner.

Area 51's security countermeasures roar into life.

37

I duck, roll. With one hand I grab Felicity, the other Tabitha. I pull them down.

Zombies roar behind us.

Bullets from the ceiling-mounted machine gun scream overhead. We press faces to the floor as hot death streaks through the air.

With an explosive, horrendously wet thunder, the machine gun chews through our pursuers.

Slowly, slowly, we begin to crawl forward. The guns are at the end of the corridor. A thirty-yard, face-down crawl and the faintest prayer that there are enough zombies to keep the gun's automated targeting system occupied long enough for us to make it.

Halfway down the corridor. The zombies keep on coming. Because they're mindless zombies. It's sort of what they do. On and on they pour into the mouth of the guns in their desperation to get to us. The stink of their detonating bodies fills the air.

"Jesus," I hear Felicity mutter. I want to reach out and squeeze her hand, but the whole desperate race for survival thing is probably more of a priority.

Three-quarters of the way down the corridor.

"We've got to be running out those zombie dudes soon," Gran says.

I risk a backward glance. The carnage is awful. I

feel my gorge rise. Bodies stacked upon bodies. More zombies clambering over the stinking, rotting pile. On all fours. On two jerking legs. On fewer limbs as the bullets keep ripping into them. They ignore terrifying injuries—holes like fists open in their chests, spilling fluid behind them. The far end of the corridor looks like it's been painted by a goth with a Pollock fixation.

Five yards to go. Four.

And suddenly silence. Another glance. Everything at the far end of the corridor is still.

Oh shit.

I risk a few inches of forward movement.

The machine gun barrels—oiled, black things, a foot long each, perforated with circular vents—protrude from a gray circular device that makes me think of Han Solo and the *Millennium Falcon*. Its servos whine loudly as I move. They fall silent as I freeze.

Four yards to go.

It's not aiming at me yet. It's aiming over my head at the back of the corridor.

How long will it take to re-aim when I start moving again?

How long will it take us to cover four yards?

"When I say go—" I glance at Felicity then at Gran and Tabitha, "we sprint for the corner."

Felicity swallows. "All right."

Tabitha adds, "Your plan is balls."

She may have a point, but I think we're twenty-six yards further down this corridor than we might have got without my plans.

"OK," I say, "three, two—"

"Wait," Gran interrupts.

"What?"

"Nothing really, dude. Just, you know, wanted to take another moment to enjoy the whole being alive thing."

I take a breath. I look at everybody and they seem disinclined to interrupt. "One. Go!"

We sprint.

The machine gun reacts like we tazed it, jerking spastically to life. Bullets stitch a path up the corridor behind us. Boom. Boom. Boom. I can hear each bullet leaving the machine gun barrels. How much goddamn ammunition do they put in these things? The barrels are almost pointing straight down. I leap, breath bursting, legs feeling achingly slow, my heartbeat the only fast thing in the world.

And then we are beneath them, beneath the mounting, out of range.

Alive.

For just a little bit longer. Alive.

This seems as good a time as any to collapse.

38

TWO STORIES UP

"Oh dude, it's seriously like they're taking the piss now."
Gran yanks his head back from around the corner.

Beyond it lie the twin doors that lead out to Area 51's hidden garage. Right in front hangs another machine gun. From the piled bodies and abundant fungal stains it seems it has been thoroughly enjoying the killing field spread out before it.

"You're sure there's no other way out?" I say for the seventeenth time.

"I know, man." Gran shakes his head. "Total fire safety violation."

My ability to be flippant runs headlong into my need to survive the next five minutes. "You know we have to get out of here, like, now," I snap. "Who knows what the hell is happening up on the surface of this city."

Felicity lays a hand on my shoulder. "It's OK, Arthur. Each thing in order. We'll deal with that when we get to it."

She's using her calming voice. But I don't need to be calm. Version 2.0 has us up shit creek, and he's confiscated all our paddles. I need everybody to get their crap together and—

OK, she's right. I need to be calm.

"There has to be another way out of here," I say,

focusing on what we can do. "Another air duct or something."

"Yeah," Tabitha grunts. "So much fun last time. Being gassed."

"So concentrate on the 'or something' then," I suggest. You can never please everybody.

I start moving, try to burn off the stress a little. I peer through a nearby door. Rows and rows of gleaming metal cabinets with a brushed steel finish. The large fungal stains smeared over three of them does rather spoil the effect though.

"Nothing here," Felicity says, leaning over my shoulder, slipping her hand into mine.

The next room we try resembles Mercurio's lab in New Jersey—long benches and microscopes. I rifle through the drawers in search of sulphuric acid or some other chemical that could help us out. White Out is the most lethal one I find. I fear the errors here may be beyond the bottle's limits.

"Never thought I'd have to break out of work." Gran shakes his head. "Thought I might back when I worked at the Pentagon. But never here."

"Pentagon?" Tabitha asks him.

"Oh, yeah, totally," he says. "I was all like secret service for a president or two. That was a real downer of a job."

Wait. What? Gran? Former secret service? Really?

"The president?" I manage. "You?"

"Yeah." Gran shakes his head. "Did not see, like, totally eye to eye on a bunch of stuff most days. Plus both first ladies totally hit on me, so, you know, that was a bummer."

If Gran is suited for one thing less than being a

CIA agent, it is being a member of the secret service. He must be terrifyingly good at something to keep swinging this stuff.

We push through the next door.

"Shit." Tabitha says. "Holy variety."

It's another storage room. That's the simplest way to describe it. Except it's storing…

"What are they?" I ask Gran.

Row upon row of gleaming metal bodies stand before us. They are approximately humanoid, stand nearly six feet tall. Narrow legs and arms bulge at the joints. The torsos are configured like hour glasses. Each one has a blank metal head, which appear to have been polished to the extent that some rather vain CIA agent can have an army of head-height mirrors.

"Oh, like, slave droids." Which is apparently a normal thing to say here. Then Gran catches himself. "Though not, like, slave in that way. Just, you know, no downloaded personality. Run off the mothership." He catches himself again. "That's, like, the cloud, you know. Steve Jobs' ghost in the machine flicking through your summer pictures looking for the one where something slipped out. At least, you know, that's how the tech boys explained the cloud to me. Except they call it the mothership." He shrugs. "We are Area 51. Be sort of wrong to not have at least one alien joke name."

"So someone would control these bodies by… remote control?" I ask, wanting to make sure I actually followed that.

"Totally." Gran nods. "'Cept since the wireless network started doing its whole siesta thing, they've been pretty much putting their feet up and snoozing. The goddamn life, man."

I look at the soulless dead things in front of me. It does not exactly seem like they are enjoying "the life."

"What sort of punishment can that body take?" Felicity asks, ever practical. But she's right, if we could get one of these things going then there's a chance we could get it close enough to the gun to do some damage.

"Oh, decent amount," Gran says. "Originally they were all, like, military specced and ready to run and gun and all that sort of groovy thing. But it turns out that your average soldier is not overly keen on the whole mechanical man thing. Really gives some of them the fear. Very low team functionality when you introduce one. Buzz killers. That's what we called them. You know, because of the soldiers' attitude. And the body count. Casualty-orama." He grimaces. "Anyway that led us to surplus-orama here. We use them for just, like, general hazardous to health stuff."

Somewhere in there, I think, was the answer I was hoping for.

Tabitha is one step ahead of me, though. She uses the extra space to tread all over my dreams.

"Won't work," she says. And even pre-empting my crestfallen question, supplies the why: "No personality to download."

The robots stand there. Soulless. Useless. It's a shame, I think, that the Clyde versions have become evil bastards trying to kill us. We could really use a hand from one of them right now.

That thought dislodges another somewhere in the back of my head. It niggles at me as we leave the room. I try to grasp it but it eludes me.

"Do you have the building blueprints in storage anywhere?" Felicity asks. "That way we could chart out the air ducts. It would take a while to clear all the gas countermeasures, but if that's all there is then we could be out of here in twenty-four hours or thereabouts."

Gran looks pained for a moment. Tabitha opens her mouth to say something dismissive.

Then it comes to me. That niggle. A serendipitous penny dropping into my outstretched hand.

"Version 2.1," I say.

"What?" Felicity asks.

"What?" Gran echoes.

But Tabitha says nothing. Which I think means my niggle is right.

"Version 2.1," I repeat. "I had Clyde Version 2.2. Felicity had 2.3. Kayla 2.4. Devon had 2.5 but she destroyed it. But you," I point to Tabitha. "You had Version 2.1. And I thought you destroyed your version, just like Devon did. But back in England, Smythe, the diplomat, he said that you hadn't."

This proclamation has multiple effects. Felicity's mouth, for example, forms a little round "o" and her eyebrows shoot up. Gran looks like someone has just introduced lemon juice to the exit-only part of his digestive tract.

And Tabitha… Well, I imagine it is the face an asteroid wears the moment before it impacts on the poor defenseless planet.

But I go ahead and stare right back.

Slowly, not once relenting in her gaze, Tabitha reaches below the neckline of her black T-shirt and starts to pull out a very thin silver chain. She pulls it over her head, wrapping it around her fist once, twice. And then, finally pulling it all free, she reveals what she had resting over her heart.

A small, gray, plastic flash drive.

Everyone is very still and very quiet. Tabitha breaks her death stare with me and looks down at her open palm. I try to read the emotions flickering there. She locks them down as fast as they wrestle to the surface. And there are just so many.

Finally she holds it out to me with a simple, "Fuck you."

Clyde. The last Clyde. Really and truly the last one now. Because... well, Jesus, there are people who are nothing but purple stains on the floor. There are bodies piled up. There's all the evidence anyone needs that the Clyde I knew is dead.

Except...

One last copy. One last chance. Held out to me in Tabitha's palm.

I take it.

And part of me doesn't want to do anything with that flash drive. I just want to keep on holding it. Don't let reality spoil it, corrupt it, overwrite it, or turn it into another psychopath trying to kill me.

"So," Gran says, his voice hesitant, "dudette. That's, like, your ex-boyfriend you were carrying around with you?"

"The time," Tabitha snaps. "This is so not it."

Felicity has more practical concerns. "Do we have a way to get it into one of those machines without a wireless connection?"

I look at Tabitha. She wouldn't have given the flash drive to me if she could not. She wouldn't have revealed this part of herself if this was about anything less than survival.

"Hey," I say, not quite daring to reach out and pat

her arm. "Don't worry. There's a decent chance he'll get immediately blown to pieces anyway."

TEN MINUTES OF BITTER ELECTRONIC ENGINEERING LATER

"Done," Tabitha says. She stands, rubbing a slightly oily hand against the small of her back. "Flash drive. Hardwired now. Part of it." She reaches out with the screwdriver and twists a screw out. A panel of buttons and switches appears. She puts her finger on the big red one, then looks at me. Straight at me.

"Don't want to do this."

She'll do it. I know she will. But it will cost her something. And she wants me to know that too.

I nod at her. And I hope she knows that it will cost me something too.

She presses the button. It's stiff and when it gives way to pressure it does so with a satisfying clunk. Tabitha pulls away like she's been electrocuted.

For a moment nothing happens. Then—

"Oh, this is not what I expected at all."

The robot's head cocks to one side. Its shoulders jerk up and down in rapid-fire shrugs.

"Wait, what operating system is this?" says the voice. It is tinny and flat, emanating from some speaker hidden within the depths of the droid's head. "God, I knew I should have studied more Linux…" Then the head jerks around and looks straight at us.

"Arthur?" it says. "Tabby? Felicity?" It looks around then seems to focus on Gran. "Either you're not Kayla," it says, "or I'm not the only one having issues keeping my consciousness in one body. So, either I'm pleased to meet you or you look lovely. I think. Probably." Its head spins a full three hundred and sixty degrees. "Oh, that's weird," it finishes.

Yes. *That's* the part that's weird.

I try to cast my mind back. To when this version was created. Back to when Clyde and Tabitha were dating. Back before there was any hint of the evil lurking within Clyde. Back before the funeral and the US and Gran.

God, this is going to be difficult to explain.

"Gone evil," Tabitha snaps at the droid. "Version 2.0 has. All other versions too. Trapped us in a US facility. We put you in a bullet-proof body. Need you to get shot and get us out." She looks away for a moment, then her eyes snap back, relentless. She thumbs at Gran. "Dating him now."

OK, so that's one way to do it.

The silver droid is perfectly still. In the way that only something mechanical can be. Inhumanly slow. When I stare at its face, all I see is Tabitha's reflection, distorted in the curve of its polished paneling. No sense for what might be going on beneath the surface.

"Oh," it says, after a while.

It is a desperately sad word. A very human emotion despite the very inhuman shell. And perhaps at least one of the actual flesh and blood people here should show some humanity.

I step forward. Step up, perhaps. I put my hand on the droid's shoulder. Clyde's shoulder. It feels cold beneath my palm. "We can talk later," I say. "I promise. There will be time. Just not now."

It nods slowly.

"That's…" it says, and there is something of Clyde's plummy tones in its electronic ones, "a fair bit to process, though I suppose Tabitha and I were technically never dating. That was another version of me and her. Very different. And if, well… you mentioned the whole turning evil thing, which, well, a relative term, I suppose. At least that's what I've always felt. All sorts of ends and means questions wrapped up in the whole moral relativity thing. But if 2.0 is ostensibly doing the whole nefarious and scheming thing… And I suppose there's no reason for you to lie. Except I'd like it if you were. But, well… of course I'm evil if you say I am. Well, not me. Him. Who is me. I'll call him 2.0. That'll be easier. Well, for me at least. Hopefully for you too. Nomenclature is always such a tricky little devil. Two horns, pointy fork, propensity for naming things. That's how I picture him anyway. But what I meant to say, I suppose, was that, you know, all things being as they are—evil 2.0, et cetera—totally up for kicking my own arse. And good on you Tabby for finding a better man than me. Or better than this other me. Can't be surprised you did. Always did question your taste in men. Glad to see it's improving." He shakes his head. "Did you say something about me needing to get shot?"

And suddenly it clicks. Somewhere in my head and somewhere in my chest.

It feels like Clyde is back.

Not a robot. Not an image on a screen. But Clyde himself. And yes, he's in a robot, but there is something about him being physical, and tangible, and right in front of me.

From Gran's expression I'm not sure how he feels about that, but both Felicity and I are smiling.

He looks at me. I see myself looking right back in his reflective visage. "Hey," I say.

"Hello, Arthur," he says, and there's undeniable

warmth in his voice. "Been a while. Well, for me, anyway. I guess this must all be a bit confusing. I'm confused. Not an unusual state for me, of course. Sort of my natural environment. You'd think I'd get used to it. But I don't. So if you have any clarity to offer on this whole being shot thing, then that wouldn't be amiss at all. Love it, in fact."

"Sure," I say. I'm not quite sure if the smile belongs on my face or not. I feel quite self-conscious about it. "There's a door we want to get through. Except there's an automated gun turret in front of it that targets movement. And the computer system is protected by three other versions of you who have been overwritten by Evil-you. So there are like four evil yous. Which really sucks."

"Wow," Clyde shakes his head. "I am really all about being evil now. I had no idea." He shakes his metal head. "You load yourself on a flash drive for a few weeks and everyone goes evil. It's like that time I went hiking in the Lake District and when I came back the Spice Girls had happened. Can't help but wonder what you could have done to stop it if you'd been a little more present." He shrugs.

"We really will talk about it later," I say. And I want to. It's like someone has hit the reset button on my friend and I have a chance to do everything over. Make everything right. I want to take that opportunity.

Except I want to do it sometime after I get my arse out of this hellhole.

39

"OK." Clyde nods toward the corner and the machine gun. "The gun's targeting is sensitive to movement, you said? Let's see how slow this body can go."

Clyde glides up to the corner leading to the door out. The body moves smoothly, with almost cat-like grace. MI37 really does have access to some very cool toys.

Gran sidles up to me. "Dude, you really think this will work?"

"Surprisingly good hearing on this thing," Clyde calls to us.

"Of course it will work," I say. Nice and loud. And with far more confidence than I actually feel.

"Bullshit meter works OK too," Clyde calls back.

Clyde reaches the corner. He hesitates. Then he shakes his head. "Well," I hear him say, "it was fun being alive for five minutes."

Then, inch by inch, he creeps out into the corridor.

And isn't shot.

He raises one foot. It takes about thirty seconds. I almost can't make out the actual movement. But then his foot is in the air, gliding slowly forward.

And he isn't shot.

Ever so slowly the foot descends.

BOOM.

Clyde flies backwards through the air. He lands, a

crashing tangle of steel limbs, tumbling over and over, clatter and smashing over the gray floor. Bullets stitch a path after him.

Clyde lies very still, arms and legs splayed. Silence returns. I can make out a great dent in his chest where the bullet struck him. But the metal isn't torn. There is no hole. The armor held up, at least to a certain extent. Something vital might have been crushed, but there's a chance...

"Clyde," I hiss. "Clyde, are you...?"

"Dented?" asks Clyde.

My breath whistles out of me. I am acutely aware that we have no back-ups of Clyde now.

"So I'm, like, guessing," Gran says, "that the whole stealthy thing is not so righteous."

"Experiments so far do seem to suggest that sort of hypothesis," Clyde agrees.

"Groovy," Gran says. Which seems a touch inaccurate. Though, I could see how Gran might find Clyde being shot again appealing.

"How many more hits like that could you take?" Felicity calls to Clyde. Which doesn't really set the right tone, I feel.

"Not wholly sure," Clyde answers, but being Clyde the answer doesn't end there. "They don't seem to have put the specs for this body in the hardwiring. Bit of a desolate wasteland in here actually when it comes to company. Just me, myself, and I. I mean not to disparage external company. Meatfolk such as yourself. Need to think of a better term for you than that, obviously. Maybe 'people.' That has sufficed up until now, I suppose. But I just mean, I can't even pick up a wireless signal, which is a bit on the atypical side."

Gran is studying the dent. "I'd guess the chassis would take two or three more hits before it gives, assuming the shooter's spacing isn't too tight."

"Well that sounds like fun now, doesn't it?" Clyde still hasn't stood up from where the machine gun knocked him.

"Get it over with," Tabitha growls.

Clyde lies still a moment longer. Then, "One way to figure this out." He whips an arm out in a blur. His metal body shrieks sideways toward us, parallel to the door. The machine gun roars, but he skids behind the protection of the corner before the tracking lines up. I hear bullets slamming into the wall.

Out of immediate danger, Clyde stands. I hear the faint whine of servos operating. "Not bad," he nods. He looks back at the corner. "Sort of thinking about doing the opposite of the slow thing. The fast thing you'd probably call it. Not to put words in anyone's mouth, but that does seem the obvious term. Even to a dunderhead such as myself."

Ignoring Clyde's word choice issues, I go ahead and ask him, "You think you can do it?"

Clyde's mirrored face is impossible to read. I see doubt, but it's my own.

"I know I'm new on this particular scene," Clyde says, "but I rather had the impression that whether I can or not might be sort of important."

"Sort of." I nod.

"Our regular 'sort of'?" he asks. "Fate of the world 'sort of' and all that?"

"And all that."

Clyde nods. I see my reflection bob up and down over curves of steel. "Doesn't really matter if I think I can or not then, does it? Got to go for it and hope for the best. Lie back and think of England and all that. Except, more run like the hounds of bloody hell are on my heels and think of England. Less of a popular saying, I realize, but more apt in this situation perhaps."

"I think you can do it," I say.

Clyde leans in conspiratorially. "Considering how things have gone for me recently," he says, "I would understand if you don't completely respect work advice from me. However, just as an observation—constructive criticism perhaps—there's a chance you might want to consider working on becoming a better liar if you want to get ahead in the whole bureaucracy thing."

He moves his head oddly, half shrugs, and then says, "Bugger. There is no way to wink in this thing."

And then, before I can respond, he's off. Just a blur of silver steel.

It's not Kayla fast. I think I've seen her approach the sound barrier. But Clyde is still fast enough that it would make a crossing guard wet herself.

He rounds the corner. The machine gun roars. It sounds like an auto wreck. Like Formula One cars armed with Uzis racing after each other around the track.

And then a great juddering scream of metal. An ugly sound, but profound somehow. Something giving way that was never meant to do so.

And then the gun is silent.

For a moment we all stand very still.

"Clyde?" I call. "Clyde?"

Nothing. Silence.

A grinding sound breaks it. Sparks crackle. At first I think it must be Clyde dragging what's left of his body back to us but there is too much bass to the sound.

Something heavy is on the move.

Oh God. What fresh hell is this?

I don't really want to, but I ease up to the edge of the corridor, and peek.

For a moment, the scene makes no sense. The world is inverted: Clyde hangs from the ceiling; the machine gun lies on the floor. I think 2.0 must have done something to gravity.

Then I see the wires spilling from the gun turret's base. I see the ragged edges of the hole in the ceiling through which Clyde is dangling.

Then Clyde drops to the ground. Behind him, the doors to Area 51 begin to grind open.

"There you go," he says. "Lot of fuss over nothing." He shrugs.

And, God, it is good to have him back.

40

A HUNDRED FEET STRAIGHT UP

As the car we've liberated from the Area 51 parking lot crests the lip of the exit ramp, white light floods the vehicle. The winter sun—bright, sharp, and sheer—slices through our eyeballs like a Friday night psychopath high on the happy juice.

There's a chance that witnessing a government facility become a mass grave has affected my metaphors.

"Oh shit, man!" Gran yells from the driver's seat and mashes the brake so hard he almost punctures the car's floor. Sitting in the passenger seat, my head bounces off the dashboard and then the door window as the car slews round.

"No. No. No," Gran repeats, his words slowly accelerating, becoming one giant slew of syllables. "Nonononononono." He slams his fists on the horn and the sound blares.

I blink, scrape at my eyes, try to free them of the momentary blinding.

And then I succeed. I try to put the blindness back.

Manhattan. New York City. The jostling thriving urban jungle. Concrete and steel cast in a twisting testament to man's ambition, avarice, and ability. New York City. The capital of the world. The bustle and animosity of eighteen million people crammed into a tiny island and forced to choke on taxi fumes and outrageous prices.

It's gone.

The buildings are there. After the initial shock I see them now. The bones of this place are still intact. But they are... hidden. They lurk beneath a deep layer of green. Plants tower everywhere. Trees have smashed through windows. Ivy has grown in great sweeps across brownstones. Kudzu envelops doorways. Lilies cover rooftops. Vines trail from street lamps. Trunks rupture the asphalt. Cars are barely recognizable beneath moss and lichen.

It's as if the urban jungle just forgot the whole urban part. And damnit, I really liked that part.

Bits of building lie in ruin. Trees have punched the corners off buildings. Vines have tightened like Amazonian constrictors around façades and lamp posts. Roots have ripped up through the street, churning the tarmac into a ruin. Our car bounces up and down as it grinds to a halt over the uneven surface.

Gran has graduated from "No," to "Shit." Still the same blur of words though. "Shitshitshitshitshit."

It's Version 2.0. He has made his move already. We're too late. Again.

I suddenly remember the list of web sites he pillaged. Infrastructure. Emergency responses. Homeland Security. And it hits me. This is more than just senseless aggression. This is a tactic. I'm sure of it. This has intended consequences. This has fail safes. As epic as this is, it's only the beginning.

The beginning of humanity's ending.

We've come close to the end of the world before, but we've never crossed over the line. Never got into full post-apocalyptic mode. Because that's what this feels like. The apocalypse.

Version 2.0 has caused the apocalypse. And I've had a beer with him.

Shit. I'm sitting in the same car as a version of him.

I look over my shoulder at robot Clyde, at 2.1 sitting in the back seat. He looks back at me.

"I did this?" he asks.

I nod, mutely.

"God," he says. "When you mentioned the whole going evil thing, you really didn't give me quite the sense of the scale of it all."

My tongue is dry in my mouth. "Really evil," I manage.

"It's a little passé now," he says, "but one is even tempted to use the prefix *über*."

"One is."

We're in shock, I think. We're trying to process something too big. Fortunately, though, that describes about fifty percent of what I do at my job. I have become relatively adept at operating with a blown mind.

"Let's assume all of New York looks this way," I say, even while my mind balks at the mental image. "He'll have gone for power centers. What's left standing? We need to work out what we have left. What we can fight with."

Fight. What the hell are we even fighting? We still don't have a clue where Version 2.0 is even located. We've got nothing except motive and so far all that's contributed to are my sleepless nights.

"Where is everybody?" Felicity is staring out of the car windows. The street is empty. No people. No animals.

I start thinking ugly thoughts about fertilizer. About

what's fueling all this growth. Jesus.

"Inside," Tabitha says, her voice a little too loud, a little too harsh. "In familiar places. Under desks. Somewhere they think is safe. Near the TV. The radio. Waiting for word."

Waiting for word. That's us. We're the word. Except what the hell do we say? *Buckle up, it's going to be a bumpy ride?*

"Gran," I snap. He's still deep in his litany of obscenity, sliding down the scale of curses. "Where do we go?"

He looks at me, and his eyes are full—just sorrow and loss. And I think about his family, his friends. How many people did he know in Manhattan? In the whole city. In the state? The country? I don't know where the outer limits of this thing lie.

"I..." he says. "I..." But he doesn't have an answer. I can see that, plain as I can see the ficus sprouting out of the middle of Broadway.

Felicity grabs his arm. Not to shake but to hold him tightly. He looks at her, still reeling.

"Basic training," she snaps. "Orientation." Her eyes are locked like laser-guided missiles onto his. "They told you about exit routes. About what to do in a National Emergency. They talked about 9/11 and the Taliban, hell they may even have mentioned an alien invasion. I don't know. I don't care. But how the hell do we get out of this fucking bear trap of a city?"

"I..." Gran says, and Felicity just goes right ahead and slaps him. The blow echoes around the car.

"Oooh," I hear Clyde breathe. Well... not breathe... but, whatever he does.

Gran squeezes his eyes shut, breathes through his

mouth. "Bridges are too exposed," he says. He's barely audible. I lean in to listen. "Too easy to hit. Stay off the bridges." He takes a deep breath. "Assess the tunnels. Lincoln then Holland. If secure proceed. If not find a boat. South Street ferry." He opens his eyes. And suddenly we have a CIA agent again. He looks back at Felicity, focuses. "Lincoln Tunnel," he says. "On the city's west side. We have to go there."

"Then put this thing in gear and go," Felicity says.

He puts the car in gear and we go.

41

It's only four blocks before we realize that Tabitha is full of shit.

The people of New York are not cowering beneath their desks. They are not in hiding. And they are certainly not waiting for us, their shining-white knights, to bring them word.

Instead, they look intent on doing us harm.

A great herd of them blocks Broadway. What must be several hundred people milling around. And I've heard New Yorkers accused of being unfriendly, but this is something else...

They are purple tongued. Black eyed. Something that isn't quite fur leaking out their nostrils, their mouths, climbing up their fingers from beneath their nails.

Clyde zombies.

Some stumble, bumping off each other, off trees, off the ruins of the street. Others, perhaps further gone into the vegetative state, stand stock still, staring blankly up. I see one whose face has given way to flowers in full bloom. Another—wearing the remains of a T-shirt proclaiming that he was once "Punk as fuck"—has a string of mushrooms sprouting up his arm.

I know I'm still having trouble processing all this because part of me is seriously trying to work out what the guy was doing wearing a T-shirt in

November. That's just madness.

Madness. Jesus. We are in the middle of detouring around a giant pine tree blocking Broadway, one of the most iconic pieces of tarmac in the world. It is time to recognize madness just got a much broader definition than some idiot's fashion decisions.

"We'll have to go around them." Gran nods at the zombies.

The George A. Romero fan in me is a little disappointed we're not going to pile through the crowd with chainsaws sticking out the windows, but Gran's suggestion is probably the sensible one.

"Which way?" Felicity scans the windows.

Gran flexes his fingers on the steering wheel. "Tunnels we want are on the west side, so…"

"Shit," Tabitha says, peering between the two of them and out the windshield.

Our eyes follow hers. Shit indeed. Staggering and stumbling the Clyde zombies may be, but they are not as stupid as you would hope someone who seems to be at least fifty percent vegetable matter might be. We've been spotted.

"Reverse?" Clyde suggests.

"Forward!" shouts Tabitha, who is apparently as gung ho about the zombpocalypse as I am. Gran, probably sensibly, ignores them both and cranks the steering wheel to the right.

The tires bounce over roots and the tail-end of the car slews drunkenly. We careen forward, the engine's horses finding their power and flinging distance between us and the horde staggering toward us. We're half a block away before the first one rounds the corner.

Then Tabitha says, "Double shit!"

"Oh my," Clyde adds for a bit of variety.

The horde was, apparently, not entirely limited to Broadway. They have leaked onto the next avenue over and are blocking our exit.

"OK dude, this might—" Gran starts, then cuts himself off using the handbrake and a large number of g-forces. I would ask him to finish his thought, but I'm busy having my face mashed against shatter-proof glass.

Our one-eighty complete, Gran guns the engine, and heads forward. But our path backwards is now clogged with the staggering, stumbling remnants of humanity. We are boxed in. Gran lifts his foot, glances in the rearview. "Triple shit," he says.

My mind accelerates as the car slows. Stopping is not an option. It can't be. Nothing good happens if this car stops. This is about speed and escape.

Man, I'd gotten away with not considering this for a fair while. I'd thought maybe I was a professional now, that I didn't have to fall back on movie clichés and Hollywood stupidity for survival, but seriously, *what would Kurt Russell do?*

Heart hammering in my throat, I reach my foot over the gear shift and stamp Gran's down on the accelerator.

The car bucks as if stung then races forward. Walk, to trot, to canter, to gallop, to a hundred-goddamn-miles per hour. Say what you like about the CIA, those boys and girls sure know how to turbo charge their engines.

"What the hell, dude?" Gran yells as his head snaps back.

"Oh crap sticks." I hear Felicity in the back seat, fumbling for her seatbelt.

"I don't mean to be a doubting Thomas," Clyde starts, his voice lilting as the car smashes up and down over the uneven surface, "or any kind of Thomas really, lovely people I'm sure, but just not my name. A doubting Clyde, I suppose, but—"

And then the first of the zombies impacts against the windshield.

Its head smashes against the glass and detonates. A massive purple smear streaks across our field of vision. Cracks radiate out.

"Quadruple shit!" Gran yells.

It's as if someone threw a can of paint over the windshield. We can see nothing. A second body smashes against the car. I hear its skull rebound against the bonnet. The dull thunk of something bouncing off a side panel. I try to convince myself that the bumps in the road are still just roots.

Gran hits the windshield wipers. Sprays cleaner fluid. Narrow streaks of visibility appear. There is something on the hood of the car. Its legs hang at ugly angles.

Gran tries to brake but my foot is still slammed down on his. The car slews left, right. The Clyde zombie flies off, over the roof and into the unknown. We smash through one body then another.

Jesus. How many of them have we taken down in the past five seconds? Clyde 2.0 doesn't need to eliminate what's left of the human race, he can just let us do it.

Gran straightens the car. We hit something else and my wing mirror flies away.

"The hell are we?" Tabitha asks.

"If I had wireless I might be able to get us a GPS signal," Clyde says as we plow through more bodies. Gran hunches over the steering wheel, peers desperately through the mess on the windshield. Smoke is coming from somewhere.

I crank down my window, stick my head out. Not my best idea.

The first thing I get is a mouthful of the smoke pouring out of the car's hood. Then I replace that with a mouthful of rotting fist.

The zombie clotheslines me. I'm not sure if it's a planned move or simply fortuitous. The car smashes into the creature and he flies into the air. His arm flails, claws over my mouth, and slams into my neck.

My head snaps back, smashes into the doorframe. The zombie, with either tenacity or really fortuitous physics, remains in place as its feet are shredded against the asphalt.

It turns, looks at me. Dead black eyes. It opens its mouth as if to speak. A tangle of white filaments, like tiny fibrous worms, spill out over its chin.

Despite the pressure on my throat, despite the wind smashing into my face, despite all I've seen in my career at MI37, I am still able to vomit.

That throws the bastard free at least. He disappears under our back tire.

I pull my head back in just in time to take another zombie in the face.

It bounces up over the hood, and smashes full-bodied into the windshield. The cracks in the glass have been growing, and apparently enough is enough. The windshield gives way with an ugly snap and the entire sheet of fracturing glass lands in my lap.

Gran takes the weight too and his hands fly off the wheel. The zombie, somehow still alive, snaps, snarls, and claws on the far side of the devastated glass. I watch its head lunge at me, bounce off the remaining framework of glass, and come back again.

Whatever solidity the windshield had, it is slowly being reduced to pebbles. The zombie keeps on coming. Keeps mashing hands and head at the glass. Fracture lines spread. The car keeps grinding and bouncing forward. I heave at the glass panel, trying to mash it and its cargo back through the open front of the car. Wind whips and slaps at me.

"Get out of here you bloody great heavy bastard," I yell. Bloody Americans and their bloody obesity epidemic.

I get a knee up under the glass.

The zombie gets a hand through it.

I heave.

The zombie grabs. Its hand clamps around my shirt lapels.

I kick the glass out, away. Everything but the zombie's hand flies away. He sprawls on the hood of the car, fist stuck through the remains of the windshield, clinging tenaciously to my throat. His body snaps up and down, like a flag in a high wind. I see the bones in his legs break as he is smashed up and down. Purple spit flecks his cheeks. I claw at his grasping hand.

"The wheel, dude!" Gran screams. "I can't get the fucking wheel!" His half of the windshield is still inside the car, still crushing him. His hands scrabble at the underside of the glass. The car careens left, right.

The zombie punches another fist at me. More glass spills down my lap, collects in the footwell.

And I swear, that will be the last sodding time I invoke Kurt Russell's name. If only for the reason this is the time it's finally going to kill me.

"Somebody bloody help!" I yell, which is not exactly the most politic way to put it, but when you're in a car barreling down a bumpy post-apocalyptic road, with no one at the wheel, and a zombie clawing at your throat... well, maybe Emily Post can shove the finer points of etiquette right up her arse.

Clyde pivots in the back seat, bunches his legs, and slams them forward against the collapsed windshield. For a moment I think it will help—mechanically powered thighs jettisoning so much unwanted cargo. Then his feet pile drive through the windshield. The whole thing fractures, dissolves. Glass pebbles fill the air. And suddenly there is no barrier between me and the zombie.

Its second hand grabs my neck and squeezes. Somewhere Gran yells. Through the blackening corners of my vision, I see him grab at the wheel. I feel the zombie's fungal juices soaking through my shirt onto my chest.

Panic, not far from the forefront of my mind, recognizes its cue and steps up to the plate. I start bucking and slamming, smashing my hands against the zombie's iron grip. I can feel the muscles in its arms bunch as it hauls itself towards me. My fingernails break its flesh, but considering it doesn't care that its legs are broken I'm not sure how much impact I'm going to have.

"Come on!" I manage with my remaining breath. But no one does. I'm too oxygen deprived to figure out why. Whatever the hell the reason is, I am not breaking this bastard's grip and no one else is.

That realization, as my hands collapse into my lap is suddenly liberating. If I can't pull him off, what can I...?

An idea comes to me. In its defense, I don't have time to think of a better one.

My vision is going dark. Operating my arms is

hard. My arm flaps once, twice, hits pleather. I try to concentrate. The zombie's breath is hot and fetid—like my dad's compost heap going rancid on a summer's day.

I clench my fist. Grip.

This better be the bloody handbrake.

I haul on it.

G-forces whirl. The zombie's grip on my throat first crushes one way, then another. I hear screaming, louder even than the shriek of the blood in my ears. The world spins. Everything is a ripping, tearing blur. Roots smash arrhythmically against the tires. We spin and skitter.

Then: the violent crunch of metal impacting on metal. The biting constriction of my seatbelt. The crisp bang of the airbags deploying. The fingers leaving my throat. The blessed rush of oxygen. The zombie, violently ripped from my throat, flies rag-doll-broken through the air, impacts against a creeper-covered wall, and becomes nothing more than an explosive purple smear.

42

It takes everyone a moment to realize we are not being eaten by zombies.

The car is a smoking wreck. It sits at a right angle across the street. We have plowed into another vehicle, our engine block impaled on what is left of its door.

Clyde reacts first. Perhaps confusion and concussion isn't a thing when you're a robot. He stands, smacking his head against the roof of the car.

"Damn," he says.

He reaches around the interior of the car, waist and arms folding in inhuman ways. One seatbelt pops then another, then another, then mine.

I try to blink away the blur in my vision and my thoughts. "Felicity?" I ask, my voice shaky. "You OK?"

It takes a few seconds for the answer to come.

"Perhaps."

I can't think of anything else to say. Clyde wrenches open my door, ignoring the bent metal. Given the state of my limbs, I decide the easiest way to dismount the car is just lean sideways until I collapse out of my seat. The road's mossy carpet is surprisingly soft.

Clyde drags us one-by-one to the side of the road. I lie there soaked in blood, sweat, and someone else's fungal juices. Not a cocktail I'm going to waste time naming. I suspect it'll be a while before I find a decent bar anyway.

"At least," Gran finally speaks, "we, like, totally lost those dudes."

"Totally," Felicity breathes. Personally I'm finding it a little early in the recovery process for sarcasm. I admire her fortitude.

"Again, I really don't want to take on the role of negative Nelly," Clyde says tinnily—he looks like he's picked up a few new dents—"but I think we're in a city full of these zombies. I'm not sure we can totally lose them. Unless you mean that we were trying to keep them but lost one and are now, all, oh no, where's my zombie? Which I don't think you are. But if you are then you're right and I'm very sorry for this whole interruption. Seeming more and more of a mistake as I go on." He grinds to a halt.

Jesus. A city of zombies. This was just our first encounter and we lost our transport. Plus almost all the good breathing parts of my throat. How the hell are we meant to get to this tunnel?

"There's got to be some way to contact someone outside the city," I say. "Some way to get someone to come and rescue the hell out of us."

This doesn't actually seem unreasonable. The US military is one of the most advanced fighting forces in the world. Surely they'll come get their own CIA boy out of a jam. Especially when it's his department's expertise that is needed to deal with this sort of disaster.

Tabitha doesn't share my optimism. "Email: no." She starts the litany. "Cellphone: no. Telephone: probably compromised. Plus this much plant growth would rip apart underground wires."

"Radio," Felicity says abruptly. "Radio could still be viable."

Tabitha nods as dubiously as it's possible to nod. Which, it turns out, is very dubiously indeed. "Possibility," she says. "Short range at least. If you have a generator."

"Dudette." Gran grins. "This city doesn't sleep. It can't afford to."

I think that means there will be generators. "So where are the radio towers?" I ask. This sounds like a plan. But we will need a conjunction of the two places for it to work.

"Ooh!" Clyde pipes up. "I know this. I remember reading a guide book. Well, I remember reading lots of guide books, but this is one in particular. About New York. Not that I ever really expected to come here. I just like guide books. Armchair traveler and all that. Truth be told, I get horribly air sick, and transatlantic boat travel is just not really viable on a traditional vacation schedule. Not to complain about the MI37 vacation policy, which I think is, given the nature of the job, actually very reasonable and much better than a civil servant friend I went to college with..." He sees us all staring. "Oh. Well, all I wanted to say was, the Empire State Building has one of these radio transmitters, if you want to go there. Meant to be magnificent views."

"The views. Of course." Felicity shakes her head.

"Well," Clyde huffs slightly, "no one said the apocalypse had to be aesthetically unappealing."

It seems safer to just ignore that and concentrate on the fact that this genuinely is a plan. We have a destination. Something to accomplish there. All we have to do now is get there. Which, I admit, does leave one final question.

"Where are we?"

JONATHAN WOOD

Gran heaves himself to his feet with a grunt. Nearby a street sign has been bent down by the weight of a bark-wreathed limb lying over it. Moss and creepers twirl up its now-horizontal length. Gran peels away leaves.

"Corner of Fifth Avenue and One Hundred and Twelfth Street. We came way across town."

"Where's the Empire State Building?"

"Down on Thirty-fourth Street. A few blocks over."

I do the mental math. Just under eighty blocks. Plus a few over. Shit.

"We have to get over there for the tunnel anyway, man." Gran looks mildly apologetic.

An angry rumble emerges from Tabitha. It resolves itself as "Stupid apocalypse."

I shrug, pick myself up, momentarily regret it, and then take a step toward the nearest street corner. "Come on," I say. "No time like the present."

FIFTY BLOCKS DOWNTOWN

We're hiding again. The lobby of some corporate tower. Creepers have broken the faux-marble counter where a security guard once lurked. Pink flowers bloom from smashed TV monitors. Roots protrude from the elevator doors.

Outside, a pack of about twenty Clyde zombies lurch down the street. Felicity tracks their movement down the barrel of her gun. Hopefully she won't have to use it. We're all down to our last few magazines of ammunition. And Felicity very forlornly told us that she has only three grenades left. I'm not sure how long she's been carrying three grenades around in her handbag, but I am officially renaming it, "Pandora's Box."

Kayla would be useful here. I suspect our progress

would be quicker with her in tow. Not just for her mad zombie-slaying skills but her ability to dice foliage like a lunch time salad.

I miss her, I realize. Good Lord, the day has come where I miss Kayla. That would be the weirdest thing this year if Clyde hadn't caused the apocalypse today.

Where is she? I wonder. All anybody said was something about a hospital. We should probably search for her, but I haven't the faintest clue where to look for her. And if anybody is prepared to survive this sort of thing it's Kayla. At least, she would be if I hadn't stabbed her. God, I hope she wasn't hooked up to any critical machines when the power went out.

The zombies pass out of sight, and after another ten seconds, Felicity holsters her gun. "I think we're clear," she says.

We stick our heads out, scan the street. Nothing moves. Zombified or otherwise.

We have seen signs of other survivors, at least, which is reassuring. A few wrecked cars, their engines still smoking. Shops with windows smashed by bricks instead of tree limbs. Plus the occasional corpse. We did, at one point, spot five people scampering across the road a few blocks south of us, but we didn't want to risk calling out, and they either didn't spot us or didn't feel like hanging around to chat about the weather and the much increased chance of being eaten alive.

Vine-covered buildings tower over us. A late afternoon sun sends shafts of pale light creeping between obelisks of steel and glass. They reflect off Clyde's mirrored face.

"How's Version 2.0 doing this?" I ask as we start skulking our way further downtown. "Whatever it is he's doing?"

"Biothaumaturgical delivery of magicodigital personality complex," Tabitha says without batting an eyelid.

Despite possibly being the longest sentence Tabitha has ever uttered it is a largely unhelpful experience for me.

"More monosyllabically?" I ask.

I am surprised the look she gives me doesn't cause more wildlife to wither and die.

"Perhaps," Clyde interjects, "I could try this one."

There's a pause for objections but none are forthcoming.

"You see," he says, "as I understand it, despite going digital, Evil-Me has not stopped being... well, this is going to sound a little big-headed, and I apologize for the fact, but, well, there are some facts and figures to support this... well, he's a world-class thaumaturgist. Or magician to the everyday muggle. And apparently getting a brain as big as the databases of most of everywhere important has not slowed that down. Sort of the opposite thing happening actually. So that's the thaumaturgical bit.

"And, now he's using plant dispersal. Well, fungal dispersal actually. Flora, let's say. But that's the 'bio' bit. And he's using the bio to disperse the thaumaturgical bit." He shrugs his metal shoulders twice. "Basically the spores are what I'm talking about. Natural but not natural. Naturally unnatural. Or possibly unnaturally natural. I'm honestly not sure. I've got a bit lost in the logic here actually. Lexical maze of doom. Oh God. Give me a second." He stands perfectly, mechanically still for a moment then shrugs violently. "No—naturally unnatural. I'm sure of it. Anyway. Magic spores. They get breathed in, or make contact or whatever and that's what delivers the payload."

"Hold up, dudes." Gran raises a hand. At first I think it's a question, but he stands stock still and silent.

"What?" I ask.

"Hear it too," Tabitha says.

I listen. And there is something. Dull and possibly distant. Down at the bottom register of my hearing. Something pounding. And slowly getting louder.

"Inside," Felicity says.

We move, clambering through a bodega's shattered window. The place smells of rotten food. We hunker behind what used to be a food counter and what is now a rainbow of fungus. So far the zombies aren't going to win many prizes for observation—assuming they give those out—but this sounds different.

The sound grows louder, but I see nothing. After ten seconds or so I turn to Clyde. "You said the spores deliver a payload," I whisper.

Clyde nods. "Yes. Not a payload like a bomb, you understand. No great big explosion and blood and guts and limbs and bits of bone fragment being flung willy-nilly all over the place. Payload, as in a great big explosion of crazy weird science magic all up in someone's brain."

His reflective head means I get to see my distaste up close.

"The spores," he continues, "release, well, I'm not a hundred percent sure, but I suspect it's some magically altered viral DNA that hijacks the victim's brain and overwrites the personality with a fairly bare bones version of Clyde's. Well... mine. Well... his evil one. Or maybe it's a pretty complete version and the spores that also colonize the infected folk could be interfering with some cranial functions of the higher variety. I'm not really sure.

"In a nutshell, it's all messed up, and it's doing really awful magic to people's insides. Plus there's some digital personality overwriting wrapped in there." He shrugs one final time, possibly for luck. "Does that make sense?"

To my surprise, it actually does, and I'm about to say, yes, but abruptly the bass of whatever is approaching becomes very loud indeed. It also picks up a not entirely reassuring way of making the floor shake.

Gran clutches his gun tight, sweeps it back and forth. "Not feeling totally chill about this, dudes," he says. He is not alone.

The building is definitely trembling now. I can see cans rattling on the bodega shelves. An algae-covered water bottle falls to the floor, rolls away. Another follows. Another. Cans spill. Cereal boxes tumble, spill. I go from crouching on one knee to both, then I have to put my hands down to try to stabilize myself. An entire shelf collapses. Glass in the food counter cracks. I see Felicity open and close her mouth. She's trying to say something but I can't hear her.

God, Version 2.0 has got something else planned. I know it. Some phase two plan. Some slow-moving tidal wave come to eclipse us all. A clean sweep across America and then onto other continents. Or he's a giant robot now. Or... or...

And then a giant foot lands in the street outside.

43

The foot is massive, pink, splayed, and most noticeably taloned. Five pink, tree-trunk-thick toes each end in long, filth-stained claws. The leg above it is coated in thick black fur.

A shadow falls. Like an eclipse. The second foot comes down. It smashes trees and rotting cars. The bodega shudders with the impact.

And then the body, fully as long as the block is wide. The gleam of one massive eye. Then the creature is scrambling up the building opposite. Its claws wrench concrete free. A long bald tail whips past, sends an abandoned motorcycle flying. And then the monster disappears.

"Rat," Felicity says.

"Great big giant one," Clyde adds.

It takes a moment for my mind to grasp the truth of this. A giant rat. That is exactly what it was. Jesus. Giant animals. Zombies hadn't even lost their novelty yet.

I'm about to open my mouth and express this sentiment when a second massive body lands in the street, then a third. The two rats hesitate a moment in the canyon between the streets, twitching and flexing. Then one after the other, they heave themselves up onto the building opposite, following after the first.

The tail of the last rat whips across the street,

smashes into a car. The vehicle spins down the road, shedding glass and critical engine parts.

And something else goes spinning too.

No… Not something…

Someone.

I see the body fall away from the tail in the moment before it impacts the car.

Before the impact… Which means whoever it was, they weren't in the car. They were on the tail.

Who the hell would be clinging to the tail of a giant rat in this godforsaken city?

I hear Felicity gasp. And then she's moving towards the store's door with a cry. "Kayla!"

Oh right. Of course that's who it would be.

FIVE MINUTES LATER

"Oh, get off me you big bunch of feckin' jessies."

For a woman we found lying in the street clutching her side, Kayla seems remarkably ungrateful for what I am going to go ahead and call a rescue. I think she'd take issue with the term, but in our defense she is not in the best shape right now.

We've propped her up against one of the shelves. She sprawls back, legs splayed before her. She's replaced her usual flannel shirt and tank top with a hospital gown. It's open at the back and when we carried her in, I got a good eyeful of the bandaging that wreathes her midriff. They were filthy. The rest of her is worse.

Except her sword. She still has that. She grips the scabbard fiercely in one hand and the blade gleams.

"I'll be fine in a feckin' minute." She shoos us with her spare hand. "Just took a wee bit of a tumble is all."

Which would be all well and good if she was

anyone but Kayla. But Kayla doesn't take any bit of a tumble. Whatever recovery she managed before the zombpocalypse began, it was partial at best.

"We have to change those bandages," I say.

"They're feckin' fine," she says. It's a fairly bald-faced lie.

I glance helplessly at Felicity. She shakes her head and starts pulling things off the shelf.

Clyde looms over Kayla, angular and concerned. "What happened?" he asks her.

"The feck is you?" Kayla's brows furrow with suspicion.

"It's Clyde," Gran says, helpfully.

Injured or not, Kayla's sword is out of its sheath and more than halfway to Clyde's neck before I manage to shout, "No!"

The blade hangs in the air. Clyde stares at it. Tabitha does too, a sort of sick fascination on her face.

"It's good Clyde," I say. "Version 2.1. Not 2.0. Our Clyde." The last good one. Irreplaceable now. But I don't add that. I need to trust myself and my emotions surrounding that fact before I go around blurting it out.

"He doesn't look good," Kayla objects. "Looks like a dented piece of feckin' shit."

Clyde shrugs. "Not to be completely disparaging, and with the greatest deference both to you and kitchen appliances everywhere, but that seems a little like the pot calling the kettle a dented piece of shit."

Kayla actually cracks a smile at that.

Felicity finishes rifling through the shelves and kneels beside Kayla. "Come on," she says. "Let me change those bandages and you tell us what happened."

"I'm telling you, the bandages are feckin' fine."

Felicity arches an eyebrow. "You are about five minutes from septic shock. Now let me change the bandages because I don't have the energy to carry you."

And that is what passes for delicacy in MI37.

Kayla complies grudgingly. She leans forward, hoists her gown to expose her midriff.

"Shipped me off to a hospital, they did," she says as Felicity begins to unwind the bandage. "Don't remember that much of it, I have to say. Blood loss and the like." She flicks a look in my direction. I attempt to sink into the collapsed shelves of rotting produce. "But there was a doctor with a nice wee bum. I remember that bit."

Tabitha rolls her eyes at that detail, but I also see her slide her hand slightly too far down Gran's back. His eyebrows pop up a moment later.

"Anyway, that was mostly it. Lights out a few more times. Came round in a bed, feeling drugged and stupid. Took me about five minutes after all the zombie shit started before I realized I weren't just high as feck." She shrugs. "Then I legged it."

Gran, who is, of all of us, the least used to Kayla's particular suite of ass-kicking powers, starts forward at that. Well, either that, or Tabitha just grabbed another sensitive part of his anatomy, but I decide to hope it's the conversation. "Just legged it?" Gran says. "What about the wound? Your sword?"

"Oh," Kayla shakes her head. "I didn't let the fecks have my sword. Some prick nurse tried to take it off me. Had to chop his finger off before he'd give up on it."

"Kayla!" Felicity rocks back from where she's undoing the final strands of bandage. She sounds outraged.

"He was in a feckin' hospital," Kayla says. "Best place to do it."

Felicity shakes her head. I swear I hear her muttering, "Ambassadors of our nation."

Personally I'm glad it was just his finger.

Felicity pulls away the final pieces of the bandage, and we all get a good look at the damage I did. There is a lot of inhaling and gasping. The wound, it has to be conceded, does not look pretty. Black stitches stand out in angry red skin, puffy and tender looking. The inflamed skin stretches out long claws over her midriff and around to her back.

"Jesus, Kayla," I hear Felicity say.

"Only a flesh wound," Kayla flips back. "Bit of antibiotic and it'll be fine."

"I'll go find something to disinfect it," I suggest.

"Better be eighty feckin' proof at least," Kayla tells me. Of all of us she seems the least fazed by the state of the wound. But no matter what face she puts on it, that thing isn't healthy.

I scrounge around the store. After a minute I discover a mostly full bottle of vodka from beneath the cashier's counter. I guess that can be a stressful job.

Meanwhile, Kayla has been encouraged to continue with her tale.

"Went to cut my way out of the hospital. Took a while. Zombie horde, giant feckin' wound and all that. Didn't go totally as planned. Bit of fleeing involved towards the end, 'cept I'm shit at fleeing at the moment. Ended up in basement. Feckers had gone and cornered me. But then the rats came in and sort of devoured the feckin' lot of them. And I figured I was a bit knackered by then, so instead of killing them there, I'd just try and fix myself to one's fur or shit, hitch a ride, and murder the feckers later. But I fell off before I got to that. And here you feckers are. Worked out pretty feckin' well, I think."

I hand Felicity the vodka bottle. If that's Kayla's idea of things going well, I'd hate to see a bad day.

"Fifty-fifty?" Felicity asks Kayla.

Kayla shrugs. "Better be thirty-seventy, given how shit's going."

I have no idea what this means, until Felicity unscrews the bottle cap, hands it to Kayla, and she promptly chugs a third of the bottle.

"Jesus," Gran breathes.

"Ah, feck off," Kayla says with a belch. "In the Highlands we call this baby's mouthwash." She hands the bottle back to Felicity. "Hit me."

Felicity upends the bottle and pours it over the wound.

Another collective inhalation. Even Clyde makes a noise, and he doesn't need to breathe. Personally I had thought delicate dabbing might be involved. This is baptism by liquid fire. I almost expect to see the skin bubble and boil.

Kayla grimaces. "Stings a bit," she comments. Then she blacks out.

44

Clean, bandaged, and still belligerent, Kayla refuses the offer of a stretcher. Or as she puts it, "Quit talking your feckin' shite."

Having reached this impasse in negotiations, we throw our hands up and head back out into the street. Kayla looks at me and then Felicity. "So," she says, "what's the feckin' plan?"

"Make contact with any survivors using the radio tower in the Empire State Building," I say. "Then head for one of the tunnels under the river. Over on the…" I glance at Gran. "West side."

He nods.

"Into New Jersey," Felicity continues. "Regroup with other survivors."

"Go find 2.0, rip off his balls," Tabitha adds.

"Yeah," Kayla nods, "but," she looks around at the devastated city, "what about this feckin' mess?"

There is a bit of a pause at that. Because honestly our plan hasn't got that far. There's been all this scrambling for our lives that seems to have got in the way.

"Erm…" I say.

Kayla looks incredulous.

Felicity seems to take a little offense at this. "The city is in ruins," she points out. "Humanity has been largely replaced by soft squishy fungus people. And now there are giant animals running around. Regrouping with a larger force is the first step in ensuring the safety of our people."

Kayla squints at Felicity. "Our people?" She nods at the building. "What the feck about these people? Isn't humanity our people now?"

Wait, did Kayla just... did she take the moral high ground? Her idea of a relaxing afternoon is stabbing people to death.

"We can't do anything for anybody if we're dead," Felicity points out with a certain brutality.

I am in the worrying position of agreeing with both women. However, I am only in love with one of them.

"Look," I say. "Felicity's right. We need to regroup. To fix a plan we need information that we just don't have at this point. We have no concept of the big picture."

Kayla nods at Tabitha and Clyde. "Them two can't figure this feckin' thing out?" She seems genuinely surprised.

"We could give it the old college try, I'm sure." Clyde plugs the conversational gap. "Though what exactly a college try is and how it differentiates itself from other kinds of trying, I'm not entirely sure. Maybe there's more drinking and mistakes involved. Would be if it's like my college tries. Or perhaps if the students were all rugby players it would be a sort of victorious and violent try. I'm not really sure. In retrospect, maybe I'll just stick to a regular sort of trying if that's OK."

I decide to side-step a pun about how trying Clyde is, and just go straight to, "OK then." Then I take a moment to work out what I'm OK about.

"So," I hazard a guess, "can we really undo any of this? Can we get rid of these plants?"

Tabitha's look straddles the previously undiscovered land that exists between dubious and scathing.

"What about this zombie thing," I ask. "Can we fix that?"

"Theoretically," Tabitha says.

"Really?" Clyde's surprise beats out my own in the race to vocalization. "I was sure you were going to give him the finger there. Completely convinced. Would have bet money on it actually."

Tabitha gives Clyde the finger. I'm still more focused on the bit where she said, "theoretically," though.

"We can really undo it?" I ask her.

"Really theoretically." Tabitha looks at me as if it's a stupid question. It probably was. "Remember Mercurio?"

"Whatever happened to the wee feck?" Kayla asks.

"His brain," Tabitha says. "We took Version 2.0 out. Left taffy behind."

"It wasn't an unmitigated success," I confess.

"Like I said. Theoretical solution," Tabitha emphasizes. "Not practical. Not yet. But... give the code a good debug..."

I think about that. And what if we could get it to work? That would be huge. That would mean the liberation of millions. Hundreds of millions. More? God, I hope Clyde's reach hasn't extended that far.

Then my mind hits a snag. "What about the fungus?" I say. I've seen brains furry with the stuff. I don't think we can just deprogram that.

"Tricky," Tabitha says. "Best bet is same spore delivery system. Co-opt. Reverse engineer people."

It takes me a moment to process that: the idea that now we need to make our own weaponized fungus to un-fungus people.

"That sounds…" I start and then stop, not sure what it sounds like.

"Theoretical." Clyde completes my sentence for me.

Tabitha gives him the finger again.

I move on. "Is there a way to move from theory to practice? Can we really save these people?"

Tabitha's face does not give me confidence. Or it gives me even less confidence than usual. "Maybe." She shrugs. "Enough time. Enough lucky breaks."

I almost laugh at that. Here in this desolation. Lucky breaks.

"Sounds like a feckin' plan to me," Kayla says into the silence. "Better one than you guys had."

"Part one of Tabitha's plan," Felicity points out, "still needs to be getting the hell out of here. Getting to somewhere where we can really hash this code out. Make sure it works."

Still Kayla's addition to our future plan is important, I feel. The hope is slim, but it is there now. We have charted a path to it. Toward victory.

We pick up the pace, cross Fiftieth Street. Just sixteen more blocks.

45

We've not gone far when Clyde stops suddenly in the street. "What's that?" He points over everyone's heads, down Forty-eighth Street. We all turn to stare.

Really the answer isn't so hard. It's a mushroom. Clyde probably could have worked that out on his own. Except... Well, it's a mushroom that's eight feet tall. The fat hood droops, brown flesh sagging in thick swaths. It's at least as wide as the fluted stem is tall, lending the whole fungal apparatus a squat appearance.

Two figures are at its base, dressed in blue uniforms. They both hold large axes and are swinging away, wreaking merry havoc on the thing's spreading stem.

"Policemen?" Gran asks.

And he's right. It's two of New York's finest.

"Is what they're doing totally safe?" Clyde asks.

I can't believe it is.

"We should stop them," I say. "Before..." But I'm not sure before exactly what. Only that it is almost certainly going to be very bad indeed.

"Priorities?" Tabitha says. "Anyone? This is all white knight and shit but: saving humanity to do."

Gran nods, an unhappy resignation on his face.

It's likely they have a point, but I can't agree with it. We don't have any idea how many people are left. Any life seems precious at this point. So I shake my head.

"We save those guys from themselves."

"Agreed." Felicity nods.

We make our way down the street, though Tabitha and Gran hesitate before they follow. Kayla leans on her sword as if it's a cane. The scabbard clicks against the remnants of the tarmac.

We're about halfway to the über-mushroom when the cops spot us. One looks up, drops his axe and puts his hand on the holster at his waist.

"Stop there and back away," he barks. He's a guy around my height, maybe got a few years on me. His face is narrow and hard. "It's for your own safety."

His partner looks up, still holding her axe. She's a solidly built Latino woman. Sweat stands out on her cheeks and forehead. "Holy shit," she says. "Is that a robot?"

The male cop considers this. "'Bout the least fucked up thing I've seen today," he says finally. "Keep swinging. You guys keep walking. Not to be an asshole but this shit ain't safe, and most of the people I seen today ain't safe. I don't want this to get ugly."

I hold up my hands immediately. Old cowboy-at-gunpoint style. "We're looking to help," I say. "I think you underestimate how dangerous that is."

The cop with the axe looks at us. "I think you underestimate how shitty a day we're having," she snaps. "Now back the fuck up."

I guess it's just an off day for everyone.

"Dudes..." It's Gran who follows me into the minefield. "I am going to reach into my pocket, like, really, totally slowly, and I'm going to pull out an ID. I am all CIA and shit, and this is all going to be cool."

The cops exchange a glance. "Are you shitting me?" the man asks.

Gran is reaching. I can see the man's fingers playing on the holster at his side, but he hasn't undone the snap holding the gun in place yet. I think he was telling the truth when he said he didn't want this to get ugly.

Gran keeps up the slow motion act. His card is produced. "I'm going to throw my ID to you dudes," he says, and does so. The man kicks it to the woman who puts down her axe and picks it up.

"Says CIA," she says.

"Legit?" asks her partner.

"Honestly?" She shrugs. "I wouldn't know a CIA ID if it started dating my sister. But I figure they've got to be piss hard to forge. Would have to be fucking stupid to do that too."

"He seem that smart to you?" The male cop looks dubiously at Gran.

"If it helps I have an ID from British intelligence," I say. "We're liaising with the CIA on this."

The man looks dubious.

The woman shrugs. "They do have a robot, Paul. I mean… you know."

The man's hand remains on his holster for a moment. Then he sags, the breath and adrenaline running out of him so fast I think he's sprung a leak.

"Oh thank fuck," he says. He bends down, hands on knees, still sagging. It takes him a moment and some seeming effort but he gets his head up enough to look at us. "What the fuck is going on?"

Policeman Paul, it seems, has found a higher authority and is seeking permission to freak the hell out. Whatever professionalism was holding him together, it is now on the verge of cracking. He doesn't have to be strong for this conversation anymore.

But if he cracks… God, these are not ideal conditions for putting the pieces back together.

"It's a terrorist attack," I say. Calm, slow, matter-of-fact. The way I delivered bad news to parents back when I worked in the murder squad. "They've got the first strike in, but we're regrouping. We're—"

"Terrorist attack?" The cop looks at me like I'm a nutcase. "There are fucking plant people! What the fuck are fucking terrorists—"

"Paul! Paul!" The woman drops her axe and steps up to him, puts her hand on his shoulder. "It's OK."

He puts his head in his hands. "Shit, Tess. I got my sister out on the Island…"

"I know. I know." She pats his back. "I got James and the kids out there too. We're going to get there. We're going to fix this. That's what these guys are telling us. It's going to be fixed."

The guy, Paul, takes some deep breaths. Tries to find somewhere calm left inside him.

"God," Clyde buzzes behind me. "I did this? I…" He trails off.

And, while it is good to have some version of Clyde back, I do wish he had better timing.

"The fuck did you say?" Paul snaps upright, hand back on his gun. He wrenches it free. "Who did this?" He jabs the gun at Clyde. "You did this?"

Out of the corner of my eye I see Kayla start to move. I almost see Paul's life expectancy like a frail thread about to be cut short. And there are nanoseconds to act.

I hate the instincts that make me do it, but I step between Clyde and the gun. I hear Felicity draw in her breath. But I'm saying, "Not him. It wasn't him," and not giving myself time to dwell on my own life expectancy.

Kayla's hand hovers on the hilt of the sword.

"He said…" Paul looks suspicious.

"It's really complicated, and involves cloned software, and serious identity issues," I say. "And it is by far the least weird part of all this. Just know this machine is not your enemy. He's actually one of our big hopes for fixing this mess."

There is suspicious silence. The atmosphere is probably not helped by Clyde saying, "Really? Thanks, Arthur. That's a really nice thing for you to say."

"Don't worry about it."

The woman, Tess, puts her hand on Paul's and moves his away from the gun. "Come on," she says. "We're all on the same side here."

After a moment, the gun goes back in the holster, and Kayla's sword blade slides back into its scabbard, and we're back to a less fraught atmosphere again. "So," I nod at the mushroom, "what the hell is this thing?"

She looks at me, eyebrows arched in surprise. "You don't know? Didn't you just say you guys were in charge?"

Seriously? I feel I've been slapped by enough weird shit today that I should be exempt from dealing with people's trust issues at this point.

"We were hit as hard as anyone, I think." Felicity steps forward before my exasperation can step in it. "Hi," she says, extending a hand. "I'm Felicity Shaw, head of Britain's MI37."

"MI37?" Paul's brows furrow.

"You know what? Just let it go." Tess flaps one hand at Paul and extends the other to Felicity. "Patrolman Tess Ramirez. Not exactly good to meet you." She grimaces.

Felicity nods. "I hear that. But to answer your question. We were dealing with a major incursion of the…" she hesitates over the nomenclature, "infected uptown. Since then we've just been trying to get to the radio tower in the Empire State Building. This is the first of these mushrooms we've seen."

"Shit, man," says Paul, finally finding some trust, it seems. "They're all over down here. One every ten blocks or so."

"They release the heads," says Tess.

"The heads?" I ask. Because… well, because she said, "They release the heads."

Tess cocks her own. "Seriously?" she says. "You ain't seen them?"

"This really is the first we've come across," Felicity says.

Tess opens her mouth to answer when beside her, the mushroom convulses. A great spasm rushes up the length of its thick stem.

"Oh shit!" Paul yells. "It's going to blow again!"

Tess seizes Felicity and me by the arms, starts to drag us away. Paul seems about to grab Kayla and do the same, but then her look makes him check himself. "Move!" he barks. She complies. Tabitha, Gran, and Clyde waste no time doing the same.

Clearly this is the moment to duck and run, but I can't help but stare over my shoulder as I do. Something is happening to the mushroom's hood. Something is peeling open and back. The smell of foul meat fills the air. Tabitha covers her mouth as she and Gran duck down on the opposite side of the street.

"Back!" Felicity barks at me.

It's good advice so I take it. Nothing good can come out of a mushroom so wide that Jerry Springer would have to airlift it off a couch. I scramble behind a car where Felicity and Clyde are hunkered beside Tess.

"Lock and load," mutters Felicity, hunkered down beside me. She pulls out her pistol once more.

"No." Tess bats the gun down. "Not a good idea."

I want to ask more but movement from the mushroom distracts me. From its splayed open heart something white, almost spherical starts to rise. I narrow my eyes, try to focus. Something like... hair? A fur ball? And then more. The white hair giving way to something smoother. Some of the hair parting to reveal... an ear? Eyes?

A face. It's a face rising up out of the flower.

And I recognize the face.

"Oh my," Clyde 2.1 says into my ear.

"You hid that narcissistic streak well," I tell him.

It's Clyde's disembodied head floating up out of the mushroom's core. And not just one, but another, and another. A great field of floating Clyde heads, each one completely white as if carved from chalk.

And they're all talking. Every single one of them jabbering at the same time.

"...well if you consider..."

"...allowing for thaumato-radioactive delay..."

"...rate of decay..."

"...terrible wrongs..."

The heads are bulbous, distorted at the temple. They drift up slowly. Ten, twenty, thirty of them. And still they come. They float up toward the sliver of sky peering down between the skyscrapers.

"The name of fuck," I hear Tabitha say from across the street. "What in the—?"

"Is that propaganda?" Felicity asks, brows furrowed.

And could that be it? Does Clyde honestly think that

he can talk humanity into committing species suicide?

"Let's just shoot them," Gran says. Loud enough for us all.

"No!" Tess and Paul yell in unison. But their cry comes at the exact same moment as Gran fires off his first shot.

To be honest, I still don't understand why they're objecting.

Then a Clyde head detonates.

It does not pop, does not deflate. It detonates. A tear of sound louder than the gunshot itself. White pulp flies over the street. Something that might have been a jaw bone embeds itself in the floor two feet from me.

And the spores. The cloud of black spores flooding out, filling the sky above.

46

Paul lets loose an obscenity, staggers back.

The cloud is massive. The width of the block. A vast sphere of night collapsing down on us.

We run. Heads down, into the wind, a full-on panicked scramble. Feet kicking over loose stones and leaves. Tripping on vines, hauling on hanging creepers. Anything to get away.

One foot goes out from under me. My balance waves goodbye and flees ahead of me. I kick with my trailing leg, with my last moments of verticality, try to get as much momentum into my collapse as I can. I leave the ground.

Felicity's arm clamps around mine. She heaves, hurling me forward in a crashing, spinning roll. My head smacks against fractured tarmac, again, again.

I lie, pant, bleed a little, and wait to see if I'm free.

When enough limbs are under my control, I pick my head up. A black blanket is settling, not a foot from me. I scramble back, but the spores aren't spreading anymore.

There's yelling. I force my eyes to focus, to search for Felicity.

Some peripheral part of me knows I've ignored three people before my eyes rest on her. But in this moment, I honestly don't care about them.

I find her, and just before the moment when our eyes

lock there is one of absolute paralyzing fear. Because I am sure there are not going to be the warm welcoming pools of brown, waiting there, just obliterating black.

But they are her eyes. Eyes that relax as the same fear ebbs out of her. The breath I take is deep and shaking.

That fear accounted for, the people still screaming become a more pressing concern.

I scan the scene. Tabitha and Gran lie sprawled, twisted, and somehow tangled in each other. His arm over her head, protective. And that's a good solid thing to see right there.

There is Clyde, standing tall, proud, and silver. There's perhaps an extra dent in his frame, but otherwise he seems unharmed.

Kayla lies on the ground at his feet, hand clamped on her midriff. Not as fantastic to see, but her eyes are full of pain, not the desire to nosh on our gray matter, so that's at least a partial win.

Which leaves…

Tess. Tess standing at the edge of the pool of black that has settled on this street. Tess standing there screaming. Screaming at…

Paul stands there. His hips are cocked to one side, almost to the point of overbalancing. His body skews in the other direction, his head back toward his raised shoulder—an awkward zig-zag of a pose. His arms hang lose. And his eyes. Oh God, his eyes.

He opens his mouth. And the fungus hasn't filled him yet. Hasn't ruined him completely, but his tongue is black as a coal miner's lung.

"Ugck," he clacks at Tess. "Garrr-fgg."

He steps forward. One horribly ruined step, lurching and sagging.

His movement seems to galvanize something in Tess, she scrambles back away. Whirls around. Sees Gran and Tabitha disentangling themselves.

"You!" She points at Gran. "You stupid fuck!" She's pointing at him with her gun.

"I said not to do it!" she screams. "I told you to fucking wait!" There are tears rolling down her face now.

Gran has his arms out wide. Tabitha is blinking. I think she took a blow to the head.

Behind Tess, Paul lets out a rumbling, "Gggrrrck," and staggers another step toward her.

"He... he..." I start, picking myself off the floor. I want to say that Gran didn't know, but the horror and the abruptness of everything is mixing with my own blows and everything takes longer than it should.

"Graaack." Another lurch from Paul.

"What happened?" Gran is saying. "I don't know... What happened?"

"Tess!" I manage to yell, because now Paul is starting to get very close, and I don't think it's co-workerly affection he wants to express.

"You dumb stupid fuck!" Tess is still having trouble moving past her rage issues. I stumble toward her. Maybe my actions can beat my words in the race toward meaning.

And then Clyde is there. Standing between Tess and Gran's prone form. Between the gun and the man dating the woman he loves.

"I'm terribly sorry to interrupt," he says, "not polite of me at all, and we've already made a pretty bad impression, I think, but I did just want to mention that I think that zombie is about to eat your brains." He points.

Tess blinks for a moment, and then spins. The barrel of her gun is inches from Paul's open mouth. His hands reach for her.

She doesn't even hesitate. Just pulls the trigger.

His head bursts apart, spraying her with blood and black fungus. He drops instantly, puppet strings cut.

There is a moment, just a moment, of utter stillness. Tess caught in her pose, gun still held. Clyde passive behind her. Kayla still focused on her wound. Felicity open-mouthed. Gran and Tabitha lying down, staring, barely comprehending. Paul's suddenly headless corpse dead on the ground.

And then the fight is blown clear out of Tess. As surely as if someone put a bullet in its over-pressurized brains. She drops her gun. Drops to her knees. Sobs start to wrack her.

Clyde steps forward, he puts a metal hand on her shoulder. "Sorry about that," he says. "Just thought you should know."

WITH THE SUN SETTING

A little while later, Felicity and I stand next to the deflated corpse of the once-giant mushroom. It is rotting rapidly back into the ground, and I have my hand pressed firmly to my nose. I have been in the presence of two-week-old corpses that smelled better than this.

"This is part of it," she says. "His contingency plan."

"Yes," I say, because that's all I want to say. I don't want to go into the cold implacable mind that came up with these things, this way of mopping up humanity's survivors.

"We should study it," I say instead. "Maybe we can learn more about what Clyde 2.0 is—"

"Talk about feckin' optimism. It's rotting into the feckin' ground." Kayla hobbles up to us, leaning heavily on her scabbard.

"Jesus," I say. "Are you OK?"

She shrugs. "Tore a few stitches or some shit. I'm fine."

Felicity shakes her head, puts her arm around me, squeezes briefly, then turns to Kayla. "I have needle and thread. Come on. Lie down and I'll fix it."

Kayla rolls her eyes but complies. Felicity starts unwrapping the bandages.

"There's got to be something we can learn from this," I say, turning back to the mushroom. Partly, I have to admit, so I don't have to stare at Kayla's wound again.

The mushroom keeps on rotting, crumbling away before my eyes until it is barely there.

"He's covering his tracks," Felicity says glancing over.

That seems unfortunately accurate. But maybe there is hope in that. If he is covering his tracks, that means there are tracks to follow out there.

I nod in the direction of the policewoman, Tess, who is sitting on the opposite side of the street to Tabitha and Gran. Clyde stands near her, a silent sentinel. "They said there were others." Then I correct myself. "*She* said there are." I don't really want to think about Paul.

God, we killed him. Not directly perhaps. But as good as. We're meant to be the good guys. The folk who save the world. And… Shit. Just look at this place.

"You're right." Felicity pulls me out of the oblivion of self-recrimination. Keeps me moving. "We'll have to find them, check them out. It's a good thought."

"Should we ask her now?"

Felicity just looks at me.

"In the morning then."

Felicity scans the buildings lining the street. "Kayla needs to rest." Kayla makes an annoyed noise. "We *all* need to rest," Felicity continues. "We need to find somewhere safe for the night."

"There are rats the size of small trucks," I point out.

Felicity shrugs. "Relatively safe."

SOMEWHERE RELATIVELY SAFE

The brownstone appears to be fairly structurally sound. At least, it should hold up as long as we don't lean too hard on any load-bearing walls.

Inside, we find a kitchen that's almost intact. There are still plates on the table. One chair is knocked over, but everything else is still standing as it was.

"*Mary Celeste*, much?" Gran says. Not even Tabitha laughs.

We hunker down in a nearby living room. Spider plants from the mantelpiece have taken over a quarter of the space but they're not visibly growing so we don't appear to be in imminent danger. Clyde offers to take watch, as he doesn't need to sleep.

Gran rustles up a campfire and we sit around it, a five-pointed star. The two couples—Felicity and I and Gran and Tabitha—make the star's base too heavy. Tess, Kayla, and Clyde are islands unto themselves. Nobody talks much. I scoop cold baked beans out of a can I found in a cupboard.

"Tomorrow then," I say when it seems like continued silence will be even more uncomfortable than breaking it. "Empire State Building. Radio tower. But before that," I nod at Tess, "Bryant Park." That's the closest location that she knows for sure has a mushroom. At least it had one last time she was there. Hopefully it hasn't released its payload yet, and we can take a look at the thing.

"We'll need new axes, I guess," I say. Tess dropped hers back at the mushroom and didn't seem to feel like going back for it.

"Shut up," she tells me. Not looking at me. "Just shut up."

I swallow hard. Lick my lips. Felicity puts a hand on my thigh. She shakes her head gently. I leave it alone.

Gran doesn't though. "Look, dude," he says, "I swear I really didn't know. I'm sorry." He leans toward the fire we've lit. His face is drawn tight. "I didn't know."

"Feckin' pillock," Kayla says. There doesn't seem to be much rancor to it though.

Tess doesn't say a word. Doesn't even seem to register that he's spoken. After a moment she pulls a blanket we recovered from the bedroom tight around her and curls up.

A few minutes later, Felicity and I do the same. I curl around her, holding her, letting the smell of her hair fill my nose. She holds my hand over her heart and squeezes.

"You're worrying again," she whispers.

"Our whole point of existence," I whisper back, "is to stop the world from ending because of magic, or aliens, or just weird shit. It ended today. I think that's reason to worry."

There's a long pause. "I've got to say it's going to hurt your performance review."

I wrestle the laugh back down into my gut. I don't think that would fly well with this crowd. "This isn't funny," I manage after a moment.

"I know." Felicity is suddenly somber. "But it's that

or scream. And I don't want to scream, Arthur. I want to fight. I want to get back what was taken from us."

What was taken from us? I do the tally. There's a city in ruins out there. Maybe a country. Millions of minds overwritten by magicodigital fungus.

"You think we can do that?" I ask.

"I think we have to try."

And she's right. Of course she's right. But... "You still think we're the good guys?" I say.

Her grip on my hands loosens. "You look out there, and you think that maybe Clyde was right?" There's incredulity in her voice.

"No," I whisper back. "Of course not. Version 2.0 is a monster. But... what we've done. Today. We killed hundreds of people today. Even if they were infected. Wasn't that monstrous too?"

I try not to think about Paul. About his black staring eyes...

Felicity suddenly redoubles her grip, grinds my fingers together, almost painfully. "Arthur, I honestly don't give a shit if we're good or bad. I just see what we have to do. And we have to end this. The sooner the better. Before it gets worse. We have to."

And that is my Felicity. Single-minded. Focused. Cutting through bullshit like Kayla cuts through skulls. And I don't have much to say after that.

But the thoughts keep rattling in my head, and it takes me a long time to fall asleep.

47

BRYANT PARK

I lie in low shrubbery trying to keep my breath shallow and my crotch free of the spikier plants.

"Well," Felicity breathes, lying next to me, "this is not exactly what we were hoping for."

Bryant Park—sitting just a handful of blocks from where we slept—is a broad rectangle of grass surrounded by tall trees and abundant ground cover. The east end abuts the imposing bulk of the New York Public Library. The other sides are bordered by a moat of road followed by towering skyscrapers. In the park's center sprouts the mushroom. It is fat and bloated. Grass has grown wild and rampant around it, a foot high at least, spotted through with hundreds of wildflowers and thistles.

And zombies. It's probably worth mentioning the zombies.

"There's, like, a crap ton of them," Gran whispers. It's not an exact count, but I think he's about as accurate as we need to be.

They stand there, arms spread, heads tilted back, staring up at the scrim of clouds covering the sky. A few stumble awkwardly about, bumping into each other and grumbling in their ugly guttural tongue.

"The hell we get to that thing?" Tabitha stares at the mushroom.

"Violence," Kayla suggests.

Tess lies to one side of me. Mostly, I suspect, because it's as far as she can get from Gran. She doesn't say a word, just keeps working and reworking her grip on the fire axe we found in the brownstone's stairwell. I worry she takes Kayla more seriously than is deserved.

"It's OK," I say to her. "We'll make our move. We'll have our pound of flesh... fungus... whatever. Just let us work out the plan then you can go all lumberjack on them."

A plan. We do need one of those. A distraction, perhaps. Something to draw the zombies away...

Then a voice breaks the silence. "What the bloody hell are you doing here?"

We freeze. All of us. The axe lies still in Tess's hands. I don't even roll my eyeballs to look.

"Oh this is bloody par for the course, this is." A broad cockney whisper comes from somewhere above my head. "Pretend I don't even exist. I see how it is. Fuckin' charming."

Oh holy hell...

"Winston?" I ask, incredulous. I slide my eyes upwards. We're hiding at the base of a broad, leafy... I actually have no idea what sort of tree Winston might be.

"Oh acknowledge me, he does. Thank the heavens for small bloody favors. Just rescue all your bloody arses out of Golem-fest 2015 and then do I get a bloody thank you, or do you all piss off out the window with nary a backwards glance? I think we all know the fucking answer to that, don't we now?"

I have a thousand questions. Where? How? Why? But of all of them the most pertinent seems to be, "Is this really the time?"

"Nice to see you bloody too, mate." Winston sniffs disdainfully. How he sniffs I couldn't say, but sniff he does.

Gran is looking around bewildered. "Do you dudes hear that or am I having a really inappropriately timed flashback?"

Tess is more to the point. "What the hell is going on?" she hisses.

"Shh!" hisses Felicity. "All of you!"

We all snap our gaze to the zombies crowding the lawn. A few have stirred, uprooted perhaps, but none appear to be getting any closer.

"Those bloody pillocks?" Winston snorts. "Don't make me laugh. They're dumb enough to have their own fucking reality show, they are."

"What," Tess repeats, "the *hell* is going on?"

"Winston," I say to her. "Animated tree. Friend of ours."

From her expression, I don't think this helps.

"Friend, he says," Winston scoffs. "Could have bloody fooled me. Discover me in a madman's lab. I save your crispy pork rasher, and then… Oh wait, I'm shipped off to another lab and nobody cares to come see how much sap was spilled in the fight. Don't know why I bloody bother."

Do other people who save the world from supernatural threats have this sort of conversation inches from fields of zombies, or is it just me?

"I am sorry, Winston," I say. He probably deserves it. If not at this exact bloody moment.

Winston hesitates, then sniffs again. "Well then," he says. "You know. Apology accepted then." Another pause. "You fucker."

Kayla chuckles.

"It is just lovely to see you again, Winston," says Clyde.

Winston starts violently, seeming to realize Clyde is present for the first time. "Bloody hell!" he says, then tries to disguise it as a rustle of branches. "You!"

A few feet away a zombie says, "Urk," but then goes back to bumping into things.

"I mean…" Winston continues, "is that… you? Him?" A branch rustles and then points accusingly at Clyde.

"Oh," says Clyde. "Of course. Should explain. Not Evil-Me. Me-me. If that makes sense. Probably doesn't. No wonder people are opposed to cloning. I mean, moral objections aside, the pronoun situation is a disaster."

Tess is itching at her axe handle.

"This is Clyde 2.1," I explain hastily. "Completely different from Clyde 2.0."

"Well, not completely," Clyde points out.

"Not helping."

Tess fixes me with a dead-eyed stare. "I swear," she says, "I am not a violent woman, but you have a lot of explaining to do if you don't want me to keep on swinging after the zombies have fallen down." Her words stab out at me from behind gritted teeth.

I suddenly see this all from her point of view. We're the CIA. The man. The bad guy from a thousand Hollywood spectacles. And she… She's Kurt Russell. The woman alone in the city gone mad struggling for survival, for sanity. Screwed over and fighting for survival. She's the heroine. We're the guys that promise aid but turn out to be responsible for everything.

Trying to be the hero may be too much of a reach on this particular escapade. Maybe I should just settle for not being an asshole.

I open my mouth. "Look," I start.

"Well," Winston cuts me off, "if you're going to get into it make it quick, because we really should do whatever the hell it is you guys are doing before the dog comes back."

Why does everyone do this to me? It would be nice to have just one conversation without a bombshell being dropped.

I tear my gaze away from Tess's slightly murderous one and look up at the tree line. "*What* dog, Winston?"

"Oh." Winston sounds surprised. "Well, you've seen the giant animals, right?"

Oh shit.

"We saw rats," says Clyde with undue enthusiasm. "Pretty impressive stuff. Not that many species can actually survive gigantism. Despite the whole dinosaur thing, most lizards just wouldn't survive being blown up that way, for example. The physics of their anatomy is all off. Goes back to the whole dinosaurs being more closely related to birds thing, actually. But—"

"Giant dogs?" I wrestle the conversation back toward a point.

"Just one. Sort of reason I'm hiding out here. Didn't really want to get involved in a game of fetch. Though if that thing comes and marks its territory on me, it's going to lose a nut. When it let loose at the other corner of the park I think it drowned a zombie. Horrible way to go. At least it would be if you weren't a zombie, I suppose. Maybe zombies are into it. Look like a bunch of kinky bastards." There is a rustle as if a leafy head is being shaken. "Brain eating and such. Weird."

OK. A field of zombies *and* a giant dog. Totally manageable. Totally...

I turn to Felicity. "What the hell is our plan?"

"Oh wait," says Winston, before she can answer, "you can go ahead and explain now. The dog is back."

Shit and… No. Just shit.

I peer for a glimpse of the creature, but my vantage point is significantly less elevated than Winston's. There are just leaves and blades of grass, and tree trunks.

And then I catch a glimpse of it.

Jesus.

Its muzzle hangs about four stories off the ground. Its eyes hit the fifth story. Its flanks—matted, scratched, and filthy—streak back for a hundred yards or more. It pads down the length of the park, foot falls making the trees shake.

"Just so you know, I am totally not trembling," I hear Winston mutter as his branches rattle together. "Trick of perspective."

"Holy crap sticks, dudes," I hear Gran mutter.

"A Rottweiler," I hear Felicity groan. "It just had to be a Rottweiler."

"You should have seen it take out the German Shepherd," Winston whispers down. "That shit was just impressive."

"Sweet," Kayla breathes.

A giant, killer Rottweiler. Of course. Just… of course.

OK. I force my mind to stop freaking out and think back. We've dealt with big monsters before. And we have Clyde with us. Clyde is our version of mobile artillery.

I turn to him. "You can still do magic, right? Even though you're a robot. Or you're in a robot. I don't know."

Tess looks like I just broke something inside of her. "Magic?" she says.

"Yes, should be able to," Clyde says to me. Then

to Tess, "It's pretty cool actually. You see there are parallel dimensions—"

I cut him off before he does any permanent damage to Tess's frontal lobe. "I swear," I say, "I will explain all of this to you once we've investigated, destroyed, and whatevered that mushroom. I swear."

Tess looks like she's debating between her desire to kill us all and her desire to imitate a sane person for another ten minutes or so. Fortunately for me the latter wins.

"Tabby." Clyde turns his head, then stops, looking I think more at Gran than his former girlfriend. "Sorry," he corrects. "Tabitha. My bad. I'm not even used to being Robocop's skinny nerd brother, let alone this whole decreased familiarity because I'm a clone thing. Work in progress. Apologies. Memories of other versions of myself and all that. Confusing. You'd think if you had a computer for a brain you'd be able to do some parallel processing or something. Or maybe you wouldn't expect that. I'm not sure about the whole computer thing. More your forte, really. Which takes me back to my point, which was about spells, and databases, and all that stuff. Any chance you could feed me a couple in a pinch?"

Tabitha looks down from him to her laptop, up to Gran. She repeats the triangle.

"Whatever," she mutters eventually.

"Fantastic," Clyde says. And he sounds like he genuinely means it. And was there some hidden warmth in Tabitha's grunt? Clyde was always far more sensitive to the nuances of her moodiness than I was.

"All right," I say to him. "So can you make the dog hurt?"

"That's never going to fly with the animal safety folk," Clyde says.

"It *is* kind of ungroovy," Gran agrees.

Good Lord. Do I really have to point this stuff out? "It's a giant killer beast of doom that will kill us all with its jaws of killing. If it just wants to play catch then I apologize for not trying to rub its belly first, but just on the vague off chance it wants to use us as particularly bloody chew toys, can we please be prepared to throttle it with its own intestines?"

"Nice," Felicity says quietly in my ear. I suppress an ill-timed grin.

"I'm not sure I know an exact spell for that," Clyde says.

"Bit specific," Winston agrees.

"Well, stick in the same thematic area at least," I say, desperately hanging onto the last fraying edges of my sanity. "Look, the plan here—and I do want to emphasize that we are all following this plan so we can get to some fairly important world-saving—is to get the dog mad, get it to attack the zombies, let them fight it out, and then come in and take down the significantly weakened dog, which, let's face it, would otherwise kick our arses."

"Speak for your feckin' self," Kayla says.

I turn to her, a little bit of a snap to my movements. "Right now," I say, "I'm not sure you'd win a fight with gravity. I think you should dial back your expectations a touch."

This doesn't endear me exactly, but it does buy a moment for everyone to just digest the plan.

"Solid," Felicity says eventually. "Clyde, light that Rottweiler up like it's a birthday cake."

"Dude," Winston says, and I think he's addressing me. "No idea you liked a taste of the crazy. Nice."

"I am *right* here," Felicity points out while I splutter for a suitable defense. "And I am more than capable of taking that axe to you."

"Jesus." Winston sounds offended. "Just trying to give your HR violation a compliment. No need to get shirty."

"Wait, am I setting the dog on fire now or in a bit?" Clyde asks.

I look at Gran. "Do Area 51 operations ever run like this?"

He shakes his head, looking as bewildered as I feel.

I turn to Clyde. "Yes," I say. "Light it up."

Clyde inclines his head to Tabitha. "Tabitha, you remember when I first learned magic and almost burned down MI37's entire library?"

Tabitha nods minimally. "Mini Chernobyl," she says.

"That spell, please."

48

"*Gorleck mal forlak cal urkur.*" Blue lines of electricity crackle up and down Clyde's spine. "*Beshat mel tekor.*" His voice booms. Zombie heads snap in our direction.

As far as incognito things go, this is not exactly in the top tier.

"*Ifllem muerto,*" Clyde bellows, and with that all concerns about the zombies' attention are pushed roughly aside.

A colossal spark… no, that word is not adequate… A massive beam of electricity—something only barely shy of being a full-grade lightning bolt—arcs out of Clyde's palm. He flies backwards, crashes into Winston's trunk. Both of them let out a yell.

And then their cries are ruthlessly and comprehensively drowned by the titanic howl of pain from across the park.

For a moment there is just sound. Input from every other sense is obliterated. An animal shriek loud enough to have physical presence. The air vibrates around me. The ground shakes. Windows smash before and behind us. Something massive slams into concrete, into walls, into trees.

The zombies come alive as one. They lurch away from us, toward the sound, ricocheting off their poorly coordinated brethren. They get one step, two.

Then it comes. Smashing through the trees on the far side of the park, close to the library. A shower of branches and raging, gnashing teeth.

One of the Rottweiler's flanks flames and smokes where Clyde's spell impacted. It bays at the zombies. Phlegm flies massively from its mouth. It swings its head down, gathers a great fungus-filled mouthful. Its jaws slam down. Limbs and skulls spill loose. Black blood stains the greenery in great spraying arcs.

Then the zombies attack. A mass of them rush the dog's paws. One foreleg rips through a stream of oncomers. I see more than one head detonate under the force of the blow. But at the back of the beast zombies clamp on to the massive feet. The Rottweiler howls again, bucks, tries to kick, but its red blood flows with the black.

I've heard it said that it's not the size of the dog in the fight, but the size of the fight in the dog, but when the dog is the size of your average four-bedroom abode I'd argue that the point is moot. Any which way, the Rottweiler is far from down.

It hacks, mashes, chomps. The zombies swarm, climb, and tear.

Felicity rips her eyes away for long enough to give me an appreciative nod. "That worked even better than I thought it—"

"The mushroom!" Tess yells. "The damn mushroom!"

We all turn and stare. And the fight is sliding sideways across the park. The Rottweiler is thrashing around, tearing at the zombies trying to clamber up its legs. And as it whirls it's getting closer and closer to the mushroom we're here to investigate. In a moment it's going to ride right over it and our whole mission objective will be mashed to a pulp.

"Oh shit." As much fun as it is to be surrounded by a bloodbath, it would be nice if it didn't crap all over our plans. "Clyde!" I yell. "Blow a hole in that damn dog's face. Save the mushroom!"

"Wait," Clyde says, "protect the mushroom or hit the—"

"Oh you dithering bastard." The curse booms from above Clyde's head. Suddenly half our cover takes off across the park at a flat out sprint.

"Fuck it!" Winston's battle cry echoes in his wake.

He covers the distance in a flat sprint. Zombies splatter beneath his feet, limbs crushed in wet black splatters. He lowers something approximating a shoulder and slams it into the Rottweiler's side.

The flaming, frothing, chomping dog bucks, howls. Winston drives his feet into the ground. Great strips of sod and turf fly into the air. Zombies leap at Winston, start clawing up his legs.

"Piss off you buggers!" Winston heaves again, the Rottweiler gives ground, sprawling across the park.

The zombies lurch on top of the sprawling pair. For a moment the park is just a writhing pack of sodden, purple-tinged bodies.

Jesus. My friend is under that.

The Rottweiler comes up first. Barking, gnashing, mouth full of bodies. Humanity's leftovers become a main course.

A bark-clad arm follows the dog, punches up, sends zombies scattering. It clamps around the dog's muzzle and Winston heaves himself up, spilling bodies as he rises.

The Rottweiler twists, lunges, and savage jaws duck under Winston's arm, and clamp around his trunk.

"Oh fuck me sideways!"

Muscles bulging, the Rottweiler hefts Winston off the ground. It holds him aloft, ignores the zombies hanging from its flanks, tearing at its skin. It shakes its head savagely back and forth.

"Mommmmyyyyy!!!" Winston's wail warbles through the air.

"He's too close," Clyde is mumbling. "I can't get just the dog."

My table leg feels stupid and useless in my sweaty hand.

And then Winston is airborne, released and flying. A tree become a twig, sailing up and away.

And then down. Crashing and smashing. Soil cresting before him like a breaking wave. Bodies flying before him. Skidding across the park, crashing inevitably towards the mushroom.

No. No.

"Do I...?" Clyde is breathless, Winston's screeching form reflected in his chrome faceplate.

"Runaway tree!" Gran yells. "Stop him, dude!"

Clyde plants his back leg. A spark flares up his spine. The smell of ozone fills the air.

"No!" I put a hand on Clyde's shoulder. The last thing I want is to have Winston blown into splinters just to save a pissing mushroom. I know heroes are meant to make sacrifices, but I'm not making one as stupid as that.

So we stand and watch as Winston bears down on the mushroom.

With a great rumble of earth, he comes to rest. Broken, bedraggled, covered in zombies, and still a yard clear of our prize. The mushroom stands untouched.

Beside me, Felicity lets out a whistle of breath.

"Close call, man." Gran is shaking his head. And he doesn't know Winston. Has no connection to him, so I can't really judge him for the decision he would have made.

"We have to get out there," I say instead. "We have to help him."

"Now you're feckin' talking." Kayla heaves herself to slightly unsteady feet.

Tess has a slightly different opinion. "Are you insane?" she asks. I have a sneaking suspicion she's already made up her mind on that one.

There again, so have I.

I break cover and run. A zombie spins as I emerge, lunges. My table leg connects with its cranium, and the thing goes down in a wet bloody splatter.

"In your feckin' eye!" I hear Kayla shout behind me. There is the damp detonation of skewered cranium.

"Winston!" I yell.

He stirs. Massive, mighty, and fallen.

"Ohh…" He sits up, clutching at the part of his trunk where his head resides. "I haven't felt this shitty since I discovered Jägerbombs…" His branches hang snapped and broken. Bark has been flayed from him, raw wood is split open, sap leaking.

"Holy shit," I say, then get distracted by the need to beat down another zombie who seems to think I'd make an excellent early morning snack. When I come back up from dissuading him, I am splattered and panting. "Are you OK?" I ask Winston, finishing the thought.

Winston blinks. Whorls of wood contracting and expanding in an expanse of bark. "Well, you know, the good part about being a tree is you're tough as fuck." He stands up, claps two branches together. "All right then, Fido, come on if you think you're hard enough."

Behind me I hear gunshots, shouts. I spin around. The zombies have discovered our little group. Gran, Felicity, and Tess have their guns drawn. Felicity snipes skulls with calm efficiency. Clyde jams out a hand. A zombie flies away. It lands in pieces.

A little way from them Kayla leans on a stick she must have found. Her other hand dispatches steel death to any zombie foolish enough to wander within a yard's radius of her post.

Winston continues to stride away from me, and while I like his attitude, I'm not as keen on his odds.

Beyond him the Rottweiler is busy thinning the zombie herd. The dog's in a pretty sorry state, but I think I know the ultimate winner of that fight. Which means when this is all over, if Winston ends up as matchsticks, the rest of us are going to have a seriously pissed off giant dog to put down.

I look down at the table leg in my hand. It is a bent and battered piece of aluminum. And it is not really going to be much help in the long haul.

Immobile she may be, but Kayla isn't going to give me her sword. And it's too much, I know, to ask for some kind soul to have left one lying around. But something pointy, at this very moment, would not go amiss.

I take rapid inventory of the park. Stalks of grass, bits of broken off Winston, enormous clods of earth thrown up by Winston's epic power slide.

Bits of broken off Winston it is then.

I grab a broken branch about four feet long, the last foot of which is one wickedly sharp splinter. It's not perfect, and the balance is for shit, but it definitely will do some damage.

I start after Winston and twenty yards later, get to try out its effectiveness.

A blank-eyed woman, apparently sick of being used as a chew toy, comes at me wielding her own chewed off arm as a club. Well, I assume it's her arm. Maybe it's not. I don't really have time to look for telling details while I'm ducking a violent swing of tattered muscle and bone.

I parry the second blow but the zombie's improvised club pivots at the elbow, around my stick, and gristle smashes into my cheekbone. I go down, blind from equal parts severed arm juice and sheer horror. I come back up hard, and with an edge of panic pounding through my blood stream.

My pointy stick skewers the woman, bursts something squishy and previously vital, then exits via the region of her spinal cord.

For an extra bonus she stops hitting me.

It isn't a flaming sword, but I am beginning to become attached to my pointy stick already.

Three punctured bodies later, I catch up to Winston.

"Pick me up," I tell him.

"What? Like I'm a mid-combat taxi service to you now?"

"Pick me up," I say, "and get me on that dog's head." I shake the stick at him.

Winston's wooden face creases. "Mate," he says, "is that like, part of me?"

Oh. That is… I think back to the woman beating me with her own arm. Not exactly a comfortable moment.

"Sorry," I try.

"Fucking savage." But Winston's hand comes down and I go back up with it. He perches me in the branches above his head.

"You got a plan with that?" Winston strides through the battlefield. Corpses squish beneath his falling feet.

"Stab it in its brains."

"Not exactly General Patton, are you?"

That seems a little unnecessary. "What exactly was your plan?"

Winston shrugs, causing me to bounce up and down. "Punch it in the face."

"Hello," I say, "I'm the kettle, you must be the pot."

"Oh, just shut your face and nut up."

The Rottweiler is close now. It's bleeding hard. The fire on its flank is out, but the wound is weeping blood and other fluids of an even less appealing nature. Zombies are on its back, ripping through fur and flesh. It's panting, and limping, but its jaws keep going down and keep coming up full. Blood and phlegm spill over its muzzle.

The Rottweiler shifts its head, sees Winston coming, growls. It's a noise that vibrates in my gut and loosens my bowels. Where the hell do I come up with these stupid, stupid plans?

Winston lunges. I'm thrown back against his limbs, then borne forward by branches and momentum.

His body and the dog's collide, their bodies smashing into each other. Winston grinding his shoulder against that weeping wound. All those broken branches. The Rottweiler howls.

I fly.

I leave the nest of branches, slam through twigs. Rottweiler hide slams into my face, thick, musty, and tasting like dried blood.

And then, as soon as I make contact, I am slipping away, careening down the dog's side. Gravity makes me its bitch. I grasp at fistfuls of thick fur, lose my purchase, gain it, lose it again. I grasp desperately, wonder why the hell I haven't let go of my stick yet. Then my arm wrenches in its socket. I wait for my grip to give way but I hang on.

My fall arrested, my feet swing forty feet above the ground. I concentrate on not dropping my stick or soiling my underwear.

Come on, Arthur. You've been through worse than this.

And while that's true, it still doesn't make going through this any easier. I need to engage my other hand if I'm going to haul myself up, but if I do that then I drop my stick and this all becomes pointless.

I hear a growl from beneath me. I risk another glimpse down.

Between my dangling feet, comes a zombie's head.

It's clinging to the dog's underbelly, hands and feet wrapped in the dog's fur, hanging upside down, but coming up, toward me.

Jesus. It's not even lunch time and the list of bad things my day has contained is beginning to get ridiculous.

I jab down at the intruding face, but my leverage is for shit, and while being hit in the face probably isn't pleasant for my friendly neighborhood zombie, it's not enough to dislodge him.

God, I need to get out of this asshole of a situation.

I prod again, with similar results. I think I heard somewhere that expecting different results from the same action is the definition of madness. As I need no help in going over that particular ledge, I decide to change tactics. Fighting isn't working. The other option provided by adrenaline is flight.

There's also another place I can jam my pointy stick.

With as much force as I can, I ram it into the dog's side. It slides in a full foot. With all that's going on, the Rottweiler doesn't seem to register the flesh wound. Which is nice because the lack of flinching gives me the chance to seize the stick with both hands and heave. The wound I've created emits an ugly wet, slurping sound. But I'm up, bracing my elbows, then my gut, then a foot on the slowly slipping wood. I balance, precarious and on the verge of toppling for a moment, before I grasp more fur, and let that take my weight.

I reach down, start fishing for the stick, pull it out, and repeat the process. Which gives me a good view of the zombie as it realizes its next meal is retreating, and increases its pace toward me. I get the stick free, jam it into the dog's side above my head again. Grab, haul.

The zombie approaches. And trust my luck to finally find one who's worked out how to get its coordination back. The bastard can move.

Now that my stick is occupied, I have to settle for kicking the zombie in the face every time it gets too close. It's even less effective than stabbing at it.

A clammy hand seizes my leg. I kick, but the zombie is really not at all about letting go of things. My grip on my stick is put to the test and apparently I should have studied harder.

Shit and—

Then Winston punches the dog in the face.

49

My entire world vibrates. I thrash about on my branch. The zombie on my ankle falls away. More undead fall from above. The Weather Girls would be happy. It's finally raining men.

One zombie crashes into my shoulder. Suddenly I'm hanging by one hand. The dog reels. I flap and fly. I grab at anything I can.

Winston's next punch lands. The world lurches again. I go from midair to eating Rottweiler hide. Zombies fall about me. The dog howls. I kick at fur, feet skidding and skittering. My hands grab uselessly.

"Not so fucking yappy now, are you, you miserable poodle-fucker."

Winston is still keeping it classy.

Somehow I find purchase. Fistfuls of fur in my hands. I heave myself in the direction that appears to be up at that moment, drag my stick with me. And finally the ground is flat beneath me. In the moment between blows I am able to recognize that I sit astride the dog's spine. The knobs of its vertebrae rise and fall like small hills.

Another punch. Apparently Winston is not someone you chew up and toss halfway across a park if you want to preserve your dental work.

For a moment this all seems rather stupid. This idea

of rescuing Winston. Of being the *X-wing* sneaking into the chink in the *Death Star*'s armor. In the distance, beyond the Rottweiler's head I can see Winston pulling back his fist.

Then the dog lunges. Brutally, savagely, jaws slamming down. I hear wood crack.

"Shit!" Winston's eye whorls go wide.

Ahead of me, the dog starts to shake its head. Winston rattles and cracks.

OK. Rescuing is back on the menu. Gingerly, I clamber to my feet.

Unfortunately this idea is not exclusively mine. Every single Clyde zombie that has survived Winston's hammer blows is sharing it with me.

The world starts to blur. The stuttering snapshot images of adrenaline and head trauma. I try to find my footing on the dog's back. Things grab at me. Blood runs down my cheek. Pain. My shoulders ache from the continual thrust of the stick. The resistance of bodies. The sound of wood on skin.

And then I run out of dog. I stand stupidly for a moment staring at empty space, trying to work out where the thing has gone. And then it registers. I'm standing between its ears. There's blood all over me. Other things. Worse things. I'm trying not to think about them.

Winston is directly in front of me. Screaming. Yelling. Cursing. Probably cursing. I can't quite tell. My head is ringing too hard. I can hear something guttural behind me, coming closer. Something I haven't killed yet.

There is a wasteland of dead below me. I can see my friends, Felicity, Clyde, Gran, Kayla—all of them. I can see them in a tight knot at the edge of the park. I can see the bodies spread out before them. A crescent of the dead. This is a massacre, a madness.

Clyde did this. Version 2.0 did this. Made us do this. He made us monsters today.

A monster on the back of a monster. And I just want this to end.

Beneath me, a foot away, one great brown eye narrows in the Rottweiler's skull. It focuses on Winston's face.

I bunch the aching muscles of my arms.

The dog opens its jaws wide. The stink of its breath fills the air. I feel the whole of its body prepare for the launch.

I plunge my stick down into that great brown eye.

The dog's jaws, prepared to snap shut, spasm. Then they let fly with a howl of absolute rage and pain. I am so close to the sound my vision blurs. But I plunge the stick deeper. I dig deep into the socket. Gouge for the nerve, for a way deeper in.

The dog bucks. I lose my footing, but I am almost up to my elbows in the creature's deflating eyeball. I dangle from its face. Sticky fluid gushes over me. Jaws snap and grind beneath my feet. I brace them against the monster's jaw bone, and then suddenly I go from elbow deep to shoulder deep.

Gore washes over me in a flood. I am soaked in it. Gagging and spitting. And I am so disgusted and horrified, that I almost don't realize the ground is rushing up to greet me. I almost don't realize that the dog is falling dead to the floor.

50

It's Felicity who makes it to me first. Felicity, gore-soaked hair plastered to her head, cheeks white with exhaustion, hands hidden beneath a thick smear of sweat and blood. She has never looked more beautiful.

She kneels beside me, pushes my hair back, examines the tears in my skin. "You," she says, and then stops and shakes her head. "You are a silly, stupid bastard."

Not exactly where I hoped this was going. A David and Goliath metaphor perhaps. Maybe a passing reference to bravery and daring.

"Killed it," I offer in my defense.

She leans down, kisses my forehead. But when she comes up there is a slightly accusatory look in her eye. "You almost killed yourself."

To be fair, that is very close to being true.

She leans in close, her eyes only inches from mine. "Arthur, it is *essential* that we all get out of here alive." There's an edge to her voice. Not hysterical, but maybe thinking about checking out houses in that neighborhood. "I can't protect you if you fling yourself at every single…" She shakes her head. "God knows if we're going to fight giant Rottweilers again. But you know what I mean." She takes my head in both her hands. "I look after my own, but you have to help me on that. Especially you."

She kisses me again. Her lips pressed against mine. Pressed there despite all the crap I've been rinsed in recently. An almost desperate kiss.

"Minor misjudgment," I offer up in terms of reassurance. The slight sheen in Felicity's eyes makes me think I could have done a better job. But that's tricky when head trauma is making the world look like it's been covered by Vaseline.

"I thought…" Felicity pauses, looks away, starts again. "We said that for this, for *us* to work… we have to trust each other. You can't betray that trust. You can't climb up a giant bloody dog covered in zombies and try and kill it with a stick. You just can't."

I think about that. "Sounds silly when you say it."

Her face contorts. Amusement, anger, passion, pain. "You," she says, and then she discards words and just holds me.

After a minute or so, someone clears their throat. Felicity pulls away. I sit up. The world spins a little, but overall I'm feeling a little more clear-headed. Gran, Tabitha, Kayla, and Clyde stand around us. We seem short on people.

I take quick mental inventory. "Winston," I identify one missing person. The one that started this whole dog and pointy stick show. "How's Winston doing?"

"He's…" Clyde starts.

"Shitty," Winston finishes. I turn, stare. He leans against the bloody flank of the dog's gargantuan corpse. Most of his branches are broken—either snapped clean off or hanging at awkward angles.

He holds out one arm. Bark hangs off it in swaths. "How the fuck am I meant to photosynthesize like this?" he asks. "I'm going to be knackered for fucking weeks like this. And the TV is bound to be shitty this side of the pissing apocalypse."

Alive. He's alive.

Slowly, and with considerable help from Felicity, I get to my feet.

"Wait," I say, another thought hitting me. And right now I'm sensitive to even those sorts of blows. "Where's Tess?"

No one meets my eye.

Oh. Oh no. Oh shit.

"No," I say. "No." But no one backs me up on that. I stumble away from the group, as poorly coordinated as one of Clyde's zombies.

"Don't," Felicity puts a hand on my shoulder, and even that weight almost floors me. But I pull away.

Because… no. No. We are not sacrificing people here. We are saving humanity. Because… because… Fuck! Fuck it! Fuck Clyde! Because we are humanity. We're a fucking species. We're part of the damn biosphere or whatever the hell it is he's trying to save. He's not saving the world, he's changing it. Maybe. I don't know. I just know that I am here to save people. People like Tess. And, God, I didn't know her, really. And I have seen other people die. People I was closer to. But… fuck. Fuck. I was going to explain to her. I had promised her. How the hell can I deliver on that now?

And then, there she is. Lying in the long grass. Flat on her back. Legs and arms splayed. Like a child making a snow angel.

"It's not your fault." Felicity has caught up with me. I am probably not that hard to catch up with right now. "You literally could not have done anything more."

"I…" I start. But what could I have done? I could

have stayed by her. Saved her. And then what would happen to Winston? Wouldn't I just be mourning someone else?

"Fuck!" I scream it at the sky. At the treetops that shouldn't be there. At this new world that Clyde has forced upon us in a monstrous attack of ego and self-righteousness.

"Make it count." Felicity is still talking. "That's all you can do. When we lose someone. When someone sacrifices themselves for you. All you can do is make it count. Make it fuel you. Go forward from here."

Maybe once, back when I first started at MI37, I would have thought her heartless, but I hear the compassion in her words now. The sorrow. And the truth. Felicity is as right as ever.

Make it count. I stand in a city park become jungle surrounded by rapidly decaying dead bodies. Make that count. Jesus.

"The mushroom," I say. "We... We have to..." It's hard to get the words out still. I am too full of emotions. Thought and speech are abstractions I can't achieve yet, I'm stuck in something more primal.

Felicity understands though. "Kayla, Clyde, Gran," she calls, "dissect that damn thing." She puts a hand on my shoulder, guides me toward the mushroom.

Clyde digs into the flesh of the stalk with motorized ferocity. His steel hands rip out chunk after chunk. Gran gouges at the thing with another splinter of Winston.

Kayla hobbles toward the fungal mass wielding her sword in one hand, leaning on her scabbard with the other, and seemingly trying to grow a third hand in order to clamp the wound on her side.

"Jesus, Kayla," Felicity sounds exasperated. "If

you're not up to this stuff, just say no and sit down."

"Feckin' up for it," Kayla spits. "Only a feckin' flesh wound."

"You were skewered, you ridiculous woman." Felicity shakes her head. "Sit down before I put you on your arse."

Kayla hesitates and then complies. I swear I hear her mutter, "Bite your feckin' legs off."

Clyde is armpit deep in the mushroom. There is a vast concavity in its side, the stalk beginning to sway. Abruptly he stops moving. "Wait," he says. "This doesn't make any sense at all."

"Stop slacking, you fecker," Kayla calls from where she's sagged.

"No," Clyde says, then catches himself. "I mean, please. If you don't mind. Sorry, didn't mean to—"

"What is it?" I cut him off, try to bring my full attention to bear. Try to get it off Tess's body, discarded, unburied in the bushes behind me.

"Well," Clyde says, extracting his arms, "I'd be the first to admit that botany is not exactly my specialist subject. Science background, yes, prior to all this thaumaturgy nonsense, but that was organic chemistry. A biology A-level in the long distant past is the best I have to offer. And, really, fungal anatomy was not a large part of even that. So there's a chance I'm going out on a limb—"

"Dude," Gran cuts him off, "the brevity thing. I know it's not yours. But, like, seriously."

"Oh, yes," Clyde says, because even he recognizes that the day you manage to annoy a hippy is probably the day when you should truncate your speeches. "Well, I was just thinking that electrical cables aren't normally part of a mushroom, are they?"

"No." Tabitha sounds like she'd like to bring her brevity to Clyde's lifespan.

"Electrical cables?" I say. Because, well, that's odd enough that I want to double check.

"I think so," Clyde says. He reaches into the mushroom again and heaves. His fist comes back out wrapped around a thick bundle of blue, red, yellow, and black wiring.

"Holy shit." It's Tabitha. We all turn to stare.

"What is it?" I ask.

"Biothaumaturgical delivery," she says, rather cryptically I think. "Thought that was how Version 2.0 was dispersing the mushrooms. Wrong. *Digi*biothaumaturgical delivery."

"Erm…" I try to parse that. "Once more, with shorter words and longer sentences?"

"Electricity cables," she says, "there to power the magic."

I nod. That's what they told me to expect. Clyde is using power cables to magically manifest his mushrooms.

"But," she says, "more than power cables there." She approaches Clyde, confidently at first, but a little more tentatively as she gets closer. Then she remembers herself, recovers, and snatches the wires from Clyde. "Red. Black." She pulls two wires from the bundle. "Electricity." She nods to herself.

I start to catch on. "You've got left over wires."

Her smile shows teeth. "Fiber optics." She pulls out a yellow wire. "Ethernet." She pulls out the blue. She looks triumphant. "Means he needs to be writing code into the spores. No wireless network means he needs to do it wired. Means he has *a network*."

I wait for more. All I get is an expectant expression, that slowly morphs into disappointment, and what I can best describe as the expression of someone who thinks I should be spayed to save humanity from my genes. It's a surprisingly specific look.

"How Version 2.0 is coordinating all this." She rolls her eyes.

I still don't get it. She shakes her head.

"I can hack it," she says.

Ohhh. Jackpot.

51

A network. A way in. Version 2.0 hid it in his mushrooms, but we found it.

"You're absolutely sure you can hack into it?" I check. After all, Version 2.0 is a digital supercomputer genius who just coordinated something that looks a lot like the end of days.

Tabitha's disdain almost oozes out of her. "Please," she says.

Kayla nods in appreciation. Gran grins like a child. "Righteous." And even I have to concede that I can kind of see why someone might be attracted to that sort of badassery.

God, the world really must have ended for me to have that sort of thought. I wrap an arm around Felicity for comfort.

Clyde just sort of stands there, and... Well, maybe he looks awkward, but maybe the body he's in was designed that way.

Tabitha takes a moment to look up from her keyboard and fistpump at the mushroom. "Your face. In it. Fucking supercomputer bullshit." She looks from the fungus to us. "I'm in."

I just manage to stop myself from asking, "Really?" because, well, there's only so much Tabitha bile I like to take in one day.

"Did I use the same password as always?" Clyde asks.

"Added a six at the end." And for a moment it sounds like there's a smile in Tabitha's voice. Then she remembers herself and scowls. "Pissing idiot even when you're an evil genius." She shakes her head.

And yet perhaps something in Clyde's posture becomes a little more upright.

God. We're in. We're doing something. We're fighting back. Well, Tabitha is.

She looks over her shoulder at me. "Now," she says. "What?"

The question catches me off guard. This is usually the climax of the movie. You hack into the bad guys' files, get the information you need, and then everything blows up while the hero smokes a cigar and bangs a hot-looking blonde.

Nothing is blowing up and my girlfriend is a brunette.

I force mental gears to engage while New York sways and creaks in the breeze around me. And really the answer is obvious.

"Your code," I say to Tabitha. "Your debugging code. Deploy it. Take over the fungus. Get that bastard Version 2.0 out of everyone's heads."

Tabitha arches an eyebrow at me. "Mercurio. End of the world. Now. Between all that, when did I get the time to fix the code? Remind me?" Her middle finger makes its traditional salute.

Shit. "Can you fix it now?"

Tabitha doubles the number of middle fingers she's erecting at me. "Sure," she says. "Go find a tent. We'll camp out a few days." Then she adds, "Dick."

"Man," says Gran. "I was just going to, like, just ask

to map the system so we can find the evil dude's servers and nuke him and shit. Love the ambition."

"Oh," I say. Because, yes, that does sound like quite a good idea. "Can we do that instead?"

"On it." Tabitha goes back to her laptop and starts tapping.

"If she finds it," I start, "well, who knows if it will really take a long time to fix the debugging code. It might not be as bad as Tabitha fears. This *could* be our moment."

"Tabitha is very good at coding," Clyde chips in. "For what it's worth."

"Man." Gran looks a bit guilty. "I was, like, totally serious about all this nuke shit. You dudes really sure about debugging and stuff?"

From the looks he gets, Gran is not backing the popular opinion.

"Talking about saving the vast feckin' majority of humanity." Kayla sits up from where she was lying down and puts the collective thought into words. "Seems kind of feckin' important." She heaves herself up.

"No, no." Gran shakes his head as she starts hobbling toward him. "I, like, get that and shit. It's just, you know, we fuck that up and we don't get another chance. We get in there and diddle Version 2.0 wrong one time and he's gonna clamp his files shut faster than we can say, 'shit, we totally boned that one up.'" He shrugs.

Felicity chews her lip. She glances at me, because she knows how stubborn I can be about little things like trying to save all of humanity. "He does have a point, Arthur," she says. "We have one shot at this. We should make sure it's the right one. We don't want to rush in half-cocked."

"What if this *is* our one shot?" I ask.

"Carpe feckin' diem." Kayla is more eloquent than I think I can be.

"Except," Gran points out, "this is, like, a totally shitty diem. Get out of Manhattan. That's, like, all of step one of this plan. Then regroup. That's step two. Then kick ass. You're like trying to mess up the order. We'll be all popping it when we should be locking it. I totally assure you that a shit show will ensue."

"Look." Kayla leans forward on her scabbard to stare hard at Gran. "Nobody likes putting foot to arse more than me. I feckin' dare you to contradict me. But where the feck is saving people in your plan?"

"Kayla." Felicity reaches out a calming hand.

"Execute the bad guy, then clean up his mess," Gran says. "Kill before spill. Totally standard operating procedure."

Felicity lays out her hands. She agrees with him. Kayla is fingering her sword hilt in a way that suggests she doesn't.

"If we see a chance," I say, "I really think we need to take it." I keep my eyes on Felicity. She will be the final arbiter here.

"Sort of arbitrary." Tabitha answers before Felicity can. She's still squatting at the base of the mushroom. I turn to look at her. "No code," she says looking me dead in the eye. "Code doesn't work as is. No time to work on it. QED, this is arbitrary bullshit."

Gran shrugs. But I won't be so easily put off.

"How long would fixing the code take?"

Tabitha echoes her boyfriend's shrug. "Fuck knows."

Gran appeals directly to Felicity. "We have to keep

moving," he says. "Get the map of the network and get out of here."

Felicity looks at me. An apologetic smile. "I agree with him," she says.

It sits wrong. I let her see that. But I'm not sure how to say it.

Tabitha goes back to us, keeps tapping away on the laptop. Her fingers strike the keyboard with increasing force. Then she throws them up in exasperation. "Bullshit algorithms!" she spits.

"What is it, dudette?" Gran looks concerned

"Maps," she says with disgust. Her face screws up. Then finally, with a savage glance at Clyde, admits, "Having problems." Another grimace. "Local server map only from here."

So we don't even get the map we need. This is all wrong. We're in 2.0's systems. We should be able to do something from here. But what Tabitha's saying is that we can't save the world from here. Even if her code was working, we could only save Manhattan.

"How do we get to the larger map?" I ask. "Is there somewhere else we can go to get it?"

Tabitha taps a few more times, examines her laptop's screen. Something between a grimace and a grin touches her face. "Irony," she says.

I look blankly at her.

She rolls her eyes. "Yes," Tabitha says. "There is. The Empire State Building."

52

OK, I'm not one for new age mysticism, or sticking burning candles in my ears, or whatnot, but that really does sound like it's stretching coincidence. Still, I'm not above trying to capitalize on it.

"Look," I say, "talk about an opportunity to seize. We have to go to the Empire State Building anyway. We can connect there to Version 2.0's larger network. We can take control. If Tabitha's had a chance to fix the code it'll be perfect."

Tabitha looks at me dubiously. "Fix the code? While walking over? To the heavily defended power base?"

"What?" I push my luck. "You're telling me there's a programming thing you can't do?"

"You'll make it work," Clyde says quietly. "I know you. You will."

Tabitha glares from one of us to the other. She opens her mouth as if to say something, then closes it again. I suspect the fact that she has to agree with one of us is causing her some sort of internal hemorrhaging. Eventually she shakes her head, then buries it in the laptop. Gran takes a slight step toward her. A step that puts him between her and Clyde. But he looks at me.

"Dude, I totally think you are rushing things," he says.

I glance at Felicity. She chews her lip. "Look," she

says. "There is no harm in Tabitha trying to work on the code while we move. That, in fact, is pretty much an undeniably good idea. And we do have to go to the Empire State Building anyway. To get to the radio transmitter and now, it seems, if we want to map Version 2.0's network. If by the time we get there, Tabitha is happy with her code then we'll reconsider." She nods at Gran. "For now the focus is recon and intel." A nod to me. "We'll re-examine the mission parameters as the situation develops." A final nod to herself, satisfied. "This is the damn apocalypse," she says after a moment, "the situation is probably going to develop."

It's a fair call. Of course it's a fair call. Neither Gran nor I can really argue with it.

"Actually," Tabitha says, "may not *have* to go to the Empire State Building."

Oh shit and balls.

Tabitha turns and looks dubiously at Gran. "Area 51 uses Google chat? Seriously?"

53

"In, like, our defense," Gran says, looking more than a little sheepish, "Google chat is really way down the contingency list."

"Wait…" I'm still confused. "Area 51 is on Clyde's wired network?" Paranoia alarm bells ring at almost deafening levels in my head. I mean, I've seen some conspiracy movies before but this is a bit of a mindfuck.

"No." Tabitha sounds annoyed. "Clyde— piggybacking his network on the existing wired one. We only took down wireless. Wired internet still there. He connected to it. Kept it live. Despite apocalypse bullshit. Area 51 also on it. Recognized my IP address. Want a passcode."

Gran holds out a hand for the computer. "You mind?"

Tabitha hesitates. Gran looks confused. Tabitha looks from her laptop to his hand, then back to her laptop. She still doesn't pass it.

"Dudette?" Gran asks. He looks a touch concerned.

For the first time in my life, I see Tabitha look contrite. "It's…" she starts. And everyone from MI37 knows what she means, but how do you explain to your new boyfriend that he is not quite as important to you as your laptop?

"Mate," Winston calls from over by the Rottweiler's

corpse, "you're more likely to talk her into the kinky shit than you are to get her to hand over that laptop."

Well, that's one way you could explain it...

Tabitha stabs a gaze at Winston that stands a chance of doing more damage than the Rottweiler did. Then, quite deliberately, she shoves the laptop at Gran. He catches it awkwardly, with an oomph of exhaled breath. For a moment it looks like he's going to fumble the thing, and I almost can't watch. Because then I'd have to watch Tabitha rip out Gran's spine and beat his corpse with it.

He manages to catch the thing before it slips, though. "Woah." He grins.

Tabitha does not.

"Fuck me, mate," says Winston. Then he considers this. "Of course, if you do that you won't get that computer again. Trust me."

Gran taps away, ignoring him. Tabitha watches him the way a prison guard watches a repeat offender.

Personally, I try to get to grips with what all this new information actually means. If we're in contact with Area 51 our reasons for going to the Empire State Building are significantly fewer.

But we *have* to go there. Whatever the potential costs, we *have* to try and capitalize on this moment.

I'm brought back to the now as Felicity squeezes my arm again. I realize I am clenching and unclenching my hands, nails leaving small crescent moons in my palms. With her free hand, Felicity makes small gestures suggesting I calm down.

"OK." Gran nods his head at the laptop screen and chews his lip. "OK."

"What is it?" Felicity takes a step toward him.

Gran stands, handing the laptop back to Tabitha, who snatches it, and cradles it to her chest like a recently recovered child. "We have to, like, get underground pronto. The subways are a death trap, but the tunnels for the PATH trains are groovy, apparently. Take us straight under the river and out into New Jersey. Evac team are chilling over there waiting to take us to Mount Rushmore."

"Mount Rushmore?" Clyde cocks his metallic head.

"You know, man." Gran shrugs. "You going to use that much dynamite on a mountain face you might as well hide a secret government facility in it, right?"

"Oh," says Clyde. "Well, yes. I suppose. When you put it like that. Eminently sensible. Not sure why we don't dynamite more structures really. Or some other explosive, I suppose. Don't want to stereotype explosive experts, do we?"

He looks around. Nobody seems willing to tackle the issue with him.

Personally I have more pressing tactical concerns. Like keeping us in Manhattan until we can try and take down Clyde. "We're still going to the Empire State Building first, though, right?" I say.

"Dude." Gran shakes his head. "We need to get below ground, like now and shit. Planes are incoming."

"Planes?" Felicity's brow furrows. "What planes?"

"Twenty minutes out." Gran shrugs. "They're taking this place out. Going to Agent Orange New York City to oblivion. We want to be well on our way, man. Like ghost gone."

Agent Orange... it rings a bell at the back of my head.

"What the hell is this color-coded bastard they're

dropping on us?" Apparently Winston is operating with a bell deficiency.

"They used it in Vietnam," Felicity says quietly. "For deforestation. Flush out the Viet Cong. Give them no place to hide."

"Thought they used napalm for that." Winston describes an expanding circle with his hands and makes kaboom noises.

"Plantkiller," Tabitha says. "Takes out grass, flowers, fungus," she pauses, "trees."

Winston heaves himself to his feet and plants great branch-like arms at his waist. "Well," he says, "that's not exactly scones and crumpets for fucking tea is it? Very fucking nice."

"It's not something I'd put in the great-for-people category either," Clyde points out. "Were I to be categorizing things that way. Which given Evil-Me's proclivities, I feel I should specify I am not. But Gran is right. None of you want to be around when that drops."

None of *us*. Because Clyde... Jesus. Every time I start to find the humanity in him I come up against this hard metal shell.

And as much as I feel for Winston's predicament... "They'll kill everyone in the city," I say.

Gran nods. "Sacrifice the infected limb. Try to spare the whole."

Jesus. Jesus that's a cold logic. Not so different from Version 2.0's thought processes.

Save the world. Kill humanity or kill the plants. Jesus. What a fucking war.

But then another thought, hot on the heels of that one, even if it's panting a little to keep up. If they kill the plants, they kill the fungus. They kill our way in to Version 2.0's system. They kill our ability to spread a cure.

"You've got to stall them," I say. "New York City is eighteen million people. We have a chance to save—"

Gran doesn't look happy. Not with me. Not with his superiors. "No," he says. "We're not trying that. Even if there's time to write it. It's untested code."

"Still haven't fixed it," Tabitha points out.

"You will," Clyde calls. "I know it."

Tabitha grinds her teeth until the frustration spills out. "Just... Shut the fuck up. OK?"

"OK." Clyde nods quick assent, stands motionless.

"Eighteen million people," I insist. I saw the pain on Gran's face when I quoted that number. "We can't write them off."

"You can't save them," he counters.

"Maybe," I insist. "Maybe I can."

Gran looks to the skies, as if the planes might already be upon us, as if he's looking for an out. He looks back to me.

"They won't hold for a maybe, man." He still looks unhappy. "Planes are inbound. And, yeah, it's shitty to do this, but this isn't our choice, man. 2.0 forced this on us, right? He killed these people, not us. You say he's so fucking smart, he saw this coming. Like prophecy and shit. This was his call."

And, I realize, Gran's one hundred percent behind the idea of planes coming in. He may be sad that it's necessary, but there isn't any doubt in him that his superiors have made the right call. His sadness isn't enough to create doubt. And in that moment I see the CIA agent in Gran. As loyal to Area 51 as I am to MI37.

"Look." Somewhat to my surprise, it's Felicity who

steps forward. "There has to be something we can give them. Some reason to buy us a little time. Just to check everything out. How long do we have?"

Gran checks his watch. "We've got less than twenty minutes. We need to move."

And no. No, that can't be it.

I need a reason to stay. And not just the people of New York. Saving people is not enough. God, it should be, but it's not. Not for Gran's superiors. Not for Gran.

I see him shooting the girl in the Mexican trash dump. This is the CIA. The movie bad guys. And they're not bad guys. They're just not heroes.

I need to give them something tactical. Something brutal and straightforward. Something like them, perhaps.

What do we have? A mushroom. A dispersal system. A network. A map of that network. A central... wait.

"The map," I say to Tabitha. "We still need the map of the bigger network, right?"

Tabitha seems reluctant to be pulled into this. "Yeah," she says, grudgingly. And I think she might just be Gran's weak spot.

"We can hack into another mushroom." Gran sees my argument coming and tries to head it off. "We can find another hub. Go in there."

"Really?" I wish I could pull Felicity's trick of the lone eyebrow ranger, perched efficiently near my hairline, but I have to heft both of the things aloft. "Can you guarantee that? Do we know that every one of Version 2.0's mushrooms is hooked into the system? Can you guarantee planes loaded with Agent Orange aren't wiping out the other mushrooms? Are you sure Version 2.0 won't realize his system has been compromised? This might be a one-time only deal."

For a moment Gran wavers. I turn back to Tabitha. "You could get that map, right? You could rip down his firewalls and lay everything he has bare. You could tell them where to drop the goddamn nuke, couldn't you?"

And slowly but surely a wicked grin carves its way across Tabitha's face. She stands up, holds her laptop out to Gran.

"Stop the planes," she says. She circles her head to include our whole merry little band. "Tell them we need more time. Tell them we need to go to war."

54

DOWN THE ROAD

"Approaching target location," Gran breathes into his brand new walkie-talkie.

We've had to abandon Google chat. Tabitha needed the laptop to work on her debugging code. Fortunately, before she logged off, the kindly Area 51 folk on the other end of the chat window were able to point us toward a stash of supplies the CIA had hidden in a secret compartment beneath the security desk of a nearby office building.

The fact that Gran seemed unaware of these stashes makes me think that he should read his interdepartmental memos more thoroughly. Assuming that the world returns to a state where interdepartmental memos are sent to Gran once more.

The really good news, though, was that along with walkie-talkies we got to restock our armamentarium. I am now the proud owner of some sleek black pistol that looks almost exactly the same as the one MI37 gave me except it has a different manufacturer's logo on it. Felicity, on the other hand, seemed particularly excited by the stash. Her handbag bulges with Pandorian horrors.

Now we huddle at the corner of Fifth Avenue and Thirty-fourth Street. The Empire State Building looms massively over us. Crouching here seems a little ridiculous when someone can just peer out of a fiftieth floor window and see us. Still, there's a chance the tree cover will help.

Then our tree sits down and says, "Bugger me, but I am knackered. Actually, don't bugger me, I'm not up for it."

"I couldn't anyway," Clyde seems to feel the need to tell him. "Lack of all the fun anatomy pieces on this model, I'm afraid."

"I feel you, mate." Winston nods and his broken branches rattle. "Made of wood, never able to get it. Fucking irony."

"Maybe," Felicity suggests, "we could concentrate on formulating a plan."

"Sure," Winston agrees. "You tell me and Clyde when you got one. We'll be here."

Felicity rolls her eyes, though the idea of Winston being uninvolved in the planning process does have considerable appeal.

"Look, dudes." Gran points across a street clogged with bushes and tangled weeds, to a doorway encircled by great swathes of kudzu. "The lobby lights are on. Place has got power."

And he's right. Halfway down Thirty-fourth Street, yellow electric light glows beyond the glass doors. "They must have generators," I say. "Or Version 2.0 spared the power source."

Felicity nods. "That makes sense. If he's running computers in there, he'll need power."

Tabitha is grim-faced. "Need to find them. The servers. Won't take long then."

"Dudette." Gran claps Tabitha on the back. "Never

let it be said that confidence ain't sexy. Because—" He shakes his head. "—mmm."

"Oh, feck off." Kayla grimaces at that.

While I am probably the last person who should complain about displays of affection toward workmates, even I throw up a little in my mouth. I'm glad Clyde is engaged in his conversation with Winston.

"Well, yes." Felicity tries to move on. "But from what we know of Version 2.0 he's unlikely to have left the front door open for us. I'm guessing we'll have some serious defenses to get through."

"Feckin' great." Kayla lets go of her sword/cane for a moment to clap her hands together.

Felicity stares at her. "What are you talking about? You can barely stand up. You are not the tip of the spear today."

"Feck you."

Felicity casually reaches over and pushes Kayla. Kayla rocks back and bounces against the corner of a building, she staggers slightly.

It is not exactly a top-notch display of super-soldiering.

"Feckin' fine," Kayla sulks.

"Back to the original point about security and stuff," I say. "That does indeed sound likely. And I've already been punched a lot today. Is there any way we could climb through the air conditioning or something?" That system is a lot less likely to be booby trapped than Area 51's was. I think it's viable this time.

"Air conditioning?" Tabitha says. "Over a hundred floors. Need to sweep them all."

And that does make it feel less viable.

Gran's radio squawks, and a static-laden voice says

something unintelligible. "Planes starting to run low on fuel, dudes," he says.

The CIA, in their infinite wisdom, have refused to ground their planes, and instead have them circling the city. Because what field operation doesn't go better when there's a ticking clock on it?

The walkie-talkie lets forth another burst of garbled static.

"Giving us a window of about an hour, then we need to be underground and running like hell," Gran says. "You know, paraphrasing and stuff."

"Groovy," I reply, but I think the irony is lost on him.

"Do we really need to sweep every floor?" Felicity stares at the upper stories. Vines have reached even there. "He can't have filled the building with his people. I don't believe that. He'll have the entrance guarded and the spot where the servers actually are. We get past the entrance, find the floor crawling with whatever he's using, and we've found where we want to be."

"That's still less than a minute a floor," I say. I'm being a bit negative, I know, but I'm still chafing at this "operational window" bullshit.

"What if we just punch every feckin' button on the elevator and see if anything tries to eat our faces when the doors open?" Kayla asks.

I shrug. It's not a perfect plan but it will at least bring the frisson of danger that most of my previous elevator rides have missed.

"Wait," Felicity says. "Will 2.0 really let us just ride up the elevators?"

Tabitha taps her laptop. "Know what controls elevators?"

From her grin the answer is clear. "You can hack the building?" I say.

She doesn't even bother with the disparaging glance. "Simple."

Gran fist pumps.

Then a thought occurs to me. I need Tabitha up where Clyde's servers are so she can deploy her code. She can't be downstairs buggering about with elevator settings.

"Wait," I say, then remember I can't talk about the code and keep face. I quickly course-correct. "What about getting the map out of Clyde's servers?"

Tabitha's face goes sour. "Shit bricks." She glances over at the building. "Need those elevators."

Gran nods. "I don't think I can climb a hundred stories in an hour. I start to get slow after like fifty of them or so."

Damnit. Now we need a hacker on the ground floor and the top one. And we don't have two.

Except...

"Clyde," I say, "could you come over here?"

Clyde looks up from what is apparently a quite intense conversation with Winston. "Of course." He points to Winston. "You hold that thought. I mean, if you don't mind. Back in a jiffy."

"No," Tabitha says before he even starts moving. "No. Not him. Not ever. Can't trust him. Cannot. No way."

"You want to nuke Version 2.0?" I say. "You have to trust him."

This isn't a definitive argument-winner but it does at least buy us enough time for Clyde to ask, "You can't trust me to do what?"

"I'm sorry to ask this," I say, "I should probably

remember this, but I'm not sure if you're a version of Clyde who knows—"

"Oh, don't worry about the version control thing," Clyde interrupts. "Totally understandable. Get confused myself. Well, not about what I know. But about what I know about other versions of me knowing. Except, well, I don't because I didn't meet them. But I imagine I would have done. Right now I just know me and Evil-Me. Well, I don't know him directly, of course. By reputation. Some similarities obviously. Big differences too. Disagree on the whole exterminating humanity thing, to take a pertinent example. But, I do—"

It's my turn to interrupt. "I'm just going to jump right to the question."

"Makes total sense. Go for it. All ears. Not literally of course. Don't have them. Just some rather well-constructed microphones placed in multiple locations—"

"The question," I say, feeling the CIA's operational window sliding closed. "Can you hack things?"

"Oh!" Clyde stands up a little straighter. "Some minor skill in that, yes. Tabby... I mean Tabitha gave me some pointers and..."

"No." Tabitha decides to lend her positive attitude to our conversation once more.

"Look," I say to her, "we need you upstairs. We need the elevators operable to do this in our time limit. We need a second hacker. We have one right here."

Tabitha doesn't budge. "Last time he was on a network—tried to kill us. Again. No. No network. He stays offline."

I look to Felicity for support. "This isn't even Clyde's network. It's the buildings..."

"Willing to take that risk?" Tabitha's dark cheeks have a red burn in them. "Willing to get a hundred stories up, have him drop us? I'm not. No."

"So you want to be the one hacking the elevator, and him to be the one plugging straight into Clyde's servers?"

Tabitha throws a hand up in frustration and looks to Gran. Her player for tie breaks.

"He's a liability." Gran at least looks apologetic.

"He's our only option for this to work." Felicity comes into play for me.

"You are a bunch of pissing plonkers, you know that?"

As a group we turn to stare at Winston.

"Care to extrapolate?" Felicity asks the belligerent looking tree. I can't tell if she's genuinely interested or just needs time to power up the punch that she's going to use to kill him.

"Not trying to be offensive or anything," Winston starts, "but I mean, you are genuinely fuckwitted." So that's one goal he's failed already and we're barely into this haranguing. "This is not the end of the world. It's *after* that. Like you guys have fucking lost already. You were meant to stop this from ever happening, and you bloody didn't. And now you finally have an arse crack thin chance of fixing all this shit, and rather than take it, you're going to argue about how trustworthy one of the five allies you have in the entire world is? I mean, seriously, what the fuck are you all waiting for? A fucking handwritten invitation?"

We all take a moment over that one. And I do believe Winston may have put us in our place.

"All right al-feckin'-ready. I'll watch him," Kayla says.

It's now time, apparently, for us to all stare at her.

"What?" she says. "I know I'm a feckin' mess. You need to be feckin' quick, and right now I'm about as fast to get off the ground as an old man's erection. So I'll feckin' watch him while you feckers go have all the fun, and if he twitches wrong I'll feckin' stab him in his feckin' eye. All right?"

Injured as she is, I would not fight Kayla over this one.

"So," I say, "I'll put you and Clyde down for elevator duty, shall I?"

"Marvelous," Clyde says.

"Whatever," Tabitha says, which is almost the most positive I've ever heard her be about anything.

"So," Felicity says, "that just leaves getting past the folk in the lobby."

But I've just had an idea about that. "Oh, Winston," I say, "as you seem so keen to get involved in this…"

"Oh piss." Winston grimaces. "Me and my big fucking mouth."

55

ONCE THE ARGUMENT IS OVER

Winston hits the door of the Empire State Building like a battering ram. Except more vertical. And with legs. And quite possibly some personality issues that need resolving.

Still, the effect is the desired one. Doors fly. Glass smashes. The sound of tearing metal booms up and down the street. If anything is going to attract attention, that seems likely to be it.

"Bring it, you little shits! Planet of the grapes is getting it in the fucking face!" Winston adds, in case smashing the doors off a globally recognized landmark wasn't enough.

For a moment there are only echoes.

Then we hear them. The growls. The guttural, jerking nonspeech of the infected.

"All right, you bastards!" Winston yells. "Let's get squishy!"

It is at this point that I am especially glad that the Empire State Building is big enough to have more than one entrance.

While Winston is battering his way through the doors on Thirty-fourth Street, the rest of us lurk on Fifth Avenue by a pair of doors that are now much less well guarded.

Felicity stares at the backs of zombies lumbering

toward Winston's massive distraction.

"Give them a minute," she says. "Then we move in."

I can feel the adrenaline tremor starting to build in my gut. Sweat dampens my palms. Counting to sixty seems to take way too long.

"Let's move," I say.

Weeds tangle the building door, but it's unlocked. We slip in. The lobby is narrow and tall, walls reaching several stories up. A large relief sculpture of the building dominates the far wall, looming over the security desk. The whole place smells of mold. I'm suspecting that's a recent change.

For a moment we stand there, waiting for the zombies to come our way, but none do.

"OK," I say when it becomes apparent nobody in the immediate vicinity wants to eat my brains. "Gran, you and I take point. Felicity, you OK taking the rear?" She nods, and I am glad Winston isn't here to snicker. "Kayla, you keep Tabitha and Clyde safe in the middle." That's as polite a way as I can think of to relegate her to less vital tasks. "Tabitha," I say, "what are we looking for?"

"Security room. Elevator controls will be there."

Gran and I slip toward the far end of the lobby. It branches in a T-junction. He goes left, I go right. We pause at our respective corners, then on a nod, both snap around.

I stare down an empty corridor. The most deadly thing I can see is a spider plant large enough that it has burst open an office door.

"Clear," Gran calls.

"Ditto."

Clyde's metal footsteps echo off the marble floor,

drowning out the others. Tabitha slips behind the security desk and starts rifling through papers. In the distance I think I can hear Winston yelling. Which means he's still upright. Maybe I should have sent Gran to help him.

"Little tense, this, isn't it?" Clyde says.

"Little."

"You know, though," he says, "I do sort of enjoy it. I mean, obviously, horrible awful circumstances, that I would give anything to not have. Humanity ending is a bit on the godawful end of pretty much any scale I can think of. But, well, when I first started doing all this, the whippersnapper years and all that, well, field operations were mostly about trying to not soil my underwear. Obviously some anatomical changes have made that less likely an outcome, but, well… I mean, I don't want to go down the whole self-aggrandizing hard-bitten agent route, because, well, you know, lack of plausibility and all that. But, well, I'm concerned I've sort of started to think of this as fun."

Part of me would love to ask him what the hell he's talking about. To say that's a really messed up way to see things. Except, God, he's right. At least in part. I'm terrified, and probably generating more ulcers than any gastroenterologist would recommend, but there is a part of me too, that feels the bite of the adrenaline, and wants to take all these bastards down.

"Totally, man," Gran says from across the hall. "Fucked up job, right?"

I actually laugh at that.

"Feckin' nancies." Kayla seems unimpressed. But Felicity runs an affectionate hand down my spine.

"Seriously." Tabitha looks up from the desk. "Less

male bonding bullshit. More letting me concentrate."

We go back to tense silence. I preferred the bonding bullshit.

A moment later, Tabitha puts her head up again. "Got it. Door location. Door code." She heads in Gran's direction. "Idiots," she adds for good measure. Hopefully she's talking about the guards.

Two corridors later and we're outside a door that used to be for employees only. Some office plants have ignored that. One ficus in particular has rendered the door code obsolete, ramming a branch through the lock.

"OK," I say, "we go in, Clyde hacks in, gets in control of the elevators, and we go up. Agreed?"

"One hundred percent groovy, man."

"And," Kayla adds with maybe more glee than I'd like right now, "I get to stab him if he feckin' twitches wrong."

"I don't mean to complain," Clyde says, "and I totally get where the trust issues are coming from, and I don't judge at all, and I really don't mean to question Kayla's judgment—she's proven herself an excellent field agent again and again, and I personally have always been a fan of her creative uses for violence, but I was wondering if maybe, perhaps we could upgrade from the whole twitch thing. Making me a little nervous."

"Just get on with it," Felicity says.

As suggestions go, it's a good one, so I open the door—

—and a zombie tries to eat my face.

It lunges at me, coming from nowhere. Or from immediately behind the door where it was waiting for an idiot like me, I suppose. But figuring that out seems like a less important issue than fending the damn thing off as its fingers wrap around my cheeks—cold and clammy and pushing painfully into my skin—and its jaws open and—

Its head explodes.

Bone, and blood, and brain matter pebble dash my cheeks. I reel back, still trying to fend off an attacker who isn't there. I hit the corridor's far wall, and the blow to the back of the head lets me realize I am still in possession of all my various component parts.

Felicity stands in the middle of the corridor, arms extended, gun still pointed at the doorway. Smoke spirals up from the barrel. I realize I can't really hear out of my right ear anymore.

Felicity holsters the gun and rolls her shoulders. "Nobody eats my boyfriend's face," she says, and heads into the room.

56

FIVE MINUTES LATER

"You're sure you're OK?"

Clyde just lets his mirror-polished face reflect mine back at him. He is too polite to say, "Yes, mum," but not by much. I think there's a chance that the near-face-eating incident has rendered me a bit of a nag.

Still, I point to the spare walkie-talkie Gran has given Kayla. "Remember," I say to her. "Constant contact."

"Not above feckin' stabbing you," Kayla comments. She glowers from beside a swollen succulent, sword gripped in one hand, the other still leaning on her scabbard.

"Come on," Felicity says from the doorway. "Clock's ticking."

And it is, damnit. We're almost fifteen minutes into our hour-long window. That's less than thirty seconds a floor. I hope it's a fast elevator.

We find it. The doors peel open smoothly. And I have to concede that the inner child in me is way too excited to run my fingers down every button on the massive panel beside the door.

Floors two through twenty are clear. So are twenty to thirty. Up to forty and still nothing. I watch the seconds tick by. The doors glide open. We stare at empty corridors. They glide shut. We jerk back into motion. Seconds turn into minutes.

"He's going to be at the top," I say. "The bastard is going to be at the top."

"Then we'll get him there," Felicity says. "We'll have time."

I glance at my watch. I am less confident. Because once we finally find the floor it's more than likely that we'll have an ocean of zombies to wade through.

I wonder how Winston is doing.

After another six floors I ask, "Should we check in with Kayla and Clyde?"

The doors glide open and shut.

"Trust them," Felicity says. She looks over at Tabitha. "We have to."

I nod. Swallow. I need to calm down. Take a breath. "Thank you," I say to her.

"What for?"

"Shooting that zombie in the face."

"He was trying to kill you." She shrugs. "It seemed like the right thing to do."

"Well." It's my turn to shrug. "I appreciate it. You have my back."

"You've got mine."

I grin.

Tabitha clears her throat.

Gran gets the hint. "So," he says, interrupting us before we become nauseating, "we got, like, you know, some sort of plan thing going on for when we get to zombieville?"

Fortunately it had crossed my mind. Unfortunately what I came up with was... "Well," I say, "I realize it's not exactly nuanced, but I was going to go with kill everything we see."

Gran nods. "I dig, man."

"I think I might..." Felicity starts. She begins to dig

around in her handbag. "In the CIA cache…" she says and trails off again. "Yes." She smiles, a warm tight little smile that I find equal parts terrifying and sexy. "Speaking of nuanced." She pulls two matte black metal spheres out of the bag. "Incendiary grenades."

Gran whistles. "Holy shit."

I feel my brow furrow almost of its own accord. "But…" I start, "won't it be hard to hack into the servers while we're being cooked medium-well?"

Felicity reaches out and takes the walkie-talkie from Gran. "Clyde," she says into it, "talk to me about your control of the sprinkler system."

57

The seventy-eighth floor. The doors glide open. The doors glide shut. The incendiary grenades clank as Felicity works them in her hand like Chinese worry balls.

The seventy-ninth floor. The doors glide open. The doors glide shut. The incendiary grenades clank.

The eightieth floor. The doors glide open—

We have repeated this so many times, I have become numb. Corridors. Corridors. Corridors. The doors are sliding closed before I register what I see.

I see... I see... Jesus, there's tons of them. The hallway is clogged with them. Office doors are open. They spill in and out of rooms. Some stand stock still. Most mill around, aimless, angry.

Gran and I stick our hands out to block the closing doors at the same moment. We all stand and stare.

Branches block the windows. Neon strip lights are infested with algae. The light is poor and stained green. The place stinks of bodies, sweat, and rot.

Slowly, Felicity raises the walkie-talkie to her mouth. She presses the transmit button with a small click of static. We all flinch. But the zombies haven't noticed us yet. Not yet.

"Clyde," Felicity whispers. "The eightieth floor. We've found them. Get ready with the sprinklers."

Jesus. Joseph. Mary. Anybody. Buddha. Allah.

Somebody. The adrenaline and the fear thunder in me. But a little part of me remembers what Clyde said down in the lobby.

I'm concerned I've sort of started to think of this as fun.

"OK," I say. "We know how this goes." My heart is beating hard in my throat. Tabitha looks like she wants to find another exit from this elevator. I can't blame her.

"You dudes are fucking crazy," Gran says. "You know that, right?"

Felicity hands him the walkie-talkie and shifts the grenades so she's holding one in each hand. "It's going to be completely—"

She is cut off by an electronic squeal. The elevator. At first I think it's sabotage, think that somewhere below Kayla is plunging her sword in Clyde's body.

But no. No, it is more mundane than that. More stupid. We pressed every button in the elevator. It has places to go. We're holding it up. And it wants us to know.

And now we know. It's just we're not the only ones. Every head turns. *Every* head. Black eyes. Purple eyes. Red eyes where the fungus has caused something horrific to rupture. All of them turn. To face us.

A noise like a hurricane through a dead forest. A dry rattle sweeping toward us, gaining volume. The throats of the zombies clattering to life. A sound of greeting perhaps. Or relief, maybe, that the long wait is over. Or maybe it's nothing. Maybe it's just all they have left. That ugly clacking sound. Maybe that's all Version 2.0 left them with.

"Oh shit."

Then they come.

The flare of my muzzle is bright in the dark

corridor. The boom of Gran's gun, deafening. The tight corridors make it easy to hit something. Bullets tear through bodies. Overpressurized heads detonate. The corridor is filled with noise and blood.

"Fire in the hole!"

The first grenade arcs our heads. Some zombies track its progress, necks craning. Maybe somewhere in what is left of their minds they know what is happening, what is going to happen.

I just keep on firing.

A second grenade flies after the first.

A zombie lunges, ducks, comes up only a few feet in front of me. I shove my gun into her face, pull the trigger. Her brains blow out the back of her head with such violence the zombie behind her goes down too.

The grenades disappear into the crowd. Uncaring, they surge towards us.

Gran kicks an encroaching zombie in the gut. His shot clips its cheek. Its head detonates. The bullet ricochets off exploding fragments of skull, skews into the neck of another zombie. It sits down gagging blood.

It doesn't matter. There is no way to overcome this many opponents. They are legion. Our bullets are not. The sheer weight of them bears down on us.

The first grenade detonates.

It is like dawn. Like the birth of the sun. It is outside of my experience. The whole world seeming to slow to a crawl so I can watch this one thing, can focus my full attention onto this moment of conception. A ball of light and heat expanding out. Its surface roiling, bubbling with rage and the desperate need to consume.

The fireball engulfs body after body. It hits the limits

of the corridor and keeps on going, becomes a roaring, raging wall of hate. I see pieces of zombie blown forward on the cresting tide of its force. Disembodied arms, legs, heads. A mist of red stains the yellow-white flare of death.

The blast of the first grenade consumes the second. A second sun. Struggling and wrestling against its elder sibling. The pair of them churning down the corridor. Ripping through the bodies.

Inside the confines of the besieged elevator, I fling myself sideways, away from the door. Opposite me, Gran mirrors my movements with a synchronicity that Olympic swimming teams would envy. With one graceful movement we both slam headlong into the elevator's wall. A tongue of white flame licks the air between us, caresses the elevator's far wall. I can smell my hair burning, can feel the moisture in my eyes evaporating.

Holy...

And then it's done. Sunset. The cataclysm over. I cling to the floor, gasping, sucking for air, the oxygen momentarily gone to feed the fire god that lived among us.

Felicity sits next to me, a slightly startled, almost starry-eyed expression on her face.

Slowly we take each other's hands, stand up. The elevator doors ping and start to slide closed. I jam my hand in the way and they retreat. I stand. I stare.

It is like a scene from the Old Testament. The hell that Bible-thumpers scream about from TV screens. Flame and misery. Body parts crisping on the floor. Smoke churns, fiery red licks in between swirling clouds.

"Now..." Felicity's voice is breathy and hoarse. She coughs. But she keeps on staring at the scene of destruction. "Now, I am become Death, the destroyer of worlds."

Gran has another phrase in mind. "Holy shit balls."

As impressive as the destruction is, there is the whole death from smoke exhalation thing to worry about. I grab the walkie-talkie from Gran. "Clyde!" I yell into it. "Sprinklers! Now!"

"On it!" the reply comes back. A moment later water rains down. Flames hiss and spit. Steam mixes with smoke. I cough and splutter and try to see.

"Come on," I say. We can't see shit, but that means whoever is left here can't see us either, and I'll take that for now. I grab Felicity's hand and pull.

Under Clyde's direction, the sprinklers become our guide. He paints our path in steam, opens corridors in walls of fire. We scuttle forward quick and tight, soaked to the bone by the raining water, steaming slightly as behind us, flames eat the rooms. Eat hungrily. Eat fast.

We figured without the foliage, I realize. Leaves and wood burn furiously. We're barely staying ahead of the fire. And we have to stay ahead. We have to find the server room fast. That cannot burn. As good as she is with computers, Tabitha can't do anything with melted slag.

"Can you slow this thing down?" I yell into the walkie-talkie.

Smoke is starting to overwhelm everything. It's hard to see, to breathe. Clyde says something back but I can't make it out over Tabitha's coughing.

There are too many pathways before us. Too many possibilities. Flame and steam and places where the fire has not yet touched.

Gran spins. "Shit," he says. "Shit, shit, shit."

ANTI-HERO

I hear bodies moving to the left. The gurgling rattle of zombie speak. I point right. "This way."

"Haven't we been—?" Felicity starts.

"This way!" I grab her arm, pull. We barrel down a water-soaked corridor. I pass a doorway filled with flames. I need more of that between me and the zombies. More fire. But I need to be ahead of it too. I need...

"The hell are we?" Tabitha peers into another flaming room.

An arm lunges out at her.

Blackened fingers snag on black cloth. A flaming fist seizing her tank top.

Tabitha flails back, drags the zombie with her, out into the corridor. It is a ruin, skin cracked and bleeding. I hear the crackle of fat cooking. Smell it. My gorge doesn't really rise—it straps on a jetpack and heads for the stars.

The zombie leers at Tabitha. Its lips have burned away. Blackened teeth splay wide. Its tongue is a charred stump.

Gran's gun barks. The arm clutching Tabitha bursts apart. Blood sprays. The severed hand falls away. Grease and ash smear over crumpled fabric. Gran fires again, again, into the body. It collapses.

Tabitha is breathing hard. Panicked, panting breath. "Through," she gasps. "The fire. It."

And then another. And another. They come out of the doorways. On fire. They come toward us. One collapses as it staggers toward us. Literally comes apart and collapses. Its arm falls off, then a leg. It goes down. Another one's head blows. But they come on. More and more of them, filling the corridor.

They're on fire. Lethally on fire. And they come on. They don't care.

They don't care.

I try to grasp that. Try to hold onto it. *They don't care.*

Jesus, Clyde. Jesus. You took that from them?

Maybe I shouldn't be shocked. He's trying to kill an entire species. My species. But this mindless self-destruction. This absence of the desire for self-preservation. It's another step further over the edge. Another part of the horror that I just can't comprehend.

But there's no time to process it. There's only here and now. And there is way more here and now right at this moment than I usually like to deal with.

Zombies keep on coming. Twenty or more of them. On fire. Only caring about killing us.

It hits me. Realization like a punch to the sternum. This plan is fucked. The question of how we will succeed is moot. Idiotic. Fucked. The only question now, is how to survive.

"Retreat!" I yell between gun shots. "Back to the elevators!"

I turn.

And turn.

And turn.

"Which the hell way are they?" Gran has lost his hippy chill. He looks desperate and trapped.

I gun down a zombie, spot something that resembles an opening. "This way!"

We move. Everything is flame and smoke and noise. A T-junction arrives, abrupt in the smoke. I spin right. More zombies. Left. More zombies. Even more. I spin back right, draw a bead on one's forehead.

There is a crash as part of the ceiling gives way. Vines rush down, spilling out of the hole. Reams of sprinkler system. Pipes sag, crack. Water gushes.

Zombies are buried in rubble, consumed by hungry fire. And all I can think is, *no. No, I wanted to go that way.*

I spin again. The horde is closer. I fire a single futile shot. I go for another, pull the trigger. The gun clicks, dry and empty as a zombie's throat.

I eject the magazine, stuff another one home. My last one. Fifteen more rounds.

"This is fucked." Gran is starting to look panicky. I'm starting to feel it.

Then I spot a door. Halfway between us and the oncoming horde. "This way!" I plunge toward it. The zombies plunge toward us. We're fractionally faster, get to the door with one second before they are on us. I use it to apply the boot. A lock pops, hinges scream.

We race through, parallel to the flames now, smoke still billowing at us, but finally out of immediate danger of being broiled alive. My lungs rasp. Too much soot and shit in them for me to get a proper breath. As we run past open doorways I see outside light spilling in. I almost want to stop, go to one of those windows, throw it open, just so I can breathe.

How did this go so wrong? It had sounded almost rational at some point. Flame to flush out the zombies. Come in fast and hard. Use the sprinklers to control everything. But the flames came too fast. And the zombies didn't care. And there are so many of them.

God. We have to get out. We can't save humanity from here. I don't even know if we can save ourselves.

Except we have to. This can't end here. I have

promised Felicity. She trusts me on this. I can't betray that trust.

I can't.

And then, there. Right fucking there. We round a corner and I see it. An open office doorway. A room untouched by fire. And computers. Hard drive after hard drive piled one on top of the other. A mad jungle of wires.

"There!" I scream, cough, hack. "There!" I point.

We barrel forward, spill into the room. Tabitha scrambles with her laptop, tries to wire it up between wracking coughs.

It's absurd. Of course it's absurd. What can we do here? How many seconds do we have? But it's the plan. It's hope. Driving us. It's the deranged part of us that makes us do what we do.

Then they come. Round the corner after us. The horde. Gran, Felicity and I take the door. Gunfire joins the crackling and spitting of load-bearing structures around us. Behind us Tabitha curses and froths.

"Fucking firewall bullshit…

"Can't design a server for shit…

"Fucking architecture, motherfucker."

On and on. And on and on the zombies come. The smoke getting thicker. Making it harder to see. And they keep getting closer, closer. Stumbling over their own dead.

"Can't hold this much longer, dudette," Gran yells. And he's right.

"Need time," Tabitha snaps back at him. And then, for good measure, "Fuck."

I'm conserving ammunition, but I'm still down to three shots.

I look to Felicity. She is grim and desperate. Soot cakes her nostrils. Her cheeks are pale and sweat streaked. But there is nothing but fire in her eyes. Fire and determination, to see this done. To save her own.

I promise to her there and then—silently but with utter sincerity—that I will make good on my promises. I don't know how the hell I'll do it, but I will save the whole goddamn world with three bullets or less. I will be the hero. For her.

And then, suddenly, she is gone.

58

The zombie comes out of nowhere. No, comes out of a doorway. Out of a fire-gutted office.

It's barely even human. Its arms are stumps. I can hear its skin crack as it barrels out in front of me, passes within a whisker of me.

Into Felicity.

And another, another, another. They pour out of the door. A great running crowd of them. I bounce off a bloody shoulder, bounce back.

And Felicity.

Felicity.

Felicity. Borne away by the tide of them. The pack pours through the corridor in front of me, out of one door and through another, bearing Felicity with them. I hear her scream.

I'm always going to hear that scream.

I stand. I reel. My vision blurs at the corners of my eyes. It's hard to get a breath.

I'm always going to hear that scream.

"Fire! Shoot! Fuck!" Gran. Gran yelling. Gran not having even seen. Concentrating on the zombies coming from the other direction. Concentrating on the threat encroaching on the server room.

"We're going to be over-run!" he yells.

"Need more time!" Tabitha yells.

Would you ever really forgive me if I saved you at the expense of the greater good?

She said maybe not. But I hear her scream again. And I realize that no matter what she says, I could not live with myself if I made that sacrifice. I could not.

I am not that kind of hero.

59

I run. Away from Gran. Away from Tabitha. Away from the mission. From saving the world.

I run to Felicity.

I slam through a doorway. Stumble, stagger, catch my feet beneath me, push after the horde. Not too far. They're still within sight. Just a room away. Silhouetted by the light of windows beyond them.

Felicity screams.

I'm always going to hear that scream.

No. Not if I save her. Not if I stop them. And as long as she's screaming she's still alive. Hold onto that, Arthur. Hold onto that.

I've raced like this before. Raced to save the life of someone I loved. It didn't go so well.

Fuck history. Fuck these zombies.

They run out of rooms, out of corridors. They dead end, before the window.

I get my gun up, fire.

A zombie is holding Felicity. I see my bullet strike him in the shoulder. See it knock him back. See him hit the glass of the window. He flails. Kicks. More of them. More of them hitting the window. I see glass crack.

No. No. No, no, no.

I barrel into the room. I shoot another, another. Heads detonate. But that's wrong, the wrong call,

Arthur. The wrong damn call. The heads don't impede the passage of the bullets. They strike the glass. One, two. The window cracks. The bodies of decapitated zombies reel back into it. The glass fractures.

No, no, no. Nonono.

I have to get to her. I have to—

I try to stop. To stamp on the brakes. But I am momentum's bitch. I am too desperate and beaten. I stagger, hit one zombie, spin off, hit another. I collide with the zombie holding Felicity. We are momentarily inches apart. She is gasping, yelling, clawing at the creature's skin. Fighting. Always fighting.

I grab her in my arms, haul on her. I feel the zombie's grip weakening.

Zombies slam into my back. Fingers. Claws. We're pressed against the glass. I can hear it creaking, cracking.

And then I have her, for a moment, I have her. She is safe in my arms.

No. Not safe. Not exactly.

Nononono.

The glass cracks.

Nonononononono.

The glass breaks.

Nonononononononoooooooo!

And then all of us—every single last one of us—we all go sailing out, into space, and down.

60

I am in the air.

I am in the air.

I am eighty stories up and—oh God, oh God, oh God—I am in the air.

I can see so much. Manhattan, the capital of the world spread out before me. I can see—finally and fully—the extent of the chaos wreaked by Clyde's plans. I can see Central Park like a ruptured tumor at the city's heart, spilling grass and greenery. I can see the trees metastasizing out of skyscraper windows. I can see the rubble of this city's broken body. The grid of roads become a grid of forest.

I can see it all.

And I don't care. The majesty and the horror are utterly lost on me. Not even the rapidly approaching ground matters yet. No, the only thing in the world I care about is between here and there, is in front of me, is falling with me, is falling away from me.

Felicity. Felicity falling. Falling to her death with me.

The air is full of limbs. Of bodies. Zombies around us. Still clawing and cawing. One of them has a hand around Felicity's neck. Its fingers are burned. Bones protrude where nails should be. I see them score bloody lines over her pale skin.

Water floods my eyes. The wind tearing at them. I

blink it away. So I can see Felicity's face contorting in pain.

No. No. I deny this end. I deny this death. No, you will not get to eat my girlfriend's face.

My pistol is still in my hand. I aim, pull the trigger. In midair. Falling down the full length of the Empire State Building. Fuck logic. Fuck you, you zombie bastard.

The gun clicks. The magazine is empty. I had three bullets to save the world. And I've used them all.

Fury. Frustration. Desperation. I don't know what fuels my arm, as I fling the pistol at the zombie. But it cracks hard against the zombie's skull. The zombie goes cross-eyed, spins away through the air. Away from Felicity.

I fall to her. Into her. My body colliding with hers. Her eyes wide, staring at me. And I wish I could read those eyes, those beautiful eyes, just one last time. But there is no time now. How many stories do we have left together? Sixty? Forty? How many seconds before we hit the ground?

Something slams into my back. It claws at me.

Seriously? In midair? Mid-suicidal leap? In the middle of my last goddamn moment of peace? Still these zombie bastards are coming at me?

I push off Felicity. The zombie spins off me. I punch it, send it spinning through midair to collide with the side of the Empire State Building. It becomes nothing but a distant smear of red.

Windows race past me. Another flailing zombie is somehow angling through the air toward me. And of course it is me who ends up falling to his death with the parachuting expert bloody zombies. Of course. Of bloody course.

God, there is so much of the building above us. So much. There can be so little left. How fast we must be going. I feel the wind ripping at me.

I swing my legs, connect with the zombie's neck. It snags my ankle, pulls me in, jaws wide. I bunch my knees, come in faster than it expects. I use wind velocity to speed the blow I direct at its temple.

Something in its skull gives way. Then its fingers do. I kick off its flailing torso, use momentum to spin through the air, and down. Back. Back to Felicity.

She is right below me. I reach out to her. And, God, there is the ground. So close. So very close. And there is so little time.

A tree. One of Clyde's fucking trees. That is what I'm going to land on. What is going to kill me. A pissing tree.

If only I could say "I love you," before the end. I start, open my mouth, manage to get out the, "I—" Then the wind rips the breath from me. There is no time to get another.

I hit the tree.

Everything ends.

61

62

?

I fly through space. Through streets. I float through dappled darkness. I am surrounded by concrete and leaves.

I look for a white light. There is only shadow. Swallowing. Enveloping...

?

Felicity. Felicity is with me. Flying beside me. Floating in and out of my field of vision. Like a broken bird. On her back. Head cast back, hair trailing.

Darkness comes again.

?

Flying. Always flying. Wasn't I flying a moment ago... Flying... down?

Except now, there is this pressure. On my back, bearing me along. Bearing me up.

So not flying.

Another word. It lurks at the edges of thought. Blurry. Vaseline-smeared thoughts. Hard to grasp. No solid edges.

Carried. I am being carried.

Carried into darkness.

Falling. Not flying. Falling. Again.

There is sound now. Perhaps there has always been sound. I think perhaps there has.

I reach the ground.

If I am falling shouldn't the ground hurt? But this is soft. As if a great hand has laid me down.

Bark and leaves. The world is full of bark and leaves.

The sound I realize is words.

"—caught you. I did, Arthur. You're going to be safe, mate."

I can't understand them. They don't mean anything to me. Meaning is water on their oil-slick shell.

Still, I try to remember them in case I can grasp their meaning later.

"Just get down into the tunnels."

Aren't I already down? What tunnels? The voice doesn't make any sense.

The tree moves. Caught by a breeze? A strong wind perhaps, because it bows back up into the sky. The voice shouts, "Come on! Come on, you fucking pillocks!"

The tree looms back down. Fills my vision, and I think perhaps the tree is going to fall on me. But it stops, lying there over me.

"End of the road here for me, I think, Arthur, mate. No room in the subway tunnels for a tree, I'm afraid, and that fucker Gran has gone and called the planes in. Big face full o' deadly defoliant for me, it seems. So, you know, when you're feeling better, kick him in the nuts for me. But you need to get down in the tunnels and away. Got you as far as I could."

Three blurs of motion enter my field of vision. They whirl around me. Between me and the tree.

There is something about that tree. Something like kinship. I don't really understand it. It's a tree. Why do I care about a tree? But a great sadness wells up in me. Something tearing free in my gut. Like a wound. The sadness welling up like blood in my throat. Filling my mouth.

There aren't words. Not here. Not now. Not this disconnected from the world. They are beyond me. My body is beyond me. I feel it hoisted up. Something behind me. Bearing me away from that tree.

"It's been real, mate," says the tree. And it's the tree talking, I realize. "Keep rocking in the free world and all that shit, you know?"

And then I am dragged down steps into a tunnel. Felicity is being dragged beside me. I see her feet bouncing off each step.

Tunnels. Is that what the tree was talking about?

I don't want to leave it. I want it to come with me. I try to cry out, but whether that has any effect, I can't tell.

The tree takes a great step. Away from me. Away from the mouth of this tunnel. It takes another. It walks away from me. I am pulled away from him.

The tunnel fills the world around me. The light of the sky retreats. But I glimpse it long enough to see planes sweeping down over the world above. Planes spouting great white clouds that fall like rain.

A name comes to me. Up out of the fog and sadness. "Winston."

And then he's gone.

63

AN HOUR LATER, IN THE TUNNELS OF THE PATH TRAIN

Beneath the Hudson river, I finally come to enough for someone to explain it to me.

"Winston's dead."

I stare, try to process the news. Try to cut through the bullshit my brain is giving me about confusion and concussion and trauma. I try to make the words make sense.

"Winston's dead."

Clyde has either volunteered or picked the short straw. His face is battered and dirt-smeared. My look of desolate confusion, reflected in his dented cranium, becomes a funhouse mockery.

"How?" I manage. It feels like I'm trying to manipulate my vocal centers with numb fingers.

Clyde twists his head. Some human expression should go here, some twisting of the features. But Clyde's face gives me nothing.

"He'd taken out all the zombies in the lobby. Very impressive actually, but…" Clyde flaps a hand, dismissing his own tangent. "He went outside and he… saw, or heard you falling. He realized what was going on. And he ran and he caught you." Clyde hesitates. "Without him you'd be dead."

I'd be dead. But I'm not. Winston's dead.

God... how? How can that be?

Dull memories of him carrying me. Of him putting me down. Walking away. Why did he put me down? Jesus fucking Christ, why did he put me down?

"Gran and Tabby burst out of the building," Clyde continues. "Going on about the plan having gone all to hell, about having called the planes in. We all had to go to the nearest PATH train. Winston carried you both. But at the train entrance... Well, the system just isn't designed for flora of Winston's magnitude. Understandable of course. Can't imagine many people thought about the evacuation options for tree-men in Manhattan. Not much call for it. But he couldn't fit into the tunnels. And..."

God. This is where the story twists. Where the deus gets to go all ex machina. But I already know the ending.

God, I don't want to know this ending.

"There wasn't time for him to get away," Clyde says. "There wasn't anywhere for him to go." Clyde spasms through another shrug. "The planes came in," he says. "The Agent Orange... He was still outside when it was delivered."

It feels like one of Felicity's incendiary grenades goes off in my gut. The birth of a sun bright and scalding in too small a space.

Clyde shakes his head, as if trying to clear it of these thoughts that cloy and clog and drag and suffocate. "Do you understand, Arthur?"

Understand? Understand that I tried to save Felicity at the expense of a city? Understand that I failed? That my friend died because of my decisions. Do I understand that?

I think I'm going to be sick. My head is between my knees. I stare at the filthy tunnel floor.

But I nod. I say, "Yes." It's lies and bullshit, but it's the only answer that will get me up, out of here, get me away from the horror and the sorrow of this moment.

After a while, I let Clyde help me up. The others gather in silence. We walk.

When we emerge into the thin light of New Jersey, I am clutching Felicity's hand tight. She stares at it from time to time, as if trying to remember what it is. Dredge up some ancient memory that fails her.

Soldiers and helicopters wait for us. Quickly, efficiently they get us on board, into the sky, and away.

64

MOUNT RUSHMORE

"Feck," says Kayla. "We've officially been in America too feckin' long." She shakes her head. "We've clambered so far up George Washington's arse, we can see out his eyes."

We stand in the Area 51 emergency control room—a concrete palace secreted inside the head of the George Washington memorial on Mount Rushmore. Analysts and researchers tap feverishly on keyboards and talk into headsets in hushed tones, saying terrifying things like, "We're down to fourteen percent control on the eastern seaboard." One wall is covered with monitors that display a variety of views from cameras located in what very well might be George Washington's stony eyes.

Mostly they show how fucked we are.

"Like, technically," Gran says, "we're located around the big government honcho's hairline."

Banter is lost on me at the moment. I focus on a handful of monitors that show ruined cityscapes. One is labeled "Los Angeles," another "Austin," and another "Chicago." City after city. Each screen shows the same vast forest stretching off forever. In one or two places, trees shake as massive animals move between them. My hope Version 2.0's attack was limited to the New York metropolitan area is exposed as the pathetic lie it always was.

For a moment, I just try to take it in. Those scenes of endless greenery. That world of forests. But I can't think that big. I can't think that wide.

Rather, my thoughts are locked on one city—

New York City is dead.—on one life in that city.

Winston is dead.

Even those two facts are too big. The consequences of decisions I've made.

A man in military fatigues stands at the front of the room, being briefed by someone from the hushed-voices crowd. We're meant to give him a situation report. Except what the hell can we tell him? We failed? We're not the heroes? Thanks to me, we're the bad guys who killed a city?

Winston is dead.

The man in fatigues dismisses his aide and nods curtly at us.

"General dude wants a natter," Gran tells us.

The man in fatigues, the General, is in his fifties, and looks a lot like he was chiseled from the same stone as George and his three presidential chums. He also gives the impression that the closest he's ever come to having a natter was yelling at his mother to starch sharper creases into his school shorts.

"New York. Sit rep," he snaps at us.

There is a group hesitation. This should be Felicity's job, but she still doesn't seem to have recovered from the fall. She just blinks twice at him.

I step forward. After all we've been through, I'm not going to abandon her now.

"So," I say. I try to put some authority into my voice, but I mostly just sound tired and defeated. "Everything is pretty fucked up, right now. The whole place is over-run with zombies. Well, it was before your planes came in. God knows what it's like now. But—"

"Son—" The General cuts me off with a look of irritation. "—I want bullshit, I'll buy me a damn cow. Now somebody give me a goddamn sit rep on New York."

It's my turn to blink at him. *Buy a cow?* Did that just happen?

"General, sir." Gran still sounds like he spent his infant years using a bong instead of a pacifier, but there's a snap to his slouch that I haven't seen before. "Attack commenced at approximately eleven hundred hours at the Area 51 New York facility. Outcome was near complete fatalities. We are the only known survivors of the facility. Manhattan Island was over-run. Primarily by the fungally compromised. Indoctrination was ongoing via an electrobiothaumaturgical dispersion network. We hacked it and located a central terminal inside the Empire State Building coordinating attacks on the city. We attempted an assault on that central terminal but were overcome by defensive forces and retreated to our evac point in New Jersey."

I stare at Gran. I'm not the only one. Where the hell did our hippy friend go?

The General considers this with a mild grimace. "Shit show, huh?"

"Sir, yes, sir." Again. Gran. This comes out of Gran's mouth. Not a, "Dude, yes, dude." Something feels off. Gran has read some new contour of power that is still far beyond me.

The General looks at one of the women perched in front of a computer. "Aerial reconnaissance on New York subsequent to air strike."

The woman doesn't look up. "Our last pass

indicated a forty percent reduction in foliation. Heat map shows significantly less activity. We are trying to confirm if this indicates a decrease in population or a transition to underground habitats."

The grimace becomes something closer to a savage grin. "Not terrible either way."

And there is something in that savagery, in that grim satisfaction, that breaks a barrier inside me. Tired grief is smothered by a choking fist of rage.

I step forward. Hell, I almost lunge at the man. Political contours be damned. "A success?" I yell. "You killed my friend." My spit laces the air as I hurl the accusation.

And, yes, I admit, mea bloody culpa. I made mistakes. I failed New York. I failed Winston. But it was *this* man who called in the planes. It was *this* man who gave the order to drop the Agent Orange.

The General turns and looks at me. His mouth twisting from grin to sneer. He steps toward me, directly into the face of my rage. As if it's nothing. "Son," he stabs me with a finger, "New York had a population of eighteen goddamn million. All I got to show for it is five fucking tourists. So forgive me if I don't shed a goddamn tear."

It is like running into a brick wall. My anger sits down hard and rubs its nose. He's right. Eighteen million. God, the totality of it washes over me. All those people. And I went after just one. After Felicity. I chose to try to save her at their expense.

Sacrifice. Jesus.

Goddamn. Winston is dead.

And Tess is dead. And Paul is dead. And Joel and Gina, the mecha pilots, are dead. Even the pretentious, uptight Kensington is dead.

It goes on. And on. The litany of the dead.

Jesus.

What would Kurt Russell do? That old standby. It seems so small in the face of all this. And what would he do? He'd not get into this fucking mess in the first place.

I want to bite back at the General. To show my own fangs. But what would I be arguing for? Can I really condone my own course of action? If I went back would I do what I did again?

I look over at Felicity.

My Felicity.

Oh God, I would. I'd do everything the same.

Shit. Maybe Version 2.0's right. Maybe we aren't the good guys. Phrases like "acceptable losses" and "forty percent defoliation" bubble up from the crowd of murmuring analysts around me. Maybe we are the monsters.

But what then? What does that realization buy me? Do I strive futilely to be better? Or do I just accept what I am?

"We needed more time," I say. "We needed to take the long shot. We needed to not be cowards." I'm not even speaking to the General anymore. It's just for me. Or maybe for humanity in general. A eulogy of sorts for the people of New York.

It's also a hideous mistake. Because the General sure as hell thinks I'm talking to him. And you don't look into a raging bull's eyes and tell it that getting angry at red blankets is a mook's game.

He cocks a fist that looks like a sledgehammer. I prepare for the taste of my own teeth.

"There's more."

Clyde steps abruptly up to us. Not quite into the line

of the punch but close enough to be impossible to ignore.

For a moment I don't think the interjection is going to be enough to save my jaw, but then the General narrows his eyes, and lowers his fist. He doesn't unball it, though. "More what?" He doesn't take his eyes off me.

"More intelligence. I mean. Data. Not IQ points. Don't mean to presume about that while…" Then Clyde seems to realize that the General is not someone who's into the whole tangential thing. He pauses, shrugs metal shoulders. "The network," he says. "Tabitha couldn't…" He gestures, then shrugs several times in apparent defeat.

He turns to Tabitha. "You say it, please, Tabby. You're terse and efficient and much better at this sort of thing than I am. I think he'll punch me if I keep going, and I realize I'm made of steel and lack pain sensors, but I've taken a fairly comprehensive beating recently, and considering my propensity for mortality and the absence of wireless for uploading a back-up, I am a hair concerned."

"Shut the goddamn fuck up," the General tells Clyde. Then he turns to glare at Tabitha.

Tabitha matches the General sour look for sour look. Actually, with their close-shaved heads, there is a certain similarity to their appearance. And though the General hasn't gone so far as to trim a skull into the back of his head, I can kind of picture him with the affectation.

"Strike on the Empire State Building," Tabitha says. "Overall shit show, yes. But some useful intelligence was retrieved." She pulls her laptop out of its shoulder bag and flips it open. "Did get into Version 2.0's system." Her look goes from sour to savage. "Did get to map it out at a national level."

And with that, the whole room goes quiet. Every

hushed mutter dies away. Every eye in the room turns to Tabitha.

The General's gaze bores into her. He doesn't go so far as to look actually eager, but there's a hunger to his look that indicates we finally have his attention.

"A map?" he says. "A national map? So you know where he is?"

Tabitha permits herself a knife's edge of smile. "Sir, yes, sir."

65

"Where is he? Where is that bastard hiding?"

I'm leaning just as far forward as the General is. Our heads are inches apart. All animosity momentarily forgotten. This is the sort of buoy-you-up-after-your-friend-died information I can really use.

Tabitha shakes her head. "Should have figured it out. Feel stupid."

She's dragging it out. We have been too eager, and Tabitha's punishing us for it.

The General doesn't take to it particularly well. He almost snarls. "If you want to play games, little girl," he says, "I'll have someone fetch you a fucking checker board, but in the goddamn mean time, you tell where the ass-fuck that little shit AI is goddamn hiding."

The General obviously hasn't had much experience working with Tabitha. You do not, under any circumstance, call her "little girl." Not if you want to keep your balls.

That said, we are in a secure military installation, and we are surrounded by a large number of heavily armed men who report to this man. Tabitha satisfies herself with simply prolonging the reveal even further.

"The heat," she says. "Should have realized. AI that powerful. Would put out heat like the server farm from hell. Heat builds up too much—everything falls down.

Version 2.0 needs a lot of cooling."

"This is goddamn America," barks the General. "I'll black ops this bullshit out of you if I have to."

But I get to the answer before the General's rage buries us in Tabitha's bile.

"The Arctic," I say, realization snapping through me. "It's the Arctic Circle. Isn't it?"

Apparently the General and I have some trust issues to work through because he looks to Tabitha for confirmation. She rolls her eyes. "Duh-huh."

Immediately the room comes alive. Murmurs elevate to shouts. The monitors flicker and whir. Forests vanish, snowy wastelands appear.

"Next fly-over?" someone shouts.

"I need thermal!"

"Who's on the ground in Alaska?"

"Canadian special forces. They exist, right?"

"Pull teams out from Mexico asap!"

The General straightens, points at Tabitha. "I need coordinates. I need goddamn specifics, and I—"

She already has the flash drive held out toward him. The General squints at it, but an aide grabs it from her before he has time to work out what it is. Moments later, the monitors show a map of the world, and begin to zoom in.

White. Endless expanses of it. Featureless.

And then, as the camera zooms closer, as grid lines expand—a small gray blip disrupts the uniformity. The camera pulls in. Three rough gray triangles grow to fill the screen.

"Resolution's for shit," the General comments.

"Working on it," says one of the aides.

I stand with Clyde, Tabitha, Felicity, Kayla, and Gran in

the middle of the whirlwind, and feel a bit outnumbered.

"I need an initial assessment of the defenses. Satellite sweeps." The General points into the crowd. Whether it's at random or he actually knows what each person here does, I have no idea. "And then," he says, "I want to know how long it is until I can have a nuke up in the air and on its way."

Hold up a moment.

"A nuke?" I say.

The General turns and looks at me. "Son, the US of A had a population of three hundred and thirteen million people yesterday. Today it's got maybe three hundred thousand. I want to make sure not a fucking molecule of that asshole remains. A nuke is only the first stop on the roadtrip of annihilation I have planned for this s.o.b."

A white-coated man at a computer raises his hand. "Sir, latest population estimates have us at around a hundred million survivors—"

"Shut the fuck up," snaps the General. "I'm trying to make a goddamn point."

And it is made. Three hundred thousand. A hundred million. Either way that's more than two hundred million people that Version 2.0 has taken from this country alone. This one country. How many people will he take in England? In Europe. In Asia? This was just the first act for him. I have no doubt there's more to come.

Except… "We can't nuke him," I say. "You can't."

"Boy—" I have been downgraded from son, apparently, "if you think you can order me around, I've got another think you can jam right up your—"

"Listen," I snap, because I don't have time for this guy to screw two hundred million people out of the best chance they have. "Version 2.0 is running an electrobiothaumaturgical dispersal network." I decide to not comment on how big of a deal it is that I just pronounced that correctly. "Thaumaturgy. That means the system requires the guy who created it to be alive, or it will collapse."

"And on what goddamn planet is there a person who wants to keep that thing up and running?" He raises a hand and whether it's to dismiss or backhand me, I'm not sure.

Still, I try to grab the time to spell it out for him. "We need it in place so we can hack it, control it, and reverse it." Now I've said that, it sounds like an awkward rap lyric from my equally awkward teenage years, but pointing that out won't really help me either. I plow on. "We can take it over, disperse a code that removes Clyde from people's brains. We can save everyone."

The General's brow creases.

"Actually, he is right," Clyde points out. I just wish he didn't sound surprised.

"Shut up, tin man." The General points to each of us in turn. "Now let me get this straight. I did not invite you here. You are not my guests. The only one among you with any sort of authority is Agent Monk." It takes me a moment to realize that he's referencing Gran's real name. "And let me assure you, that ain't much authority. Way I see it is you are the guys who were meant to stop this, and it sure as shit ain't stopped. So now it's my turn. And I am nuking this bastard. And that is the last goddamn time I am explaining myself to any of you. You have problems, you can deal with them outside of this base, in between the zombie attacks. Otherwise, find a way to be goddamn helpful, or get the fuck out of my face."

"Erm, sir." It is the lab-coated hand-raiser again. "About those nukes…"

"Your next words better be about how far we're going to shove them up this AI's goddamn asshole." The General seems to be a man very much in touch with his own feelings.

The lab-coated man looks around in the same way a rat does when it realizes it's cornered. "Erm…"

"Spit it goddamn out."

"I'm getting information that nuclear is not going to be an option for at least a week. There was massive damage to the, erm…" he flicks an eye at the MI37 crowd, "facility where we're keeping them." The air quotes he's using are almost audible. "The computer network is considerably compromised. We're not getting anything off the ground."

The General's eyes narrow. "You shitting me, son?"

Lab-coat gulps. "Sir, no, sir."

The General whips around, his fury carrying his body with it. "Goddamn it!" The hushed murmurs go quiet again.

I look to Felicity but she's still looking pained and slightly confused.

Shit. I really wish I didn't seem to always end up being the person who said these kinds of things… "If we send in a strike team," I say, "get into those buildings—" I point at the gray blobs on the screens, "—get some serious computer—"

"Shut the goddamn motherfucking hell up!" the General almost screeches. The room quakes with his anger. He screws his face up in concentration, points to me, and looks at Gran. "Control him," he whispers. When he opens his eyes, he seems to have regained some level of control. His point switches to Tabitha. "Heat, you said heat. Heat would fuck him up."

Tabitha shrugs, unfazed by the theatrics.

The General whirls. "Thermal devices. On his location. We melt his ass and watch it sink to the bottom of the ocean. Then we'll nuke him next week." He nods to himself, apparently satisfied. "Now someone get me an ETA on a strike force. And someone else get this English prick out of my face."

I am really starting to not like this man. And, hell, maybe this is all my fault. But it's not my fault alone. I take a step toward him.

Gran's hand stops me. He puts it square in my chest.

"What do you want to do, dude? Piss him off more?" Gran looks at me, imploring.

And he's right, I realize. Neither yelling nor kicking nor screaming is going to change anything. I need a new angle of attack. I give Gran a quick nod, and beat a tactical withdrawal for now.

OUTSIDE THE CONTROL ROOM

The door closes and I can't contain myself any more. "Nuke the Arctic? Melt a great hole in it? Drop defoliant on New York? What if we win this fight…" I shake my head. "I mean, what about *when* we win this fight?" It's important to maintain the right attitude. "I mean, we're becoming the very shits Version 2.0 claimed we are."

Yes, Arthur, that's the right attitude.

Felicity puts a hand on my arm. "We need to talk," she says. She still looks pained.

"I know!" I sweep my arm around the group. "We have to turn this shit around. Obviously we can't just grab the General by the horns and turn his head, but—"

"No." Felicity shakes her head. "You and me. We need to talk." She looks to Gran. "Where can..." She shakes her head. The pained look is back but doubled now. "Somewhere private. Please."

SOMEWHERE PRIVATE

A few moments later, Gran is closing a door on us. Felicity and I stand in another of the small gray rooms we seem to spend so much of our lives in these days. The dull chipped table and windowless walls almost look familiar. Just a beaten up space that no one cares much about. Give the room a white board and I wouldn't be able to tell it apart from any other place on earth.

I step closer to Felicity. I'm still worried about her. About the fall. Her concussion.

"You OK?"

She grimaces. "Not really."

"But you've got a plan? A way we can turn this around?" Felicity is the smartest, most sensible woman I know. If she's got something, then I know it's going to work.

"No, Arthur," she says. "I don't."

That catches me off stride. I pull my eyebrows down, trying to figure out what angle she's working.

"I need to sit down," she says, and pulls out a plastic chair, slumps into it. She puts her head on the table. "I feel like shit, Arthur," she says. "I do. But... Fuck." She pulls her head up. "We have to talk."

"About what?" I feel like I should know this. Like this is something I should have seen coming.

"New York. The Empire State Building."

I close my eyes. Something rolls over deep in my gut. She's right. Of course she's right. But time is slipping away. There will be time for recriminations and debriefs later. We need to focus on forward motion.

"We can still pull things back," I say. "We can still hack Version 2.0's network. Maybe now we know his central location it will work out even better."

She looks up, her brown eyes looking big in her pale face. "Did you believe that when you came after me? Did you honestly think it would all work out fine when you abandoned Tabitha and Gran?"

"I didn't abandon..." I start. It's a knee jerk defensive action. And her eyebrows bounce up. Because she's too smart for that bullshit. Even concussed. And I owe her more honesty than that, even if I don't want to be honest to myself.

We look at each other for a long time.

"You would have died if I didn't come after you." That's what I have. All I have.

She nods. She knows it's true.

"Don't for a moment think I am not grateful for that," she says. "That I don't love you for that. That I didn't want you to. I was screaming for you to come and save me. And when you did..." She shakes her head. "God." The smile on her face almost breaks my heart. "You jumped out of the Empire State Building for me. You mad bastard."

"For you," I say. And that's it. That's my excuse. All I have. Her. It was for her.

And that seems to be what breaks the smile. "I know," she says, face crumbling. "I know. God, I know. But it can't be for me, Arthur. It can't. It's too big." She's starting to cry. "It's too much. Eighteen

ANTI-HERO

million people." She swallows hard. "Eighteen fucking million people, Arthur." She shakes her head. "They're dead. Even if this mad plan of yours works and we can unprogram the rest of the country. Even if that happens, eighteen million people in New York are dead and gone. Because... Because..."

She whoops in air, trying to keep enough control to carry on speaking. "Do you know what Agent Orange does to people, Arthur? What it does to the land they live on? For generations. And we let that happen. We made that decision." She puts her head in her hands. "You made that decision." And she can't suppress the sob any longer. "For me."

I stand there. And I want to hold her. I want to protect her from this sadness. This guilt. But I can't. It's me. It's me she needs protecting from.

"I..." I start. But is there an excuse? There is no General in this room for me to blame, to shout and rail against. I just have to face my own culpability, the simple honesty of her accusation.

"I wasn't strong enough," I say. Because that's it, in the end. The simple truth. "I couldn't do it. I couldn't." I realize there are tears in my eyes too. "I couldn't, Felicity." I take a step toward her, but can't take the next one. Too much confusion and hurt are in my chest.

"I know." She sits up, wipes her eyes, smears mascara. "I would have done the same thing."

And I find a smile somewhere for that. She has given me that.

She shakes her head. "That doesn't make it right, Arthur. That doesn't make it good. I understand what you did, and... God, I forgive it. If it needs forgiving. I don't know." She holds her head.

"So, there's no problem——" I start.

"Of course there's a fucking problem, Arthur! Eighteen million people are dead!" The vehemence in her voice seems to catch us both by surprise. "I swore, Arthur. I swore to stop this. And I didn't. So I don't forgive *me*. I was too weak. I exploited a weakness I knew was in you. I screamed for help. I shouldn't have, but I did. And I can't forgive that."

"That's an impossible standard," I protest. And I believe I'm right. "You can't blame yourself for being human." I hold my hands out to her. "And it's going to be OK." I don't know if it's an empty promise or not, but it's all I have. It's hope. And that's enough for me. That's always enough. It's at the core of us, of the good in us. "We'll make it better. We'll fix everything."

She's shaking her head. "No," she says, blunt and hard. "We can't. It's already done. Eighteen million lives. For mine. That's done. It can never be undone." She looks me straight in the eye. "I let my sister down *eighteen million* times." Her voice sounds stretched, raw. She lets her gaze fall, seems to be unable to look at anything. She curls up on herself, recedes into the confines of her own arms.

"This can't..." she says from the depths of her sleeves. "I can't..." And then, "We can't..."

"I love you," I say. Those three words that I wanted to say as we fell down the Empire State Building. The ones I had no breath for. I say it now. To stop this. This sensation of the ground giving way beneath me. I cannot have it give way.

I am not strong enough.

"Fuck, Arthur." She slams her fist down again. "No. No." She closes her eyes. "I know you do. I know. And

I love you. But that's not enough now. Not here. There can be no more saving damsels in distress. The stakes are too fucking big. We've screwed over a whole city for this idea of 'us.' Let's not screw over a whole country."

And I get it then. What she's saying. Why we're here. I understand completely. But I cannot accept it. No more than I can accept that I killed eighteen million people.

"We can't keep doing this, Arthur," she says. "We can't be together. We have to end this. Whatever is between us. We have to."

"No," I say. "No, this is a bullshit reason. We didn't call in the planes. We didn't drop any chemicals. That was not us."

"Winston's dead."

She wields the fact at me like a weapon. And I almost go down on one knee.

"One of our own." She twists the knife. In her own side as much as in mine. "Our friend. Someone we swore to protect. We caused him to die. You and me."

"No," I say. But there's no strength to the word.

"Winston's dead," she repeats. "Because of me. Because I screamed at you for help."

"No."

But yes.

"We're over," she says. "I am ending us. For our own good. For the world's good. For the sakes of our friends. This is at an end."

But no. No. I can't let this go. Not after everything we have survived. Everything we have fought. After surviving a fucking fall off the Empire State Building. After fighting zombies in midair. This? We end here?

"Just because we break up won't stop me from loving

you. From caring for you. From wanting to save you."

The words break against her like the tide against a rock. As surely as my heart breaks. As if it dropped eighty stories and hit the New York sidewalk.

"If the moment comes," she says, and she seems to have some degree of control now. The tears are over. Her skin is pale, and her cheeks red, and make-up is smeared down her cheeks, but she is in control. "If you need to decide again between me and the greater good, think back on this moment. Think back on the pain I am causing you here and now. And then make your decision."

She pushes out the chair, stands, moves to the door, and walks away.

And then it is my turn to sob.

66

Time passes. I don't bother paying attention to how much. Eventually the door opens behind me.

Part of me leaps. Felicity, it must be Felicity.

But it's not.

"Well, you look a bit of a feckin' pussy right now, don't you?"

"Go away," I tell Kayla, with a degree of force that suggests that I have lost the will to live.

"You want to start another fight, you best be willing to stab me one more time." She hobbles toward me. Her scabbard strikes the floor—an extra footstep. She sits heavily beside me.

I look up, pull my head out of my arms. She leans back, regarding me, her long red bangs almost in her eyes.

"Felicity?" she asks. Not unkindly. Not combative. Not mocking. Just a simple question.

And I can't say it. I can't hear the truth now. I can't hear, "yes," so I just look away.

"Feck," Kayla says.

"Yeah," I manage. That is a truth I can get behind.

We sit in silence. Not a companionable one. It's just the only way I think either of us knows right now.

"You're meant to tell me she'll come back," I manage after a while. A phrase hanging between humor and accusation.

"Feck, man." Kayla shrugs. "I don't know. Maybe she will, maybe she won't. Seems like a bit of a minor feckin' problem compared to all this other shit, you know?"

I don't have the energy to be outraged or offended. I just look at her. *Et tu, Brute?*

"Feck." She shakes her head. "Not like that. You know me, Arthur. I don't do all this compassion bullshit. Shit feckin' sucks for you right now. It's going to keep on sucking. But at least Shaw's alive. Plenty of folk you can't say that about these days. *That* seems like the bigger feckin' problem to me. And I appreciate that none of this perspective shit really feckin' helps, but what the feck else do you want from me?"

I don't say anything. There's nothing really to say. She's right. She can't do anything. A piece of nihilistic philosophy from her lips to my ears.

"This won't make you feel better either," she says, "but time really does heal. Tomorrow this won't hurt so much. And then less the day after. And it'll be too slow. And it's a shitty truth, really, but it is a truth. And that's the closest you're getting for sympathy from me, and probably more than you feckin' deserve, you enormous feckin' pussy."

I nod again. Someone could tell me I've won the lottery now and I'd just nod. A self-imposed numbness. Because it is easier.

The door opens again. "Is everything OK? I don't mean to interrupt... Well, I have interrupted, so I suppose I do mean to. Kind of hard to deny the intent behind an activity that is only really designed to do one thing. So, starting over I *do* mean to interrupt, but I hope it doesn't interfere with some deep heartfelt moment or interrupt some epiphanic juncture..."

I catch motion in the corner of my eye. Kayla's hand

slowly inching toward her sword. And Kayla's patience does not extend as far as Clyde's preambles. I manage to drag myself out of the mire of my own head long enough to save everyone from decapitation. At least I still have the power to save some lives.

"Felicity is done with…" I struggle for a word. "Us. Me and her." I can't carry on. I submerge back into the depths of my gloom.

"Oh, God," Clyde says. "That's not the best news on the face of the planet. Though considering the face of the planet these days, I suppose, it's actually not the worst. Not that that helps of course. Sorry. Should be carrying on, telling you how over-rated the whole plural pronoun business is. How the love of a good woman is something for romantics and dead poets, and that you and I are stern men of action, and we save worlds, and that women will throw themselves at us, and we'll have different ones every night. And not once think about that long lost embrace of the one woman that we thought maybe we could perhaps spend the rest of our lives with. That we felt really understood and—"

"Not feckin' helping," Kayla points out.

"Oh, God," Clyde says in a small voice. And suddenly he is sitting at the table next to me, his head as far down as my own.

"Sorry," he says. "Going to be a bit despondent for a bit."

"Oh," I hear Kayla moan. "This is feckin' perfect. Any more feckin' pussies in this room and I could start selling feckin' kittens."

Clyde looks up at me. "Sorry," he says, "bit self-absorbed and everything."

"Same here," I manage.

"Can we skip to the bit where you two grow your feckin' balls back?" Kayla asks.

Clyde ignores Kayla. His head reflects my own misery back at me. "Just wait until she starts dating a CIA agent named after your maternal grandparent. That's the really spectacular part."

Kayla looks at us both in mild disgust. "Are you seriously going to make me play Dear feckin' Debbie, here?"

Neither of us seem to have an answer.

"Dear feckin' Debbie," Kayla spits at us. "My girlfriend fecked off and appears to have taken my balls with her. What the feck do I do?" Another scathing glance. "Dear No-dicks. Grow a feckin' pair. Love feckin' Debbie."

I close my eyes. "Seriously. This happened to me about an hour ago. I think this is a reasonable mourning period."

Kayla looks genuinely astonished at this utterance. "Do you remember what the feck is going on out there?" she says. "That hundreds of millions of feckin' people have been turned into mushroom zombies or some feckin' shit by his broken feckin' twin feck?" She nods at Clyde. "No you do not have a feckin' hour to be a whingy feck. Prioritize your shit, Arthur Wallace, afore I come and feckin' prioritize it for you."

Part of me wonders if this is meant to be a pep talk. I decide against it. It feels like it resembles a beating too closely.

"They're just going to blow him up," I say. "Or melt him. Or something. It's over apparently. Thanks for the cooperation, we'll take it from here. That sort of bollocks." And some of the anger at that does leak through the numbness.

"Hmm." Kayla pantomimes musing for my benefit. "You know what might help solve that problem?" She cocks her head to one side. "Oh yes, I remember now. *A pair of feckin' balls.*"

Clyde finally bridles at this. Which is a rare enough occurrence to be notable. "You know," he says. "Anatomically speaking, this is a robot body which is built without any sort of genitalia, and so any sort of insufficiency in the gonad region is not exactly—"

"Shut the feck up," Kayla tells him.

So he does.

She stares at him. "Seriously?"

"Seriously what?" He sounds as confused as I feel.

"I tell you to shut the feck up and you do? That's it? That's your whole feckin' defense mechanism? Haven't you saved the feckin' world or something?"

Clyde and I exchange a look.

"Well," I concede. "We did do that a few times."

Clyde nods. "I remember that."

"So why the feck would either of you shut up when someone tells you to?"

"Well," I say, "you do have a history of stabbing people…"

She throws up her hands then winces and drops the left one with another wince. "So do feckin' you." She rubs the top of her stomach. She shakes her head. "At this feckin' point, if someone starts to play the dick swinging game with you, you don't curl up and take it, you get yours out and you beat them about the head and neck a few times."

"Again," Clyde starts, "anatomically speaking—"

"Metaphor!" Both Kayla and I cut him off at the same moment. We exchange a glance. I don't think either of us are entirely used to synchronicity.

"Wasn't this entire conversation, at some point," Clyde asks, "and I understand I may be mistaken here, but at *some point*, wasn't it meant to be about us feeling shitty about being dumped by women?"

I actually smile then. Despite it all I smile. Because something about this feels familiar. Something about… camaraderie. And it really does feel like sitting with Clyde in a way. With my old friend.

Kayla ignores both of us. "If you don't want these CIA pricks to melt Version 2.0, then stop them."

"I tried that." I shrug. "They have an army."

"That's an unfair size advantage," Clyde says. "If this was a boxing match they wouldn't allow that sort of match-up. Not that it is a boxing match. But if it were. Which it's not. Sorry, I don't think I'm contributing much."

"Big feckin' change that is." Kayla rolls her eyes at Clyde. Then she seems to decide that a new policy of ignoring Clyde would suit her best and she turns to me. "Look," she says, "let me put this in sword-fighting terms. You can't stab a man in the face, what do you do?"

I shrug.

"You stab him in the feckin' back." And there is the savage expression on Kayla's face we at MI37 all know and love, and also secretly crap ourselves about. "You can't change the CIA's minds about this up front, you just smile, say yes, go to the feckin' Arctic with them, and do this your own feckin' way. Simple enough."

I exchange a look with Clyde. He shrugs. "They still have an army," he points out.

Kayla hasn't finished grinning. "Yeah," she says, "but you've got feckin' me."

67

LATER, IN AN AIR HANGAR SCULPTED INTO THE BACK OF TEDDY ROOSEVELT'S HEAD

"You're not goddamn coming."

Kayla looks murderous.

The General considers this look. Apparently, it measures up. It's probably the look his mother gave him while he breastfed or something similar. "Look," he says, "if I could take you over numb-nuts here," he nods at me, "then I would. But you've got a hole in your gut and he's not. If stabbing him would make a difference I'd happily do it."

Around us soldiers bustle into DC-10s, propellers buzzing hungrily. Shouts of "ooh-rah" and "hup, hup" occasionally break through the din. The General, Gran, and the MI37 crowd stand negotiating at the back doors of one of the massive transport planes.

Felicity, standing next to the General, gives a small cough. She won't look at me. But she does at least cough when someone suggests perforating me.

I want to go to her. It is killing me to not start imploring her. To beg her to see the mistake this is; to see how little difference this will make to my performance in combat; to just hold her; to shout that breaking up because you care too much is the stupidest damn thing I've ever heard.

But I don't. Now is not the time. Kayla was right. The world's problems are bigger than mine. I need to keep my shit together.

The General, oblivious to my inner conflicts, looks at Kayla and shakes his head.

"You're goddamn grounded. The rest of these limeys have bought themselves a ride." He looks at Tabitha. "Though you better live up to these grandiose fucking intel promises you're making." He turns to Gran. "Agent Monk, you're holding the goddamn leash, understand?"

Gran nods.

Kayla looks at Felicity, appealing.

"No," Felicity shakes her head. "Absolutely not. You're recuperating."

Kayla's knuckles go white. But then she nods, and stalks away.

The General nods at Felicity. "Firm hand," she says. She doesn't acknowledge the compliment. And she still doesn't look at me.

Our plan needs Kayla. I lean over to Clyde. "This could be a problem."

"Really?" Clyde sounds surprised. "This is Kayla we're talking about."

"She *is* recuperating."

"Yes," Clyde nods, "that's a point. We should probably assume that, running the whole way, she'll probably be a few minutes behind us."

THREE HOURS LATER. ABOVE THE ARCTIC

I am generally unenthusiastic about airplanes. Freezing winds that shake the plane like a toddler in a temper tantrum do nothing to consolidate my enthusiasm. Still, making my discomfort apparent in front of thirty-five marines armed with assault rifles and military-grade testosterone seems like a mistake. At one point I go to squeeze Felicity's hand for comfort then remember that along with the rest of the world, my personal life has gone to shit. The gesture becomes a clumsy stretch and yawn that almost leads to me punching her in the nose. The hand grab might have been less awkward.

What makes it worse are the googly eyes Gran is making at Tabitha. She, though, is largely ignoring him in favor of a small black box covered with a variety of blinking LEDs.

Gran grins at her. "You like your new toy."

It is, we've been told, one of the wireless jamming devices they've been using to take down the networks around the US. The general assumption is that Version 2.0 probably did not turn off his own router despite the kindly urgings of the US government. As none of us want to end up with our brains going on a permanent holiday, this is DARPA's slightly-more-upscale version of Tabitha's tinfoil-lined hats.

"Going to backwards engineer the shit out of it," Tabitha tells Gran. She blows a kiss at him.

God, their relationship survives all this shit, and mine doesn't. Ugh.

I have a few hours to contemplate that before the largest of the marines—who I assume gained command by clubbing all challengers to death with his enormous ball sack—stands up at the front of the plane. "Approaching drop zone," he barks. "Ready!"

"Hoo-hah!" is the popular response. It's a little bit like being at a convention of Al Pacino impersonators. Albeit extremely militant Al Pacino impersonators.

Though, at this point, odder things have happened in my life.

Gran looks over at the MI37 crowd. "You dudes all cool?"

While I am untrusting of aircraft, once I am in them I am predisposed to stay in until we once more reach terra firma. My hopes of that detonated on the appearance of the term "drop zone," much like a body impacting on an ice field.

"Not really," I confide.

"Sort of banking on the durability of flash memory a little more than I'd like," Clyde adds.

Felicity doesn't say a word. Just stares stony-faced into the distance.

Then the back bay of the plane is opening and men are lining up. I hesitate.

"Dude!" Gran claps me on the back. "You're going to dig this. It is, like, a total rush. I mean," he points at the distant ground rushing past a mile below the plane's open maw, "we are literally high right now."

"Well," I say, "it'll be nice to have a parachute this time."

Gran looks briefly concerned. "Oh yeah," he says. "Sensitivity and shit. Sorry, man." Then he gives me a thumbs-up and grabs a massive looking assault rifle off the wall.

"Going in hot!" yells the huge marine, I assume because knowing this is going to involve being shot at is totally the motivation we all need.

I close my eyes, concentrate. I have a plan. I am going to take control. We are going to prevail. We are going to save the world. From Version 2.0. From the military's desire to use brute force. We are turning back the clock on the zombies. We are going to fix this. All of this.

I stand up. My legs shake but I master it. I take one step, then another. I walk to the back of the plane. I stare into the freezing, howling night. And I do not look back. Instead, I leap out into everything that is to come.

And I plummet like a stone.

68

The wind roars. It has teeth that rip. I shut my eyes and feel the tears freeze. The thick thermal fatigues I'm wearing become a rather pathetic joke. God, I'm going to lose a limb to frostbite before I even land.

If the plane ride was Gran's high, then this must be the crash. Not that I've ever taken a narcotic associated with a significant crash, but if it involves plummeting screaming toward the promise of certain death, then this is exactly like that.

Something starts beeping on my chest, a shrill scream that slices through everything, and for a moment my heart stops. It is the sound of things going wrong.

Then I realize it's the altimeter that they strapped to my chest, and I yank the parachute cord before I get turned into a pancake.

After that things are significantly more peaceful.

We land in a surprisingly tight circle. The snow crunches beneath our feet, packed hard and frozen. No one sinks in or starts to make snow angels. That, I suppose, is a good sign for the professionalism of the mission so far.

Similar groups of marines land around us, describing a loose circle about a mile in diameter. We surround our target. Pale moonlight bounces in sharp jagged edges off the endless reaches of snow. In that light, I finally see it—the home Version 2.0 has built for himself.

Tabitha's eyebrows rise. She shakes her head. "Egomaniac bullshit," she says with a look of mild disgust.

"Well, that is a little embarrassing, one does have to admit." Clyde nods.

They rise out of the ice like pyramids. Blunt triangles of steel, and glass, and stone. Mist boils up around their base, obscuring the seam they form with the ice.

"Well, that's just silly," Gran says. "I mean, that requires, like, resources. Labor. I mean, how the hell does a dude get himself a workforce in the Arctic Circle to build a Fortress of Solitude?"

Personally, I think it looks more like the structure from the end of *Watchmen*, but I also get the feeling that no one would care for that observation right now.

"He might not need an imported workforce," Felicity muses. "Maybe he can just grow one. Or build one. Or whatever the hell he's doing now."

There was a time when I loved it when Felicity talked. When I knew what would follow would be smart and clear-headed and cut through all the bullshit. And now, in some ways, is no different. She's right. It's just she's also right in a way that feels like someone is kicking me directly in the chest.

"Come on," I say to the marine leader. "Let's go and blow them up already."

He looks back at me. "Intel," he snaps. "On-site assessment. Defenses?"

And I thought Tabitha had a gift for brevity. I resist the George Orwell nuspeak reference and instead try to be helpful.

"Erm…" is probably not an auspicious start. The

marine's expression certainly suggests so. "Well, so far," I rally, "he's relied mostly on golems. Though there's really nothing here that he could use to…"

"Snow," Clyde interrupts me.

"What?" The marine leader and I are twinned in our confusion.

"Oh." Clyde's posture suggests he'd look sheepish if he had a face. "I mean, well, basically you can make a golem out of any solid substance provided it can articulate." He waves his arms around to demonstrate. "Well, actually, technically, it doesn't have to articulate, but it would be pretty pointless to do that. Unless you're the sort of sick, twisted bastard who likes to be surrounded by animating forces trapped in inanimate matter. But I can't really see even a perverse pleasure in that. Though, who knows. I didn't know I could turn into a world-destroying psychotic, and that hasn't stopped it from happening."

Quietly, and quite deliberately, the marine cocks his gun.

"Oh." Clyde goes quiet for a moment. "Snow golems. That's all I was saying really. That could be it."

The marine leader narrows his eyes. "You telling me," he says, "in all seriousness, that I've got to look out for killer snowmen?"

Clyde looks away. I study my gloved hands.

"I suppose so," Clyde finally concedes.

The marine closes his eyes. He keeps them that way for a long time. Then he touches his throat mike. "Intel suggests to be on the lookout for…" He hesitates and then glares at Clyde and me in turn. "For animated snow creatures," he says finally.

There is radio silence. Then, eventually, inevitably,

"Repeat that, snow leader one. Please confirm, animated snow creatures."

The marine leader looks so murderous I am suddenly sad that Kayla isn't here yet. I think the two of them would probably get along.

"I confirm: animated snow monsters." Another baleful look.

But the only response is, "Copy."

Killer snowmen. Sometimes I hate my job.

The lead marine points his rifle at the pyramids and checks his scope. "Five hundred yards to target," he says. "Advance two hundred. Move out."

As one, the marines stand. They move with incredible synchronicity, as if operating at the behest of some great military hive mind. For my part, I do what I can to stay low and out of sight. And to not be too painfully aware of where Felicity is at all times.

Two hundred yards later, we come to a halt. Around us other groups of marines do the same, drawing the net tighter. The marine leader looks at me, back over the clean ground we've covered, and then back at me. "Snow golems," he says with disgust. "If you think fucking with me is a fun game then—"

"Dude." Gran holds up a hand, cutting him off. "These dudes are the experts. They say snow golems are a threat, they are like a threat times nine." He looks at me. "Right, dude?"

"Right." I can't help but smile. Times nine. Really.

The marine leader shakes his head. "All right. Two hundred more yards. Move out."

We sneak forward another five paces. And then, from behind, comes a rather desperate sounding, "Sir!"

We freeze and glance back. A lone marine is back

where we were just sitting. He has one leg bunched beneath him. The other... the foot has sunk into the snow. The ice crust has given way and his boot is stuck. He tugs on the limb to no avail.

"Get it together, Jenkins," snaps the marine leader. "I said move out."

"Trying, sir," says the poor chap, Jenkins, who I think might be getting spill-over ire that's really intended for me. I take a step toward him.

"Leave him," snaps the marine leader.

"I got it," says Jenkins waving at me. "Just seems—"

To our right gunfire suddenly breaks out. Sharp and harsh against the silence of the Arctic night. Our heads snap up. We stare, trying to work out what is going on. And then—from the other side of the pyramids—another eruption of sound.

"What's going on?" I hear a man breathe.

With violent suddenness, Jenkins sinks up to his hip. I hear a sharp crack, a noise that sounds profoundly wrong out here in the snow and the peace. The marine, Jenkins, howls. It was the snap of bone.

"Holy—"

And oh shit. This is it. The marines whirl their guns about, but they haven't realized what is happening yet. They're well-trained operatives to be sure, but weird-ass shit is not their job description.

It's mine.

I start sprinting toward Jenkins.

"Sir!" Jenkins yells.

Then comes another brutal crack. Another. Another. Jenkins's body folds like a rag doll's. His leg smashes up into his nose, bloodying it. His pelvis and spine defy anatomy. Jenkins is ripped down, a bloody bag of breaking bones torn into the snow.

"They're in the snow!" I yell. "The golems are in the snow!"

The response is stunning in both its immediacy and violence. Bullets tear into the snow at our feet. The ice crust becomes a broken mirror, plumes of white erupting up into the air.

Five seconds later everything is still.

The marine leader stares at me. "They still below us?"

It takes me a moment to realize it's a genuine question. "I…" I'm panting, still picturing Jenkins's body as it folded up and was dragged below. "I don't…" I turn and look at Felicity, then realize I don't want to and look at Gran instead. "The fruit golems didn't go down from one bullet," I say. "We had to chop them up. Snow is…"

"I don't think bullets are going to do it." Clyde is shaking his head and shrugging in unison.

"Golems." Tabitha has her laptop open. "Death requires physical disruption."

"I do not have time for a fucking anatomy lesson!" the marine snaps. "Enemy forces still at large!" he barks at his men. "We are still hot!"

Then it comes at us. A hundred feet away, the ground ripples, swells, rises. It rises until it occludes the night sky, until it encompasses the world. A vast tidal wave of snow and ice. Soldiers open fire, but it does as much good as shooting any wave. The golem comes on unheeding and uncaring. It towers above us. Massive. Undeniable.

And then it crashes down.

All about me, bright glittering white becomes cold frozen dark.

69

Snow fills my mouth, my nose, my ears, my eyes. I choke on it. It bears down, a force greater than the simple weight of the snow. A bone-crushing, spine-cracking, teeth-grinding pressure. A giant's hand squashing the flies that have disturbed its slumber.

This golem—it is nothing so pedestrian as the trash squid. Nothing so terrestrial. Version 2.0 has transcended the limits of form. This creature is just a ball of will and spite, sent here to keep us away. It is malleable, angry destruction and nothing else.

I try to find purchase in the snow. Try to heave upwards, to arch my back against this pressure.

Nothing.

I grit my teeth at the effort, at the cold taking root in me. I feel a trembling in my limbs.

And nothing else.

I gain no lift, no purchase. I try to suck in breath, but there is nothing. Just blackness, frozen pressure, and the creak of my sternum.

My body turns on the faucets full force, pours adrenaline into my system. But there is nothing I can fight, nowhere for flight. I have no options.

I heave again. Achieve nothing again.

No. This can't be it. I have fought too much and too hard. I still have to win Felicity back, goddamn it. I try to push, but my arms feel weak. I need oxygen. I try to suck some through the snow but just end up with a mouth full of ice for my troubles.

Fairly essential physiological systems start yammering in my head. Panic trying to override the system. Some evolutionary alarm siren starts screeching at me to just fix this, to do some ridiculous insane Kurt Russell shit. But there is nothing. Just crushing paralysis.

I think a rib is going to give. If I'm still conscious at the time then that will really suck.

And then, abruptly the pressure leaves. And I am aware enough to feel it. That hand moving away. And hope rises in me. A bright golden flower blossoming in my chest.

I heave.

I heave.

Nothing.

I heave again.

Nothing.

I push a final, desperate time, with the last of my will and strength. But even with the golem gone I am buried too deep. The sheer weight of snow is now too much for my oxygen-starved muscles. That is why the golem left. It wasn't whimsy. It wasn't a distraction. Its job was simply done.

I am already dead.

70

I work my hands, try to clear space, try to get to my mouth, to find some air. But I can't feel much now. Everything is numb.

Felicity. That is my last thought. That I didn't fix that. Not the disaster we are leaving behind. Not humanity's tenuous fate. Felicity. That is my regret.

I push one last time, achieve nothing, lie still.

At least this is a fairly awesome way to die. Crushed to death by a snow monster. That is a small comfort, I suppose.

Something brushes my cheek.

I try to flinch and then realize I can't. It seems like a minor concern anyway. I'm more bothered by my body's insistence on trying to breathe. It seems fairly pointless now.

The same thing pokes my cheek. And seriously. What the hell? In my final moments, is there no damn peace?

And then it is not just one thing poking me, but five. And then it is a hand. A hand touching me. Human contact. And then the hand claws down my face, tears away snow.

Air. Freezing, icy air that rushes into my lungs, makes me choke and cough and retch. But air. Breath. Life.

My body, still trapped, tries to buck, to convulse. Each breath is a frozen knife blade keening into me, but I cannot get enough. I suck at it, slurp it down. More and more. Like an alcoholic left alone among the taps. Air. Life. God.

The hand is joined by its twin. The pair dig, scrabble, clear more of my face, my shoulders. They grab me, heave. I give half-hearted kicks. And then full-hearted ones, the air catching, the strength coming back to me. My numb limbs feeling a mile away. A distant slow motion thrashing. Coordination not quite mine yet.

And then the snow releases me. I emerge, sloughing ice, coughing, spluttering still. I curl fetal, shivering— the world's ugliest, coldest newborn.

But I am alive. I was saved.

"Dude! Duuude!" A hand shaking me. A voice calling.

I uncurl. It seems ungrateful not to. And there is Gran. Gran. Of all people, it is Gran who is leaning over me, who has his face creased with concern.

"Holy shit, man. Thought I'd gone and, like, lost you there and shit." He shakes his head. "We've got to fucking move, man. This shit is insane."

He grabs my arm, heaves. Somehow I find enough resources to comply. I stand up. Around me, marines are desperately digging. Bodies emerge. Some stutter, stagger, and cough. Like me. Others…

Others just lie dead.

Gran. Holy shit. Gran. He… Jesus, he saved me.

I see Tabitha and Felicity hauling Clyde up and out. He keeps thanking them and saying he was quite all right. "Whole not breathing thing was actually quite helpful."

Gunfire swirls around us. Muzzle flares shoot stuttering illumination through the icy night. Marines not involved in pulling their compatriots out of the snow stab assault rifles at the empty night, wild panicked looks on their faces.

Felicity's eyes flick to me. Stay there for just a moment. And I think she may say something, express some gladness that I am alive. And then she lowers her head. Looks away.

So, near-death isn't enough to get her to take me back then. Good to know.

Well… good might be an overstatement.

"You cool, man?" Gran says. Part of me is aware it's not the first time he's asked.

Suddenly—and I cannot quite identify the impulse behind it—I grab him and hug him. He fucking saved me. I thought… Jesus… I can't think about that. I can't think about Winston. I can't think about the lives this path has cost so far.

This isn't over. I need to get my head back in the game.

I stagger toward Tabitha, grab her by the shoulders. "Bullets," I say to her. "Y… Y… You said…" I fight my chattering teeth. "You said th… th… they wouldn't work. What the h… h… hell will?"

"Bullets, indeed worth shit," Tabitha nods. She looks at the marine leader instead of me while she says it. He hears, turns. "Golems," she says to him. "Need to disrupt the form. With snow, you can't poke holes. You can't slice. The body will reform. You need more. Need explosives."

The marine leader stares at her for a moment. Then he turns to his bewildered, shivering troops. "Grenade launchers hot!" he barks.

OK, why the hell have we not been using them before?

"Move out!" the marine yells. "Close on hostile compound. Go! Go! Go!"

As we start to move I realize that I am decidedly short on the whole grenade front. Instinctively my eyes snap to Felicity. She is still pointedly not looking at me. And when did it become so hard to ask Felicity for grenades?

And when exactly did asking Felicity for grenades become a normal part of my life?

"Erm," I say. "Do you…"

She stabs a hand into a pocket, yanks out a black cylinder and shoves it at me. She mumbles something, but it's lost in another burst of gunfire.

"What?"

"Five second fuse."

"Thanks."

And nothing else. No eye contact. Just take the grenade, and then she jogs away from me, toward the other side of the group.

Gran claps me on the shoulder. "Ready to blow the living shit out of some spooky magical shit, man?"

The weight of the grenade suddenly feels very, very good in my hand. I look him straight in the eye. "Hell yes."

71

The marines accelerate, running hard and fast. My arms and legs complain. The stitch in my side bites. My ribs ache. Everything still feels painful and disjointed. But I honestly don't care because each step gets me this much closer to blowing the living shit out of Version 2.0's compound.

This is ending today. One way or another.

I glance over at Clyde, running parallel to me. Sparks crackle up and down his spine. He holds one hand out in front of him, like an old-school priest warding off the dead. Except the old-school priest's palm never doubled as a boom-stick.

The ground ripples to our side. Clyde pivots on his mechanized waist and his shoulder joints rock with the force of the spell. Magic tears into the ground. The ripple goes very still.

Clyde. Coming with us to kill himself. Some shattered-mirror version of himself. His ex-girlfriend and her new boyfriend by his side. I don't think people get much better than Clyde. He's been through a world of shit, and he is still the same person, affable and smiling. Still trying to save the day. It's funny, if all of humanity were as good as Clyde, then I don't think his evil self would be trying to kill us.

Suddenly the surface layer of ice before us cracks,

shatters, bursts upward. Something massive rears up. I have the vague impression of a snarling mouth, of vast paws. The thing stretches up, ten, fifteen yards into the sky.

I fling my grenade. I am not alone.

They smash into the golem, sink into the snowy mass of it. And then, as it crashes down toward us, they erupt. First one, and then all the others, a rippling wave of destruction, tearing the thing apart, ripping through it until it is nothing but powder on the night wind.

"Hoo-hah!" the Pacino impersonators yell. We run on.

Gran runs alongside me. He carries the same rifle as the marines. A fat tube under the barrel emits a short cough, and a moment later a suspicious looking bulge in the ice to our right is a much less suspicious looking crater.

Gran. The hippy CIA agent. The man who saved me. The man who shot a little girl in Mexico. Who seems to have brought Tabitha comfort in these dark days. Who maybe could have stopped the Agent Orange attack on New York but didn't. Who nodded when a general told him to write off two hundred million lives. Who saved me.

And beside him is Tabitha, head down, laptop clutched to her chest. She looks grim at the best of times, but now she has a look of implacable fury. Running toward Version 2.0. And of all the versions, this was the one she knew. The one who was once flesh and blood. The one whose bed she shared. The one she should truly fear, perhaps. But if ever there was a girl who could sublimate fear into hate... Well, maybe Version 2.0 picked the wrong girl to dump.

The ground suddenly gives way beneath us. A cavern opening up. We plunge down. But the grenade launchers hack up projectiles even as my feet seek purchase. I land in a blizzard of torn apart snow. And whatever meant to trap us down here lies still.

We scramble up the sloping snow wall. Out onto the frozen waste. Only seventy-five yards to the compound wall now.

There is one absence in our group. Kayla has not made it here. Not yet at least. Though she must be coming. She would not miss this. This opportunity for violence. Though that paints her too narrowly, I think. She will do the right thing. Sometimes—despite all the violence—I suspect she has the strongest moral compass of us all. She can stare unflinching at what must be done, and do it. Whatever it is. Because she thinks it needs to be done.

Plus, I suspect, she does not trust us to pull this plan off on our own. Maybe after New York, she's right.

The ice erupts to our right. The biggest golem yet. And this one does make a few gestures toward anthropomorphism. It is not as reassuring as I had hoped. Not arms that long, nor fists that big, nor claws that sharp.

The marines swivel, aim—

Something massive drops out of the sky. The golem disappears in an explosion of snow and steel.

A mecha. It stands in the billowing debris of its enemy. Squat, powerful, grey steel bedecked with chains of ammunition and badassery.

Another mecha lands a few hundred yards away. And another. The cavalry, plummeting from the sky. Because, well, screw subterfuge at this point. We've hit the let's-use-grenades point pretty early on.

A golem rises behind the mecha nearest us. A jagged

spiteful ball of ice shards, smashing up, like a haymaker from Mother Nature.

The mecha swivels. Massive cannons at the end of titanic arms tear into life. Flame and lead rip through the golem and tear it apart. By the time it connects with the mecha, it's nothing but collapsing slush.

Boo and yah.

We thunder on. Explosions paint the night yellow and red. My ears sing in the warbling upper frequencies that I will never hear again.

In the flickering light I pick out Felicity at the far side of the group. My Felicity. Or... God, I don't know where we will stand after all of this, she and I. Is this just temporary, this break? Will she see past this moment? I hope so. God, I hope so. But... Part of me knows she did the right thing. I fucked up in New York. Massively. Monumentally. And I would repeat the mistake over and over and over. I would do it happily. How can we allow that situation to perpetuate?

A hero sacrifices. And I cannot sacrifice her. And the world needs a hero.

Maybe Gran can be the world's hero. Maybe Felicity. Maybe they are stronger than me. I hope they are.

The wall of one pyramid slopes up massively before us. Steam billows up around us.

"Prepare for breach!" the marine leader yells. "Johnson, on my—"

And then our fearless leader yells no more.

A jagged spike of ice lances up out of the ground, catches him full in the gut. There is an ugly tearing sound, meat being cruelly sheared. The spike rips through him, lifts him bodily off the ground. A tattered strand of intestines, caught on the spike, is torn out the gaping hole in his back, steaming and dropping. The marine gags once, and is still.

The marines, highly trained killers that they are, pause and blanch.

Me, well, I almost piss myself.

More spikes come. And the marines' instincts kick in. And the grenades fly. And within three seconds the spikes stop. But ten men are dead. Become punctured, bleeding rag dolls.

Shit. Shit. Version 2.0, you fucking bastard.

The marines look at each other. The one called Johnson swallows.

Then his face hardens. "Prepare for breach!" he bellows.

I wonder if any of them can speak at the lower decibel end of the spectrum. Maybe it's all the explosions. Maybe he thinks he's talking at a normal volume.

Then Johnson leaps into the steam clouds. The whole unit waits. A moment of collective breath holding. Around us the world continues to erupt. I see a mecha go down under a tidal wave of snow and ice. Another is buried up to its waist, arms thrashing as ropy tentacles of ice try to bind it. Another lacks one arm but is still firing. Marines swarm around the machines, guns firing, grenades flying.

Then Johnson comes flying back, erupting out of the steam. "Fire in the hole!" he bellows.

The words are barely out of him before the explosion catapults him forward. He skids over the ice. When he comes up, blood is trickling from one ear, but he's grinning.

Red light floods through the steam. A bright beam

from deep within the pyramid. Spilling out like blood from a wound.

The marines swarm forward. Pour into the breach.

The MI37 crew take a moment longer. We stand there, panting, exhausted, flooded with adrenaline, staring into the light. Gran, Tabitha, Clyde, Felicity, and me.

Then, without a word, but as one, we step forward.

And we're in.

72

Heat. Pounding, pulsing heat. It comes in waves. Sweat springs out on my skin, soaks into the thick fabric of my Arctic gear.

We stand in a triangular corridor, tall walls curving up to a blunt point, reminiscent of the building's overall architecture. Small archways punctuate the corridor's length every ten yards or so. The walls between are strung with thick horizontal cords that press up against... I cannot quite place the material the walls are made from. It is thick but translucent. Almost like rubber. Red light pulses behind them, rushing down the corridor's length in waves. I reach out to touch it. Felicity slaps my hand away.

"Don't." She even looks at me for half a second to make sure her point is heard.

"I don't mean to be overly graphic," Clyde says, "but does anyone else happen to feel a little bit like they're standing in the middle of someone else's colonoscopy right now?"

Well, I do now.

It doesn't help that the place is swelteringly hot either. I paw at the zipper of my thick fur-lined jacket, then rip off the glove to help me remove it.

"Venting heat," Tabitha says. "Version 2.0 is. Funneling it from the servers to here. To dissipate." She too reaches out to touch the odd rubber walls. Felicity again slaps the offending limb away.

"Don't," she says. "We don't know—"

"Just blew a hole in the wall." Tabitha shakes her head. "Think he knows we're here."

She touches the wall. The substance gives slightly, stretching out, pushing between the cords that are strung between the arches. She pulls her hand back and makes a face.

"Gross."

It is a remarkably succinct summation of the place. I would have gone with fetid, close, and oddly clammy. But the brevity is not as strong in me.

"This way." Gran ignores us and points down the corridor. The backs of the marines are visible as they march forward.

"I don't mean to be a bother," Clyde says as we head in the direction indicated, "but I think it's probably worth mentioning, well... maybe this is just self-interest and if so, I hope you pardon the intrusion. As I stated up front, my desire for the bothering thing... not huge. But I did want to at least point out that I'm going to start experiencing some major malfunctions in approximately the next ninety seconds if we don't get somewhere cooler. My fan is about to crack an axle as it is."

As we have survived snow and ice monsters, I am not going to see us go a man down due to bad air conditioning. "Clyde," I say, "punch us a hole through that wall."

"What?" Felicity says, looking at me like I'm insane. "No." At least she's looking at me.

"Look," I say, "I'm field lead. I don't want to watch Clyde's more important electrical parts melt. We need to get out of here."

"Thanks, Arthur," says Clyde. "I appreciate that."

"Dudes," Gran says, "we, like, really need to stick with the marines."

"We leave that wall standing," Felicity insists. "If you want to get shitty about rank, I'm the director of MI37. Your boss." The red in her cheeks isn't just because of the heat, I think.

"Look, dudes." Gran puts up his hands. "Technically I'm in charge of both of you on this one, and we really do need to, like, stick with the dudes with the grenades and dubious political beliefs about violence."

"About forty-five seconds," Clyde says. "Not to add undue stress to the situation."

"Shoot the damn wall," I tell him.

"Arthur!" Felicity snaps.

"Dude?"

"Sorry," Clyde mutters. Then the muttering makes less sense. "*Melfor cal eltear mor kel lethar.*" And then his arm bucks, and the wall quakes.

Cords snap. Rubber tears. Fluid spills. A great gush of warm mucus splashes out of the hole Clyde has punched in the wall. It soaks through my clothes, warm and clammy. Tabitha is almost bowled over, hoisting her laptop above her head in the last moments. Thick ropes of the fluid drain down from her elbows as it runs down the corridor.

"Fucking gross." She spits and the wall mucus sprays from her mouth.

"What the hell?" Felicity stares at her ruined clothes.

Still, despite the vileness of it all, Clyde has made a conveniently man-sized hole in the wall. He's the first to step through into the darkness beyond. "Oh, that is so much better."

"Dude." Gran throws his arms up at me. "The whole marines thing. Organized strike and shit, man." He gives me the kicked puppy eyes. "I'm responsible for you guys."

Felicity isn't bothering with reprimanding me. She just looks pissed. And that hurts. Way more than betraying Gran's trust regardless of whether he saved my life or not.

"We're not going a man down on this," I say. I look directly at Felicity. "We protect our own."

She looks away. And I didn't mean to do that. I didn't mean to get angry. That doesn't help my cause. But it is done. I need all this done. I need this over so I can concentrate on trying to fix my life.

Gran shakes his head "Fucked up, man."

Tabitha gives me a thumbs-up. "Way to go, team player."

"Well," Clyde calls from the other side of the wall, "I, for one, really appreciated it. Not to discount other people's opinions. Totally valid. But the whole staying alive thing is a big motivator for me."

"Seriously," Gran says. "We can't go that way, dude. The marines are that way." More pointing ensues.

"What?" I ask. "We're going to have Clyde punch holes in the wall every minute or so?"

I do not want to follow the marines. I want to get the hell away from and ahead of them. I want to get somewhere where I can talk Tabitha into ignoring her boyfriend and his superior officers, and into hijacking this mission so we can fix things properly. But it's probably not time to mention that bit.

"I could actually do that," Clyde says. "The punching holes in walls thing. I charged the battery on this body way up, I've got power to spare."

Not helping.

"What the hell we still doing here?" Tabitha asks. "Marines that way." She points.

It's three against two. Democracy is not on my side. So, in at least one way, it is sort of a good thing that Clyde chooses that moment to say, "Oh shit."

"What the hell?"

From through the tear in the wall there is a crunch and a bang. As of something very hard hitting something like Clyde with a great deal of force.

I don't waste any time. I plunge in after Clyde. I know an opportunity when I see one. And, also, you know, less mercenary things, like going to save my friend.

And then I sort of wish I hadn't.

Some... thing stands over Clyde. An abomination. A patchwork nightmare.

The room we've broken into is dark and noticeably cooler. There is light, but it's as if a miser is in charge of the bulbs, only willing to let a few dark blue rays slip through his fingers. I can just make out Clyde's body on the floor, reflective highlights picked out like stars in a night sky.

Above him, the *thing* moves. Massive and pendulous. I can't see all of it. Just what the patchy light picks out for me. And part of me wishes there was no light at all. So that my imagination could supply me with more mundane horrors.

A leg. I concentrate on the leg. A goat's perhaps? A deer's? But it's too small, too frail for the quivering bulk above. For the... Jesus. I close my eyes a moment. Try to unsee things—

—*a scab of scales, of scars, hair bursting between*

in ragged tufts. Nails skewing from raw flesh. Muscle beneath translucent skin. A cluster of eyeballs, some red, some weeping. And the teeth, the teeth. God, the teeth—

It growls at me. A sound more felt than heard. A rumble in my gut. The bass line to night terrors.

"Oh shit."

It moves. I move. My hand flying to my gun, snapping out.

It's less than a foot away when I start firing. I get two shots off. I see, as if in slow motion, the spray of blood, the massive gush of fluids as if the thing's contents are under pressure, as if I hit some massive boil.

Then it hits me. And in the battle of beast versus firearm, this isn't even vaguely fair.

I sail through the air, collide with the wall. Sag.

It advances.

Where are the others? I think. *Where are the cavalry?* And: *We really should have stuck with those marines.*

Saliva trickles down from the thing's mouth… mouths… it trails up my leg. If I hadn't already soaked them in vile wall phlegm I might be upset about it. But I'm being preoccupied by the imminent death thing.

My fingers aren't working terribly well, but I manage to get a halfway decent grip on the pistol.

The beast growls and I almost drop the gun. But I get a second hand on the damn thing and opt for shooting it in the face instead.

It doesn't seem to care much.

And then, there they are, the cavalry. I knew they'd remember me in the end. Felicity firing her pistol, Gran letting fly with the assault rifle. And that seems to attract its attention.

It seems to attract a lot of things' attention.

Something scuttles past me. The clack of limbs on a hard floor. And then Felicity is screaming and flinging something away. And I can just catch glimpses of the things crawling down the walls, over the floor, in the crackle of muzzle flashes. I fire. I fire. I fire. I empty a magazine into the room, try to ignore the sounds the impacts make. The crunch of shells. The wet slap of something akin to and yet not quite flesh. The splash of fluids. The room stinks of gunpowder and offal.

I crawl toward Clyde's fallen body. Around me the madness goes on. On and on. The big thing falls, its gut opening up and then more things scratch, and crawl, and tear out from its deflating corpse, scrabble toward us, barking and baaing, screeching and cawing.

"Fall back!" Felicity yells, and she is right. So very right. But the hole through which we have come is blocked off now. Something viscous oozes out of the broken cords, filling the space with a tough gelatin surface. While I claw and tear uselessly at it, Felicity empties another magazine.

"Shit." I am reduced to curse words and sweating. Something comes out of nowhere, out of shadow and a depraved mind. A midnight horror of tentacles and teeth. It flies up over Clyde's unconscious form. My bullets catch it in midair and it detonates in a spray of foul-smelling fluid that stings my cheeks. I drop to the ground gagging.

"Fall back!" Felicity yells again, but she's not the only one who doesn't seem to know where to fall back to.

"Felicity!" I yell at her. "You still have any incendiary grenades?"

In the muzzle flash of her pistol I see her brow furrow.

"Again?" Gran asks me. "Really?"

"We need light."

"And an incendiary grenade is your answer? Dude!"

"We need to clear this room." Felicity's pistol re-enters its holster.

"Fucking nutzoid bullshit." Tabitha is caving in the head of some unspeakable horror with her laptop. I don't know if she's talking about the situation or our way out of it.

"Last one," says Felicity staring rather forlornly at the grenade in her palm.

I reach down, grab Clyde under the shoulders. "Help me!"

Gran shakes his head. "We have to move, man. We can't. He's too heavy."

I heave, and damn, he is right. Clyde is not exactly light. I won't leave him behind, though. "Please!" I beg.

But Gran is backing away, pushing Tabitha behind him. Something comes down from the ceiling at the pair of them. A mouth on a tentacle. Spines or teeth or... Tabitha's laptop blunts its jab. Gran's shot severs the stem. The mouth drops gnashing to the floor, while the stalk it was mounted on pours blood in a thick stream.

"Fire in the hole!" I don't think Felicity is really warning anyone. Just a little prayer to the gods of pyromania.

One whole wall of the room seems to detach itself. An arcing fist of gristle and bone. *Meat wallpaper*.

I heave on Clyde. Heave. He scrapes heavily on the floor.

Then Felicity is next to me, grabbing one arm, pulling with me.

"We protect our own," she says.

And the room bursts into light.

73

Flame envelops the creatures skittering across the floor, swallows the ones clambering along the ceiling, and cooks the ones on the wall to a fine medium-well crisp.

It also gets what's left of my eyebrows, I think.

In the sudden whitewash of light—there is the door. Right bloody there. A sheet of metal embedded into the flesh of the wall just a yard from Tabitha and Gran. I point, shout, yell. Gran understands, turns, heaves open the exit.

Something wraps around my leg. Something muscular and slimy in just the opposite of my favorite combination. I kick. It heaves. I lose my grip on Clyde. For a moment I hear Felicity scream. And even as I prepare to join in, part of me thinks, *well, at least she screamed. At least she cared enough to do that.*

And perhaps it's that thought that gives me the strength to kick free, to scramble desperately to my feet, to stamp on that fucking tentacle as it snakes toward me once more. Stamp again, again, again. Until the tentacle doesn't end in reaching flesh, but in flat, mashed meat paste.

Whatever it is that the tentacle belongs to, whatever it is that is howling in the darkness—I don't hang around to find out. I just run. I grab Clyde's arm, and I pull.

Gran and Tabitha are holding the door. Flames race after us, licking and cackling.

We spill through, my legs tangling with Clyde's frame.

Tabitha slams the door, but it bounces open again. Flames spit through the opening.

I stare in horror. And then I see Clyde's legs. Clyde's legs are blocking the door. I heave one last breathless time. My arms scream at me. But Clyde moves.

"Now!" I scream. "Shut it now!"

Tabitha slams the door home, just as something massive collides with its far side. It scrabbles madly against the metal, but the door doesn't give. The scrabbling dies away and hell is shut out for just a little longer.

ONCE EVERYONE IS FEELING A LITTLE MORE SANE

"USB stick," Tabitha says. She jiggles something inside Clyde's head. "That's all. Came loose." She flips a panel closed and tightens a screw with a practiced twist of her multi-tool.

"Oh my stars and garters!" Clyde sits up with a yell, and scrambles backwards. Then he stares around at us. He becomes very still. "Did I just say that out loud?"

"Garters?" I ask.

Clyde turns his head away. "Boot-up term," he attempts. No one buys it.

Gran is behind us pacing back and forth. Tabitha steps away from Clyde and goes to him.

"You OK?" I ask.

He turns and looks at me, and for a moment I think he's going to actually snap at me. Something we are doing is actually cutting through his permanently relaxed attitude. Then he exhales hard.

"We need to get moving, man. Do the whole melting thing and get out of Dodge. This place is messing with my calm, you know? Leaving the marines. Scary monsters. I just want to plant my thermic charges and get this mission done before this Version 2.0 dude does any more harm. You dig?"

Do I dig? Well...

"Are you really totally fine with just melting Version 2.0 and dropping him to the bottom of the ocean?" I say.

Everyone looks at me. I feel like the bad apple spoiling the whole bunch. "No," I shake my head. "I don't mean we should save him or rescue him or any of that. I kind of got over that when he killed most of everybody. But back in New York, we had a chance to do something better." Felicity is already looking away. My stomach churns. "And I know," I say, and God I hope they can hear how heartfelt this is, "I *know* it was my fault we failed there. But do we seriously not even have to try here?"

Gran looks pained. He opens his mouth.

"Fucking liability." Tabitha cuts him off. Her finger stabs at me. "You are. Fucking forget about long shots. Put your head down. Do the plan. Save what's left."

I look around the room. Clyde has turned his head away as if avoiding anyone's eye, but I'm pretty sure that's because he doesn't want to publicly disagree with Tabitha. Gran does the shrugging for him. And Felicity... I don't know. I just don't know.

"Let's move," Gran says, deciding to ignore my outburst. "Come on."

That's normally my line. But Gran is in charge. That's what we were told. His is the mind I need to change. If he goes, then Tabitha will follow, I think.

And Felicity... Well, if I get Gran and Tabitha it will be four to one at worst, and the democracy thing could work out there.

We move through the room, looking for an exit. The light is blue, not red, but it pulses the same way the light in the outer corridor did. And the walls are the same—gelatinous, translucent, shot through with slightly organic cords. Peristaltic waves run down the cords, the wall bulging with them.

"Is this place... alive?" I ask.

Gran ignores me, keeps moving. Tabitha sticks to his side. Felicity is still only talking to me when she absolutely has to reprimand me. But Clyde turns. "Not to cut you off," he says. "Totally into the celebrating of individuality through the expression of unique thoughts and all that sort of thing. Open communication is the foundation of any endeavor. All of that. Really means a lot to me, but, you know, on the other hand, I was really trying to not think about that."

Which seems fair enough. Except now I *really* wish I wasn't covered in wall mucus. How long does that stuff take to dry anyway?

At the far end of the room is a puckering in the wall absent of cords. It is for lack of a better word a...

"Sphincter," Gran says. If his nose wrinkled up any further it would be between his eyebrows.

Clyde snickers. "Sorry," he says immediately. "Completely immature response."

I look around for another exit. For another steel door. There is none. Just the...

... sphincter.

We have to push through it. We have to. There is no other way. And right after destroying two-thirds of humanity, this may be the worst thing Version 2.0 has done.

We all hesitate. "Fine," I say, because I always seem to be the one who says these sorts of things, and I might as well give in to the gravity of group roles now, "I'll go first."

I push through. It is unspeakably awful. There is nothing else I want to say about it.

The room beyond is, again, vaguely organic. The architecture remains slightly too gelatinous for comfort. Here, though, the biological is mixed with the mechanical. Or, is... punctured by it. Thick bundles of electric wires spear up through the floor and twist toward great hulking machines. Some of these are nothing more than dull steel boxes. Others, though, have a delicacy that suggests complex lab equipment.

At the center of the room is one that looks to me like a torture device designed by H.R. Giger. The central component is a large fluid-filled sac punctured at many, many points by thin spider-like limbs. Inside the sac the limbs end in fine, sharp-looking needles. They glisten slightly in the dull blue light. The limbs themselves arch back away from the sac to connect with a more utilitarian looking metal box. The box is as punctured as the sac but this time by electrical wires and tubes of a more biological nature. They emerge from the floor to penetrate its sides.

Clyde steps toward it with a low murmur. He reaches out a hand, and touches the sac. The side dimples slightly under the pressure of his hand. He almost strokes it.

"What is it?" I ask him.

"Shit." It's Tabitha from behind me.

"What is it?" I repeat.

"Can't have this," Tabitha says. "He can't." She shakes her head. "This is future tech. Impossible now. No." She shakes her head again. "No."

"Is there a problem here?" Felicity is all business, gun drawn, expression stern.

"It's a printer," Clyde says. Somehow despite the lack of breath in him, his voice sounds breathy. "A 3D printer."

That triggers a few neurons in the old gray matter. 3D printers. Machines capable of receiving a three-dimensional blueprint and printing the object. Layer after layer building up. The mechanics of it escape me, but as I understand, while they are not exactly commonplace, they are a practically realizable technology. Which begs the question, why is Tabitha freaking out about it?

Then Clyde supplies the answer.

"Except, well, it's a biological 3D printer."

Now that I haven't heard of. But the implications are plain enough.

"He's printing life forms?" My voice heads for the higher octaves. Maybe it thinks its feet are going to get less soaked by the creepy up there.

"Monsters," Tabitha says. "Back there." She thumbs over her shoulder at the room we just firebombed. "From here." She points to the machine.

This has gone from mad science into genuine horror movie. In the Kurt Russell oeuvre, this is the *The Thing* and I never watched that bloody film.

Clyde turns to me. Fully to me. Like I'm the only person in the room. "This can build bodies," he says. "Not just monsters. It can build…" He can't quite say it. Not all of it. Something is choking him up. But I can't quite follow.

"What?"

"Good spot," Gran says. "Like, never would have caught that myself." He puts his assault rifle to his shoulder.

"No!" Clyde screams, but it's already too late.

Gran opens up, full rip. Bullets tear through the sac, fluid sprays wildly, the arms snap and sever, the metal box tears apart, cables and cords whip and snap away.

Gran lowers the gun. "Groovy." He blows smoke from the barrel. "Like, the last thing we need is 2.0 having reinforcements, right?"

Clyde takes several fast steps toward Gran. And for a moment I think I've had it all wrong, all backwards, that this Clyde is nothing but another lie, another trick, another dashing of my hopes. I think I am going to steel fist exit a meat skull.

But the energy seems to sap out of Clyde. He stands, a limp metal form before Gran. Everything about him sagging. "A body," he says. It's so quiet I can barely hear him. "We could have used it to make me a body."

Oh. Oh God. Oh, how could I not have seen that? I stare at Clyde's hopes and dreams splattered across the room.

Gran blinks as realization hits. "Shit, dude," he says.

Tabitha stares from Clyde to the machine, to Gran's gun, then back to Clyde. A tight loop of realization and confusion.

"On, you know, the plus side," Gran says—and I have a distinct feeling he shouldn't—"like, the robot body is way more durable and shit. Way groovier in a fire fight."

And I was right, he shouldn't have said it.

Clyde grabs him by the scruff of his jacket and hoists him clear off the floor. I realize Clyde's mechanical body, while skinny, is over six feet tall. Gran is not. Clyde holds Gran close to his face.

"I am a human fucking being!" Clyde shouts. The mirrored surface of his face actually quakes. And this is Clyde categorically and unmitigatedly losing his shit.

I've never imagined it before. I don't think I'd have been able to imagine it. And perhaps it might be funny in some circumstance, because it is so unlikely, so unrehearsed, so incompetent in some ways. Clyde is not equipped for this sort of rage.

But knowing him. Knowing his pain here and now. No, this is not funny.

"I am not a robot!" he yells. "I am not a fucking machine! Not a chip or a program or a string of ones and ohs. I am a fucking person trapped in this horrendous fucking body and it's shit. It's all shit. And I could have changed. I could have fixed it. I would have… I would have… I would have…" He stops. Or the rage runs out. Or he realizes who he is and what he's doing and sees the look of horror on Tabitha's face. Whatever it is, he turns and stares at his hand, and then opens it, and Gran drops to the ground. "I would have been me again," he finishes.

I want to look to Felicity. To follow her lead. Or to judge mine from her. But that path is closed.

"It might not be the only printer," I say. It sounds a little lame.

Clyde just shakes his head.

And then, again—*again*—Gran opens his mouth.

"No," I cut him off. "Not now. Just let it lie."

But he won't.

"Dude," he says, "I'm not, like, trying to be a dick about this, or anything—"

But he's going to be.

"—peace and love are totally my thing, but I don't want anyone to have any false expectations about what we're doing here." The pained expression again. "We are razing this place to the ground, dudes. We are not saving anything. We are not doing this slowly. We're just here to fuck up its shit, you know?"

There is a pause of substantial length. Because, well… that, at the very least, is not why Clyde and I are here.

I wish Kayla was here. Just another body to add weight to the cause. And, also, because I think Gran may have a mind that is difficult to change. He is a man of commitment. No matter his outward demeanor, there is inner steel in Gran, and I'm not convinced that I have the strength to bend him. He *believes* in the marines' mission here.

Clyde starts to walk away, past the shattered machine, into the depths of this place. "Fine," he says.

But I don't believe for one moment that it is.

74

Another sphincter door. It is no better than the first. Another room that's organic enough to make my own organs quiver in revulsion.

We are strung out now. Clyde leading, me just behind him. Gran and Tabitha in a tight pair some distance back. Then Felicity, dragging at the rear. Keeping her distance from me.

If I could just sell her on my plan… If I could get her on board with the idea of changing the nature of this mission… And she would want to save people, wouldn't she? But there is no way to discuss it with her. No way to get her alone and implore her.

And if I was alone with her, would I really beg her about this plan? Or just to take me back? How selfish am I? Maybe it's better that I don't know.

Another sphincter door. I swear they're getting worse.

"Dudette, fancy smacking me upside the head with a GPS reading?" Gran asks Tabitha. She responds with a list of numbers.

"We're going down," he says. "Floor's, like, sloping and stuff." Then louder, for all of us to hear, "Hold up, dudes. I'm going to go ahead and plant the first charge. Be like thirty seconds and then we groove on, 'kay?"

Nobody really acknowledges him, but we do stop. I glance at Clyde, but he's been in his own personal hell since the 3D printer went boom. I look at Felicity, but she keeps her eyes on Gran.

What do I say? What stops Tabitha from yelling at me about long shots?

Gran pulls a black cylinder from his backpack. It's about a foot long, bulges in the middle where a digital readout and several buttons lie. Gran starts to press them.

"We're proving him right," I say. I have no idea if this is the right tactic or not.

"Who, man?" Gran doesn't look up from setting the bomb.

Tabitha rolls her eyes.

I push on though. "If we damn everyone Version 2.0 has taken from us," I say, "if we just write them off, then we're the species he says we are. Selfish idiotic destroyers ruining this world."

"Fucking long shots!" Tabitha spits, her bile frothing over. "Fucking stop it!"

So this wasn't the way to avoid her saying that. But I can't let Tabitha derail me.

"No," I snap back at her. "No, I won't. Because it's too big. Too important. This is the tipping point. We determine the future of humanity here. This is not a light decision."

"Why it's too big to fuck up! My whole point!" Tabitha turns her back on me, apparently no longer able to bear the sight of my idiocy.

"That's exactly why we have to go for the long shot," I insist. "We have to be better than 2.0. We have to hold humanity to higher standards."

"So, what, dude?" Gran sets the thermic charge down by his feet. I can see the air rippling, distorted by heat shimmer around its top. "If humanity doesn't live up to your standards, and I mean, like, *your* standards, then Version 2.0 is right and we get thrown in the disposal unit. That's not, like, totally groovy thinking."

"If we don't live up to that higher desire, then humanity can't escape the disposal unit." I'm trying desperately to hang onto this argument, to not get caught up in my own frustration. I aim for the higher ground. "It's not about what I believe. It's about the two hundred million people who will die if we don't try to help them."

"They're already dead!" Tabitha yells, spinning back around, unable to simply ignore me.

And God, it's so frustrating, because in the end… "*You* are the one who can save them!" I yell. "You! Your code!"

"He's right."

And finally, finally, thank you. Someone has my back.

"Shut the goddamn fuck up!" Tabitha screams at Clyde.

"You could do it," Clyde keeps on, quiet but definite. "If anyone could, you could. I know it."

"Shut up, you goddamned machine!"

"Dudette…" Gran lays his hand on Tabitha's shoulder.

"What?" She whirls on him too. "Like this is viable?"

He shakes his head. "No. Of course not."

"Yes," I demand, "it is. We're at the center of Version 2.0's network here. We put the code in his servers. We distribute it to all his mushrooms. He deprograms everyone for us."

Gran looks at me. "Seriously, man? Just, like, think it through. For your plan to work we need to take down the wireless blockers. And if we do that, we, like, all lose our minds. Like instantly and shit."

"And he—" I start.

"He distributes your code?" Gran looks at me, incredulous. "No way, man. He's, like, a super genius. He rips your code out and wins. And yes, I totally get that this way sucks, but it's the way we have, man. It's what Version 2.0 has left us with. Let it go, dude. Just chill, and blow him up, and shit. It's cathartic, man."

While Gran may have saved my life moments ago, right now punching him in the face might be a little cathartic.

"I could help," Clyde says. "I could fight him. He is me. I could—"

"Dude," Gran sounds like his patience is slipping too. "You really need to chill. Like, he tore apart the brains of three of you already. He'll do it to you too." He shrugs, as if somehow throwing Clyde's signature move back in his face.

And finally, because I can resist it no longer, I look to Felicity. She is staring at the thermic device at Gran's feet. The heat shimmer has expanded halfway to the ceiling. But then, for a moment she looks at me. And all I can say to her is, "Come on. Please."

She opens her mouth.

Suddenly a great vibration runs through the room. Something massive and decidedly unhealthy sounding. One wall bulges awkwardly. I hear a fleshy ripping sound and then a gush of fluid. Somewhere a wall has given way.

"The hell?" I stare around.

"Sweet," Gran says.

I fail to see the saccharine he's referencing.

"Guessing this isn't, like, the first device planted." Gran nods at the device at his feet. It is belching out heat. Sweat has broken out all over my forehead.

And that's just great. Another ticking clock. Just what I needed today. Why are there no threats to the world that I can just get to in my own damn time?

"Felicity," I say, "you know what I'm saying is right."

She looks away, and then back. "I know it would be

nice if it was right. But Gran—"

"Jeez, man. You are, like, so into making me be the dick today." Gran shakes his head. "I want this to be awesome for us. We take down the bad guy and shit. That's what we do today. We're not doing your thing, man. We're not. I'm sorry but there's no way it's happening. It's ungroovy."

There is something in the way he says it which sets off alarms in the back of my head. I don't think I'm the only one who senses it.

"Or what?"

Another boom from somewhere not as far away as I'd like.

Gran looks at me as if I'm genuinely crazy. "What do you mean, or what, man? I mean, like you're going to come to blows with me on this? It's not happening, dude. It's, like, no way and no how coming together in beautiful harmony. We need to talk about something way more chill and get out of here before the timer on this thing goes kaboom. You dig, dude?"

"Would it come to blows?" I ask. And I remember Winston. I remember him saying that Gran called in the planes. I remember being asked to kick Gran in the nuts. And I dismissed it. I blamed the General. I thought Winston was just upset at the world. But… what if he wasn't?

I remember again the little girl with her brains blown out before we could save her.

What if Winston wasn't wrong? What if Gran killed him?

Gran just looks sad. "Dude… I… This is ridiculous, man. We need to go. Come on?"

"Would it come to blows?" My voice is raised. I will

not move. And even Tabitha is looking at Gran now.

"Dude…" Gran shakes his head. He goes to speak and I see the exasperation on his face, and I get that I'm being a dick to him, but this is too big to sweep aside just because it's socially awkward. I'm not letting him take that exit. And Gran sees it. He sighs.

"Dude. I am here to save the world today. From Version 2.0. And from you if I have to. There. You fucking happy, man?" He shakes his head. "Can we go now? Do this thing?"

And there it is. Out in the open for us to see. Our role here. Our place. And that's what I have. That's what I have to show Tabitha and Felicity. And maybe they agree with Gran. But maybe, just maybe…

Tabitha steps toward Gran. "Come on."

Shit. Shit and balls.

But then Felicity says, "No."

And God, oh God, it is like a supernova in my chest. I almost don't care what she's objecting to. She is agreeing with me. She is with me. Here and now, on this, *she is with me*.

Gran looks at her.

"No," she says, "it's not right."

"Dudes." Gran looks genuinely distraught. "I don't get this. I mean, fuck, man. This is the easy bit. We're in. We kill things. We chill. I don't… I don't…" He looks to Tabitha for support.

She looks disgusted by all of us. "Fucked. In the head. All of them."

Gran shakes his head. He looks beaten. And maybe… "I like all you guys. Like, hugely. MI37 is awesome. Don't do this."

"That's it." Felicity stabs a finger at him. "That. Right

there. That's what I won't fight for. That's why you're in the wrong. Because you care for us but you'd throw us to the wolves anyway. No. I say no to that. We protect our own. And, yes, Arthur's idea is stupid and idiotic, but God, it's necessary. He's right. We need to be more than the people that survive. We need to be heroes."

"Jesus!" Gran throws his hands up. "If I'd known you guys were into hallucinating so much we could have had serious fun, you know. You're talking about throwing away everybody. You understand that? Everyone in the world."

And what if Gran's right? Everything he's saying makes sense.

Except the thought of his victory makes me feel sick in my gut. I could not live in the world he'd leave us with.

"We can find a way." I feel like a preacher in the desert, desperately trying to convince my flock.

"Without me you can't." Tabitha has her hands on her hips.

"We have Clyde," I snap back.

"Thanks, man," says Clyde. "You are like an awesome over-confident friend. I really appreciate that."

OK, maybe we do need Tabitha.

"I'm sorry," I say to Tabitha, "you have to come with us."

"Hey…" Clyde sounds a little hurt.

"*Have* to?" Tabitha says at the same time.

But it's Gran's reaction that really captures my attention. Because apparently the line you do not cross with him is the one where you say that his girlfriend has to come with you.

The barrel of his gun points straight at my face.

75

"Dude," Gran says. And there really is such pain in his voice. The pleading in that word is as heartfelt as any plea I have made to him. "I'm begging you here. Chill the fuck out and come along with me. Let's be totally radical and cool about this. Can we do that?"

But abruptly Gran's gun is not the only one drawn.

"You put that goddamn thing down." Felicity has a bead on Gran's head. "You understand? You put that down this instant."

Oh my God. She… She… What the hell is happening here? How did this happen?

This is New York all over again. A plan falling apart all over again. People are going to die again. Sweat is pouring off me, though part of me realizes that's as much to do with the skyrocketing temperature as with the tension.

I need to get this under control. "This is insane," I say. "No one is going to shoot anyone."

"Just Version 2.0, right?" Gran's gun doesn't waver from my head.

"You put that fucking thing down!" Felicity's calm is definitely in question. And despite everything going on in this room, part of me just wants to rush over and kiss her and thank her.

"We need to just talk," I say. "That's all. All of us sit down and talk and think about this."

The heat is a physical presence in the room. An oppressive force pushing down on us with sweaty palms.

"There is no discussion, man." Gran is still pointing the gun. "We have orders and shit, dude. Chain of command and shit."

"Never really was Arthur's strong point that," Clyde says. "Not judging of course. Just an observation. If you want it. Probably don't—"

"Shut up, tin man," Gran snaps. For a moment his gun wavers away from me in Clyde's direction. I twitch and the gun is back on me.

"Put! It! Down!" Cords stand out in Felicity's neck.

"This is crazy, dudes." Gran still sounds sad. "I'm going to have to take you in and shit now. This isn't how this was meant to be."

"I will reset your thoughts right here and right now." And I know that tone in Felicity's voice. She is not joking.

Someone is going to die here. I realize that suddenly. This is the immovable object and the unstoppable force. I am as stubborn an arsehole as Gran. And I don't know which one of us is the hero anymore. I've lost that. But… Jesus. Jesus.

There is one way to settle this.

I turn my back on Gran. "I'm going to find the servers," I say. "To do it my way. You do what you have to do."

There is a moment of absolute silence.

"Not completely convinced on the whole wisdom aspect of this plan," Clyde says.

The heat shimmer makes the entire room seem to quake.

"Put the gun down!" Felicity is reliably consistent on this point.

"Arthur. Dude. Don't make me do this."

"I'm not making you do anything."

I take a breath. I think about how maybe, just maybe, Kurt Russell might be proud of me in this moment.

I take the step.

There is a noise like the world crashing down.

I wait for the pain, for the numbness, for the end.

It doesn't come.

But the sound goes on, crescendos.

I spin just in time to see the room's ceiling collapse.

76

The blast sends me sprawling. I slam into something hard and unyielding and in a moment of startling clarity realize that it's Clyde's chest. Then something falls on my head and clarity decides to take a short sabbatical.

I fumble through fog. Lost.

An ugly hacking noise breaks through the mist. It brings me back to the present. Eventually I identify the noise as my own breathing.

I pick myself up slowly. My head rings. I put a hand to it and it comes away sticky with blood.

"Hello?" I yell. My voice sounds tinny in my damaged ears. No one answers.

The room looks like a bomb went off. I think it probably did. The ceiling has collapsed. A great ragged tear opening up the room, spilling steel struts, twisted machinery, and sagging organic matter. Everywhere I look, things are coated with wall mucus. Smoke and steam billow, occluding my vision.

"Hello?" I yell again. Then I remember the room of monstrosities we encountered earlier and hold my tongue. I don't want to attract any undue attention.

With another momentary flash of clarity I realize that if I collided with Clyde then he is likely to be somewhere nearby. I start searching the floor. Reflective metal catches my eye. I scrabble at the rubble covering it. Clyde's legs appear. One of them twitches weakly. I heave away a chunk of machinery. It's heavy, but more pleasant to remove than the unidentifiable wall-organs spilled all over him.

Someone nudges me while I work and I wheel around grabbing for my gun. But it's Felicity. My Felicity. Safe. Alive. And my heart leaps. Actually leaps and hits me somewhere in my throat so I can't breathe for a moment, only gasp. And then I grab her and seize and hug her savagely.

She stands stiffly. Lets me work through the hug. Lets me realize that she's not going to respond. I let her go, step back, slightly embarrassed. But she had my back a moment ago. She pointed a gun at Gran on my behalf. This fight is not lost yet.

She chews her lip. Then, "Come on," she says through the ringing in my ears. "Let's get Clyde free."

Nothing is certain as we set about the task, but I go about Clyde's rescue with renewed strength. Within a few minutes we have his torso clear, then finally his head. Its once reflective surface is scarred and dented. There's something about the damage that suits him. It has, for want of a better word, personality.

"OK," Clyde says. "Not to cast aspersions on the people who built this body. It's taken a machine gun round full in the chest and walked away, and I definitely like that about it. And the whole battery-operated thing is a great boon for a magician. But I do think we are reaching its stress limits. And if Evil-Me is listening I would deeply appreciate not being hit again."

I have more practical concerns. "Where's Tabitha?" And then, because even though he just pointed a gun at me, he did save my life earlier, "Where's Gran?"

Felicity points to the tear in the ceiling. The deluge of rubble below reaches up to the tattered hole, making the world's most horrific ramp and neatly bisecting the room.

"They were on the other side of that," she says. "So they're either still there or they're buried."

"They're still there," I say automatically. It's what I have to think.

"God. Tabby." Clyde stares at the rubble. "I mean, I think we should search for her. Make sure she's OK."

"She's OK," I say. She has to be. It's an absurd thing to be certain about here, in this place where everything is designed to kill our species, but she has to be.

"We should search for her," Clyde repeats.

"No." And Felicity always had the strength for the hard calls. "There's no time. We have to press on."

And do what? We need Tabitha to put the code into Version 2.0. We need her for this plan to work. But she can't be buried. She can't be... be... She can't be under there.

"We do need to find a way around," I say. "Find a way to get to her."

"Didn't you say Clyde could do it?" Felicity asks me.

We both turn to look at Clyde.

"Well, erm, yes, about that," Clyde starts. "I figured... Rhetoric and all that. Figured we were all exaggerating slightly on the whole being-able-to-do-it front. Sort of maybe figured that some groundless bravado on my part might help the situation... and, well, it was all poorly conceived now, I see, but I was trying to get them to think something along the lines of 'resistance is futile.' And, you know Tabby, always reluctant to let me near a keyboard. And, given the circumstances we're in, you can sort of understand why, I imagine. Not that me wiping out a species was probably ever on her list of major concerns, poor girl. More of a concern about files in general. I hesitate to use the phrase 'control-freak,' but, well, I just did say it and it's out there now..."

He's babbling, pawing at the pile of rubble, shifting a few pieces here and there. But honestly, if anything is under there and it doesn't have a military-grade steel chassis, then, well, we all know what's really happened to it.

"What about this?"

Clyde and I turn from the rubble to see where Felicity is pointing. And there it is, lying on the ground. Lying out from the rubble.

Tabitha's laptop.

The case is dented, smudged, cracked on one corner. Clyde steps toward it, almost reverently. A priest approaching a holy relic. His hand hovers over it.

"She doesn't let go of it," he says. "Never." There's horror in his voice.

"She does," Felicity says, "if someone grabs her unexpectedly around the waist and flings her out of harm's way. Now stop pussy-footing around, grab it, and make sure it works."

Clyde picks up the laptop. Something about it looks right. He and the computer share an aesthetic right now. Scrap metal chic.

He hesitates again. "She would never let me turn it on."

I see Felicity's jaw tighten. "A moment ago she was standing by the side of a man who was pointing a gun at Arthur's... at one of my agent's heads." I don't call her on the adjustment. I can't tell if it's a good or a bad sign. "I don't give a shit what she's let you do. We're here to save the human race, and you need to pull your finger out of your output port and figure out if you can help us do it."

Somewhere in the swirl of events I need to work out how I feel about Gran pointing a gun at my head. What I'm going to do if he survived.

He survived. He has to have survived. Despite it all, I want him to have survived.

But… After Version 2.0, he and the military are the greatest threat to humanity I can think of.

And he thinks I am.

There isn't a way around this. Nothing neat or simple. If I see him again I'm going to have to fight him in one way or another. Trick him. Trap him. Something.

Shit. Shit and balls.

Clyde has the laptop open. The screen, mercifully, blinks to life. Uncracked and whole. Clyde's fingers move over the keyboard, reluctant at first, then with increasing speed.

"It's all here," he murmurs. "All good to go."

There is another boom from deep within the building.

"Then we should be too," Felicity says.

I look at her. At Clyde. "We're decided then?" I ask. "Screw the military's plan? Shoot for the moon?"

They both nod. And our path is set.

77

The most obvious exit is up, so we take it, scrambling up the fallen wreckage and through the tear in the ceiling. While it does involve a certain amount of stepping-on-unspeakable-squishy-things it is distinctly preferable to a sphincter door. I try not to think about the possibility I am squishing Gran and Tabitha's corpses into a slightly finer grade of pulp.

The architecture of the rooms above resembles that below. It has two doors, both of the hideous sphincter variety. We pick one, push through.

As we work our way deeper into the compound, the organic theme is developed, worked and reworked. Subtle noise permeates the structure—a low gastric rumble in the corridors. In one place, a wall is lined with slowly waving cilia. Fungal structures intrude into passageways—great yellow brackets, drooping gray stems.

"I don't know about you," says Clyde, "but I have to say I am not at all down with Evil-Me's sense of aesthetics. I mean, I get that it's creepy and weird, and that's great for dissuading folks like you and me, and being all ominous and stuff, but considering he spends way more time here than we do, it seems, ultimately, like an exercise in cutting off your nose to spite your face."

I'm not sure what to say to that.

"Just to highlight," Clyde adds, "in the face of any

upcoming fracas, that we are very different people."

I give him an encouraging smile. Felicity just shushes him. Long term, hers is probably the smarter plan.

TWO CORRIDORS FURTHER ALONG

Felicity comes to an abrupt halt. She holds up her hand. "Do you hear that?"

We stop and listen. I don't.

"What?"

She shakes her head, concentrating. "I thought I heard... grunting perhaps."

Grunting doesn't sound awesome. In fact, I can think of no circumstances in which I would want to walk in on anyone who is grunting.

"Do you have any sense for which way we should be heading?" Clyde asks. Which seems a little late, as we've been making our way through these rooms for about five minutes now.

"The cords in the wall," I say. I almost think of them as vessels now, though I resist using the word. They branch and bisect, a pattern somewhere between arterial and tree-limb. "They're getting thicker." And the chances of Version 2.0 locating himself near the nutritional heart of this place are fifty-fifty at best, but it's all the navigation I have.

"Shh," Felicity hisses again.

We freeze again. And this time I hear it too. I turn around. "Is it coming from behind us?" I ask. "What is it?"

"You know, actually," Clyde jumps in, "not to be presumptuous or anything, but I think I know what that's reminding us all of."

I eye him. "What?"

"Well," Clyde says, mulling it over far too slowly for my taste, "to me, it totally sounds like those zombie chaps from back in New York."

Oh shit.

"Damn it, Clyde," says Felicity.

"Was I wrong?" he asks. His metal shoulders slump.

"Opposite," I tell him.

"Oh!" For a moment Clyde sounds cheered. And then we get to the implications. "Oh," he says again.

"Probably best to start running," I suggest.

What we break into is probably best described as an enthusiastic limp at this point, but we all make a valiant effort. In the end it gives us about a ten yard head start.

Then they come. Lumbering, jerking, staggering, pouring out after us. The walls give way with sickly pops as the zombies push through. They don't rupture. Rather, polyps bud off, erupt wetly, spew zombies into our path. I can see them thrust themselves against the far side of the walls, transitioning from dull silhouette to looming presence. A sphincter door unleashes more of them, pushing toward us, hands searching.

It's an oddly quiet chase. The zombies lack speed and grace, but so do we. We all stumble forward, trying to overcome limbs that have seen better days. There is the guttural clacking of the zombies, my huffing breath, Felicity's soft cursing, and occasional clank of Clyde bouncing off a protruding piece of wall. That is all.

I stagger and the zombies gain a yard. One buds from the wall next to me. I feel its fingertips graze my shirt every time my pace falters. Then I put another yard between me and it, struggle to maintain the gap.

But we cannot get ahead, can only be driven on. We

come to a T-junction, turn right. The way is blocked. Left seems like a decent option in retrospect, so I opt for that. And then the zombies are ahead of us, bursting one-by-one from the wall.

Felicity's gun barks, takes down one. Takes down another. But then one explodes out of the wall right beside her. It claws at her. She kicks it in the gut. It smacks back against the side of the corridor.

Something in its neck convulses. Some alien anatomy grafted there. The zombie tilts its head back, the whole thing pivoting back around the jaw, stretching the mouth inhumanly wide. There is a glimpse of blackened teeth and tongue.

Then something erupts out of the creature's distended neck, thrusts out between the teeth. A bulbous mushroom stem pointing like a gun from the jaws. It bulges violently.

Felicity throws herself sideways a moment before the mushroom's hood erupts. The zombie collapses. Black spores fill the space where it stood.

78

Felicity rolls. I grab her arm, help heave her to her feet. Clyde grabs me under the shoulder. Together we drag her free.

Felicity blinks in surprise. I desperately search her eyes for a sudden blossoming of blackness. For signs of fungal infection. But there are none. She got free in time.

Then she's pushing up, yelling at me to get a move on. So I get my move on. But the zombies are closing tighter about us. Another emerges right in front of me. Its neck convulses. I punch it in the throat and it gags violently. Then its neck distends under the force of some internal detonation. Purple blood tinged with black sprays from its lips.

I just killed someone. Someone I could have saved.

On. On. Deeper in. Our pursuers a constant presence, constantly closing. We duck down one corridor, another. We wrestle through one sphincter door. More zombies await us.

Necks bulge. Spores disgorge. Great vomited clouds of them. We duck and weave between them. I try to hold my breath but it is coming too raggedly. Around us the whole structure seems to creak and quiver. Distant explosions wrack the place. The sense of imminent disaster is heavy in the air, like a headwind I need to force my way through.

Why the hell didn't I bring a sword? Why the hell didn't I ask the marines for one? I shoot zombies again, again, again. One more magazine down. Another. I slam the final one home. And it is not enough. A pitiable defense against the numbers opposing us.

I put my head down, do my best to gain some distance. The others do the same. We race zombies and our own cramping muscles. And somehow we stretch our lead from three yards to ten, to fifteen, to twenty.

We come to a confluence of tunnels. Three of them fusing together. A massive cord rises in the floor, distorting its surface in a rough curve—some major artery in Clyde's compound. This has the feeling of something important.

A few yards down the corridor, emerging from the gloom—a door. An honest-to-goodness door. Not a sphincter, or portal, or cloaca, but a real door. It's made out of steel. It has rivets.

I edge ahead of Felicity and Clyde, slam my weight against the door, heave. Nothing happens. Behind us, our lead narrows. Then I realize the door pivots, up and to the side. I tug laterally and the door swings up. I usher Felicity and Clyde through then scurry after them.

The room beyond is vast. A great hangar of a hall. It lies empty now, but there is a sense of latent heat. As if something vast was just here. Version 2.0's zombie army perhaps? Something worse?

"We should get out of here," I say. The place feels off. I hate to think of the things that could bud through these walls. The last thing we need is some zombie version of the dog we fought in Bryant Park.

"I am a huge fan of that plan," Clyde says. "Willing to start a convention in its honor. PlanCon. Everyone will come. And then immediately leave, I suppose. Thematically that would be the thing to do at least. Maybe not such a great convention actually."

"Yes," Felicity agrees. "You guys move on up ahead."

Wait…

I turn to her, try to read her expression. "All of us," I say. "All of us move on ahead."

Something impacts against the far side of the door.

"No." She shakes her head. "This is a natural choke point. This is an easy hold. I can delay them. I can get you the distance you need."

"No." I shake my head. This is an absolute. Non-negotiable. I do not leave the woman I love behind to die.

"What happens if I don't do this, Arthur?" She finally looks me in the eyes. And I see nothing but conviction there. "What happens if we get to those servers? How long could we buy Clyde to do his work? Enough? I don't think so."

I want to argue with her. I want to grab her and just run. But I can't and I don't. Already I know she's right. I know that we couldn't buy him enough time. But there has to be another way. This can't be it.

"Someone has to make a stand here," Felicity insists. The door starts to pivot open. She lets a zombie get an arm through then slams it closed. The arm is severed with a meaty "chunk," and proceeds to spray black fluid across the floor. "Someone has to buy you the time you need."

"I'll stay," I say. "You go with Clyde." It's all I can think of, and as soon as the thought comes it's obvious.

"No." Felicity shakes her head, definitive.

"Why not?" I say. "It makes sense, you're… you're…" I attempt to put it into words. "…So much more than me."

"No," she says again.

"You have to." Desperation is setting in. Zombies are clamoring at the door.

"No." A third time. And then she almost says something else, but she swallows it.

"You have to let me stay." I beg her. I beg her with everything I have. "You know how I feel about you. You know I love you. I don't care what you've said. How you feel. I know I should but I don't. I love you. It's that simple. So I can't let you stay here. I can't let you… you…" I struggle against the word. "I cannot let you die for me. You have to let me stay."

I'm almost on my knees. Some godawful parody of a proposal.

Felicity turns away, turns her back on my words, faces the door. And that's it, I think. It really is over. She just pointed her gun at Gran because I was one of her team. She's done with loving me. That's not a factor in her decisions anymore.

It's over.

Then Felicity says in a very small voice, "I…" She hesitates. "I'm…" She shakes her head. "I'm not strong enough, Arthur."

I stare at her. She looks back at me. I look at the mouth that said my words. "I can't leave you here," she says. "I just can't. I don't have it in me."

"I…" I say. "I can't…" But she's said it. They're her words now. I have lost my ownership.

"I tried, Arthur," she says. "I tried to be better than I am. Better than… I don't know, us. Not you and me specifically," she flounders. "But that idea. That concept of us. But… God, I protect my own, Arthur. You're my own. Us. We're each other's. I don't…"

Something in my chest is fracturing. That I am hearing this now. As she is asking this of me. To let her sacrifice herself. I don't know where I'm standing.

"This is your plan." She puts a hand on my chest. "Not mine. Yours. You need to be the one to fix this. I honestly don't know if I can. You don't think you're strong, but there is a force of will in you…" She bites her lip, bites off her sentence.

"If they come through," she says. "*When* they come through, I won't let them eat me, or whatever the hell it is they do. I'll make sure it's the spores that get me. I won't be dead."

Jesus. Jesus. I'm reeling. The image of Felicity as one of… of… Shit. As one of those. Her eyes gone. Her mouth. Her fucking mind gone. No. No. No.

I shake my head. She grabs my shoulders, pulls me toward her. My head down to her level. "Because then you'll save me, Arthur. You'll make your plan work. And everyone who's infected will be safe. Will be free. I will be free. I will be alive. Because of you."

I try to take it in. All of it. Felicity's life riding on my plan. My long shot. Can I live with that? Jesus. And why did it seem easier to put the rest of humanity on the line?

I remember New York again. The Empire State Building. Seeing her carried away from me. Seeing her being taken to die. I remember diving out of a window to save her.

I remember letting a city die because of that.

I can't do it again.

I can't let her stay here.

"You go." And I'm begging now. Pleading. "You save me."

"I love you, Arthur," she says, so suddenly, so abruptly that it stops me right there. "I love you so much." She leans in and she kisses me. Her lips pressed against mine. And such incredible softness. Such heat. A warmth spreading through me, flooding me. And for a moment I am lost to it. To her. Just lost.

She pulls away. "I love you. And once you save my life, I cannot wait to date you again." She blinks at the tears threatening to spill. "This is all fucked up. It always will be. But we will work something out. Now let me get this shit over with, and go save the world, goddamn it." She's smiling despite the tears in her eyes. "Go do that thing that makes me love you." She nods. "Go on."

The clamor against the door is getting louder. The walls either side of it are starting to bulge. Felicity glances away from me and shoots into the spongy surface. The bulge deflates.

I stare at her. God. She's willing to do this. She believes… well, maybe not in my plan, but in me.

Do I?

God, I staked the future of my species on this. How can I back away from that now?

I try to say OK, but I can't. The lump in my throat is too big, too hard to shift. Instead I just pull out my pistol, eject the magazine.

"Take this," I manage to say. "Say you'll take this."

"You'll need—" she starts.

"You'll need it more." She won't deny me this. If she expects me to walk away from her here…

Oh God. Oh Jesus. Oh fuck.

"OK," she nods. Then, "Remember there's still one in the chamber of your gun. If you need it."

I nod.

"I hate to be the one to do this." Clyde puts his hand on my shoulder. "But unless we start moving, all this noble sacrifice business—which is amazing by the way—it isn't going to matter much."

We can't be doing this. This can't be the way forward.

"Go," Felicity says. "I love you."

"I love you."

She smiles. It's beautiful and perfect. It lights her up like a city at night. And then she turns away, and faces the door.

Clyde takes me by the arm and pulls me away.

79

We've turned the second corner before I get my emotions under control enough to insist, "We have to go back."

But we don't.

Clyde keeps pulling me along, drags me forward step by tumbling step. "Sorry, Arthur," he says, "but the whole point of nobly sacrificing yourself is so someone else can achieve something. If they don't go ahead and achieve it, that rather undercuts the whole point of the sacrifice."

I wish he wasn't right. He remains stubbornly so. I plant another foot in front of the other.

But she's back there. She's behind me. I can picture her, the slow-motion of my mind's eye dragging out every agonizing second. I see every shot she fires. Every one that finds a home in a zombie's skull. Every one that isn't enough to stop the tide. And then I see her waiting. See them coming for her. And I see that she has no way to defend herself.

How long will it take? Is it over already? Is she still hanging on?

What if she isn't infected? What if they move too fast for her? Or her resistance makes them angry? Scenarios bifurcate, become fractal in my head. Only one constant swirling at their heart.

I left Felicity to die.

I feel nauseous, dizzy. The edges of my vision have lost their focus. *We have to go back. We have to go back.* It's the rhythm of the blood in my veins, of my feet on the floor. *We have to go back.* But we can't. We mustn't.

Clyde is right.

The floor lurches. At first I think it's some psychosomatic sense of vertigo seizing my gut, but then Clyde staggers too, grabbing at the wall for support.

"Holy shit," he says. "I think we're sinking."

Sinking. Exactly what the marines want. To send Version 2.0 to the bottom of the ocean. And given the way things were the last time I saw Gran, he may not mind if I'm on board.

I wait for another lurch, but it doesn't come.

"From the department of not-so-great-news," Clyde says, shrugging a few times, "the rate of ice melt is going to keep accelerating. We really do need to move."

I know. I know. I think I can hear guttural sounds chasing after us. Distant, but not retreating. I can't tell if it's in my head or not.

The wall to my right bulges abruptly. I stagger, spin, raise my pistol. One in the chamber, Felicity said. One shot. And it could be the one thing that prevents her noble sacrifice from being a pointless one.

The wall ruptures.

"Well, that's just feckin' gross."

I stop, stand perfectly still.

"Kayla?"

She stands there in front of me, dripping mucus, hair lank and matted, soaked flannel shirt clinging to her equally soaked tank top.

"Well, feckin' obviously." She paws some of the goo from her brow.

"You came," I say. It's obvious, but I'm so stunned that I have to state the obvious. "You're here."

She ran. All the way from Mount Rushmore to the Arctic Circle. With a hole in her side. And she cut into Version 2.0's compound. Past the golems. Past the zombies. Even for Kayla this is an act I can barely believe.

"You're here," I say it again, trying to get a handle on the enormity of the fact. I grasp her dripping arms, make sure she's solid and real. She is.

"Well." Kayla looks rueful. "I had to come. You'd gone and left without a feckin' sword again. Feckin' neglectful it is." Her face softens slightly. "I would have brought you one but I didn't see any lying around. So it's just mine, and you aren't getting your feckin' paws on that. So I'm just here to tell you to remember next time." She shrugs.

She's here. Kayla is standing right before me. And behind me, somewhere, is Felicity. And suddenly it feels as if there's a chance that Felicity's sacrifice will mean something. That I can turn this around. Or that Kayla can do it for me.

I hug her. Covered in mystery snot or not, I don't care. I cling to her. Because she is the promise of a good break finally. Because she didn't give up on us.

"Get the feck off me." Kayla wrestles away with ease. She looks up and down the corridor. "Where the feck is everybody?"

Jesus. How to explain. How to tell her she's the only thing that's gone right since we left Mount Rushmore.

"Gran is... opposed to our course of action," Clyde says. "We had a bit of a tiff about it. Then the ceiling collapsed and we rather lost track of him and Tabby after that."

"Feckin' Americans," Kayla says but seems to have little to add after that. "What about Shaw?" She looks at me. "You finally detached her from your hip?"

And God, how to say it? How to explain?

But then there is no time, and no need. We have dallied too long with this reunion. With a grunt and a growl, Felicity comes charging toward us.

80

Part of my mind simply unhinges. This cannot be. I have to deny reality.

Felicity's sacrifice was worthwhile. It was meaningful. She bought us time and space. We are using that time and space to get ahead of the zombie horde. To buy ourselves time. So we can save the world. So I can save Felicity.

That is what is. What has to be.

So she cannot be here. The horde cannot be here. We have not wasted the lead she gave us this way. We have not wasted her sacrifice. Because no. Just no.

I stand there. Just stand there.

To my left I am half aware of Kayla blurring into motion. Zombies rush toward us. Kayla chops one in half, a long diagonal slice from shoulder to hip. The zombie falls in two pieces. Kayla spins. Her blade flashes. Another zombie is bisected at the waist.

I barely see it. I am completely focused. On the zombie that is not there. That cannot be there.

Her hair hangs lank, darker than I remember it... than it would be if it really were Felicity, if it could be her. And the eyes are the wrong color. Not a dark rich brown but a purple-black. Felicity's lips are a delicate dark red, not that lifeless blue. Her nails are well cared for, not black claws at the end of frozen hands.

She... it... staggers forward. Even less coordinated than her brethren. Newborn perhaps?

No. No. No.

To my right, Clyde extends an arm, mutters words. A zombie comes apart at the seams. Arms and legs and head and torso spilling apart. A crackle of electricity and the chest of another flexes from concave to convex. It collapses in a bloody, frothing heap.

The zombie that is not there walks on. Walks past the death of her fellows. Walks toward me.

And there is something still beautiful in this... this... thing that is not, cannot be her. There is some echo of her in the angle of the cheekbones, the curve of the brows, the shape of the eyes. Some echo of a woman I love.

Kayla's blur of violence moves toward her. Clyde does too. Piling up bodies either side of her. Making a channel for her to move through. Kayla decapitates, amputates, maims. Clyde smells of ozone.

She walks toward me, down a channel of the dead. Like a bride toward her groom.

I am aware of the gun in my hand. One in the chamber. That's what she said. One bullet if I truly need it.

If I need it to save her.

I raise my gun. I can see her face beyond the end of its barrel. Can see her black eyes locked on mine.

And once you save my life, I cannot wait to date you again.

The gun drops from my hand. I can't. I just can't.

She reaches me.

Her arms are wide. Like a lover's. She embraces me. Clutches me with stiff arms. And I hold her back. My arms fold automatically about her. And her body is so stiff, so rigid, so unlike her. And yet somehow so familiar. The way this curve fits here, the way her head comes to right here.

I look into those eyes. Those lost black eyes, and she stares into mine. She tilts her head back, as if for a kiss.

I remember those kisses. Softness pressing hard on my lips. The taste of her lipstick. The smell of her perfume and her hair around me. Her, so much of her. My Felicity.

I lower my head toward hers.

And her jaws open wide.

81

"Feck!"

The shout is distant, barely registering. All I can see are those eyes, that mouth. Darkness to drown myself in. To make all my problems go away.

A sharp harsh noise emerges from Felicity's throat. And part of me wishes she would not have done that. That she would not have ruined this final embrace with her new tongue.

Then her head lolls back, and the stiffness flees from her body, and she is limp in my arms.

Kayla pulls the blade free of Felicity's body. The blade is stained black with infected blood.

All the strength flees from me. I drop her. Drop Felicity. She falls to the floor.

She falls to the floor.

She falls to the floor.

"Close one that." Kayla nods at me, and whirls away. Zombie limbs fill the air.

I drop to my knees. Stare at Felicity. She lies there on her back. Arms splayed. A broken bird. A dropped book. She lies in a pool of black blood. It expands in short oozing pulses.

Pulses.

Her chest rises and falls.

Her throat works.

Because she's alive. She's still alive. Holy shit.

My mind races. First aid courses. The recovery position. Tilt the head back. Clear the airway. No. No. That's not right. Five pumps, one breath. Or is it no breaths now? Just pumping. No. No. Pressure. Apply pressure to the wound. Stop the bleeding.

I flip her over. I see the puncture in her back straight away. A tear in her jacket haloed by blood. I slam a hand down on the wound and press, put all my weight into it. A grating gurgling sound emerges from Felicity's throat. No matter what has been done to her vocal cords there is no mistaking that cry of pain.

But it doesn't matter. It doesn't matter if it hurts. It only matters if it keeps her alive. Her arms twitch weakly, trying to grab for me. I ignore them. Blood is seeping between my fingers. I need something like cloth. Something absorbent to help the clotting.

I take my hands off the wound, jam my knee into it. A fresh moan emerges from Felicity. With shaking hands I rip at my shirt buttons. But my hands are quivering too much. I grab my collar and yank. Buttons pop. I don't care. I tear off the shirt, jam it over the wound. Black blood flows into white cotton. I hold it there with my knee, work off my belt. I start working the belt under Felicity. I'll tie the shirt there. She'll stabilize. It'll be OK.

"What the feck are you doing?"

I don't even look up. "It's OK," I pant. "She'll be OK."

"Did they feckin' bite you?"

I glance up at Kayla, standing over me, a confused, almost horrified look on her face. She has her sword out. Blood and gore drip from the blade into Felicity's hair.

I bat the blade away. "Move that fucking thing!"

She keeps on staring at me. And I don't have time for this. I go back to the belt.

Kayla shoves me roughly aside. I sprawl back off Felicity's body. She stares at me, at my eyes. "Are you feckin' losing it, man? We're trying to kill the feckers."

"No!" I yell. And I am trying to be rational, to not blame her for this, to not go for her fucking throat. But the fury is raging at the back of my throat and in my voice. "Not her. Not her!"

And then Clyde arrives. Finally. He stands beside Kayla and looks down, looks at Felicity, looks at me. "Oh no," he says. "Felicity?"

"Felicity?" Kayla's eyebrows go on an orbital trajectory. "Oh, you are feckin' kidding me."

"We've got to stabilize her," I say, scrambling back toward the body, grabbing the belt. Stop the bleeding. There's still time.

"Oh shit," Kayla is saying. "When the feck did this happen? I didn't know, Arthur. You've got to understand I didn't feckin' know."

"I know!" I snap. "Just…" Red tints my vision, things start to blur, but I force it down. I need to focus here. Focus on Felicity. "Just help me."

"OK, OK, OK." Kayla and Clyde kneel. They help me with the belt. Kayla applies crushing pressure. Clyde folds the fabric to clot more effectively. And together we dress the wound.

82

We stumble on. Stumble deeper. Everything hurts. My body. My soul. My head. It's trying to contain too much, to hold onto this one stupid fucking plan I once had, this idea I had to save the world. But it seems ethereal now, slipping between my fingers.

Kayla carries Felicity across her shoulders. The weight doesn't seem to bother her. Felicity twitches and growls. She claws lightly at Kayla's back, but achieves little. She's weak, getting weaker.

Does the fungus interfere with the body's healing process? I've seen how fast the zombies rot away. What if it stops her from healing?

I can't afford to think like that. I have to focus. I have to find the heart of this place. Find Version 2.0. I have to kill him.

This place feels oddly absent of him. Where are his stand-ins? Where is his omnipresent face looming over me? Does he think this vision of biology and architecture fused speaks for itself?

I thought I knew him. When I see Clyde in front of me—I know him, don't I? Yet this thing his twin has become. This force for… is it evil? This place is so alien it seems to exceed such a simple definition. And his goals, as twisted as his methods are, they're noble. That's still the truth.

Everything is twisted around. Has become a wracked body wrapped around Kayla's shoulders.

We round a corner, following the major artery that we picked up back before the hangar room. Another door. Clyde pivots it wide and we duck through. Another massive chamber. But this one isn't empty.

Wires. And wires. And wires. They rise out of the floor like trees. They branch and splay through the room. They form rafters above us. A great web of them.

Clyde reaches out to touch a bundle before us. "Neurons," he whispers.

I squint. It doesn't help me see the metaphor any more clearly. "What do you mean?"

Clyde looks around. "If this building was a creature… Well, it's not. It's a building. We're walking around in it. Sort of definitional, I suspect. Well, actually I'm not sure what the definition of building is. It's always that way— you know what a word means, but then defining it is a whole tricky mess. And, well, as buildings go, this one does blur the line regarding the whole creature-building divide, which, I have to admit, has never appeared blurry before. But if one discarded the building aspects of this place entirely. Just hypothetically of course. Not some sort of construction work I'm suggesting, just an exercise of the imagination. But if that were the case, then I would really think of Evil-Me as the brain of the creature that I'm positing here. But from the brain come the nerves. The neurons. And as Evil-Me is all digital and everything and not organic—going back to the whole hypothetical thing here, well then the neurons, the individual nerves will be wires."

"Why the feck are you talking?" Kayla is primed for violence, not metaphors.

"Oh, well, you know, cultural-biological imperative. Man as a social creature. That sort of thing. A general species-specific desire to share insight and knowledge. The collective experience. Plus, it should be fairly easy to track these back to Evil-Me's servers. So that seemed relevant."

Kayla narrows her eyes. "I can never tell if you're trying to piss me off or if you're just a guileless feckwit."

Clyde shrugs. Which may suggest the former. Or the latter. Damn. I don't know. I don't have the energy to work on team dynamics right now. Instead, I grasp at the sense that we're finally coming to the end of this goddamn maze.

"Which way?" I ask.

"I think—"

Clyde is cut off by a massive whirring noise. As if something vast and industrial has sprung to life. A sound that summons images of buzz saws five foot tall and aimed at James Bond's crotch.

"What the hell?" I turn around searching for the source.

The wall to our left seems to be the culprit. But there is no machinery, just wires and space.

Noises with invisible sources… They always work out so well…

The wall bulges suddenly—an alarming streak of white manifesting as the rubbery building material stretches then tears.

A colossal buzz saw. Six feet in diameter. Teeth an inch wide. It tears through the structure. Arterial cords snap and fly. Mucus sprays. Wires spit sparks. The whole room reverberates with sound, with echoing destruction.

The whirring blade retreats, comes back again,

slices diagonally into the deflating material. A great flap of wall collapses messily on the floor.

The marines pour in.

There must be fifty or more, all quick stepping to the frog march fandango. They push in, guns and bad attitudes on full display.

"Plant charges," booms an electronically amplified voice from the darkness beyond the tear.

And then the saw's owner steps into the room. A massive mecha, ten yards high at least. The saw has replaced its right fist. The end of the left arm looks like something that resulted from the ill-fated coupling of a glove and a bulldozer. The legs are equally sturdy and functional. Steel plates riveted around pistons. Three splayed toes grasp the uneven floor with hisses of pneumatic pressure.

The torso is less substantial—a cage of thick steel bars. It reminds me a roll cage awaiting the car chassis, although someone has equipped this roll cage with a fairly substantial motor and a control panel that wouldn't go amiss in an airplane.

And sitting inside that cage, behind those controls... Well, long time no see, Agent Gran.

83

"Tear this shit out, dudes," Gran yells, the steel mitten of his left hand pointing to the wires. To back up his point, Gran jams the buzz saw through one bundle of wires. They sever with a shower of sparks. Marines set about hacking at others. One guy just opens up with his rifle. Copper shreds and flashes.

Panic alarms start ringing in my head. I turn to Clyde. "What chance is there that some of those are pretty critical to the wireless communications network we're looking to hijack?"

But Clyde isn't looking at me. He isn't looking at Gran. He stares at one figure standing near the mecha's feet. A figure clad entirely in black. White tattoos standing out sharply against her dark skin.

He stares at Tabitha.

Oh, thank God, she's alive. And despite the circumstances, despite the fact that she's standing beside someone who threatened to execute me not so long ago, I smile. I have no idea how this will play out, but right there, that is someone we didn't lose.

I glance to Felicity, still slung over Kayla's shoulders. Her hands have stopped clawing. I can still see the shallow pulse in her neck. But only just.

Then Clyde steps toward Tabitha. He raises a hand in greeting. I try to bat it back down but it's too late.

He's already been noticed. Guns swivel.

Gran is among the last to twig. A bundle of wires comes apart and he notices everyone looking our way. Aiming our way. His saw whines to a halt. He looks too.

"Dudes?"

Despite knowing the pilot, it seems an unlikely phrase to come out of such a hulking machine.

Gran takes heavy steps toward us. Tabitha moves with him, scurrying to keep up with the machine's massive footsteps. When Gran stops, she stands before him, extending a hand toward Clyde.

"Laptop," she demands.

Clyde steps toward her.

"No," I say.

Clyde hesitates. Looks back at me.

"We need that," I say. "Tabitha's not with us on this. So we keep it."

"My damn laptop." Tabitha's hand is still out. Her mouth set.

"No," I repeat.

Clyde looks between us, torn. For a moment I think I've lost him, the laptop, my cause. And then he steps back in line next to me.

"Dude." Perched above us, Gran sounds like he's somewhere between exasperated and amused. "Seriously? Still? There are, like, fifty marines here. You are not doing this. Give it up already."

Fifty marines. I look over at Kayla. She looks back. And doesn't blink for a moment.

"Just put Felicity down somewhere safe," I ask her.

She rolls her eyes.

Gran looks between the two of us. "Dude. You are not seriously suggesting..." He looks down at

Tabitha. "He's not is he, dudette?"

Tabitha stares straight at Clyde. "Give me the laptop."

Clyde shrugs so fast and so many times I think he's going to blow a fuse. "I can't," he says. It sounds like it pains him. "Arthur's right. And we have to save Shaw now."

Tabitha glances at Felicity for the first time. "Shit." She turns to Gran. "He is. They will." She shakes her head. "Stubborn arseholes." Though maybe there's an edge of respect in that last statement.

Gran joins the head-shaking crowd. "Well," he says, looking at me, "this sucks. I really enjoyed working with you."

"OK," I say to Kayla, ignoring Gran, "time to put Felicity down."

"Wait." Tabitha steps in front of the mecha, suddenly seeming to realize the impact of her words. She looks up at Gran. "Arthur's not going to negotiate. But you…" She shakes her head, "you don't have to actually shoot—"

Gran isn't even looking at her. He turns to the marines.

"Weapons free."

84

The world erupts. The floor hits my chin. The air above me fills with lead. Felicity slams into the ground next to me. She lies there, eyes staring, breath shallow.

I keep my head down while Kayla works. I don't want to see this. I want everyone to live. I want everyone to be saved.

But that can't be. That's not the way the world works. Bad people. Bad things. Bad decisions. And sometimes, just very bad shit happening to good people. Bad things like Kayla.

Clyde is to my right, muttering, bullets ricocheting off him. I hear the crackle of electricity and the cry of a man flung across the room.

I reach out and hold Felicity's hand.

Oh God. She is so cold.

Something hits me in the head. I flinch back, with a spectacular kind of violence. Around the time I land, I realize that it's not a bullet and that I'm not dead. I stare up, searching for an assailant. There's no one nearby. But one of the marines' assault rifles is lying where I was.

"A little pissing help," Kayla yells.

She's between two men. One aims the butt of his rifle at her head, the other the barrel. She ducks under both, almost too fast to track, comes up on the far side of the pointed weapons, arching her back—a dancer in the ballet of combat. She flicks her sword. The butt hits one man's head, the blade hits the other. Blood blossoms. The men fall, victims of circumstance and head wounds.

Gunfire to Kayla's right. To her left. But she's gone, weaving up and down and round. Her blade spins up, and I swear I hear the whine of a bullet deflected by the blade. She rolls, comes up at a marine's feet. Her sword comes up with her—skewers him, balls to brow.

There are three men behind her, their guns raised.

I don't want anyone to die.

I grab the assault rifle, aim low, and pull the trigger.

The largest thing I have fired in my life is my government-issue pistol. This thing is about ten times bigger. It leaps, slams back into my shoulder. I grunt as bullets spray around the room.

I release the trigger. The barrel smokes.

"I said feckin' help, not hinder, you feckin'…" The end of Kayla's insult is lost to gunfire and bloodshed.

Shit. Shit. Shit. This is so messed up. I have no idea if I hit anyone. If my bullet took the brains of a man following orders, fighting to defend what he has been told is right. Jesus.

I tuck the rifle tight in against my shoulder. Aim low. Not to kill. I don't want to kill.

The end of the gun disappears in a spray of sparks and fragmenting metal.

Gran's buzz saw lands five inches in front of my face. It chews into the floor, with a grinding, mulching whine. I stare at rotating metal, feel the wind of it whipping past my face.

I sprawl back. Gran is a few yards away. He wrenches the saw out of the ground. It hangs above me. And then it doesn't.

I roll fast and hard, bouncing over the uneven surface as the saw slams down, chews through more of the floor. I come to a stop as I hit a bundle of wires.

Gran whirls the mecha around, the saw blade chugging and jittering over the ground, spraying floor shrapnel at me. I roll back over the wire bundle as shards sting my face.

I'm still holding a truncated gun. I have no idea why. I throw it away and try to figure out a plan.

Gran. Gran coming for me. Gran massive and armored and with his mind set. I'm the enemy now.

Shit. Shit. Shit.

How is Felicity? Is she safe?

No. *Concentrate*.

Footfalls. Close. Coming closer.

I scramble to my feet, put some distance between me and Gran. He lacks range. The wires will clog him. I am small, and—in this particular scenario—comparatively nimble. That's an advantage. I can use that.

But as I hear his buzz saw chew through another bundle of wires, I remember my earlier thought. If these are the neurons of this place, which ones do we need? How damaged can Version 2.0 become before we can't use him?

I need to end this. And I need to do it fast.

I double back, swing around, head for places Gran has already punched through. Where he can cause no more damage. I stumble over marine body parts.

Where is Kayla? Maybe she can help me?

Unfortunately, one of the many problems with being chased by someone ten yards tall, though, is their stride-length. I've spent the past month getting more rigorous exercise than I ever imagined, but I get about eight strides in, about three seconds to formulate a plan, and then I hear the rush of air behind me. I duck instinctively. The buzz saw whistles over my head. I scramble up, on all fours, then running once more. The buzz saw swings again. I duck, roll.

The blade swings closer this time. I swear my back brushes the flat of the blade as it swings. I swear I nearly piss myself.

Where the hell is Kayla?

Then I understand the way the marines are spread out, all facing one spot. They have, against the odds, pinned her down. I sprint parallel to her hiding spot, behind the line of their guns, catch a glimpse of her, hunkered below some organic outgrowth in the floor.

Clyde is proving more elusive, if less fatal. He's over on the other side of the room. Every time a marine lines up a shot he extends an arm, and they go sailing through the air. Marines are bleeding and bruised, but they're not giving up.

"Battery getting a touch on the low side!" he yells across the room. Then, "Probably shouldn't have revealed that!"

Where the hell do I go?

And then that's not a problem anymore. Because there's nowhere left for me to go.

The wall comes up hard and fast. I slam into it, just getting my palms up in time to not take the blow in the face. I feel the give of the rubber, the resistance of the thick cords. I spin, look at what little ground I've gained.

Gran advances. His saw buzzes.

Behind him, I can see Tabitha. I sort of expect a look of grim satisfaction on her face. Me finally coming to the sticky end she always knew I would arrive at. But she is standing in the middle of the room and screaming something at the top of her lungs. One word. Over and over. I can't make it out over the noise of the saw, coming closer, closer.

Despite the proximity of messy, violent death, or maybe because of it—some part of me desperately trying to escape the situation—I narrow my eyes and try to read that word.

"Stop! Stop!" Over and over.

And maybe… Maybe…

Gran glances at her. Then back at me. And if he knows what Tabitha is saying, then he doesn't care. His face is set. No hippy weakness. No peace and love. Not anymore. The chips are down. And I don't have the winning hand.

He steps toward me.

Behind him a marine grabs Tabitha, shoves her roughly to the ground. I see the wide startled stare. The mouth open to shout. Then her head hits the floor. When she comes back up, her mouth is bleeding.

Gran steps a little closer. My only hope is to time my dodge correctly. To move at the same moment he moves. To move in the right direction. So do I go left or right?

Is Felicity OK?

Concentrate.

Behind Gran, Clyde bursts into motion. He starts running, hand out like a cannon. I see the marine who grabbed Tabitha fly roughly through the air. One impact. A second. A third. Clyde guns at him. The marine rag-dolls across the room.

Gran steps closer. I edge right. He follows.

Clyde skids to a halt at Tabitha's side, leans down.

516

He offers her a hand, helps haul her to her feet. They stand staring at each other for a moment.

Tabitha darts forward and grabs the laptop from under Clyde's spare arm. A bullet ricochets off Clyde's skull.

Oh shit.

But then Tabitha stays there. Stays right by his side. She doesn't run. Doesn't head for the safety of the marines. Just stands there looking at him. Blocking the shots.

"It's over," Gran says to me. Oblivious to this drama. His jaw is set. "Sorry, dude."

He pulls back his arm.

Left or right?

Concentrate.

Gran lunges.

He swings his arm in, left to right.

Concentrate.

85

I dive left. I dive toward the blade. I dive toward death.

But I dive low.

The blade is hot, is screaming white at the edges. The air around it ripples as it is whipped and heated. Massive teeth chew up the space between it and me. They are directly in line with my eyes. They fill my vision.

Then I am beneath the blade. It screams over my head. And Gran buries it into the wall.

He eviscerates architecture. Mucus floods out of the great gash, a massive sticky tide. It catches me, carries me, extends my dive, sends me skidding over the floor. Out from beneath the shadow of the blade, as it stutters and rips deep into the wall. Across the floor. Beneath the mecha's outstretched arm. And then I am, just for a moment, in line with the body of the beast. Just for a moment, in line with the open cage of the mecha. In line with Gran.

And as I dive, I pull my gun.

Felicity's voice. Felicity's intensity. Looking me in the eye. "Remember there's still one in the chamber of your gun. If you need it."

The hero sacrifices.

Not just himself.

Not just his loved ones.

Not just people.

Ideas. Ideals. Promises. Dreams. Hope.

The hero sacrifices.

I just wanted to save everybody.

I skid across the floor. Feet from Gran, from his wide staring eyes. From his good cheekbones and better teeth. From his easy manner. From his love for Tabitha.

And I shoot him.

86

The bullet catches Gran in the throat. There is a great spray of blood and bone. Vital elements of his anatomy are ripped away and spread around the back of the mecha's cage.

I have time to think that at least the end will be quick for him.

Then I skid out past the mecha. Past Gran. The sweep of the fluid ends and I land, bedraggled, stunned, and sprawled in the middle of the rough floor.

My arms are still held out before me. My hands still grip the gun. I can see Tabitha staring at me. Staring at the unmoving mecha. And she knows.

The marines know too.

And I am lying in the middle of the floor with nothing that resembles cover near me.

The air comes alive with bullets. Desperately, I roll back the way I came, toward the shelter of the mecha's corpse.

Bullets slam into the steel frame. I keep my head down, try to piece together the action from noise alone. From the ricochets I can tell the marines are moving. How long will it take one of them to circle round? I listen for sparks, for mumbled gibberish, for a sign that Clyde is still standing. I listen for Tabitha coming for my blood.

The mecha looms above me. The massive suit of weaponized armor. And… God, I don't want to look up at the corpse hanging in the cage above me. I don't want to look at what I've done.

But there's a chance the mecha is a solution to my on-the-verge-of-being-killed problem. If I used the buzz saw as some kind of shield, maybe I could herd the remaining marines out of here. Like I'm some sort of massive mechanized sheep dog or something.

It's not the best plan, but it's pretty much my only one. I risk a glance up at Gran. His head lolls at the sort of unnatural angle only permitted by a partially severed neck. Blood slowly oozes out of the wound. Which means his heart has stopped.

Bile splashes against the back of my throat. I swallow hard, wincing as acid scores my tonsils.

Jesus. What have I done?

But I know exactly what I've done. I made a choice. About what sort of person I am. About what I'm doing here. About my level of commitment.

I killed Gran for my plan. I can't be squeamish now.

I lever myself up, trying to be careful about the angles between me and the still shooting marines. I look at the straps holding Gran's body in. If I can get over the basic horror of moving Gran, they shouldn't be too complicated. Then I glance at the controls.

Oh balls…

It looks like an aircraft's flight deck got a videogame controller drunk and knocked it up behind the bike sheds. A bulging swarm of dials and buttons, joysticks and toggles. I have about as much hope of mastering it as I do of becoming impervious to bullets.

Which means I'm down one plan, and back at zero again.

Bullets hit the steel frame. From a new angle. The

marines are moving to flank me.

"Clyde!" I yell.

"Happy to be of assistance as soon as I lay my hands on some jumper cables."

Crap sticks.

"Kayla?"

"Feck off."

Plans do indeed appear to be sparse on the ground. I consider yelling Tabitha's name but in the shadow of her boyfriend's corpse that might be considered pushing it right now.

Then another feature of the cockpit draws my eye. Small black cylinders. LED read-outs.

Gran's thermic charges.

I glance back at the mecha controls. But no, they still don't make sense. And honestly, I'm more likely to get a handle on demolitions before I am on advanced robotics.

I grab one of the thermic charges, examine it. The LED read-out is a timer. Three unlabeled buttons sit below it. Can't be that hard. I try one of them. The timer grows bright.

00:00:50:00.

There seem to be too many numbers, but... erm... I need to get it down from fifty minutes, I guess. I press another one. The numbers flicker and jump.

00:00:30:00.

I go back to the first button.

00:01:00:00.

What the hell? What sort of mad logic... Back to the second button.

00:00:40:00.

OK, this makes no sense. I press the third button just for kicks.

The numbers spring to life. A dizzying blur of LED. The final two are nothing but a transitional glow, moving too fast to be read. The forty speed counts down to thirty.

What the hell?

The numbers keep on screaming downwards. Not slowing. Not measuring minutes. Thirty becomes twenty in the blink of an eye.

Down to twenty.

Seconds? Forty meant four seconds? Who the hell measures time that way? Who has numbers for hundredths and thousandths of seconds? What sort of insane bomb-making psychotic, CIA, bastard…

There is no time to aim. Only to fling it wildly, desperately away. A mad hooked shot around the frame of the mecha. I snatch my hand away.

There is time to hear the *oof* of whoever the bomb hits, and then to think, *shit, they got really close*.

Then it detonates.

87

A solid wall of heat. It slams into me like the palm of God. I crash back, impact against the flat blade of the mecha's saw, still embedded in the wall.

My head rings. My vision blurs as my eyes go into separate orbits. I blink, stagger. There is shouting and shooting. The sound of gunfire moving.

Away?

What happened…?

A marine. A marine had snuck up on the mecha. Must have been less than ten yards from me when I threw the bomb. Just dumb luck that I hit him.

Jesus. The bomb hit him.

God, I am trying to not kill people here. I think I just atomized one of them. Jesus…

The sound of gunfire stabilizes. Gains a new source. I can hear where they are. Further away now. Holy crap. That worked. I drove them back.

If I can just keep pushing them back… Push them back and not vaporize them… I grab another charge from the mecha's case. I press the first button.

00:00:50:00.

Is that five seconds? That doesn't make any sense. Then it should be a five and not a fifty… Bloody military nonsense.

Screw it. I press the middle button. The numbers

spring to life. I fling the bomb as high and as hard as I can. To the marines' left. Try to get them to move back toward the rip in the wall they entered through.

The bomb is not exactly aerodynamic. Still I get some decent distance on it. I hear it clunk and roll. I risk a glimpse under the mecha's saw arm.

It goes off like a firework. A blistering star of fire arcing through the room. I see the air quake at the heat ripple. See it tearing through bundles of wires. Tearing toward me.

In the movies, people duck away from explosions. They out-run fireballs. Movies are way better than real life.

The shockwave slams into me. It's worse than the first one. I feel the heat rip over me, through me. Feel the impact of it in my gut. Taste blood. I fly backwards. And thank God that 2.0 made these walls spongy. I am cushioned between arterial cords, then the elasticity snaps forward, slamming me face first into the ground.

Cries. Yells. Gunfire. Running feet.

I pick myself up, dribbling blood. I think I may have knocked a tooth loose. Some dull, numbed part of me wonders if I can get it fixed while I'm still in the US. Avoid NHS dental care. That said, I just blew up at least one marine, so the chances of the US being a very fun place for me after this are slim enough to make Kate Moss look chubby.

Marines. I am throwing bombs at marines. What the hell am I doing? These men are just following orders. Goddamn shitty orders.

I risk another look. The room is a disaster. It looks like… well, it looks like a bomb went off in it. Which it did.

Bundles of wires hang in tattered rags. Plastic bubbles around copper. The floor and walls are scorched. Fires flicker, spit greasy smoke into the sky.

The marines hunker around the rip through which they entered the room. A bristling mass of weaponry and scorched machismo.

I grab another thermic charge, prime it, throw. I have no interest in seeing how accurate I am this time. I just hunker down and wait for the detonation. It comes early and seems, to my damaged ears, to be located higher up. The marines shot it in midair? The concussive explosion rips through the air around me. The mecha at least offers some protection.

The heat in the room is sweltering. I don't know how these charges work, but when they go, they really do belch out heat. I can hear creaking and tearing from above. The sound of something giving way. Shouts and cries.

"Move!"

"Fall back!"

"Oh shit!"

And still I hunker and wait. After a few moments I risk a glimpse. The devastation is markedly worse. Something that lies between infrastructure and internal organs sag from the ceiling. Fluid pulses down into the room. It hits fires and steam mixes with the smoke.

But the marines... The marines... I can't see the marines.

"Can we leave now?" It's Clyde's voice.

And I think we have to. I grab the fourth and final charge from the mecha, scramble toward his voice.

"You see an exit?" I call.

"Great big feckin' hole in the wall next to you." Kayla's voice is close.

I hesitate, glance over my shoulder. That does indeed look like an exit.

Kayla emerges from behind a pile of smouldering wires. Her shirt is smoking and noticeably more tattered than when we entered the room.

"What about Felicity?" It's my first response. It shouldn't be. I should be asking how Kayla is. If she's injured. But I don't care about that as much as I do about Felicity.

Let me not have hit her. Let her still be OK. Let the bandage have held. Please. Please.

Kayla rolls her eyes. "Feckin' priorities," she mutters.

Clyde staggers out of smoke toward me. He looks like he's barely functioning. Sparks spit out of tears in his joints. His once mirror-shining head is just a smudge of scorched metal. One leg is bent and grates with each step.

And Tabitha. He is supporting Tabitha.

God, what do I say? What can I possibly say to make this right?

It's not even right. What a fucked up fantasy the idea of doing right was. It was just necessary. But how the hell do I explain that?

But Tabitha doesn't even look at me. It's as if I don't exist. She just walks forward, eyes staring, fixed on the mecha. She is bleeding from a gash along her close-cropped scalp. Clyde helps her past me and she doesn't even blink as I interrupt her field of vision. Her eyes just glide over me.

Kayla takes off at speed. Possibly Mach one. We move toward the tear. She makes it back as we push between the torn skin between the rooms. Felicity is on her shoulders.

"Is she—" I start.

"I'm not bothering carrying round a feckin' dead woman." Kayla muscles past me through the tear.

I can hear the marines shouting back at their own makeshift entryway. The rally is coming soon. I need to seal this exit.

I eye the last thermic charge. We may need it up ahead. But… God, I don't think we can go much further. Might as well shore up the distance we've managed so far. I manage to wrestle the timer for what looks like ten seconds, chuck it fifty yards or so away, turn, and push my way out of the room.

88

The shockwave hits the wall behind me at the exact moment Tabitha's fist hits my jaw.

She unslings her arm from around Clyde's shoulder, pulls it back, and slugs me. She strikes up, compensating for the height difference, catches me under the jaw. Me and the wall both quake. The wall doesn't go down. I do.

Then she's on me. Hitting, kicking, biting, scraping. I should defend myself, should push her away, but I just killed her boyfriend. It doesn't seem right to defend myself. I deserve this.

Someone grabs her, pulls her off me. Kayla, I see, as one of my eyes starts to swell. I'd love to put something cold on it, but everyone else here seems to be in the middle of melting something.

"Get yourself under feckin' control," Kayla hisses at Tabitha.

"Killed him! Bastard killed him!"

I slowly pick myself up. I don't really feel like it, but there's nothing much else left to do. Tabitha stares at me vindictively. All I can do is nod.

"Did you not feckin' see him chasing Arthur around with a big feckin' chainsaw hand? If it'd been me, he'd have been lucky if I just stopped at shooting him the once. Be wearing his feckin' testicles as a necklace right now, I would."

I wish I could tell if Kayla just had a really dark sense of humor or if she really was borderline psychotic.

"What the fuck happened?" Tabitha spits at me. "What about your bullshit speeches? What about being better than that?" She wipes at her eyes so fiercely it's almost a clawing motion. "Can't you go a fucking month without killing a boyfriend of mine?"

Fuck. Fuck. God, and she's right. What the hell sort of person have I become? When I shot Clyde—when all this started, I suppose—Tabitha had just started dating him. Admittedly he'd been possessed by evil aliens, but... I shot him.

A line from *Macbeth* comes to me. "I am now so steeped in blood, t'would be easier to carry on than to turn back." Something like that anyway. Is that who I've become?

Except I never did like that play. Too much fate and fatalism. Macbeth never seemed to really want to buck the tide. He just took the path of least resistance, and gave into the embrace of tyranny. Isn't fighting that impetus the whole thing I'm fighting for? Wasn't that why I shot Gran? Or at least some less pretentious version of that?

"He was going to doom us all," I say. "I didn't want to do it. God, I didn't want to. But he was going to throw humanity away. And we can save them."

I don't know if the big picture will really mean anything against something so brutally personal, but it's all I have.

"Yeah," Kayla says. "That and the feckin' thing with the chainsaw."

Tabitha stalks toward me. She looks down at the laptop in her hands, at my head. And then she swings it back like a cricket bat, ready to knock me for six.

There is an ugly grinding noise, and the blow never comes. I stop wincing long enough to see that Clyde has caught Tabitha's arm.

"What would you have done, Tabby?" he says. "In Arthur's place?"

She pulls against his restraint, and I hear his elbow joint crunch in a decidedly unpretty way. But she doesn't break free. She glares at me again, still murderous. "Given in!" she shouts. At both of us, I think. "Been less of a stubborn fucking arsehole."

Clyde stays there, holding her. His voice is low and calm, like the ocean without a breeze. Something intimately human in those mechanical words. "Would you really?"

"Fuck off!" Tabitha suddenly turns from me, from him, pulls hard, breaks away. Clyde's arm coughs out sparks, drops limp. She claws at her eyes again.

"Shouldn't have done it," she says. "He shouldn't have done it."

"I know," I say. "But—"

"Not you!" she snaps. She whirls. Fire white hot in her black eyes. "Him. Gran. Shouldn't have done it. Didn't think…" She pushes a hand over her scalp savagely. It comes away red with the blood of the cut there. "When he pointed the gun at you… Bluster. I fucking assumed bluster. Fucking idiot. Me. Him. You." She claws more blood from her hair. "Shit. Shit. Shit."

"I'm sorry," I say. The words seem so little against the deed.

"Shut the fuck up." Tabitha agrees with me.

"It's done." Kayla steps between us, Felicity still on her shoulder. Felicity slowly dying on her shoulder. "So shut the feck up and move on. Deal with this bullshit later. When there's time for consequences."

And that makes a certain amount of sense, but, "No." I shake my head. There has to be an accounting for actions. That's part of this too. Part of being worth saving.

I step toward Tabitha. Into the heat of her rage. "I am sorry," I say again. Only words, but they need to be said. "I didn't want to shoot him. If I could have seen a way out of it, then I wouldn't have. If I was a better person, perhaps. But the stakes are what they are. And it's not all my fault. But it is some. I accept that. I acknowledge that. I want you to know that I understand it. That I will make amends when I can. In any way I can. I can't make this right. I can only make it seem less pointless. And I will if I can. I promise you that." I look her right in the eyes. "It's all I can promise. But I mean it."

We are locked there for a moment. Her grief meeting mine. The heat of hers, the numb chill of mine. But Felicity is there. Right there. Reminding me of why I am here, of everything that I am trying to do. And in the end it is Tabitha who looks away.

"Fuck," she says.

"I'm sorry."

"Say it again," she says without looking back. "Once more. Dare you."

I shut up. And take a second. Just one. Just to take stock. The mental and physical inventory. And it's not good. We're in the middle of some slowly collapsing biological horror house, which is quite possibly sinking into the Arctic Ocean. All of us have been beaten to within an inch of our lives— possibly closer—and pushed way outside of our moral comfort zones. We're traumatized, exhausted, and about five seconds from giving out. And as far as I can tell we have still done piss all to save the world.

I look around me. Another dark, fetid little room. It smells vaguely of offal. And I'm sad I know what offal smells like.

But there is a bundle of wires. And it is fatter than anything that was in the room beyond. It snakes away from us. So there is still a trail to follow.

I take a breath, as deep as my battered lungs will allow. "OK," I say. "Honestly, as ridiculous as it is to say, nothing has changed. The plan is the same. We find Version 2.0, we find his servers. We take them, get into them, Clyde puts in Tabitha's code, and we hijack the wireless signal." I look over to Tabitha. "You do still have the wireless box, don't you?"

Tabitha reaches down to something hanging from her belt.

"Wait." It's Kayla. She holds up her hand and stares at me. "*That* is your plan? *Feckin' still*? Revising the feckin' thing didn't cross your feckin' mind?" She looks incredulous. "That's what I've been feckin' fighting for?"

I stare back at her. She has caught me completely off guard. How can she not know this? I think back to when she rejoined us. And she missed… But… I look back at the gash in the wall behind me, sealed now with rubble.

"Those people…" I say. "You killed… You fought…"

"Yeah," she almost shouts. "Because I thought you had some sort of better feckin' plan. Some sort of reasonable feckin' idea how to get a feckin' handle on this feckin' shit of a feckin' mission, you feckin' dumb feck. I mean, are you feckin' shittin' me?"

And finally, something just gives way in me. Exhaustion finally wears away whatever usual restraints I have. And I realize that I am just fucking sick of all this.

"Yes!" I bellow at her. Psychotic tendencies be damned. My lack of a sword be damned. "*That* is the plan. That's what we have." I can feel the muscles in my neck straining, trying to get the volume up to match the flare of anger. "And if you have a better one, then why the fuck didn't you mention it earlier?"

I wait for impact. But sod it, I stabbed her once. If it comes down to it…

Kayla squints at me. "Jesus," she says. "Feckin' temper on you."

I want to tell her not to push me, but I don't think that line works unless there's movie lighting on you. Instead, I just keep on staring, keep on trying to force my will out through my eyes and beating and crashing into her mind.

She holds out her hands. "Al-feckin'-right then, but nobody say I didn't say it was a feckin' stupid idea."

It takes me a moment to realize I've won. That she's acquiesced. "What?" I say, not quite willing to relax.

"No, man." Kayla shrugs. "Power of conviction and shit on your side. Just…" She shrugs again. "I mean, usually you're all, but what about this, and, we should've…" I am not entirely excited by the nasal whine she puts on when imitating me. I am fairly sure that's not representative. "But, you know, if that's what we got." A final shrug. "Feck it."

Holy shit. I just stared down Kayla. I knew it could be done but… by me? I wish Felicity was conscious to see that. Well, I wish she was conscious in general. And not stabbed. And not a zombie.

God. This plan had better work.

"OK," I say, letting a modicum of the tension slip out of my shoulders, feeling my neck return to a more normal state.

"Thing is," Tabitha says, not really looking at anyone, "she has a point."

"What?" I look at her. I can feel the anger coming back, like air blown into a balloon of tension in my shoulders and back.

Tabitha tries out a sneer and then seems to think better of it. "Your plan," she says. "It *is* shit."

89

I feel my fists ball. I mean, that's it. I am done. I have shot Gran to get this far. I will beat down every member of MI37 if I have to, and reprogram the bastard myself if...

"Fixable," Tabitha says quickly. "I mean... I can. Fix it."

I realize I have taken steps toward her. And that I've stopped breathing. I let the air hiss out of me, and back up.

"Sorry," I say, partly because... well, it's probably been ten seconds since I last said it, and partly because the idea of trying to do this on my own is spectacularly stupid. I need help. I always have. MI37 is a team, that's our strength. I need to rely on that now.

"So how do we fix it?" I ask her.

"Version 2.0 will take Clyde apart," Tabitha says. She looks at him, but not his face. Just his dented and battered torso. "Did it to the other versions. Will do the same here. No difference. Foregone conclusion."

"So," I say, "you go in. You hack him."

She shakes her head. "Can't. He's..." The next words seem to take significant effort. "...too good. For me." She kicks at the ground with a force that makes me think she's hoping it has some sort of pain nerves connected to whatever system Clyde is running on.

Shit. Piss and shit. Because if we can't hack him...

God, I don't have a plan. Holy crap, I killed Gran for a plan that won't work.

"You *have* to…" I start.

"No." There is enough force in the word to stop a charging rhino. It certainly stops me. "I cannot. Can. Not. Not an option. Forget it."

"But—" And there has to be a but, even if I don't know what it is.

"Can fix this. Said I can." She shakes her head. "God. Men. Listen. Open fucking ears." She takes a deep frustrated breath. And I can understand that. I need to get a rein on myself. Except Felicity is right there. I can hear the clock ticking to the slowing beat of her heart.

"OK," I manage. "How?"

"Trick him," she says. "We have to."

"Erm…" It's Clyde this time. "The whole super genius AI thing. I mean, speaking as an AI, the whole parallel processing thing… Not trying to brag here, mind you. I'm no super genius. Or regular genius. Hasten to add. Cambridge degree notwithstanding. And OK, that does sound like bragging. But I was totally going in the opposite direction, I promise."

My knuckles are whitening again.

"Anyway," Clyde continues, "I just wanted to say that if Version 2.0 is, as we keep on mentioning, a super genius—and I think given the whole end of the world scenario and twisted science thing we have going on, then we have a certain degree of confirmation that he is—then I just wanted to put in a slight query on the whole feasibility of tricking him."

"Blind spot," Tabitha says. "He has one. Big and obvious."

Really? Because…

"I hadn't feckin' noticed," Kayla says.

That.

Tabitha rolls her eyes. "Us."

Again with the really. Because…

"He doesn't exactly seem to have any issues with trying to squish any of us so far," Clyde says.

That.

Tabitha shakes her head. "Doing forty fucking questions here? Not us." She sweeps her hand around the room. "Us." The circles become wider. "Humanity. He thinks the worst of us. Thinks we want to survive."

And again…

"We feckin' do."

That.

Tabitha smiles. It is never reassuring when she does. It is a tight, efficient and slightly macabre thing when she does it.

"So," she says, "we die."

90

"We what now?" I'm actually quite pleased my confusion allows for that many syllables in a sentence. It's normally much more of an "erm" thing.

"Clyde goes into Version 2.0," Tabitha says. "Gets taken apart."

Clyde nods. "Which is why I'm not going to do it, right?"

"Why you'll do it." Tabitha doesn't bat an eye as she looks at him. "You give Version 2.0 the codes to unlock the wireless boxes. In a way that means he doesn't realize we're giving them to him. Thinks he's killing you but he's being sabotaged."

Clyde cocks his head to one side. "But he *is* killing me."

"Yes." Tabitha still doesn't bat an eye. She turns to me. "Version 2.0 controls Clyde. Gets box. Takes down wireless block. Invades everyone's heads."

My brows are creased enough it hurts. So far this sounds a lot like the whole doomsday scenario we're here to prevent. "But what about the bit where we distribute the code to un-fungus everyone?" Did I miss that bit?

"It's in your head," she says.

The brow creasing pain problem is not solved at this point.

"I spike you," Tabitha continues. "Version 2.0 goes

into your brain. Starts overwriting. But my code is there, waiting for him. You are the trap. You spring. You tear him apart. Code distributes, propagates, deprograms and de-funguses." She nods, then seems to reconsider slightly. "Theoretically."

I nod. Slowly. Very slowly. "So he overwrites my brain."

Tabitha nods. "But you're spiked to take it back." A pause. "Theoretically."

I look over at Clyde. Sacrifice. It all comes back to sacrifice.

"How feckin' theoretical?" It seems like this should be more my concern than Kayla's, but then I consider that if the spiking fails then my brain isn't the only one that goes down. If we fail... Jesus. Yes, "how theoretical" is probably a question every remaining human has a right to ask.

Tabitha looks pained. "Untested code. Unknown system. Biothau- maturgical interactions." She shakes her head. "Very theoretical."

Kayla curses for a very long time.

Clyde nods in my direction, his head wobbling on his neck as he does it. "Why put the code in Arthur's head? Why not mine?"

Another eye roll. I think Tabitha does them partly to comfort herself. "Need to bring down wireless system then spike. If you have the code, we spike too early. And Arthur over me and Kayla because…" Tabitha looks to Kayla. "Fuck it, I don't want anyone to data-dump in my brain. Crazy bullshit."

"Feckin' right." Kayla nods with unusual enthusiasm.

Well, that's just lovely. Except, considering it's essentially me and my plan that have brought us to this point, I'm not really in a good place to negotiate. I just wish we could change the phrase "data dump." It sounds a little too close to the idea of taking a digital shit in my skull.

Actually, given my experience of having the old Clyde deposit all my sword-wielding knowledge, that isn't so far from the truth.

Nobody looks happy. Not even Clyde, and he doesn't have a face.

God. This could kill Clyde. Again.

"Can we copy Clyde?" I say. "Before he goes in there."

Clyde looks at Tabitha. She almost looks at him. I can see a muscle working in the corner of her eye.

"No." It's Clyde who speaks. "Not anymore. I think we've all had enough of copies of me."

"But…" I start.

He looks at me. "If this all goes to hell," he says, "who's going to reboot me anyway?"

"But if it doesn't…" Because there's the rub. Directly there.

Clyde looks to Tabitha. His body groans with the movement. "Will the code work on me?" he asks. "Deprogram me?"

Tabitha shrugs, still not looking, her eye still twitching.

Clyde nods, as if that's what he thought all along. He turns to me, doesn't say a word. Just looks.

I look from him—burned and blackened—to Tabitha—battered and bereft—to Kayla—just angry, still angry. And then to Felicity, balanced across Kayla's shoulders. My Felicity. Her hair is lank and stained with purple.

And this is it, right? This is what we have. This is where I've led us. This is the point I've killed people to reach.

At least if I'm wrong there won't be anyone left to tell their children what an arsehole I am.

"Sod it," I say. "Let's do this."

91

TWO MINUTES LATER

So far, "doing this" has been a mostly static affair. At least I've been lying down for most of it. That does mean that almost all of my muscles have seized, but honestly that's a minor complaint compared to the fact that I've not had to shoot any close friends in the face during that time.

On the other hand, I have allowed one close friend to sit down next to me and pull out large amounts of his innards.

Tabitha perches above Clyde's chest compartment, multi-tool in hand, poised like the grisliest of eighteenth-century surgeons. Clyde, his inner electronics splayed out before him, forms the midpoint of a circuit that also includes Tabitha's laptop and my head. I think the laptop may be getting the best part of this deal. Kayla, who is holding wires against my scalp, also seems to be having more fun than is really appropriate.

Tabitha shifts from dissecting Clyde to sitting cross-legged in front of her laptop screen and begins swearing so hard that it could conceivably make even Kayla blush.

Her fingers keep pace with the curse words, a drill beat tapping on her keyboard punctuated by crescendos on backspace.

"Everything OK?" This is not the most reassuring way to go into battle.

"Shut up," Tabitha tells me, which I think is about fifty percent of what she says to me, but then she carries on as if she hadn't. "Ugly code. No time to fix. Just... Jesus." More backspacing, more typing. "Don't know what I was thinking. Oh wait..." More tapping. "God, just going to comment out half this crap. It's all circuitous." She shakes her head. "Need more goddamn time."

She looks up. "Ugly. Will suck. As close to working as it's going to get." She nods to Kayla. "All right. Going to zap him."

I swallow hard. Just when I was starting to enjoy lying down.

"Look at it this way," Clyde says, "I did it last time, and I can't possibly have been as competent as Tabby is going to be, and you survived that."

Which, actually is kind of a reassuring thought, and—

BLACKNESS

Ow. Goddamn but ow.

VERSION 2.0'S HOUSE OF FLESHY HORRORS

"—he OK?"

"Slap him."

Someone slaps me. Why am I being slapped? I decide to tell them to stop it.

"Thwurr wah."

There is either something wrong with my ears or my tongue.

"I think he's coming round."

I followed that. It's my tongue then.

"I'll slap him again." That voice definitely has a Scottish brogue.

"Thto paht." OK, that was still pretty pathetic.

I am slapped again. I almost feel like I deserve it. Plus, thinking *is* clearer now.

"Stop it." My voice still sounds thick enough to make it sound like I spent the night in the company of Mr. Jack Daniels, but I'm understandable.

"I think I should just give him a slap one more time."

"I don't think you should. He's bleeding."

The world starts coming back into focus. Kayla is there, Tabitha. It takes me a moment to remember the thing that looks like a badly abused toaster is Clyde's head, but then that snaps back and I manage to wrestle free and sit up.

"I'm fine," I say. My tongue is still less than limber.

Kayla and Clyde back up to give me space, but Tabitha doesn't. She reaches out and pulls down the lower lid of my eye, stares critically. Then she pulls back, holds up a hand.

"Fingers. How many?"

"Three." That one is easy enough.

"Nausea? Headache?"

I nod and wish I hadn't. "Both," I say.

She nods back. "Mild concussion," she says. "Nothing worse."

It occurs to me that the mild concussion may not be due to the recent data dumping, but rather the week I've been having, but I'm not in the mood to point it out.

"All right." Tabitha stands up. "Final check." She looks me in the eye. "Mary Poppins," she says. Which is weird.

Or it's weird right up until my mouth flies open and

I start spurting out gibberish. "Zero, one, zero, zero, zero, one, zero, zero, zero, one, one, one, zero, one, zero, one, zero, one, one, zero, one, zero, zero, zero."

I clap a hand to my mouth. Tabitha smirks at me.

"The hell?" I ask her.

"Check," she says. "Make sure the code took. Sub-program. Every time I say Mary—"

With the hand that isn't over my mouth I point as threatening a finger at her as I can.

"The trigger phrase," she corrects with an eye roll, "you say that. Means the code stuck. Means we're good. Quit bitching."

"What does it mean?" I ask.

"What?"

"What I just said."

She eye rolls and looks away, but I think I catch the smirk again. I glance at Clyde, but he has the advantage of looking like a badly abused toaster to obfuscate his emotions.

Honestly, in the face of things, it's probably the least of my concerns.

"OK, then." I survey the scene. Clyde has tucked most of his insides back in. "Are we ready then?"

"If that's what you want to feckin' call it." Kayla looks dissatisfied with something. Us, I suspect.

I point to the bundle of wires I spotted earlier. "We follow that then."

So we do, into a dark corner of the room. There is yet another sphincter door. It is not quite as bad this time. I think the spectrum of bad things that can happen to me may have broadened and it's a question of relativity. That's a better option at least than the idea that I may be getting used to them. Some things you just don't want to ever lose their horror. Seal clubbing, war crimes, sphincter doors. That sort of thing.

Then it's a corridor. The bundle of wires grows fatter. Small tributaries joining the main flow. We keep on. I'm leaning on the wall. Tabitha, who seems to think her work is done now, stares ahead and stumbles over her feet. Clyde hisses and sparks. Kayla is probably the most together of all of us, but even she seems to be favoring her right foot over her left.

Another sphincter door. Not distant enough for the horror of the last one to have really faded. I force my way through anyway.

And there it is. Finally. Finally. Because as little as I know about computers, this I recognize.

Version 2.0.

92

He is massive, monumental. This must have been how the ancients felt when they stood at the foot of the Colossus of Rhodes. How New Yorkers felt when the first skyscraper rose.

He is a tower, fat and squat, but no less dominating for that. A black towering stack of server after server after server after server, stretching up toward a roof so distant it makes me think cathedrals lack a sense of ambition.

He is wreathed in wires. Like a cloud. Like a halo. They twist and twine about the vast stacks of him. A labyrinth of them leading from port to port.

LEDs blink and flicker up and down his prodigious length. Blue and green flickering up into the gloom, adding ethereal light to the room.

"Fuck me," Tabitha whispers from behind my shoulder.

The heat coming off him is enormous, is almost a cage about him. Vents in the walls hiss clouds of freezing vapor into the room. I see them strike the wall of heat, shrivel and waft away. They are not enough.

The marines' plan is working. Version 2.0 is dying. The cool of this place is retreating, will not be enough to keep his systems online much longer.

Another moment of hesitation, of second-guessing my own wisdom. Then Kayla pushes past and puts

Felicity on the ground. Felicity is very pale. And there is no time for hesitations now.

But Clyde does. He stares at the twisted version of himself that towers before and above him. It is so alien. So very evidently unhuman. So very not Clyde. Anti-Clyde. And now the two of them will be forced together. And annihilated.

There is no time for hesitations, but I do not question Clyde's. I do not push him. He stares at himself, and he stares at his own death.

Maybe we can save him. Maybe. Maybe.

Of all the thin hopes I have, that is perhaps the thinnest.

I look to Felicity again. At the ruin she has become. But memory overlays the woman I love onto the zombie at my feet. As she lies close to death, I also see her as she lies in bed on a Sunday morning. Her hair spread-eagled on the pillow. A slow smile spreading across her face. The light filtering through the air, like dust settling.

That moment. That is what I am here for. That is what I am fighting for.

"When you're ready," I say to Clyde.

He hesitates, shrugs. "That's not something I'm ever going to be. Let's just do it when I'm not."

Tabitha reaches into a pocket, produces a blue ethernet cable. "This. Use it."

"Thank you." Clyde reaches out and takes it. But then his hand hesitates, still in hers. Her dark fingers against his silver ones. "I..." he starts. "I still... I'm sorry, Tabby, but I... I still..."

She nods. "I know."

I try to read her expression, but I can't. Her eyes are for Clyde alone. And maybe that's as it should be.

Maybe that should be for him alone.

He nods. "Thank you." He pulls away, walks toward the stack.

We follow in his wake. Clyde fiddles with a panel in his head, flips it open. He plugs one end of Tabitha's cable in there, then turns his attention to a row of ports before him.

"Here to sabotage," he says quietly, to himself. Psyching himself up perhaps. "Here to damage. Here to damage. Here to damage." He turns, swings his head back to stare at Tabitha one last time. And then without looking plugs in the other end of the cable.

93

I brace myself for... For...

Clyde stands there, static, a puppet with his strings cut. His battered limbs hang as straight down as they are able. His head sags. The only sign of life a blue blinking light besides his cable.

"Is it—" I start.

Then Clyde jerks upright. His body comes to life. I peer at him. And of course he is just the same beaten up shell. But what ghost lingers in the machine?

"Did it—" I start. But apparently today is not a day for finishing sentences.

"Well," Clyde says, cutting me off. "That was incredibly stupid."

And then he backhands Tabitha so hard she leaves the ground.

I stare. The violence is so casual, so brutal and it comes from nowhere. Tabitha's feet are in the air, her body spiraling, head twisted to face a hundred and eighty degrees from her feet. Blood sprays from her mouth, a spiral about her, tracing her path.

She lands, body still twisting, a mess of limbs.

I step back from Clyde.

No... No, I step back from Version 2.0.

Except I don't move fast enough. Version 2.0 steps forward, a quick one, two. The ethernet cable snaps out of the port behind him, whips in his wake. His hand darts forward, a swift flat blade. It slams into my Adam's apple. I drop gagging and spluttering to the floor.

Kayla lunges, swings her blade. Clyde slams out a hand. Her blade impacts against his palm, bites deep into the metal, the blade travelling through into and up his arm.

And wedges there.

Version 2.0 twists his arm. Kayla wrenches, but for a moment the blade is stuck and that is all the time 2.0 needs to step inside her guard and deliver a headbutt. His steel head collides with her flesh and bone one. She drops.

Kayla is down.

I'm still trying to breathe, on the floor, fighting my own closing throat. Air hisses into me. A too-thin reed of air. And what if he just kills us? We didn't think of that, did we? What if he kills us out of spite before he takes over the minds of everyone in this place? What then?

I see him glance over to where Felicity lies. And no. No. Not her. Spare her more harm. Spare her. Spare her.

He shakes his head. "Sentimental," I hear him say. Then he reaches down and rips something off Tabitha's belt. A small black box lightly smattered with LEDs. The wireless jammer. He flips down a panel. His fingers tap.

And something about his pose relaxes. He turns to me, cocks his head to one side.

"Hello, Arthur," he says. "Goodbye, Arthur. Welcome to the family."

And then the pain begins.

94

It is a hot lance thrust directly into my frontal lobes. An agonizing, spiking burst of pain that I think will drive the sanity out of me. A vine racing through my whole body. It is too much to bear.

And then, somewhere in the depths of my head, the bud of pain blooms. It swells and is everything, is the totality of my world. It begins to drive the *me* out of me.

I cannot take this. I cannot.

I am eclipsed. Done with. Discarded.

AND THEN I INHALE

My eyes stretch. My mouth is an "O" too large for my face. An attempt to open a release valve on the pain.

But the pain is gone.

It catches me by surprise, trips up my scream and the exhalation comes out as a gasp. My hands fly to my chest, my arms. A rapid physical inventory. I am whole. Not a cut or bruise upon me. All the damage of my trip through Version 2.0's compound is gone.

I actually feel good.

And it's not just me, or my skin. My clothes too. They're whole. Not a rip or a tear. Not a stain.

What the hell is going on?

I look around. I know this place. I'm in Felicity's apartment. I'm in Oxford. It's Sunday morning. I don't

553

know how I know it, but I do. Something in the lazy light drifting in through the kitchen window.

Felicity's apartment.

Felicity.

I take off at speed, race through the room, shouting her name. Into the living room. Not there. But she has to be here somewhere. Because if she's here then maybe she's not dying on the floor somewhere.

Dying on the floor…

Wasn't I…?

What the hell is going on?

I lose momentum as I approach the bedroom door. Something is wrong. I can't be here. It makes no sense. I was in Version 2.0's compound. We had… What the hell has happened?

Felicity was lying on the floor. Zombified. I was about to save her. Wasn't I?

A sound from beyond the bedroom door. Someone shifting about.

Did I save her? How could I have forgotten something like that?

Another sound. And she's in there. She has to be there. I have to have saved her. I have to.

I push open the door. A familiar room. The familiar Georgia O'Keeffe prints on the wall. The familiar flowers on the bed stand. Familiar white sheets on a familiar bed.

But not Felicity.

Clyde.

He sits perched on the foot of the bed. Not metal Clyde. Not towering server stack Clyde. But flesh and blood and meat Clyde. A few years younger than me. A scruffy beard on his chin. Glasses. A tweed jacket. Bloody Clyde.

There is an expression on his face that lies somewhere between amusement and embarrassment.

"Hello, Arthur," he says.

I work my jaw a few times, use it to buy me some time. "Hello, Clyde," I say.

He shrugs. "Well, more or less."

My brow furrows. Is it not Clyde?

And then it comes back to me. Those last agonizing seconds. The image of Clyde's metal body standing over me, staring down at me. My throat closing. The wireless jammer turned off.

"Version 2.0." I close my eyes.

"Bingo."

Oh balls. "This is all in my head, isn't it?" I say. I open my eyes, stare into that oh-so familiar, oh-so mocking face.

"You know the answer to that," says Version 2.0.

So, yes. Yes, this isn't real. None of this is real. He's in my head. He's overwriting me. Right now.

"Yes," says Version 2.0. "Yes, I am."

So he can read my thoughts.

"It's not exactly James Joyce," says Version 2.0, "I'll tell you that."

"Oh piss off," I tell him.

"Case in point." Version 2.0 smirks.

I stare at him for a moment, at what he's become. And a great sadness fills me. This man used to be my friend. And now he's a monster who's killing me. And I can't fight him. That would be useless. But I would love to understand him.

"What happened to you?" I ask. "You used to be the best of us. Jesus, the version we were working with still was."

Version 2.0 shakes his head. "I'm all I've ever been, Arthur. Really, I am. Honestly, I think I've changed less than you think. Which sounds a little presumptuous, I realize, but, well… that's just it, Arthur. My perspective has changed. Because of who or what I am now. That's all. I see things differently. I see the bigger picture."

He sounds genuinely sorry for a moment. The smirk faltering. And I can almost believe him. But… God, I have seen too much horror done by his hand to give him a free pass. Hell, we are having this conversation while he is in the middle of bloody murdering me.

"You're angry," he says.

"Can you really justify what you've done?" I ask. "You're trying to make an entire species extinct."

"One species." There's an angry snap to Clyde's voice this time. "One. Do you know how many species mankind wipes from the face of the earth every day? Do you have any clue? Or do you walk about in blissful, uncaring ignorance? Do you assume that someone else will take care of it? Well, I am taking care of it now, Arthur. And it may be presumptive, and arrogant, or some other thing I used to think was important. When I thought humanity was important. But honestly, Arthur, what makes humanity special? What distinguishes them?"

He's a zealot. That's the word. He is beyond reason.

"Those are hurtful words, Arthur." But he's smirking again. Masking anger as humor.

I try a different tack. I don't really know why. Everything is already in motion. Everything is already too late. But I want to believe that he could be saved.

"I get it," I say. "I get that we're a shit race, doing shit things. But what about hope, Clyde? What about the long shot?"

Clyde shakes his head. "It's probability, Arthur. It's math. And it's cold, and it's uncaring, and it's so... what is your word? Inhuman. It is inhuman. But it *is*. That is the world. And you can fight against it, but it will roll over you and not give the slightest damn."

He's talking about himself.

"I might as well be."

These interjections into my mental monologue are getting tiring. Everything is tiring. Fighting Version 2.0, fighting for him, or for what he could be, is tiring. Fighting for him to be better.

God, maybe I was wrong. I have staked everything on hope. On a long shot. But here, with him, with someone who used to be my friend, is there no hope?

I look at him, and I don't see it. And I know then, no matter what I try, what approach I take, this will not work out. There are no heroes here.

"No, Arthur, there aren't."

His voice is cold, implacable. There's nothing of Clyde left in it. No room for hope. No room for humanity. And maybe when hope dies, so should the hopeless.

"Well then," I say, "I can't be sorry about this."

95

For a very, very long moment absolutely bollocks all happens.

Clyde looks deeply perplexed. "Arthur, what the hell are you going on about?"

Shit. It's not working. No! I can't think about it. He can read my mind. Don't think about the... Pink elephants. Pink elephants. Think about pink elephants.

"Don't think about what?" The arch-villain relaxedness seeps out of Version 2.0's pose. He stands up from the end of the bed, advances.

Pink elephants. Pink elephants. I picture them cavorting about the room.

"Don't think about what?" The whole room quakes with the force of Version 2.0's shout. Storm clouds form outside the windows. Water stains obscure the art prints. The sheets blacken with stains.

Pink... elephants...

The elephants rupture. Bloody and messy and physical. Their guts littered about the room. A mass of gore, their bodies turned from pink to red.

Version 2.0 advances on me. He looks murderous. But considering this is halfway through the actual murdering event, that seems a little late.

"Don't—"

The word is a physical blow. It sends me spinning

back, slamming into the wall.

"—think—"

Another blow. Plaster cracks underneath me. And this isn't real. This is in my head. Except it's not really my head any more.

"—about—"

The force of it drives me back through the wall. Plaster and bones break. I scream in agony. I think Version 2.0 can do anything to me he wants in here.

"—"

The last word doesn't come. I am braced for the final brutal blow, but it doesn't fall.

Clyde stands still, his mouth open, ready to speak the word, but he cannot get it out. Instead, his mouth goes round. He puts a hand to his forehead, winces as if in sudden pain.

"What?" he says. Just normal volume. Just a normal man. My pain is suddenly gone, my bones whole again.

"What did you do?" he gasps. He drops to one knee. Both hands go to his head. "What did you do to me?" He speaks through gritted teeth.

And it's my turn to be sad. So very sad, as my old friend kneels before me, curled up in agonizing pain.

"What did I do?" I say. "I gave up on you."

AND THEN I INHALE

The room is gone. There is no transition, just an abrupt vacuum where once it was. Version 2.0 is gone. And for a moment, I am almost gone too.

I can feel… everyone. I can feel minds. Thousands… hundreds of thousands… millions… hundreds of millions. I can feel all of humanity, all of the minds Clyde has overwritten inside me.

There is not room. I think my skull is going to cave in. I think I'm giving way.

I am Arthur. I am…

I am everyone, everything. I am the world. The hope, the future.

There is too much of me. I am on the floor staring at my hands, laughing and choking. I am a marine staring at the gun I was firing. I am a mecha pilot. I am a helicopter pilot trying to grapple with my controls, trying to work out if I want to plunge into the Arctic wasteland or struggle for the skies. I am a woman in an Alaskan village. I am her husband. I am a man in New York staring at the desolation of the world, feeling the agony of the burning clouds still ripping through my skin. I am the horde of zombies closing in on him, stumbling and staggering and with his scent in my nose and the need to kill him in my gut. I am a mushroom growing, spreading, spitting out myself.

I am Arthur. I am Arthur.

I am architecture. I am blood vessels and steel ribs. I am wires. I am machines. I am infrastructure and advancement. I am connected.

This is the spike, Tabitha's code bomb. This is me taking over Version 2.0's servers and ripping through him. This is me doing to him exactly what he was doing to me. What he did to everyone. I am tearing him out, putting them all back. All of them. They were all on his servers. And now I am the conduit through which they all return.

I am Arthur. I am Arthur. I struggle for the thought, for the memory of myself.

But I am others too. I am Tabitha in a swirling fog of unconsciousness. I am Kayla wondering how the

fuck that little arsehole managed to land a headbutt.
I am Clyde.

I am Clyde.

Somehow in the swirling miasma of souls, of
thoughts, I can feel my friend. At least some part of
him. Damaged, in pieces, but there. There is some
part of me that is Version 2.1. And from there I can
feel a piece of 2.2, 2.3... and there... yes, 2.4 as well.
Fragments of someone, pieces. Barely enough to stitch
together. But they're all there, 2.1—the version who
sacrificed himself for us—strongest of all.

*I am architecture. I am blood vessels and steel ribs. I
am wires. I am machines.*

Machines. I am machines.

I remember Clyde staring at the ruins of a 3D printer,
at the machine that could make him human once more.
And I remember promising him that maybe there were
more. I remember how hollow that promise felt.

But it wasn't.

I can feel the machines here. Every single one in this
sinking tub of a building. I am the goddamn building.
And I know exactly where the other 3D printer is.

And then it's all fading. All coming apart.

I am Arthur. I am Arthur.

I am rushing back to my body, my self, my physicality.
My arms, and ribs, and legs, and aching, aching throat,
they are me, undeniably me.

Desperately, with the last remnants of my
connectedness I grab the remnants of the versions, the
tattered bits and pieces of my friend. I tear through
Version 2.0's palace. I can feel the tattered wires like open
wounds. I slam into electronic dead ends. But I race on.

Even as I do the place slips through my fingers. I

am not it. I am just a man in pain. A man on the floor, curled up and useless.

And then I am back, flickering into the building. And I am there. I am at the controls of the printer. Shoving Clyde into it like carrots into a juicer. And things worked out for Dr. Frankenstein, right? Nothing went wrong with his attempt at stitching back together the dead pieces of a man.

I can't give up. I have to have hope.

We protect our own.

And then suddenly I don't know what I'm doing. Suddenly I am staring at controls that were once part of my body, my architecture, and now they are like a discarded limb, lying useless before me. They are slipping away from me. And suddenly I don't know how this machine works. I don't know how to save Clyde. And how the hell do I take this long shot?

I am rushing back to myself. I am losing control. But in this last fleeting moment, I feel it inside me. The last spark of Version 2.0. And he understands this printer. He built it. And I am beyond desperation. I am into nanoseconds. So I reach down into myself—unsure of how I even do it—reach to that last bit of me that is him, and I shove that into the machine too.

And then it's gone. The printer. The building. It slips out of my consciousness before I know if it worked. Everything is ripped out of my hands. I race away.

And then… then I am Arthur. I am Arthur.

And I am alone.

96

WHO CARES HOW LONG LATER

When I come to, there is a barrel pointing at my face. It is attached to a very large gun, which itself is attached to a very angry looking marine. He looks a lot like he is considering pulling the trigger.

Behind him is the towering mass of Version 2.0.

It is on fire.

The marine hauls me roughly to my feet. My throat aches. Each breath hurts.

But I am me. I am not Version 2.0. These marines are not. No one is, in fact. Which means…

Holy shit, it means we won.

I look around. Look at the survivors. The victors. Tabitha is on her feet too. Another marine has a gun trained on her. There are many marines, I realize. Sweat slick, their shadows long and quivering in the light of Version 2.0 burning.

Do they get it? Do they realize this is victory?

Another marine stands over Kayla. Her eyes are open. She looks at me. And I see the sparkle of imminent violence there, waiting to be unleashed. She can get us out of here.

I shake my head.

We won. We saved humanity. But we didn't wash it free of its sins. We killed people to get here. I will make sure we answer for that.

Something else lies on the floor. A dull battered piece of machinery. Something that looks like a badly abused toaster on top of a battered torso. Bent limbs, smoke drifting from them. Clyde's mechanical corpse.

Except... except... I remember those last moments. The last dash to preserve my friend.

So maybe that's not his corpse.

Maybe...

I go to scan the room, knowing that we're nowhere near the 3D printer I found, but just in case, just maybe... And then my eyes fall on her. And all other thoughts leave me.

Felicity. My Felicity.

She lies there. Not twenty yards away from me.

The marine's gun is inches from me. And I do not care.

I break and run to her.

There is a shout from behind me, from the marine, and a blur of movement from Kayla. A shot rings out, and at the same moment a grunt. The bullet goes well wide of me, of Felicity. It buries itself in the ground.

"What in the name of goddamned hell?" a voice shouts from the pack of marines.

But then I am on her. On my Felicity. My hands on her. Running up her sides, feeling her. Her physicality, her real-ness. And I am turning her head. Her brow is soft and clammy with sweat. Her eyes are closed.

I reach to pull back one eyelid, and then I cannot.

We kicked Clyde out of people, but... but... what about the people he infected? That wasn't just digital. Can Tabitha's code really have removed a fungus?

I don't think I could bear it if it hadn't worked. To

know we had done so much and yet have achieved so little.

To know Felicity was dead.

My finger hovers above the pale skin of her eyelid.

"Someone get that goddamn dumbass back here and goddamned cuff him already," says a familiar voice from among the pack of marines.

I don't dare know. But I cannot not know. I have to. I don't want to. I want to. I have to.

I push back the lid.

And my heart stops.

Clear. Her eye is clear. Is clear brown. Is *her* eye. My Felicity's eye.

For a moment she stares into nothing, and then she twitches. Her whole body convulses. A great wracking shudder that runs the whole length of her body. Her arms flop. Her feet kick. Her eyes roll wildly.

"No!" I shout, but I don't know what I'm protesting, what outcome I'm trying to avoid. All I know is that she has to be OK. She has to be. That is the world I fought for. The one she is in.

She convulses once more, curls up, tight and fetal, rolls over, face pressed to the fleshy floor.

And then she retches. Massively. Epically. The sort of retch that J.R.R. Tolkien could write a three volume tome about. There are emotional peaks and troughs to this outpouring of vomit. Felicity coughs, and gags, and finally flops to the earth.

A vast pool of purple vomit lies before her. There is fur in it.

"Jesus," I hear a voice from behind me say.

It's out of her. That's all I can think. And I know then that she'll be OK. Because it's lying on the floor in front of me. All the poison, the infection, all of it voided from her body.

She lies on her side, panting weakly.

The marine who has come up behind me grabs my arms. He pulls them back roughly. I feel something close around my wrists.

Felicity's eyes swivel up, fix blearily on my face. And she smiles. She smiles. She smiles. It is so bright it makes the fire behind me seem paltry.

"Knew you'd save me," she says. "Told you." And then she closes her eyes, and they pull me away.

IN THE CORRIDORS

We move at speed. All around us the tunnels quake and crash. Collapsed ceilings send us in circuitous routes. Violent lurches send me to my knees. The marines do not help me to my feet despite my bound hands. I elbow my way up against tattered walls. And then I run some more.

We enter a room and the smell almost drives me to the floor. A hundred people, all on their hands and knees. Each one bowed before a pool of purple vomit.

"What in the goddamned hell?" It's the General. He was with the marines who found us. So far he is not entirely sure what happened with Gran, but he knows we're in the shitter. He stares at the room.

"Zombies," I say. "They used to be. But we freed them."

"Fucking refugees." Apparently even saving the human race won't make the General happy.

They round them up. And then we run again. This place is sweltering. Sweat pours off me. I'm so tired, my eyes almost droop. But I force them open. I am looking for something.

For someone.

Clyde has to be here somewhere. Some version of him. Surely. I saved him. It was a long shot. But… This worked. Why can't that?

We pick up more recovering zombies. Most are half-naked, shivering from the rigors of pouring the fungus out of their system.

There are so many of us now, it feels like some sort of mad carnival. The marines are outnumbered ten to one, then fifteen to one. People, slowly coming back to themselves, yelling and weeping, laughing and screaming. These people have thrown off a waking nightmare and the sudden sense of freedom is so foreign that it leaves them devastated, struggling to deal with it.

Kayla runs beside me. Felicity is back on her shoulders. My Felicity. Injured, but stable. The infection out of her. Saved. Kayla bears her easily enough. Still indefatigable. Still only ruffled, it seems, by briefly having her mind evacuated out of her body.

And Tabitha too. Tabitha runs with us. But the toll on her seems to have been greater. She lived her worst fear today, I think. I can still remember her, lying in Clyde's grave, clutching her tinfoil-lined hat, screaming about Version 2.0, wanting to overwrite her mind. And then it happened. And then we killed him. A man she had loved once. Her second bereavement of the day.

Gran is not with us. His absence feels like a hole in the crowd.

We pass through rooms devastated by the marines' ingress. Walls riddled with bullet holes. Smashed crates, smashed machinery. The bodies of mangled monstrosities, products of Version 2.0's mad experiments.

And I don't see Clyde.

We round a corner, see another collapsed ceiling.

The marines waste no time, there is none to waste. They open fire into a wall. It collapses under the hail of ammunition. We pour through.

And I don't see Clyde.

But then... I hesitate in the flow of the crowd. A devastated machine in the center of a room stops me. A fluid-filled sac, punctured by spider-like limbs ending in needle points. The whole device supported by a utilitarian metal box.

It's the printer.

But the needles are broken. The wires are snapped. And the sac is empty.

He is not—

"Tabby?"

I barely hear the word. Only realize it was said when Tabitha freezes. A marine grabs her arm, pulls, but it's as if he heaves on stone. She stares at a shadowed corner.

The crowd seems to sense something is happening. Marines unsling their guns, point.

"Tabby, is that you?"

I can see Tabitha's jaw working. See her eye twitching.

And out of the shadows steps a man. Naked, his hands cupped over his manhood. He is tall, though not quite my height. A few years younger than me. His hair is disheveled. A scruffy beard is on his chin. And despite it all, despite his obvious confusion, his nakedness, there is something almost collegiate about him.

Holy shit, it worked. It actually worked.

"Tabby?" he says. His voice shakes.

Her jaw works.

"Clyde?" she says.

"Tabby," he says again.

And her tears fall.

97

MOUNT RUSHMORE, THREE DAYS LATER

They put us in a cell inside Thomas Jefferson's head.
I wonder if that's part of a convoluted metaphor or
just an accident of architecture. Everyone else is too
preoccupied by the whole being-put-in-a-cell thing to
discuss it.

It's not exactly how I hoped things would go. We piled
out of Version 2.0's compound about two minutes before
the whole structure sunk into the ice. We were packed
onto helicopters like sardines. Rotor blades struggled
against the weight of all the occupants. We raced low
over an ice cliff, and I wondered if we would fall.

But we didn't. We came back here. And our
questions were ignored, and me and Tabby and Kayla
were herded into this cell. And the only soldier we've
seen since has been the one who brings our food. And
he makes your average rock look talkative.

Still, they did bring me one piece of good news.
Felicity.

She lies on a low crib beside the cell's bed. They
returned her from the infirmary early this morning. I
sit on the floor beside her. Her arm drapes over the edge
of the cot and into my lap. I hold her hand tightly. I do
not want to let go. I never want to let go. Never again.

When she first came back, quite a lot of kissing

ensued. I saved her after all. My Felicity. The woman who sacrificed herself for me. For the world. My hero.

Kayla made barfing noises from her corner of the cell. Tabitha just sat and stared.

That's pretty much all Tabitha has done since we got here.

Since she saw Clyde.

I rebuilt him. I really did. As he was. When I first met him. When Tabitha fell in love with him. I don't know if it was the right thing to do. I think it was. I hope it was. But I still remember reaching for that piece of Version 2.0 to get the printer to work.

Back in the compound, when we found him, he called out to Tabitha, and she recognized him, and she knew. But that was it. That was the whole moment. Then the tide of humanity got in the way and pulled him away from us. We lost track of him after that.

He hasn't been brought to the cell yet. I don't know if that's a good or a bad thing. But Tabitha hasn't said a word since she saw him.

The scene is interrupted by a rattle at the door. I stand up immediately. It is early for food. Mid-afternoon. But does this signal good news or bad? Is this our release or a bullet to the back of the head?

The door opens.

Of all the people I considered, none of them were Duncan Smythe, the British civil servant who sent us on this little journey across the pond.

"Ah," he says, "there you are. Marvelous."

He is still thin, still with his comb-over and mustache, still with his umbrella. I have no idea what to say to him.

Kayla shifts. There is something of a caged lion in

the movement. "What the feck is going on?"

"Ah." Smythe blinks at her. "Quite the question, that is. Quite the question indeed. I mean," he shifts his umbrella from one hand to the other, "quite a few implications there. The world outside you might mean, for example. Quite a lot going on there, or so I'm told. The briefs they write about these things. Veritable novels they are. But for the most part it's happy reading at least. Always nice to have an upswing in events. The general North American populace is a big feature. The long-term effects of the fungal infection, which now, thankfully, seems to have retreated from these shores."

There is a chance that the slight incline of the head in our direction is an acknowledgment of some sort. But perhaps he is just shifting his weight.

Kayla seems unimpressed. She stalks a step toward him. "I mean," she says, "what is feckin' going on with us." Her finger travels a circle, describing the occupants of the room.

"Ah." Smythe clears his throat. "A smaller issue, but in some ways a trickier one."

That does not sound exactly like good news.

"The Americans are quite angry at you," he tells us in his unruffled way. "A lot of talk about you murdering some marines and a CIA agent. A lot of talk about insubordination, and threatening the lives of soldiers, and even conspiring against the human race."

"We saved the human race," I can't help but point out. Because it's bloody true.

Smythe acknowledges this fact with the briefest flicker of a smile. "Yes," he says. "Yes, there is that."

A pause.

"And?" I push.

Another flicker of the lips that may just be a smile. "Well, in the eyes of Her Majesty's government that does rather make the Americans' position untenable," he says.

Felicity stirs on her bed. "And what does that—"

"What about Clyde?"

It's Tabitha. Finally standing from the corner she's been sitting in for three days. Her knees pop loudly. "What about him?"

"Which one?" Smythe arches an eyebrow.

"You know which fucking one," she snaps.

"You are speaking about the version of Clyde Marcus Bradley that was recovered in the aftermath of the attack on Version 2.0, I assume," he says.

"He's not a version," I say. Because he's not. I don't want to hear that word ever again. He's Clyde. The one. The only. Ours. I rebuilt him. I brought him back flesh and blood.

"The Americans are quite concerned about him," Smythe says, in his quick, smooth way.

"They're concerned over nothing," I say. "He's not Version 2.0. He's the old Clyde. He's on the world's side. Humanity's side. He's its bloody hero." My whole body is rigid. I am ready to fight on this one, and right now I don't feel like my track record is too bad.

Smythe inclines his head again, and then he nods. "Yes," he says, "I am rather inclined to agree with you."

And then Smythe steps aside. And there, standing behind Smythe, he is.

Clyde.

He stands there, shoulders stooped, head tilted to one side, slightly embarrassed look upon his face. They have found him glasses, and a tweed jacket, and corduroy trousers. And he is Clyde.

A sound escapes Tabitha. Something more than a gasp. Something a little deeper, a little throatier. Clyde's eyes lock on hers. She takes half a step toward him, then hesitates. He opens his mouth, but the words seem to catch.

And then she is on him, flinging herself across the room and crashing into him, knocking him back a step. She buries her head in his chest, locks her arms around his waist. And holds him. Holds Clyde.

After a long, long moment he looks up from her. There are tears in his eyes. I think there are tears in mine as well.

"Hello, chaps," he says.

Felicity's hand snakes out and clutches mine.

And like that we are together, and we are whole. MI37. The world's long shot. And we came through. Somehow, despite it all, we pulled it off.

"Well, come on then." Smythe clears his throat once more. "I rather think it's time that everyone got to go home."

ACKNOWLEDGEMENTS

A great many thanks to the usual suspects: Jeff and Ann Vandermeer, Paul Jessup, Natania Barron, Moses Siregar, Sam Taylor, Michelle Muenzler, Mark Teppo, Darin Bradley, Ennis Drake, and Sally Janin. These are the people who encourage, cajole, and inspire me along the way. Thank you to my agent, Howard Morhaim, who makes pretty much all of this possible. Thank you to everyone at Titan for giving this series new life, especially Cath Trechman, Miranda Jewess, Tom Green, Ella Bowman, and Katharine Carroll. Also thank you to the team at Amazing15.com for the awesome covers. They make me smile. And finally, as ever, thank you to my wife Tami, for her continued and unflagging support, for being wiser than me, and for generally being the best person I know.

These are the people responsible. Now you know who to blame.

ABOUT THE AUTHOR

Jonathan Wood is an Englishman in New York. There's a story in there involving falling in love and flunking out of med school, but in the end it all worked out all right, and, quite frankly, the medical community is far better off without him, so we won't go into it here. His debut novel, *No Hero*, was described by *Publishers Weekly* as "a funny, dark, rip-roaring adventure with a lot of heart, highly recommended for urban fantasy and light science fiction readers alike." Barnesandnoble.com listed it has one of the twenty best paranormal fantasies of the past decade, and Charlaine Harris, author of the Sookie Stackhouse novels, described it as "so funny I laughed out loud." He has continued the Arthur Wallace novels with *Yesterday's Hero*, *Anti-Hero*, and *Broken Hero*, which are all available from Titan Books. He can be found online at www. jonathanwoodauthor.com.